SUMMERSEA

SAMANTHA HARTE

DIVERSIONBOOKS

Also by Samantha Harte

Cactus Heart
Timberhill
The Snows of Craggmoor
Kiss of Gold
Hurricane Sweep
Sweet Whispers
Autumn Blaze
Vanity Blade
Angel

Diversion Books
A Division of Diversion Publishing Corp.
443 Park Avenue South, Suite 1008
New York, New York 10016
www.DiversionBooks.com

For more information, email info@diversionbooks.com

First Diversion Books edition March 2015.
Print ISBN: 978-1-68230-092-3
eBook ISBN: 978-1-62681-661-9

One

Miss Witherspoon Embarks Upon a New Life

Rhode Island: Monday, May 27, 1889

Betz Witherspoon's hired carriage swept along the narrow dirt road with orderly grace. Outside, the afternoon hung still and sun-drenched, the quiet broken only by the crunch of the wheels and the muffled thunder of the carriage horses' hooves.

The meadows on either side of the road were like deep green oceans. The sky was high and pale, a breathless, timeless color that made her feel especially vulnerable and alone.

She heaved a ragged sigh and unclenched her fists. She should not feel uneasy. Bright, competent and unattached, she should have no trouble securing this position. But once before, she had ventured beyond the overprotective circle of her family and had been beaten back. She didn't want to make another mistake. She couldn't fail again.

Now that her brother no longer required her help with his motherless children, Betz could move back to the family home. It was her house, after all, left to her by their mother seven years before. She could take up residence there and live in simple seclusion, waiting for old age.

But Betz wanted something better. She wanted a life of her own. Love was too much to hope for at this point, but she did want to live fully to feel the surge of her existence coursing in her veins.

The carriage turned at last at a high iron gate. The Ryburn house—Cyrus Wood—loomed at the far end of the broad, white gravel drive. Gray stone walls, greenish slate roof, dark window trim…

it stood silently like a judge in chambers, stern and uncompromising.

At once her pulse leaped. Because of the simply worded letters she had received from this place, she had thought it would be an ordinary house. This was a mansion. She felt suddenly overwhelmed and unsure, but moments later managed to summon her courage, and resisted ordering the driver to turn back.

It would probably all be over in a matter of minutes, anyway—the introductions, the interview, the discussion of her qualifications. Then she could move on to other possibilities. This position had intrigued her because the pay was so inordinately high. And the woman who had responded to her newspaper advertisement had seemed eager to meet with her. The other positions offered would not have paid enough to keep her in decent shoes.

As the carriage rolled to a stop, Betz drew the sweet spring air into her lungs. This was what it felt like to be alive, she reminded herself. Only the dead felt no sense of apprehension.

Her heart was pounding. The other applicants were surely far better qualified she thought. Her clothes were worn and out-of-date. Her education had been scanty, at best. But she would try. No one would stop her from doing that.

The driver climbed down and opened the carriage door. She gathered her heavy black worsted skirts and made a graceful exit down to the white graveled coachway. If nothing else, she knew how to appear utterly composed.

At least eight gables were visible along the front of the house. Dozens of multipaned windows caught the glinting afternoon sunlight. The enclosed veranda stood in deep shade next to a conservatory with misty windows. Lovely rhododendrons, lilac bushes, and a magnificent southern magnolia were in full bloom in the yard. The place was so quiet, it reminded Betz of a mausoleum.

She climbed the steps and tapped at the broad white door. For a brief moment she half wished that she might slip away unnoticed. Surely, if she begged, her brother would take her back…if she explained her dread of living alone and apologized to his pretty, new, young, spoiled, demanding little witch of a wife…

Trembling Betz was spurred to courage by an anger she had not realized smouldered so deep within her. If they did not appreciate all she had done for six years—cooking, laundering, nursing, and managing the entire household—well, she would just offer her services elsewhere!

She knocked more loudly and tugged on her gray kid gloves. Straightening her back, she fixed her expression to what she hoped was a convincing display of backbone.

A uniformed, red-haired maid with lively eyes opened the heavy door. The unexpected aroma of Far Eastern sandalwood incense wafted out. Distracted by the exotic fragrance, Betz stammered over her first words.

"I-I'm here to see Lady Agatha Ryburn, if you please."

"Do come in," the girl said, curtsying. She adjusted her ruffled cap and eyed Betz. "Oh, you're young, you are. Her don't like young ones."

The reception chamber was surprisingly unadorned and small, Betz, thought, resisting the urge to ogle the crystal drop chandelier.

"I'm nervous," she whispered under her breath. "Do you think I'll do?"

Eyes widening, the maid surveyed Betz's homely black jacket and traveling skirt. Then she shrugged.

"It's been a long morning, it has. Her's been receiving applicants since ten. Tough old biddy, if you ask me. Her's testy and contrary, and I'm glad she's only here a few months of the year. Scared of her, I am. Excuse me. I'll announce you. Stay right here, dearie. You'll do as good as anybody."

Betz offered the maid her engraved card, printed only that morning on the way from Boston. It read: Elizabeth Jane Witherspoon—not Betty Carlyle, which her brother George insisted was her name. Only *he* used Betty as a nickname. And only *he* insisted that she must still use her married name, after so long.

As the maid slipped through another set of glass doors etched with elaborate twin R's, Betz heard from the depths of a long, hushed hall, "And who is it this time?"

The maid closed the door, leaving Betz feeling as though she had intruded into an alien world. For the offered pay, she had expected a large family of children, but she heard only the ticking of an untold number of clocks. Seconds later, the maid opened the door and beckoned with a smile.

"You may come in," and the clocks began a cacophony of tolls, dongs and tinkles. Betz chuckled and straightened her shoulders. It was, most assuredly, four o'clock. Perhaps this was when a new life would begin for her.

Admitted to the reception hall, Betz stifled a gasp of appreciation. The hall opened to impressive carved arches, and a broad, herringbone maple floor protected by an elaborate Persian carpet. The house seemed to be welcoming her into its lovely chambers.

On every curiously carved, black walnut table stood a collection of brass goblets from India, or ivory elephants from the Orient, or zebra figurines from Africa. She had thought such treasures available only in museums.

"Come along. Madame will see you in the conservatory. I'll bring tea. Through here."

The formal parlor was a study in Victorian perfection with a black marble fireplace dominating the room and an elaborate set of brocade chairs and settees to delight the eye. In one corner stood a porcelain peacock, glazed a most astonishing turquoise color.

Through a pair of tall glass doors, she followed the maid into a vast conservatory resplendent with myriad exotic plants.

Betz was assailed by the deep rich fragrance of fertile, dark earth. The air fairly dripped with heat. The golden light that fell hot and soft from filmy side and overhead windows gave her the feeling that she had stepped into a tropical paradise. The profusion of plantings thrust large waxy leaves in her way as she swished along a path of reddish brown quarry tile toward a sun-bright potting area along the far, glass wall.

A stout woman wearing a dirty canvas gardener's apron over an astonishingly ornate bustled silk gown was busily pruning an overgrown plant. Like a pirate, she rustled and swished as she plundered the thick dark leaves.

"Impudent thing...the ignorance...the waste..." Her accent was purely American, not English as Betz had expected because of her title. And her voice was striking, with a deep, commanding rasp that caught Betz by surprise.

"Excuse me. I'm Elizabeth Witherspoon, Lady Ryburn. I'm here to interview for the position of companion to your granddaughter. We corresponded..." She felt like an awkward schoolchild called before a most forbidding headmistress.

Though the woman's mouth was thin and turned down, the blue eyes she lifted to give Betz a thorough appraisal were merry. There seemed a subtle spark of humor in the deep creases that framed her impersonal smile.

"I know who you are, Miss Witherspoon. You're late. Call me Agatha, if you will. I'm thoroughly tired of hearing my late husband's name bandied about as if he still lived, dear soul. I took back my maiden name some years ago, you see. What do you think of that?" She went on studying Betz, unconcerned about her dull black attire.

Lady Ryburn's aging face was feathered with wrinkles. Her iron-gray hair had been hastily twisted into a careless little knot, and one of the buttons on her sleeve was undone. She looked breathless and impatient, and her eyes were as keen as Japanese steel.

Betz felt suddenly that this woman was not as formidable as she wanted to appear.

"I think it's admirable. I did the same."

"Ah, so you've been married?"

Betz swallowed. "Yes, ma'am. I mentioned that in my letters."

Lady Ryburn regarded her with piercing blue eyes.

"You're very tall."

"Five feet seven and three quarter inches."

"Honest. Precise. You are, however, far too young. Most applicants—there have been seventeen, including yourself—are closer to my age."

Betz kept her gaze level with Lady Ryburn's. Her tremulous courage was wilting. She said, "I'll be thirty-six in the fall, Lady Ryburn."

Lady Ryburn seemed amused.

"From my vantage, that is exceedingly young. Recount your reasons for wanting the position. I've read your letters, of course, but I want to hear the story from your own lips, without benefit of belabored composition." She returned her attention to the impudent plant, frowning at it. "And I am not a 'lady.' That's a title I merely adopted, the way southern gentlemen take up the title of colonel. I've been unable to shake it off."

"I see. Well, I cared for my widowed mother until her death when I was twenty-seven—"

"Ah, a spinster so long."

"I didn't think of myself as one, ma'am. I had no particular desire to marry. Yet shortly after her death I submitted to the encouragement of well-meaning friends and relatives and made a marriage…to an unfortunate young…gentleman. The marriage ended in divorce an insignificant time later." Betz resisted balling her fists. She saw no point in hiding the truth. She had been a fool, and that was that.

"Ah, you failed to mention the matter of a divorce in your letters, Miss Witherspoon."

"The information is easily found in the county clerk's office. I only speak of it to those I feel will understand."

"Do you believe your unfortunate marriage qualifies you to chaperone a thoroughly incorrigible fifteen year old child who has been polluted with a disgraceful upbringing?" The woman's raspy voice was emphatic.

"I do. I feel it is my strongest qualification, Lady—what may I call you, if you prefer not to use your adopted title or the name Ryburn?"

"We'll attend that later. How might your marriage and divorce qualify you?"

"I know firsthand the sort of tricks unscrupulous men will use to turn the head of an unwary young woman. Unlike spinsters and formerly well-married widows, I can speak from experience when warning a headstrong child of the pitfalls of flirtations and dalliance. I was once well-off and innocent. I am living proof that seduction leads to a life of hardship."

"I see. Then I take it you are bitter to the core." Lady Ryburn had ceased pruning the plant. Her expression had grown intense, fixed on Betz.

"No, I admit my former ignorance. I speak of it so that you will understand that I'm aware of the dangers awaiting a pretty young heiress." Betz hoped she sounded like the sort of stiff-necked chaperone this matron would require. Secretly, she felt as stuffy and didactic as her brother George.

"And since your divorce, Miss Witherspoon? What have you been doing?" She untied the gardener's apron and laid it aside.

From behind them came the soft rattle of a china-laden tea table on wheels. Lady Ryburn indicated an arrangement of ornate white wicker chairs in the far corner. She proceeded to throw open several misty French doors, revealing a breathtaking view of the rear lawn and gardens.

Betz momentarily forgot what she had been about to say. So much beauty...what a wonderful place in which to sort out her future...to approach it cautiously...and avoid mistakes.

"Do go on while my girl pours. You like jasmine tea, I hope? I brought it back the last time I was in Hong Kong."

Startled to think this old woman traveled so far, Betz sat, tightly laced her fingers, and began again.

"After my divorce, I was taken in by my brother George. His wife had died. I looked after his four children—as if they were my own—until two weeks ago, when his new wife of three months asked that I leave."

Lady Ryburn held her fragile Chinese cup in midair.

"And how might this further qualify you to look after my granddaughter?"

"I was very good with my nieces and nephews, but my sister-in-law wanted to tend her stepchildren herself. I didn't care to remain where I might interfere with the success of my brother George's marriage, or Cynthia's duties as stepmother." She managed to keep from mentioning the unpleasant things that had been said when she was asked to leave.

"You don't paint yourself in particularly flattering colors, Miss Witherspoon. Do you have a poor opinion of yourself?"

Betz felt her strength returning. Of one thing she was sure. She had done an excellent job with George's children.

"No, I don't believe I do. I'm just not interested in misrepresenting myself. Might I ask why you require a companion for your granddaughter?"

"As I mentioned, she is incorrigible. I have a son, you see, somewhere in this curious world. She is the illegitimate result of one of his hapless liaisons. She was presented to me not so very long ago as heiress to my husband's estate…and my collections. I have no doubt that Cordelia is indeed my son's child. The resemblance is evident. My concern is that she is very pretty. I do like her very much—undisciplined as she is. I am nearly seventy, and so it is unlikely that I shall produce any more heirs." She chuckled to herself.

Amused, too, Betz felt it would be imprudent to add her own chuckle. She was surprised to realize that the woman was far older that she appeared.

"What of other grandchildren?"

"Ah, well, that is for my lawyer and executor to fret about in due time, isn't it? My immediate concern is to educate my grandchild to finer tastes, to prepare her for a finishing school, and then, the proper education."

Betz's pulse leaped again.

"You believe in education for women?"

"Such a question. Do I look like a simpleton, Miss Witherspoon? Of course she must be educated. But until she has been tamed and civilized, she won't last a day in any of the places I have in mind for her."

"And you want me to tame and civilize her?"

"Mercy, no! You'll pardon my bluntness, but a woman of your social background, as wholesome as it surely was, simply hasn't the training. I believe you're very well read. I did read your letters of reference most thoroughly. And I do believe you possess the honesty and strength of character I require during this coming spring and summer season. I've made plans to travel abroad, you see. I do so every year. Of late, I have thought each trip might be my last. This year's itinerary takes in all those corners of the world which I have neglected. It is to be, you might say my last good-bye, my final sojourn into the bazaars. If Cordelia proves unsuitable as an heir, I shall simply leave my collections to museums. She may have the house to do with as she sees fit. That would have pleased Cyrus..."

"Then you would require me only through August?" Betz relaxed still more. She had worried about taking on something lengthy.

"I expect to be gone that long, yes. If you and Cordelia get on, we might make further arrangements later. And you shall not have a free hand entirely. I have friends who will look in on you both and report back to me. I shall expect a certain amount of effort on your part. You did indicate that you had some training in the arts. The dear child is utterly devoid of all social graces. If you could only hear what punishment she gives a piano...and her voice..." She shook her head, sipped and chuckled softly. "I shouldn't wonder that she might already be beyond your help or mine. She might not even be a virgin, and *then* wouldn't I have a time finding a decent boy to marry her! But I will leave that for you to discover during my most regrettable but necessary absence. I would like to return to find my granddaughter receptive to the care I would like to lavish on her in my declining years."

"Am I to assume that you have decided to hire me, then?" Betz asked blinking with surprise.

"Oh, yes, yes. You are quite right, Miss Witherspoon. Your unfortunate marriage, and the divorce, which I did have my lawyer investigate, are convincing qualifications. You look quite taken aback. Are you having second thoughts?"

Betz wanted to shout with delight, but she reined her pleasure.

She had gotten a position! Wouldn't George be surprised, the dour old fuddy-duddy.

"Can you tell me specifically what my duties with Cordelia will be?"

"Certainly I can, and I will if you'll be so good as to sit back down. You may call me Agatha Dunwitty. It's not an elegant name, but then I myself am not an elegant woman."

"I disagree!" Betz interjected.

"Oh, indeed! There were years when I was the stuffiest old thing on two legs, but when one reaches my age, certain things fail to impress. One morning I looked at my stiff neck and my upturned nose and my haughty rich widow's expression, and I said to myself, I said, Aggy Dunwitty, you've become an old biddy witch."

Betz laughed in spite of herself.

"I come from plain stock. So did Mr. Ryburn. He earned every penny he made—he was a genius as a merchant. No doubt you've shopped in the Ryburn Department Stores. All his doing. And then, poor dear, he dropped dead one day. There I was with all this money, and a lofty reputation to uphold. Let me tell you, it was a relief to get so old that what I did no longer mattered."

Betz found that a tantalizing thought.

"That's when I began traveling." Agatha went on. "And I haven't stopped. So long as I'm in Nepal or Tahiti or Mozambique, the upper crust thinks I'm still that bejeweled stuffed shirt they once knew. That's why I took back my maiden name, to remind myself that I had too few years left to waste with my nose in the air."

"Miss Dunwitty, I think I like you very much," Betz said, unable to hide her pleasure.

"You have a charming smile. And thank you. If you find Cordelia too much for you, perhaps you might consider being my companion when I return. This tour will be my last, for I'm simply not as strong as I once was. But enough about me. You would like to meet Cordelia. She has been eavesdropping behind the Boston ferns for the past several minutes. Do come out, child and take some tea with us. Meet Miss Witherspoon. She's going to take you in hand this summer. Mercy, did I fail to tell you where you shall keep yourselves while I'm traipsing about?"

A bank of delicate leaves parted and a slender blond girl crawled out. Her delicate white muslin gown was dirtied at the knees, and her long thick braid was mussed. She brushed something from her cheek, leaving a smudge. Strolling forward as if wearing hip boots, she extended a dirty hand.

"Hello," she said.

Smiling, Betz stood and shook the girl's hand. Cordelia Ryburn was lovely, and would likely ripen before her very eyes that summer.

"You may call me Betz. Your grandmother and I have been discussing you. Can you join us for tea?"

Making a bored face, Cordelia dropped undecorously into a wicker chairs nearly upsetting it.

"I hate that dusty-tasting stuff. Where are we going this summer, Grandmother? Why can't we stay here?" She sounded annoyed and far from childlike. A certain anxiety darkened her round blue eyes.

"I am off to New Delhi in two weeks. You can't stay here because Albert is here. It isn't proper. And he has worked for me since he was nine years old. He doesn't deserve to be dismissed simply because a flirtatious bit of baggage like you has come along. Miss Witherspoon will take you to Summersea until I return in August."

Betz stiffened. She turned to her new employer and said nervously, "Summersea is a...resort. A very nice one near Newport, said to be part of the Newport social scene..."

"I, too, read the dreadful tabloid, *Society Topics*. All foolishness. You mustn't be intimidated."

"But Miss Dunwitty—"

"Call me Agatha, if you please."

"Miss Agatha, you were quite correct to assume that I haven't the social graces to properly prepare Cordelia for a finishing school. I thought I would be a companion...here. I most certainly know nothing about how to guide her through a summer...there."

"Grandmother," Cordelia interrupted, "I hate the name

Cordelia! Can't I please have back my own name? And what is this place Summersea?" The girl's blue eyes conveyed alarm.

"It's a prestigious oceanside spring, dear. If you behave, Miss Witherspoon may allow you to swim. And you must learn tennis and croquet, and when you're not fumbling about with your manners and which fork to use, she is going to give you voice and piano lessons. I dare say, she might instruct you in a bit of sketching and painting as well. It's going to be a full summer. I would appreciate your cooperation, my child."

"Miss Agatha," Betz interrupted. "You might do well to reconsider your decision. I will hardly know how to conduct myself, as a servant, in such a place. How can I teach Cordelia to conduct herself as a young lady of privilege? I would do far better here, alone with—"

"Nonsense. You'll be a companion and chaperone, not a mere servant. If I had a maiden sister I would ask her to look after Cordelia, and she would be considered a guest at Summersea and treated accordingly. But I have no relative to call upon. I am convinced that you, Miss Witherspoon, will do. Don't allow those stuffed shirts to diminish your stature as my employee one iota. How do you think Mr. Ryburn and I learned to stiffen our necks and hold our noses in the air among the upper crust? We came from a background little different than your own, or from that which Cordelia remembers.

"Now, I should like Cordelia to be exposed to such persons. She will live among them, if she marries well. If she does not, it won't be for lack of trying. If Cordelia had been raised here, she would now be a budding little stuffed shirt, and I would send her off to public school to have a little honest humility knocked into her. As it is, the reverse is necessary. We are all born into a hard and unequal world. I should like to spend much time with Cordelia in my remaining years. I would like to be able to stomach her company."

"I hate the name Cordelia!" Cordelia shouted, making a fist. "I was born Cherry Rose, and that's what I want to be called."

Agatha smiled, indulgent.

"Perhaps the name is a bit too much for you, dear. But your

given name is more suitable for cockney strumpet, and I should hate to give my old friends at Summersea the wrong impression. I have the distinct feeling that you and Miss Witherspoon are going to have a fine time this summer, and I shall be very sorry to miss it. Let's have the remainder of our tea, shall we? Then I shall outline what I expect you both to accomplish before I return."

Two

The Journey to Summersea

Thursday, May 30, 1889

Seventy-two hours later, Miss Elizabeth Jane Witherspoon and Miss Cordelia Norbit Ryburn, who still insisted upon being called Cherry, found themselves riding in the Ryburn private railroad car. The richly appointed parlor-sleeping car had not been used since Cyrus Ryburn died, fifteen years before.

In dusty grandeur, they sped south toward the Rhode Island shore. The pale sky was clear, the verdant hills fragrant with spring. The rhythmic clack of the wheels on the rails lulled their thoughts.

"I didn't like my grandmother at first," Cherry said. With her cheek pressed clumsily against the windowglass, she was braiding the fringe on the drapes. "She seemed so old. I was scared of her huge, old house. But after a while I could tell she was young in her heart. That's when I began to love her. I wanted to please her. Otherwise, I would have run away."

"In the few days I've know your grandmother, she's had quite an effect on me, too," Betz said, feeling surprisingly comfortable with her new young charge. She laid her hand gently across Cherry's busy fingers. "A young lady doesn't fidget with the fringes."

"I'm bored in this car with nobody to look at! I guess I am glad that we won't be stuck in that big old house all summer. Aren't you? I got lost three times. Grandmother doesn't like that house much. She only keeps it to show off."

"Miss Dunwitty doesn't strike me as the sort who shows off," Betz said. "How would you like to go forward and sit a while in the coach section? I haven't traveled much in recent years, so I'd like to see who's going to Summersea along with us."

"Can we?" Cherry's round cheeks flushed. She looked contrite. "You're nothing like the others."

"What others?" Betz asked as they made their way forward. The plush private car's atmosphere had been suffocating. The dull maroon fringes had reminded her horridly of George's somber main parlor.

Once in the half-filled coach car, Betz directed Cherry toward a pair of empty seats. Cherry flounced into her seat and heaved a sigh.

"This is nice! You're not like my other *companions*," she said sarcastically, and crossed her legs. At Betz's frown she straightened, pressed her knees together and folded her hands. "Grandmother made you think I'd been at her house just a little while, didn't she? I've been there three months. I've had four companions. I drove them all away in less than a week."

"Such an accomplished terror you are, Cherry. What will you do to drive me away?" Betz chuckled, adjusted her hat, and settled back a little. To set a good example, she knew she mustn't touch her back to the seat, but the rocking coach was relaxing her. She wished she could unbutton her snug jacket, unfurl her hair to the breeze that blew in through the nearby window. Of course she wouldn't. She had long kept her natural impulses under strict control.

"I won't cause you much trouble unless you're cross with me. Then you'll be sorry." Cherry watched Betz with keen blue eyes the exact shade of her grandmother's.

Betz let the challenge fall. She had no intention of provoking the child to rebellion.

"I'll be very careful, then," she said in a mildly teasing tone.

Cherry looked disappointed, then thoughtful.

"You're not a very happy person, are you, Miss Witherspoon?"

Finding it very odd that the girl would say such a thing, Betz said, "I'm content," and settled back a little more. She was having a wonderful time—on her own at last.

"Maybe you're content, Miss Witherspoon, but you're not

happy. You've gotten old, and you've given up. I think you're bored with the world, but you don't have enough gumption to do anything about that. I won't be like that when I'm old. I can tell you that much." Cherry gave a firm nod of her head and then squirmed around in her seat to ogle the other passengers.

"Tell me about yourself, Cherry," Betz said, hiding her discomfort. She patted the child's knee to encourage her to settle down. "I know only a little about your mother."

Cherry shrugged. Her flat straw hat was askew, and its ribbons began to flutter as a broad-shouldered gentleman in the seat ahead raised his window. Now the wind was full in their faces.

Remembering her obligations as chaperone, Betz stiffened her back and tapped the man's shoulder.

"Would you please close the window…"

He twisted around, fixing her with piercing dark brown eyes. His very dark, wavy hair was brushed to perfection. Alarmingly attractive, he didn't smile as he memorized her features one by one. Then his gaze dipped. She was immediately on guard, her heart skipping.

"…the draft…" she said, her voice strained, pointing toward the open window. Oh! she hadn't been looked at like that in years!

"Sorry, ladies," he said briskly. His accent was American but not distinguishable. He closed the window and returned to his thoughts, giving Betz the well-shaped back of his head.

"Tell me about your marriage," Cherry whispered loudly, "… *Miss* Witherspoon."

"Another time!" Betz whispered. "I would like to know how you came to be with your grandmother." The girl *was* incorrigible!

"Didn't she tell you?" Cherry began pleating her skirt.

"Y-Yes, but I'd like you to tell me, too." Betz found her thoughts in a jumble.

"You had a childhood, playmates, a place to sleep, schooling. She didn't tell me about that." She stilled Cherry's nervous fingers, wishing she could still her own heart. The man sitting in front of them was terribly attractive!

Scowling at her now motionless white hands, Cherry said, "Sometimes you sound stuffy. Is is because *he's* listening to us?"

A hot blush crawled into Betz's cheeks. She stole a look at the man. While he appeared to be lost in thought, his hooded eyes moved from passenger to passenger.

Suddenly she was fully alert and tingling with alarm. He *was* listening! She motioned to Cherry to be silent.

As the pause in their conversation lengthened, Betz watched him shift his position. He consulted his pocket watch and stood. Turning to Betz as if recalling that she was there, he placed his derby on his thick dark waves, tipped the brim and then strolled to another seat toward the front.

Turning the seat so that he might sit facing backward, he greeted a startled passenger who looked up from a book. Producing a pack of cards, he queried with his brow. The passenger declined, and so the attractive man took up a newspaper from the empty seat next to him and began to read, with a scowl on his face.

That was odd, she thought. If he had wanted to listen, why had he moved away?

"I don't care for gentlemen who wear hats like that," Cherry was saying with eyes narrowed. "They remind me of bill collectors."

Betz gave a startled little laugh.

"You've had experience with bill collectors?"

"I used to hold them off while Mama slipped out the back way. She couldn't always pay. She was very pretty. Men liked her a lot."

"And that's how you came to find your grandmother, when your mother needed money?"

"No, my mother died." Cherry fell silent a moment. "She was killed by a runaway cab horse."

Betz studied Cherry. The girl's expression was tragic.

"Grandmother doesn't know. I just told her that Mama got sick. She was…some of the time." Cherry made a fist with her thumb sticking up. She tipped her thumb toward her mouth in a drinking gesture.

"Oh." Betz felt embarrassed for the girl. "Did you…uh, ever

meet your father?"

"Just because I was born on the wrong side of the blanket doesn't mean I never saw Papa. I did. Plenty of times. But then he stopped coming around. I think he's dead, too, but I'm not sure. If he wasn't, he would've come for me himself."

Betz was aghast at the girl's honesty. Then she noticed the attractive stranger's eyes.

"That man is still watching us," she whispered. "I was wrong to speak to him. It would have been better to have our hats blown off than to create the impression that I was willing to talk to a stranger."

"He has a nice face," Cherry observed, smiling. "Do you like him?"

"What a question! I know nothing about him, favorable or otherwise." Betz was suddenly overly warm. She did like his face, and his physique, and the way he dominated the coach car just by being in it. She could not remember when a man had had a more profound effect on her!

"You sound just like my grandmother. Are you terribly old, Miss Witherspoon?"

"No, I—if I seem stuffy, Cherry, it's because…I was brought up in a very gloomy house. I'll tell you more about it sometime. And the past has hurt me. Besides, I'm…shy."

"You don't look shy! You look as if you know everything. What do you suppose he finds so interesting about us? And everyone? Look at the way he watches people. He makes my stomach flutter."

"He's wondering about how much money we're carrying. He'll watch as we prepare to get off the train, and he'll find an excuse to follow. He'll offer to help us with our baggage, and then he'll grow increasingly friendly. Perhaps he'll insist that we share a carriage to the hotel. And then…"

"Is that how you met your husband, the unfortunate young gentleman?" Cherry's eyes shone with mischief.

"*I* was the unfortunate. He was luckier than any young man I ever met. He got everything from me. My money, my innocence, my…Let's not talk of that. It's long in the past. If I seem morose it's because for the past six years…I was mother to my nieces and nephews. Now I won't see them until Christmas, if I'm even asked to visit then." Her voice caught. George had been so ungrateful. "It's a lonely thing to be an unattached woman in today's world. There should be more opportunities for women. How lucky you are that your grandmother will educate you. Marriage isn't your only recourse. My education was meager and too shallow for me to become a teacher. My talent in the arts is minimal. All I know how to do is cook, mend, and tend the elderly…"

"And you know about men." Cherry's eyes remained bright. "Tell me!"

"I know about one man. And you shall not hear the details. You need only look at me to see where giving in to seduction leads. Would you like to carry all your belongings in one trunk and two carpetbags for the rest of your life?"

"Everything that's important to me is right here," Cherry said as she patted her reticule, her blond curls falling in a sunny cascade over her shoulder.

Betz wondered suddenly what it must be like for such a very young girl to be cast upon the world, into such new and exacting circumstances. She knew how she felt—awkward, conspicuous and insecure. The poor dear. She patted Cherry's still hands, wishing there was someone to pat hers.

"All the things in my trunks are from Grandmother," Cherry said softly. "We didn't have much, Mama and me. After her funeral, I spent two weeks in an orphanage, and what little I had left was taken away. I never got my things back. I was afraid that I'd have to stay there forever. But a friend of my father heard about what had become of me and sent someone to take me to Grandmother's." Cherry lifted her face, and her troubled expression began to brighten. "I made up my mind that I wasn't going to like her! But I did. And yet I'm still scared. Grandmother wants to change everything about me. Even my name." She looked about as if she had lost herself. Then she looked at Betz imploringly. "She must not like me very much."

"Your grandmother loves you dearly, Cherry," Betz said,

understanding perfectly how the girl felt. "But you're in a new world now, and you must learn how to get on."

"You remind me of Mama," Cherry went on. "With you, I don't feel so…alone in the world. For a while all I had left was my grandmother. And she was a stranger. When I was taken to her house, she looked at me like she was seeing a ghost—my father. And do you know what she said? I'll never forget!"

"What did she say?" Betz circled the girl's shoulder with her arm.

"She said, 'I knew I hadn't raised a saint. I knew there had to be at least one child somewhere in the world. Come in,' just like she'd been expecting me. I had been sure that she'd throw me back into the street. You know how rich people are. But she gave me the best room, and bought me so many presents. I wanted to please her. I still do. I wish she was with us now. She might die in those strange places where she goes. Then where will I be?"

She would be an heiress, Betz thought with a shiver, prey to every swindler from coast to coast.

"Your grandmother looked very strong. When I'm that old, I'd like to be like her," Betz said to distract the child's fears. "Of course I haven't much money now, and I won't likely have much when I'm old. If I had listened to my brother and let him choose a man for me, I might have my own children now instead of…"

"Instead of me?" Cherry looked anguished.

"Oh, no, I'm delighted to be with you! I was about to say that if I had not chosen my husband myself, for all the wrong reasons, I would not be so confused now about what to do with my life. I hope I can teach you all the things that your grandmother expects. We'll have to be on our best behavior. I'd hate for a poor report to reach her when she's ten thousand miles away."

"Who do you think she'll have spying on us? That gentleman? He's still watching you."

"Not me, Cherry. Us."

"No, he's looking right at you, just as if he would like to come and ask your name! This is ever so exciting!"

Betz tightened her mouth and looked away.

"Thank heaven we're coming into Huntington Station. I've already made a terrible blunder, and we're not yet off the train. Don't make a move to get up until the train is almost ready to pull out. We'll make a very speedy exit, and he'll never be the wiser. I don't care for gentlemen who play at cards. It's a mark that they're not gentlemen at all. He is your first lesson, Cordelia. Never, under even extreme circumstances, speak to strangers."

"I hate that name!"

"Nevertheless, in public, you will be Cordelia and I will be Miss Witherspoon—Oh, I think he's going to get off here, too! It's too much." With her heart fluttering, Betz watched the wavy-haired, handsome stranger stand. She felt mesmerized—by the way his shoulders filled and strained the wool of his new-looking coat, by the way his gaze swept the passengers knowingly, and finally, by the way his gaze stopped at her.

They watched him tip his derby to the man in the seat across from him. Betz noticed that his suit was well-tailored but not terribly expensive. Again he consulted his watch; Betz wondered if it was gold or nickel.

He tipped his hat as he passed, catching her eye for one piercing moment, and then he exited at the rear of the coach car. She had never known anyone to look so directly into the essence of her being. It was as if in one brief instant, he had touched her soul. She shivered, alarmed that such a thing might be possible.

"Hadn't we best get our things from our car, Miss Witherspoon?" Cherry asked softly, beginning to giggle. "I do think you're taken with him! Mama used to get taken with men on sight just like that. But she was a bad judge of character."

Taken aback, Betz regarded her charge. Which of them needed a chaperone, she asked herself as she hurried Cherry back to their private car. The train was hissing great clouds of vapor as they debarked with their carpetbags and bandboxes.

"Luckily for you," Cherry went on, "I am a good judge of character, and I know that that man in the derby is honest and true."

She giggled again, behind her hand. "See the way he wears his hat on the back of his head? He's not stuffy."

On the platform, Betz saw nothing of the beautiful rolling green hills. She didn't even think of the vast Narragansett Bay, less than a mile away. Overhead the gulls were wheeling and calling, and the air was tart and cool. But Betz was aware of only the gentleman pacing at the far edge of the nearly deserted platform.

He seemed consumed with nervous energy. His thoughts must be churning, for he looked about as if observing everything, and yet he seemed absorbed.

As she wondered what to do about transportation to the hotel, there was a flurry of activity, and an open carriage drew near to the opposite end of the platform. A tall buxom woman in gray satin and plumage waved hello as her driver handed her down. The driver headed for where Cherry's trunks were being off-loaded at the side of the train. Amid billows of vapor, Betz and Cherry waited as the conductor and driver made arrangements for the trunks to be delivered to Summersea. The buxom woman in the huge plumed hat drifted forward with a measured walk, and reeked of expensive toilet water.

"You must be Miss Witherspoon. And *Cordelia.* What a delight…" Her observant gray eyes were sharp on the girl. Betz worried about how much she knew about Cherry. "My dears, I've known Lady Ryburn for years and years. Now, come along you two. They've been at work on your suite ever since word of your imminent arrival reached us. I'll have so many young people for Cordelia to meet. And you, Miss Witherspoon, should get on splendidly with my maid and the other servants. They have perfectly nice accommodations in the rear."

Betz was not able to get in a word.

"Now, Cordelia, dear," the woman blustered, "you must try to remember everyone I introduce to you. You're only a few years from your coming out, so you haven't much time to make the right impressions. I know several young gentlemen at Summersea who will be smitten by you, simply smitten, but you mustn't let them turn your head. The young man your grandmother and I have in mind for you won't come along until next month. His father's in railroading, one of those Wall Street giants we all admire so much."

"Excuse me, madam, I don't believe I caught your name," Betz said, her voice sharp. Agatha had said that she was not to be treated like a servant.

"Why, I'm Felicia Ellison, wife of the Randolph Ellison... Ellison Steel. If you were one of our regular nannies, you'd know who I am."

"I'm not a nanny, but a companion. Might you be so good as to direct us to the hired carriages?"

The woman looked stricken.

"I wouldn't dream of allowing you to arrive at Summersea without escort or proper introductions. Agatha has been going off to foreign lands so long she's forgotten how things are done here. And, of course, *you* can't be expected to know, being hired. You *must* come along in my carriage, Miss Witherspoon. I insist. That's why I'm here, can't you see? I will be very upset if you don't allow me to escort you."

"Very well," Betz said, squirming and still annoyed. "Will you be reporting to Lady Ryburn on a weekly or monthly basis?"

"Reporting? Why, whatever do you mean...do you *know* that man, Miss Witherspoon? He's *staring* at you."

As she was about to follow Cherry onto the carriage, Betz turned. The wavy-haired gentleman was openly watching her.

"No, I don't." She felt another wash of awareness flood her body. "Do you know him, Mrs. Ellison?"

Mrs. Ellison stiffened and said, "Not well, surely."

"A bill collector," Cherry said with mischief in her eyes.

Mrs. Ellison faltered, gaped at Cherry and then dismissed her. "Children are to be *seen* and not heard, my dear. *Remember* that. Now, Miss Witherspoon, tell me all about your people. You've fallen on hard times, I take it. What does your father do? Might I know of other families where you have been a nanny?"

At the woman's brusque reprimand, Cherry's face reddened

and brows drew low. Betz was about to lay her hand soothingly on the girl when Cherry sprang from her seat in the carriage and vaulted to the ground, petticoats flashing.

"Cordelia, no!" Betz whispered, inwardly groaning.

"Whatever has taken possession of that girl?" Mrs. Ellison asked, pleasantly scandalized, as Cherry dashed toward the wavy-haired stranger.

"Excuse me, Mrs. Ellison, I'll fetch her. Cordelia isn't used to correction from anyone but myself. I'd appreciate it if you'd be good enough to remember that only I am to instruct her in manners. You may have been told, or will soon deduce, that she has not had the same upbringing as the other young people who frequent Summersea. She…lived…abroad, many years…among savages. You'd do well not to antagonize her."

Leaving Mrs. Ellison repeating her word "savages," Betz climbed hurriedly from the carriage. She almost ran after Cherry, who was accosting the wavy-haired gentleman. He was grinning broadly.

Cherry's words were loud and delivered with youthful authority. "…been staring at her, and I can tell you right now, she's not that kind, so be off with you before I call the sheriff!" She stamped her white high-button shoe and her slim body quivered with indignation.

"Cherry! Hush, and come back to the carriage." Betz seized the girl's arm. "I've just told my first lie for you, so you'd better not say a word until we are safely locked in our rooms. Now we'll have to make up some sort of story. Oh, if only I had not spent the last six years telling bedtime tales! Sir, I beg your indulgence. She has no manners."

He removed his hat and bowed.

"But impeccable loyalty. I admire that. Forgive me, Miss, if I was staring. I meant no harm. I thought I recognized you."

She dragged Cherry back toward the carriage. "That's another of their ploys, Cherry! Why would you speak to him after I—"

"But he's not a stranger now, is he? We were talking about him, and he did look like he knew you, staring at you like that." Cherry looked delighted with herself.

"We don't know this man's name! We weren't introduced! Cherry, if you don't listen to me, we'll get right back on that train. I won't be responsible."

Imagining tongues wagging already, she was secretly furious with herself for caring a whit what anyone might think or say. And yet, her job was at stake. She mustn't fail again. She did not allow herself to falter as Cherry's face folded into a stormy pout.

They were almost beside the carriage when the man called out, "Excuse me, Miss Witherspoon, but might I share your carriage?"

"You gave him my name?" Betz hissed at Cherry, mortified.

"All I said was, 'Miss Witherspoon does not care for your staring.'" Cherry had the decency to try to pretend bewilderment.

Betz stopped, drew breath into her lungs and stiffened her back. She was trembling.

"Join Mrs. Ellison in the carriage. Now I will be forced to speak to him. Go on. I don't want you to hear this."

Reluctantly, Cherry moved away.

Betz turned back to the grinning man, his derby in hand. She approached as if nearing a precipice. He was altogether too attractive to be borne, and she felt as conspicuous as if she'd shed all her clothes.

"Please forgive my young charge, sir. I cannot offer the hospitality of my hostess's carriage. I only just met her. And I will ask that you p-please refrain from speaking to us again." He looked down on her with those piercing dark eyes, obviously amused.

"I beg your pardon if I intruded myself, Miss Witherspoon. I meant no harm."

Mrs. Ellison called out in an affected falsetto, "Miss Witherspoon, do ask Mr. Teague to join us! I recall now seeing him at Summersea. For a moment I didn't recognize him. That awful derby...It's quite all right, dear, if I say so."

Betz's already shaken confidence wilted. Mortified, she turned and marched away. She was well settled in the carriage beside Cherry by the time the gentleman climbed aboard and sat opposite her. Their knees touched, and she felt a tingle of alarm spread throughout her body. Her reaction to this man was altogether too intense.

Keeping her eyes lowered, she endured the introductions.

"May I present Miss Witherspoon, Cordelia Ryburn's nan—companion. Yes, you do recognize the name, my dear man. Ryburn Department Stores are the place to shop. Miss Witherspoon, this is Mr. Adam Teague. I'm told that he's from out west."

"Chicago, ma'am," he said, grinning ever more broadly. As the carriage got underway, he focused his attention on their buxom hostess. "And has the weather improved since I left, Mrs. Ellison?"

Mrs. Ellison took a benign expression of superiority. Her eyes fixed on Betz's bright cheeks, she cooed, "Oh, *certainly*. It's been quite *soporific*. Miss Witherspoon will likely enjoy an hour or two from the rear servants' lawn. We guests, of course, get a *glorious* view of the beaches. My shell collection is extensive by now. We're making plans for the opening summer benefit, and you simply must come. I had thought you had left us, Mr. Teague."

"I had business in Providence," he said.

"Well, now that you're back I insist that you come to the benefit. Do tell us more about yourself. I've seen you skulking about Summersea's upper corridors. You have us all quite curious."

"There's nothing to tell. I'm here for my...hayfever." He shrugged modestly.

"I see, and you must be feeling quite well, I should think. Do come to the benefit, won't you? There are so few men at Summersea. Just widows and families and...ladies such as myself with husbands promising to come on the weekend...who seldom do."

"Miss Witherspoon is invited, too, I hope," he said.

Betz's collar began to feel too tight.

"You needn't concern yourself about Miss Witherspoon feeling left out of the invitations. There will be some sort of amusement that night for the servants, surely. She won't feel left out."

Mr. Teague said, stroking his chin, "She doesn't look like the sort to be relegated to attics and downstairs servants' halls."

Betz glanced at him, speechless. She could not remember the last time a man had given her a compliment.

"Why, Mr. Teague," Mrs. Ellison cried, "who among our guests would invite a servant to a hotel function such as our benefit? It just isn't done. And I'm sure Miss Witherspoon knows that to accept such an invitation would be clearly improper. Even if she was asked, she would decline. Wouldn't you, dear? She knows her place."

Betz found the woman as insufferable as George's wife. And, she had not been told she would be treated in quite this way. Mr. Teague folded his tanned, well formed hands over his hat.

"A companion isn't quite the same as a scullery maid, and I, a vacationing businessman, am no different from one of the leisure class. Times are changing, Mrs. Ellison. Class differences are dissolving."

"Not so much as that, surely!"

He gave an expression of innocence and Mrs. Ellison looked aghast.

Cherry Rose had cheeks as red as flame. Her eyes darted from Mr. Teague's smirk to her companion's stiff posture and thinned lips, and devilment made her smile. Cherry could see, if no one else could, that her companion and the unconventional Mr. Teague were meant for one another!

Three

The First Afternoon at Summersea

Struck by the serenity of the village of Huntington Station, Betz eased back in the carriage. With the unsettling Mr. Teague still watching her, she turned her attention to the quaint village tumbling toward the mast-studded docks not far distant.

A steady parade of opulent carriages was meandering the brick streets. Though no one watched from the windows of the scattered small houses, the elegantly "got-up" passengers were on display. The ladies in their ostentatious hats and fashionable silks were preening for each other, nonchalant in the extreme, but preening just the same.

"…was built twenty or so years ago to get away from the larger resorts. We always used to go to Cape May, but we've found Summersea a very nice place—smallish, of course, but it'll do. There are three other resorts nearby now…" Mrs. Ellison indicated the carriages, looking jealous, "but Summersea is still pleasant enough. And the summer climate is congenial."

"If you like fog," said Mr. Teague.

Mrs. Ellison sounded offended.

"That's part of its charm. I find the entire area very restful to my nervous condition. I've been so undone since—" She caught herself, avoiding what was apparently a hurtful subject, and took another tack. "We do have to put up with a certain amount of mixing with the masses here at Summersea. The management doesn't seem to think pricing out the riffraff is part of their function. But you'll find we're able to keep the class distinctions quite clear. I will be happy to help you to choose those with whom Cordelia should associate, Miss Witherspoon. You can't be too careful in these...*changing* times, as Mr. Teague has been kind enough to point out."

Betz's attention began to wander. Mrs. Ellison's voice faded into the background.

Ahead was a dirt road—watered to keep down the dust as the elegant afternoon procession wound its way through town and and then to the roads leading to Huntington Beach Resort, Cape Helen Hotel, and Summersea. The shadows were growing long across the tall grasses, and the sun was turning the air to gold.

Mrs. Ellison kept up a steady prattle as they made their leisurely way from town into those drowsy shadows. Cherry craned her neck, looking for likely beaus. Mr. Teague had lapsed into scrutinizing Betz with a kind of abstracted attention. This would have unnerved Betz, but she had become mesmerized by the bay that emerged broad and gray-blue ahead.

Everywhere the colors were muted, smudged together as if in a pastel drawing. The sky was dusty bluish white, the grass not green so much as reminiscent of green. Since it was late spring, the blooming trees were casting off faded petals of pink, white, and rose.

As they turned at the crest of a gradual hill, they could see Summersea a half mile distant. The hotel with sweeping grayish-white marble steps leading down to foot-printed sand, stood perched on the rim of a broad cropped lawn and lush garden.

Summersea itself was varied and irregular in the Victorian fashion, with weathered gray shingle cladding, and fancy stickwork on the many wraparound porches. One side was a huge glass rotunda that was likely the ballroom.

The carriage road cut through a field of wild miniature white daisies toward the hotel's front. The air seemed so still, the sun gently warm.

On Summersea's lawns were a scattering of abandoned white chairs and a few groupings of pigeon-shaped matrons all dressed in dark sun-absorbing worsted. A few lads lounged in the grass near the tennis pavilion. Some little girls in white muslin dresses were having a tea party with china-head dolls beneath a huge red-and-white-striped umbrella.

The carriage drew to a halt before the imposing, rambling building. All the windows were thrown open. On the breezy, shaded verandas were gentlemen reading newspapers or bent intently over checkerboards.

When a woman in heavy foulard satin came out onto the nearest porch, Mrs. Ellison resumed her prattle with, "That's Mrs. Myrtle Fitch, of the Newport Fitches. Cotton mills, you know. She is a very exacting woman. They're here this summer with their daughter Lyddie, the poor dear. They're calling her a widow, but I hear…"

She lowered her voice as a uniformed steward came around with two tiny yapping dogs on leashes. He turned them over to Mrs. Fitch's unsmiling care, and the thin woman started down the steps past the halted carriage.

She gave only a curt nod of acknowledgment to the newcomers. Her gaze never reached Mrs. Ellison, who whispered, "I hear poor Lyddie's bridegroom just ran off, just disappeared into thin air. It's the saddest story."

Mr. Teague tipped his hat, saying, "Mrs. Ellison, I suspect we must hurry just a bit. We're holding up the other carriages arriving from town."

"Oh, certainly—goodness, there's that awful Mr. Howard! Now Miss Witherspoon, I will warn you of that man, there in the white boater. *He* is what we refer to as *nouveau riche*. It's just terrible that the finer people here are forced to associate with upstarts like that, but he simply makes so much money. I'm told his factories are perfecting interchangeable parts for railroad equipment…"

"Want to buy some stock, Miss Witherspoon?" Mr. Teague asked in a joking tone.

Betz didn't know what to say. He seemed to be making fun of someone. She knew not who.

"…usually go to Saratoga, but of course, they can't this year, what with poor Lyddie needing rest. All their friends there know all the truth, just as I do. And I suppose we are a bit less straitlaced here. The old guard mixing with the *nouveau riche*...it's all quite modern, don't you think, Mr. Teague?"

He failed to respond. He was still watching Betz, who was coloring like a schoolgirl.

Adam thought Miss Witherspoon more attractive than average. Her auburn hair was done up in a severe style, but thanks to the breeze tendrils of it were escaping at her temples and nape. He didn't think he could accurately guess her age, if pressed, thirty, perhaps. She wore her years well.

Beneath a tailored black jacket, she wore a sheer white muslin blouse with understated inset lace; he liked the way it accentuated the paleness of her skin as it lay across her beautifully rounded bosom.

He didn't go in much for delicate women. His tastes ran to the more robust. But there was something about her...He felt a new stirring of interest, and was annoyed. His boredom in this place must be acute. He wished himself in Providence, involved in more stirring pursuits, without Mrs. Ellison's voice droning at the edge of his consciousness.

Suddenly, he snapped his mind to attention, as the insufferable woman said,

"...Victoria Whitgift herself. I have it on good authority that she is due to arrive with her grandson some time in late June. Now, she will be the one Cordelia will want to impress. The woman is the last word, simply the last word among the old guard families."

"Is she very rich?" the young heiress asked.

"Heavens, yes! Land, banking, railroading. Name the concern, and her late husband was involved. Her son, a formidable lawyer, was heir, of course. He married very well indeed, and she has a single grandson. Raised on the best of everything, a dear boy, he's twenty-one now and quite the handsome blade, I'm told. A bit spoiled perhaps, but aren't they all? The Whitgifts will be looking over the fresh young hopefuls for him this summer."

"Hopefuls?" Cherry inquired.

"The *ingénues,* the debutantes, dear. The young lady they pick for Master Drew must be groomed to the most impeccable standards. There are rumors that he is quite taken with the governor's niece."

"Which governor?" Miss Witherspoon inquired idly.

"Why, New York's, of course. What other would be worthy of mention? Now, Cordelia couldn't hope to do better. Why, by her coming out she could be unofficially engaged to him, and then wouldn't her future be assured! Her dear grandmother Lady Agatha is surely the only person of my acquaintance who can match the Whitgifts in wealth. It's astonishing. Cyrus Ryburn began as nothing more than a common merchant. But in terms of capital, the Ryburns, along with the Whitgifts, put the Fitches, Howards and Reinholds—and the rest of us, surely—at a decided disadvantage. Now, the Reinholds, of course, are in banking. They have the double suite directly across from—"

Teeth clenched to keep himself silent, Adam climbed down from the carriage. He had heard all this innumerable times before. He was about to go on up to his room before he realized that Mrs. Ellison was holding out her hand to him.

"Mr. Teague, if you would be so kind..."

"Pardon me, madam."

Her gloved hand felt steamy as he helped her step from the carriage. Wondering how the woman might look without that titanic corset, he stifled a laugh. "Have a good afternoon, ma'am, ladies..." He tipped his hat to the outspoken, bright-eyed young heiress.

Cordelia whispered something to the flushed Miss Witherspoon. Miss Witherspoon stiffened and looked horrified.

Pursing his lips to hide a chuckle, he turned away.

Mrs. Ellison, gesturing toward the veranda where an assortment of chairs and rockers were lined up, indicated a young family seated nearby. "They dismissed their nanny," she said. "Couldn't pay her, so I hear. Oh, don't run off, Mr. Teague! You must join us for tea!"

"You'll forgive me," he murmured, stepping away.

Catching Betz Witherspoon's eye, he wondered briefly why she looked at him with such knowing detachment. He determined once for all that she was not the one he had mistaken her for on the train. She was only what she claimed to be, a companion.

For all her attractive qualities, particularly the direct, unaffected way in which she appraised him, he did not detect much promise in her cool smile. Her reddened cheeks, however, were another matter.

Still intrigued, he tipped his hat again. "I have some things to take care of," he said, and started up the broad wooden steps.

The tottering Misses Hobble called hello to him as he reached the door, and as he tipped his hat to the elderly ladies he caught a fragment of Mrs. Ellison's loudly whispered comments.

"...he's attractive, *certainly*, but there's an air of *mystery* surrounding him. Claims to be in *shipping* but one might wonder if he's from the boardroom of a recognizable firm or merely the *warehouse*. It's the hat, I think. Not a boater, but a derby." She clucked disapprovingly. "Clearly a city man, I'm sure. No one here has a clue to his connections, and that is very suspicious. Still, he's quite pleasant. I wonder what he was doing in Providence. He doesn't talk much about himself. I always say to myself, when a man is as *closemouthed* as that, he has something to hide."

He turned, pinning Mrs. Ellison with his inscrutable smile.

"Yes, Mr. Teague? Have you changed your mind about tea?" Mrs. Ellison asked in a singsong tone.

"No, ma'am."

The young Cordelia, he noted, was watching and knew that he'd overheard. It was likely that Mrs. Ellison had intended for him to be discomfited by her poorly hushed comments. He was tempted to ask when her husband might be arriving. Lyddie Fitch-Harve wasn't the only abandoned woman in the vicinity. Then he chided himself and turned back to the shaded interior of Summersea. He had no reason to expose the buxom Mrs. Ellison's well-hidden heartache. If she didn't want anyone to find out that her husband had refused to join her at Summersea this season, it was not his business. Besides, she was a Niagara of information.

Inside, he plunged headlong toward the stairs and the stuffy silence of his third-floor cubicle. There he could be himself before descending again for the tedious trial of evening supper in the dining room.

And he made a mental note that when next in the city he must buy a new hat.

Summersea's vestibule was a typical Victorian buffer between the outside world one could not control and the exclusive inner world. With dark, carved woodwork and rich wallpapers and a wide maple staircase that caused in Betz a surge of appreciation, Summersea's public reception hall had a grandeur only money could buy.

A little girl with perfect corkscrew curls was seated at a Chickering box grand piano in the reception parlor to the right. Beyond were the closed French doors to the ballroom.

The child was listening to a man of about forty who combed his hair perfectly smooth across his thinning crown. He lifted his eyes, caught Betz's idly curious gaze and nodded.

Taken aback at first by his open familiarity, she then wondered if she was becoming too stuffy. Or was she somehow inadvertently encouraging gentlemen to approach her? Clearly, she had been out of circulation so long that she could no longer tell the difference.

"What do you think?" she asked Cherry about the hotel's quietly elegant interior. "I'm awed." And frightened, she added to herself. She felt far out of her element. She had taken on too much.

The girl was properly awestruck, too, craning her neck like a tourist, and gawking. It would certainly take some effort to give her the "I've seen it all, and I'm not impressed" look so common to the rich.

Across from a parlor cluttered with chairs, tables and potted palms was a dining room which could seat perhaps fifty. It had marvelous stained glass windows done in twining vine designs. It overlooked the side garden, and the pale, seemingly motionless expanse of sailboat-dotted bay beyond.

Even the interior had that same hushed feeling as the grounds and surrounding countryside. Subdued spring sunlight spilled from the windows and reflected on the brilliant, linen-draped tables.

The desk clerk seemed to be expecting them and directed them toward the stairs.

"I'll get you settled before I find my room," Betz said.

"Won't you be staying in the Ryburn suite?" the clerk asked, summoning a bellman for her carpetbag.

"Well, I…"

Mrs. Ellison immediately took charge, "Miss Witherspoon is hired and—"

"Begging your pardon, Mrs. Ellison, Lady Ryburn's instructions were to put Miss Witherspoon in with Miss Ryburn. Is that acceptable, Miss Witherspoon?" The young man's cheeks were reddening.

"If Lady Agatha wants it that way…" Secretly pleased and relieved to think that she would be looking after Cherry at closer proximity than the servants' quarters in the rear, she followed the bellman up the elegant staircase.

"Don't be late for tea," Mrs. Ellison called, but her expression had turned cold.

"We'll do our best to join you."

In the second floor south wing she and Cherry were ushered into a suite of three rooms—a central sitting room flanked by two sleeping rooms with individual balconies overlooking the beach. Though not luxurious, the rooms were pleasantly airy, with a breathtaking view of the bay.

Cherry plunged into the rooms like a colt, and selected her bed by bouncing on it and mussing the covers. She went out onto the balcony—the doors and windows were all open to the tart sea breeze—and flung her arms wide.

"I like it! I wish Grandmother were here! She would quiet that ghastly—" she stretched her mouth in an exaggerated haughty tone— "*ghastly* Mrs. Ellison!"

"She may not be all that bad. Your grandmother arranged for her to meet us at the train."

Cherry made a disgusted noise and tossed her curls.

Betz had been instructed that all services and gratuities were prearranged, and so all she had to concern herself with was Cherry's welfare. They would take only one meal per day in the dining room—the midday dinner, which would serve to gradually expose Cherry to Summersea's guests, light conversation and table manners. Breakfast and supper would be in their rooms under less stressful circumstances.

The room held several trunks containing gowns for Cherry's dazzling debut into the summer social world. More would arrive weekly, and anything else might be ordered from a seamstress in the village. Agatha had prepared Betz for all this.

They had their own wash room with hot and cold running water, and fresh towels. The place was not equipped with the latest lighting. They would use candles or kerosene lamps.

Cherry chose the sleeping room with twin canopy beds covered with hand-knotted, fringed netting. The floors were painted wood, the wallpaper simple in design.

Betz's room had green flowered paper and a four-poster bed with posts that rose to an inch from the ceiling. On her balcony she stood looking out over the lawn and broad beach, to the blue wash of the bay beyond. The breakers rolled in and out lazily. Gulls wheeled overhead and terns ran along the sand. To the north the shore grew rocky and treacherous. She could see a hazy hint of a pavilion perched on a promontory, and wondered if it was part of the hotel grounds. At once she wished she was there, alone, safe from prying eyes.

She wondered what the children were doing, and George, with his pretty young Cynthia in charge of what Betz had come to consider her own home. She had a queer, unsettling feeling of being cut away from that life. She had felt she was suited for it, and she had expected to lead it for the rest of her days—as maiden aunt and substitute mother.

But then George had remarried, and later when Cynthia said rudely that she didn't need a housekeeper or nanny, Betz had been surprisingly ready to answer to an advertisement in the nearest city newspaper. She had answered the reply offering the most pay and found herself accepted by Agatha Dunwitty, almost without question. It was all so very sudden.

None of that was so unsettling, however, as the feeling that she was not as distraught over leaving the strict life and household behind as she might have expected.

She felt strangely free. Like a small craft drifting leisurely out on those waves, she drifted. True, she moved toward a summer of convention more strict than anything her brother could imagine. Yet she *was* drifting.

She had misled Cherry somewhat when she had said that she missed the children. She didn't miss them as much as she thought she should. She didn't find herself grieving for a married life of her own, either.

For the first time in her life Betz was, in essence, alone. She found it was not so terrible a state. She wondered if something was seriously wrong with her, that she wasn't sizing up each male she saw and secretly measuring him for a wedding suit.

Trying to summon a desire to be married again, she found instead a desire to go on as she was. Turning from the view, she took off her hat and jacket. Then she set about planning Cherry's daily routine, allowing for long walks on the beach and a trek to that rocky point she had seen from the balcony.

Tonight she would not be cooking a rigorously dictated meal for George, nor overseeing the bathing of four reluctant though adorable children or reading them bedtime stories. Tonight she would not lie awake listening to distant whispers and sighs coming from George and Cynthia's bedchamber.

Instead, after a quiet meal in the Ryburn suite, Betz might retire with a book and think her own thoughts. Cherry would do a bit of studying.

At Summersea, Betz expected to rest and refresh herself and generally be her own person. It all seemed too good to be true.

And it was.

Four

Summersea at Dusk

"We'll unpack first and when I've gotten my bearings in this suite, perhaps we'll go down to tea. We have a lot to talk about before our debut in the dining room tomorrow afternoon."

"But I want to go out! I want to get my feet wet! You're not going to get tiresome on me suddenly, are you?"

"We'll do those things tomorrow, except that I'm not too sure bathing is allowed here," Betz said, keeping her voice low. "I didn't see anyone wading when we arrived."

Cherry heaved a sigh of extreme vexation.

"You must follow my lead here, Cherry. We have to be very careful about all we say and do. One misstep and your reputation could be forever ruined."

"If I'm too careful, I'll molder here!" Cherry cried. "We're here to have fun! Grandmother said so! Don't you remember how, *Miss Witherspoon*?" She emphasized Betz's name as if trying to provoke an argument.

Betz smiled indulgently.

"We have the whole summer. You do want to please your grandmother, don't you? You don't want to make a mistake."

"I want to please Grandmother, yes, but not any of the people Mrs. Ellison thinks are so special. I'd like to put a gag in the mouth of that one, wouldn't you? What do you think she's saying about us at this very moment?" She struck an affected pose that was astonishingly like the refined haughty attitude Betz had been thinking

Cherry would never be able to mimic. "That Miss Witherspoon…" Cherry said, imitating Mrs. Ellison's tone, "is rather out of her element at Summersea. One will not expect her to ever fit in. Not on the servant's lawn. Not in the dining room, surely. And that young Cordelia…" Her drawn expression became even more droll. "She is just the most uncivilized creature ever to set hoof on our sacred soil. Why, did you see her running about in the sand just now as if she was enjoying herself? Now that won't do. Not at all."

Eyes popping, Betz burst into a laugh.

"Where did you learn to speak like that? You could be an actress!"

"I know what they'll think of me here, Miss—Betz. They'll think I'm not as good, but I'll show them." She flounced to the nearest chair and sat with one foot curled beneath her. "I'll play their silly games, and I'll even make eyes at the *right* beaus, but it'll all be for show, just as Grandmother said. And then I'll be able to go on a world tour with her and meet *real* people. You don't think Grandmother will die in Persia, do you?"

"I believe she was headed for India. And no, you mustn't worry." The girl seemed pathetically fearful of being left alone.

"I did like that Mr. Teague, though," Cherry said, leaping up and dashing for the balcony. "I wonder what he's doing here."

"Not trying to impress anyone, I don't think," Betz said absently. An image of his robust features and pent up energy came to mind. With an unwelcome shiver of excitement, she pushed the thoughts away.

"There, I knew you liked him! It was written all over you."

Betz was afraid Cherry was too correct. She had to smile, then.

"I suppose it can't hurt for us to take a short constitutional. I need to think."

"You can take a constitutional. I'll take a walk. Last one to the rocks is a stuffed shirt!"

Cherry dashed out the door and down the hall, her high-buttoned shoes clattering like a child's. She paused, drawing up her dignity as she descended the stairs. Alarmed, Betz followed at a breathless pace, unwilling to call out a reprimand that might be heard by those having afternoon tea in the dining room.

Cherry hiked up her skirts and was running across the sand the moment she had skidded down the broad marble steps. Betz gave up hope of checking her abandon.

At Cherry's age, Betz had been secluded in her mother's house, faced with ten more years of nursing her ailing mother. There had been no carefree summers for her, no well-intentioned matrons grooming her for a good match.

Only once had Betz felt that free. Within three months she'd been married, prisoner to a new kind of social convention, that of her husband's inescapable rule. The honeyed words that had poured from his lips had been hypnotic. The bruises his fists left had shattered her innocence.

Only once had she defied convention by seeking a lawyer and getting her divorce. From that moment she had behaved as she had been previously taught, convinced that the only way to the dim duskiness of the future was the given and accepted one.

With renewed resolve Betz marched after Cherry, alarmed that she had momentarily allowed the girl to escape the very chains that could assure her a happy, well-kept future. The suffocating rules of society were necessary, if Cherry hoped to avoid the personal shame Betz had known as a divorcée. If Cherry failed to make a good start in society, she had no duty-bound brother to take her in. Without Agatha, Cherry was doomed to become a common creature as her mother had been.

"Cherry! You mustn't run! And do stop showing your petticoats! What will they all think?" She could feel eyes boring into her back—and hated her own words—as she rushed after the girl.

Somewhere deep inside was a voice urging her to throw off her shoes and splash into the surf, but she ran on, with her corset crushing her ribs and constricting her lungs, her heavy skirts dragging her down to earth like a thousand hands.

She paused once and turned to look back. Summersea stood like a a back-lit shadow, frowning across the beach like a worsted-clad dowager.

The bay was so broad with the tide coming in. In a few hours the waves would reach the marble steps. The world suddenly seemed overwhelming in its complexity.

The Pavilion at Sunset

In the hotel, Adam Teague stood in his third floor cubicle, near a small circular window in one of the many gables, watching the two figures rushing toward the rocky shore.

Gilded in the sunset, their shapes made wavy and indistinct by the thick old glass he was peering through, the two women were growing ever farther apart. The first found the trail leading up to the pavilion at Fog Point and clambered up the many crudely constructed wooden steps. The second slowed to a walk, resigned. He wondered if Mrs. Ellison was watching them, too.

Then Adam looked at his watch. It was time for him to prowl the halls. He expected nothing out of the ordinary to happen, and that annoyed him.

Cherry scrambled up the last of the wooden steps that cut between the trees crowding the point. The pavilion stood at the very edge of the rocks, dappled by elongated afternoon shadows. Behind her to the west, was a brilliant orange and pink sunset. Before her was the coming darkness of night spreading over the vast bay.

Shivering, Cherry turned to face the sunset. The pavilion was about twelve feet across, circular, with a picket railing, peaked roof and benches all around. She could hear the surf crashing below as the tide advanced. Her companion's footsteps were loud on the steps as she made her way up from the sand below. Cherry wished she could be alone a while longer, yet it was comforting to know Miss Witherspoon was near.

It was comforting, too, to think that her companion cared enough to follow. Another sort of chaperone might have left her to find her way back to the hotel alone.

Cherry felt so out of place—not just Summersea, but in the world. Everything she did or said or thought was under someone's sharp disapproving eye. She felt like a bug in a jar, trapped and yet terrified of being set free.

If only Mama hadn't died, she thought, still furious at the way things had changed so suddenly. She had loved her mama, certainly, though she had never received the attention she craved.

Throwing out her arms to the chilling breeze, she turned to face the darkening sea. She felt a rush of panic, and stood fast to endure it. What could be worse than being orphaned? What could be better than to discover a wealthy grandmother? If only she knew how to be what was expected of her.

"So, there you are," Miss Witherspoon said, panting as she topped the last step. "That was quite a climb! This corset will be the death of me."

"One hundred twelve steps," Cherry said, darting to kneel on the bench. She leaned out over the rail.

When Miss Witherspoon said nothing more, Cherry stole a peek at her companion. Betz stood, feet apart, face into the sunset, eyes closed while her breathing grew even. Her hair had come loose and was feathering thick tendrils all around her face and shoulders. Her cheeks were flushed prettily. Standing like that—without her traveling jacket, wearing only the long black skirt and sheer muslin blouse over several layers of propriety beneath—she looked alarmingly young.

Absently, Miss Witherspoon gathered her unruly hair and then finally opened her eyes. She looked annoyed as she plucked pins from the smooth auburn waves and held them between her lips. For an instant a cascade of auburn tumbled down her back to her waist. Facing the wind so that it would smooth tendrils back from her face, she quickly twisted and knotted her hair into submission.

"You have beautiful hair, Miss Witherspoon. Do you ever wear it down? For a dance, maybe?" Cherry asked.

"I'm far too old for that," Betz said with a smile. She entered the pavilion and took a seat close to Cherry. Twisting to gaze back at the darkening sea, she hooked one leg beneath the other and sat for some time, looking thoughtfully at the horizon. She seemed very young indeed.

Then Betz realized Cherry was staring. She caught herself in the casual pose, straightened, and primly folded her hands. Bringing her knees tightly together, she contemplated the assortment of dry leaves caught beneath the benches.

"We can come here as often as you like, Cherry," she said gently. "But I do think we had best be back in our rooms before nightfall. I can't tell you how bad it would look for us to be out alone. I ask your cooperation, Cherry."

Asked so nicely, Cherry found she could not bring herself to refuse.

As she followed Betz down the stairs Cherry thought about the interesting Mr. Teague. He *was* a guest at Summersea, not some bit of riffraff. He was the most interesting person she'd seen here yet. And the most real. In Cherry's opinion, Miss Witherspoon needed someone like that.

The Second Day

Friday, May 31, 1889

Precisely at eight the following morning, Mrs. Ellison tapped on the door urgently. Betz was still seated beside the breakfast tray, munching an apple muffin and trying to convince Cherry that the only way to learn piano was to go down to the reception parlor, sit before one, and receive instructions.

"In front of everyone?" Cherry had just cried. "I couldn't! I won't!"

Betz had nearly reached the door when Mrs. Ellison popped

her head in, gaped at Betz's dressing gown and then surged in.

"Well, you certainly look comfortable here together. I was just saying at breakfast that I was certain you were up, but I couldn't imagine where you were. I knew you wouldn't want to miss a perfectly wonderful morning like this." Mrs. Ellison saw the breakfast tray then. "Oh, you're dining in. Aren't you feeling well?"

Cherry rolled her eyes to one side and gulped her freshly squeezed orange juice. She would have escaped to the balcony if she hadn't caught Betz's admonishing look.

"Good morning, Mrs. Ellison," Cherry said, "Did you have a comfortable night?" Her voice was an overly polite singsong, exactly like Mrs. Ellison's.

"Oh, well I...I've come to take you out for a morning promenade with the rest of us. All of my dearest friends will be along. Emma, Gettie, Millie, Myrtle and Lyddie...It's a long walk to the spring from the road, but worth the effort. I know you'll enjoy meeting everyone."

"We'll be along in a while," Betz said.

"Oh, *you* needn't rush, dear. I'll just wisk Cordelia away and you can dawdle along later if you like. Just everyone will be along, Cordelia, and it's ever so stimulating. You know, I heard the most regrettable thing. The Marshes haven't paid their bill. They should never have come here if they couldn't afford it, but some people will go to any lengths to be among the privileged..." She looked pointedly at Betz. "Come along, Cordelia, dear. We mustn't keep everyone waiting." She cocked her head as if to say that Betz couldn't be expected to know how one got on at Summersea.

Not wishing to make a scene by refusing to let Cherry go without her, Betz nodded. "You can go along if you like, Cher—Cordelia."

Cherry made a face, wanting to be rescued from the insufferable promenade.

"But I'm not dressed!"

Mrs. Ellison threw up her hands in mock exasperation.

"You helpless children of privilege...you've probably been waited on hand and foot since birth. I've been wondering about your very interesting *background,* Cordelia. Where, exactly, did you live among savages? I don't recall a single word about Agatha Ryburn's son being an African hunter. I don't recall any professional *bent* whatsoever, if truth be known. But then one does lose track of the children of long-lost friends."

Cherry's mouth hung agape. The woman was moving into her room as if preparing to assist with her dressing. Cherry darted to intercept her.

"I'll be right out, Mrs. Ellison. Please ask everyone to forgive me for keeping them waiting."

Blustering, obviously disappointed at being prevented from looking through the belongings hanging in Cherry's wardrobe, Mrs. Ellison took her leave.

"You handled that very well, Cherry," Betz said the moment the woman was gone. "I'm somewhat doubtful that you need me to teach you deportment."

"You won't leave me with her all day, will you? I'll run off!" Cherry cried. "I will! I'll hide myself away for days and days!"

"I won't leave you alone with her any longer than it takes to dress, reserve time at the piano and order artist's supplies from the village. Do mind what you tell her about...Africa."

Cherry grinned as she flounced into her room.

"Betz, you've stuck your foot in it this time!"

The Invalid

Cherry had been gone nearly a half hour by the time Betz completed her chores and appointments. She was just turning from the desk clerk when a belligerent looking nurse in black gown and starched white apron rustled across the hall from the dining room. She smelled faintly of tobacco smoke.

"Are you ready, Mr. Bonaventure?" the nurse called loudly.

As Betz started for the door to the veranda, the nurse added, "Oh, you—Miss? Would you hold the door for us?"

Betz turned. The nurse was now pushing a young man in an elaborate chair fitted with wheels. His face was astonishingly handsome. He couldn't be more than thirty-three, with thick brown hair and hooded dark eyes.

For an instant, Betz thought he gazed at her rather harshly. Then a benign smile tugged at the corner of his mouth, and he looked at her so intensely that she wondered if he was as sickly as he appeared.

She held the door while the nurse wheeled him onto the veranda, then stood a moment longer watching the black-clad woman adjust his plaid lap robe. He folded his hands in his lap, the picture of docility, and gazed wistfully out across the lawn to the beach and breakers. The nurse turned up his collar against the strong morning breezes.

Two elderly ladies in black shuffled over from around the far corner of the veranda, the shorter supporting the taller.

"Good morning, Mr. Bonaventure. Were you able to sleep?" the delicate tall lady asked, stopping to observe him.

"Miss Hobble, how kind of you to ask after my health," he said, taking her hand and brushing the top of it with his smiling lips. "You look especially lovely this morning. Have you changed your hair?"

She dimpled, resisting the urge to pat her carefully arranged snowy curls.

"You're such a dear to notice. Isn't he a dear, Gettie?"

"Sister, I have always said, and still do, that Mr. Bonaventure appears to take a keen interest in everything around him. It's the nature of an invalid. You're looking well, Mr. Bonaventure. What news from your doctor?"

"Nothing encouraging, I fear," he said. Then he brightened. "But we can continue to hope."

"Excuse me, sister, I mean to introduce myself to our new guest." The shorter woman nodded a curt good-bye to the man in the wheelchair and strode forward. "Good morning, Miss Witherspoon. I'm Gertrude Hobble. Everyone presumes to call me Gettie. My sister Millie is gushing over the very handsome Mr. Bonaventure. A very safe beau, and I suppose, pleasant to look at. I hear that Agatha

Ryburn has come up with a granddaughter. Isn't that remarkable. What can you tell us about this Cordelia?"

Rigidly on guard, Betz escaped having to answer, because a tall, gangling old man with spectacles askew and a wiry, gray goatee plunged through the doors. His easel and sketch box caught on the screen, and his stretched canvas displaying a half completed oil seascape nearly dropped onto the gritty veranda.

"Ladies, if you would, give a man some space. Yammering females…standing in doorways…makes a man wonder why their tongues don't fall…Jehoshaphat, these damned breezes!" He marched on down the steps, struggling as the winds caught his canvas like a sail. Muttering words they couldn't make out, he disappeared across the beach.

"Pay that old fool no mind whatsoever. He's a nuisance. I don't know why he's allowed to stay," Gettie muttered.

Millie Hobble joined her sister. Looking sweetly on like a tall, white-haired child, she said, "So this is our new guest. When we heard Agatha was sending us a grandchild for the summer, our astonishment was complete."

"Hardly," put in her sister. "We all knew Harry Ryburn would come to no good. African hunter, indeed. We're not fooled, Miss Witherspoon. A chance-child from the slums. I'm too old to keep quiet on what I think is proper, and what I think is not."

Frowning, Betz looked first from the sweet-faced Millie to her brittle elder sister Gettie.

"My employer gave me the impression her granddaughter would be among friends at Summersea."

Gettie Hobble sniffed her opinion. "If Agatha thinks her world travels impress us, she's mistaken. She has not seen fit to visit with us in years. Not a card or letter, since I can remember. Agatha has thoroughly neglected us all. Snubbed, might be a more fitting description. And you, sister, must stop fawning over Mr. Bonaventure. He is too young for a maid of sixty-one. Your reputation is spotless, and his connections are tenuous, at best."

Behind them, Mr. Bonaventure coughed into a handkerchief.

As the coughing fit worsened, his nurse wheeled him out of earshot.

"You've offended him, sister! said Millie, alarmed. "It's such a shame, and he's such a wonderful-looking man. That's how it is with consumptives in their last months, you know. Robust until the last gasp. Gettie, I wish you wouldn't speak so loudly. How he must feel now..."

"Everyone here knows my opinions."

"But he heard you, and the dear boy is at death's door—"

"Excuse me, ladies," Betz interrupted. "I promised to join Cordelia and the others. They're taking the waters..."

"You'll never catch up to them afoot, Miss Witherspoon, Gettie said, "They go out to Poonsocket's Pond by wagon and walk the rest of the way to the spring. You'll have to wait until they get back. Did you sleep through breakfast?"

Betz turned away, pretended not to hear the question, and hurried down the steps. She wouldn't dignify the old woman's insulting question with an answer.

Not having the slightest idea in which direction Cherry and the others had gone, she wandered across the lawn. Skirting the deserted tennis pavilion, Betz found her way back toward some outbuildings where the hotel staff had their rooms.

Across a dreary-looking enclosed lawn where several children's play tables and an abandoned wicker perambulator stood, two youths in long white pants sat beneath a tree. When they caught sight of her, they remained silently motionless hoping that she wouldn't notice the trails of smoke lifting from their concealed hands.

The servants' and children's lawn, she concluded. She wondered if she might feel more comfortable there after all.

The hotel grounds hugged the sandy shore. Beyond, the eccentric artist had set up his easel and was attempting to paint in spite of the wind buffeting his canvas.

Near him, a man in shirt sleeves was seated in the sand. He saw her, Betz was certain. She couldn't go back now. To avoid him would be too obvious. With reluctance, she walked on, headlong into the scrutiny of Mr. Adam Teague.

Five

A Morning on the Beach

As Betz passed behind Mr. Teague, who was sitting in the sand with his knees up and his tanned forearms crossed over them, she thought it peculiar and rude that he said nothing by way of greeting. He might at least be polite.

The drenching sun highlighted his wavy brown hair and accentuated his aggressive profile. He was squinting into the morning brilliance reflected from the placid bay, and that made a series of attractive wrinkles fan from the corners of his eyes, framing his upper cheeks.

In that casual pose, he radiated restrained energy, his hands large and well-formed, long fingers laced between his knees, capable looking. She thought it odd that she should notice his hands, and find them so…compelling.

Still he didn't acknowledge her arrival on the beach. Feeling ignored, she made her way across the deep sand with as much grace as possible, to stand several feet behind the windblown artist at his easel.

The old man struggled to make a stroke with a wide brush, his white hair shifting in the breeze like beach grass. Finally, he stood back, cursing mildly under his breath. He jerked off his paint-daubed cap, slapped it against his thigh and replaced it on his head. His spectacles glinted in the sun, blinding Betz when he turned to her.

"Can I do something for you, dear?" he asked rather gruffly, throwing back his head to observe her through the flashing lenses.

His graying goatee was wiry, his poorly trimmed mustaches turned up slightly at the tips. As he grimaced at her, she could see that one of his front teeth was broken, giving his half smile a rakish air.

"Please continue, sir. I didn't mean to interrupt."

He went on looking at her, his mouth half-open, his eyes masked behind the circles of reflected sunlight.

"Surely you have an opinion of my work. Every female in creation does."

"I'm not qualified to make any observation, but the painting gives me a warm, peaceful feeling. The colors make me feel serene, like a sunny summer morning."

Closing his mouth, he gave a huff of disbelief and turned away to make several more strokes on the canvas.

"Damnedest thing I ever heard a woman say. They usually say it's very good, or the style is admirable..." He stood back, pushed his spectacles back to the bridge of his nose. With the brush, he left a yellow ochre blotch on the narrow bill of his cap. "One woman once had the audacity to say that I might think to sell a few of my paintings. She thought my talent had some merit."

Betz thought a moment and then smiled.

"Something tells me, sir, that her remark struck you as obtuse. I would venture to guess that as an artist you are world renowned."

"Obtuse? Stupid is a better word. Of course, my paintings are good. They tell me that in New York the critics especially like the sand—" The wind buffeted the canvas, threatening to send it sailing to the beach. "I've reached a conclusion. Any canvas that hasn't fallen at least once gets a handful of sand just to satisfy the stylists in New York."

The old man stooped and took up a handful of sand. He twisted to look at Betz from the side of his glinting lenses. He seemed to be daring her to stop him from throwing the sand at the wet painting. Betz felt as if the old man was testing her wits. She longed to please him with the correct answer, but couldn't imagine what he might expect of her.

"I'm sure you know the effect you want, sir. Surely the opinion of others doesn't concern you."

"Jehoshaphat, an intelligent woman! Adam, my friend, take note of her." Dropping the sand, he stepped back and seized her arm, leaving a trace of zinc white on her muslin sleeve. "Look here, at this, dear. I want to achieve the glare, the brilliance of the morning. The shimmer of the water, the heat. Summer!"

She stared into his painting, mesmerized by the genius of his seemingly effortless technique. A sultry feeling stole over her as she admired what he could do with mere paint. She watched in fascination as he applied rapid strokes, capturing the feeling of a day at the beach.

Then she was aware of Adam standing directly behind her, so close that the currents of breeze around them were altered. The color rose to her cheeks, and her flesh tingled. She resisted glancing back at him, but she was no longer engrossed in the painting.

"This is Warren Woodley," Adam said softly, as if in a private conversation. She recognized the name at once. Her best friend Otila Watkins owned a small Woodley landscape; she had paid dearly for it.

"Not world renowned, dear," the old man said, laughing a little. "Notorious, perhaps. I'm staying at this godforsaken nuisance of a hotel because it's the best I can manage this season. What is your excuse, my dear?"

Betz could see from the old man's crinkled eyes behind the lenses that he was teasing.

"Work," she said simply. Feeling breathless because of the solid, very masculine man standing so near, she couldn't elaborate.

"Ah, well that explains it. Give an old man some silence now, if you please." Mr. Woodley turned away.

Betz had to glance back to get Mr. Teague to give her space to back away. She stumbled in the giving sand as if tipsy, her mouth dry and her entire body trembling. Her mind was a blank. "If you'll both excuse me…"

She could see a brightly painted wagon back beside the hotel's veranda. Matrons wearing black and girls in white dresses were climbing down from it. Mr. Teague just grinned down at her and then muttered something beneath his breath to the artist. Then he moved to Betz's side as she made her way across the sand.

"Let me assist you, Miss Witherspoon." He cradled her elbow with a firm grip.

"Not necessary," she said, her pulse leaping.

"Planning to stay long at Summersea?"

As the matrons turned one by one to watch her approach alongside Mr. Teague, she said, "The summer," trying to walk more quickly and escape his searing touch.

"I hear there's a benefit tea, or ball, or something of the sort, to be held in another week. Mrs. Ellison was referring to it yesterday on the way from the train. You remember, when she was trying so hard to put you on the servant's lawn?" His voice was hushed, intimate, his touch still most unsettling.

Betz began to tingle.

"If you're thinking of asking me for a dance—"

"No, I wasn't thinking of that," Mr. Teague said, "but if you find yourself not included…when it comes to snobbery, the people here are worse than the Vanderbilts and Astors. You'd think we were among millionaires the way they put on the dog. But as I was trying to say, you might consider accompanying me to Newport. I know of a number of amusements there."

"I couldn't possibly," she said, turning to look up into his appraising dark eyes. Betz's step faltered. She felt flattered beyond reason, and flustered because her refusal was so emphatic and automatic. If she were not a chaperone…

"A pity, Miss Witherspoon," he murmured. He gave a slight bow and turned away.

With her mind whirling, she watched him head back in the direction of Mr. Woodley.

She had forced herself to do the right thing. Now she felt as if she had missed a train. She wanted to run after him, waving her arm and crying yes, yes! she would go anywhere with him!

She stumbled and caught her breath. What a startling thought!

As Adam strode away, his shoulders powerful beneath his shirt, his waist so broad, his thighs sturdy and well-developed, she was undone to realize again her physical attraction for this man…in such a particularly unsettling womanly way. She had thought herself immune to it, cured of it, purged of it by an ocean of tears.

She stumbled again and paused to fuss with her shoe, wanting to avoid the matrons who seemed to be waiting like vultures. For the moment, she wanted to speak to no one. She wanted only to understand her feelings. If she had been anywhere else, under any other circumstances, she might have accepted Mr. Teague's clearly improper invitation.

Straightening, she brushed invisible sand from her hands and strode on. Thankfully, she thought, she was safe from such dangerous choices here. She could have nothing to do with Mr. Teague, nor any other man. She must be perfectly behaved at all times.

But her confusing reaction still unnerved her. As she approached the ladies waiting beside scowling Cherry, she suddenly thought how thoroughly she disliked them. When they greeted her in their mirthless, superior manner, she was secretly angry with them for standing between her and the freedom to do what she wanted with her life.

Felicia Ellison, by virtue of her acquaintance with Betz the previous day, spoke first. "Well, dear Miss Witherspoon, we're so glad to see you're finally up and about this fine morning. You're certainly welcome to take the waters with us any morning that you so desire, but of course, you must rise a bit earlier."

At Cherry's side, Betz found it surprising that the girl said nothing in her defense; she had after all, been up at dawn. Then she noticed that Cherry's cheeks were flushed, and her eyes ablaze. Alerted for trouble, Betz fixed her attention on the introductions.

"I see that you were talking to that Mr. Teague again. Well, never mind. Later I'll speak to you privately on the subject." Felicia then indicated the eldest woman in the group.

Myrtle Fitch wore her silvering blond hair brushed severely back from her high, thin-skinned forehead. Her sparse brows frowned eloquently over small, sharp eyes that reminded Betz of a fox's. She was thin, and wore a gown similar to the severe lifeless gray one she had worn the day before.

Introduced to the woman's pale daughter Lyddie, who looked about twenty, Betz scarcely had time to smile before the girl was jerked away by her disapproving mother and hustled toward the veranda.

Felicia then introduced a heavier matron who smiled wanly and said, "How very pleased we are to have the pleasure of Cordelia's company this summer." Then she turned away, done with all tedious niceties.

"And this," Felicia said with feigned regard, "is our lovely Lillian, Mr. Howard's wife. Have you met Leon Howard yet, Miss Witherspoon?"

Betz shook her head.

Lillian was the mother of the darling four-year-old who had been practicing the piano the day before. She also had a fifteen-year-old stepdaughter. From the sneer on the girl's face and Cherry's studied silence, Betz knew at once that the two girls had clashed.

Felicia nearly forgot to introduce an attractive young woman who seemed touchingly eager to be included and then sent her on to the hotel with Cherry. She then turned to Betz, giving her her most sincere frown of concern.

'*Dear* Miss Witherspoon, I feel it is my *duty* as an old friend of Lady Agatha's to *warn* you that Mr. Teague, while certainly an *attractive* and congenial man, is not a wise choice of company for you. While in another setting you might expect to get on very *nicely* with Mr. Teague, I feel you would be wiser not to encourage him here."

"You're very kind to advise me, Mrs. Ellison," Betz said rigidly.

"I knew you'd understand. One simply can't be too careful these days. A Chicago man...why, he might be just *anyone.* And, as Cordelia's chaperone...well, you see the implications."

"Implications?" Betz felt herself growing angry.

"Why the dear child has only a *ghost* of a chance of acceptance here, appearing as she has from the very depths of nowhere. And now with this incident at the spring this morning to start things off…" She plucked a fan from her reticule, snapped it open and fluttered it before her face. "Oh, my."

"You certainly must tell me about it," Betz said cautiously.

"I feel entirely responsible, of course," Felicia said breathlessly. "I swept the dear child away this morning, not thinking, not remembering your very wise and prudent warning that the child… well, *where* exactly were these savages, Miss Witherspoon?"

Betz didn't answer.

Blithely, Felicia went on, "I asked her, of course, but Cordelia just said the most extraordinary thing. Something about the darkest avenues of the world, among creatures so vicious that a female by the time she was twelve—twelve!—could not hope to possess a single remaining virtue!"

"Oh, dear," Betz muttered.

"Such scandalous talk before the tender ears of the Fitch and Reinhold girls! I must say I was faint, simply faint! And leave it to that cheap little Howard creature—not fit to sit at our tables at dinner, I can tell you, and her stepmother is no better—that cheap little creature asked if Cordelia still retained any of hers!"

The fan fluttered, and Betz felt dull with dread for all that remainder of the summer promised. If this was any indication of how people at Summersea behaved…

"You needn't go into detail about the incident, if you're so distressed, Mrs. Ellison," she said, knowing full well that the woman was savoring every instant of the recounting.

Felicia took a deep breath and went on. "I don't know *what* possessed Cordelia to attack with such a vengeance. It was done in such a sweet way that I cannot help but wonder what goes on behind her dear little face. Why, Cordelia looked right at Marietta Howard and said quite distinctly—I won't soon forget!—that she had more than Marietta. 'More than you.' That's just what she said."

"I see," Betz said flatly, growing impatient.

"She meant *virtues* you see, dear. I was speechless. I'm terribly concerned about what Marietta's father may say to you when he hears. He can be quite unpleasant."

"I'm sure I can handle it," Betz said, not sure at all.

Felicia went on as if she hadn't heard Betz say a word.

"I'm so upset about what Agatha will think when she hears, too. Insults and slurs…so common. How *will* we keep this out of the tabloids?"

"Tabloids?" Betz asked, thoroughly bewildered.

"We're all concerned about public gossip. The lower classes are so morbidly curious about us, don't you know. If Marietta can't hold her tongue, it's only a reflection of her background, you see. If Cordelia acts the same…well, I can only imagine what the better families will think of her. I'm concerned about her future, her standing, her reputation."

"I will certainly discuss the matter with Cordelia at some length," Betz said, trembling with irritation.

The pair of elderly sisters came out onto the veranda, and Felicia smiled distractedly and murmured, "How nice." Glancing at the sisters almost as if she feared them, she started away toward the tennis pavilion. "We'll see you both at dinner, I trust. One o'clock, sharp. Try to be on time."

The Dinner Debut

Betz found Cherry sitting cross-legged on her bed. Sighing, she plucked off her hat and went to stand in the breeze coming from the open balcony doors. She unbuttoned her jacket, wishing she had had more time alone on the beach. And now she must think how to approach Cherry about the incident with Marietta Howard.

Cherry still looked grim as she met Betz's quietly encouraging gaze. Finally she shrugged.

"Marietta made me furious! She was acting so high and mighty. I know her kind! She's a cheap little thing. I saw her wave to two of the waiters, and I think she knows the man who was driving the wagon this morning. I saw him put his hand on her backside."

Betz made a face of disbelief, but Cherry nodded.

"She didn't think I noticed, but I did! And, Betz, what am I going to do about this awful story you made up? Savages!" She glared at Betz, her fists balled, her cheeks aflame. "Everyone's asking me where I grew up, and Grandmother told me I mustn't say anything about the mills and factories, or the beer halls and…"

Betz waved her silent, fearful suddenly that the walls of the suite had ears.

"I am terribly sorry about that," she said. Crossing into the sitting room, she removed her shoes and poured sand into a small waste can beneath the table. "I spoke on impulse. I truly don't know what to do about it. I didn't think it'd be so hard to get along with well-bred people. We haven't been here a day and I've allowed you to make several blunders."

Cherry scowled, with a frightened pinch to her eyes.

"And Grandmother would be angry with me if we had to leave, wouldn't she? Well, I just won't talk to anyone, anymore! I'll stay right here. And rot!"

"Nonsense. We're going down to dinner soon, and you'll do just fine. We'll just have to try a little harder. We'll have a practice session right now, and you'll see. You'll show them all that you're as well-behaved as a girl raised with nuns."

Cherry scoffed, and then giggled. She took a seat at the sitting room table, watching as Betz named all the silver in a place setting. Betz called off the uses of a dozen dishes and goblets. They talked over the proper forms of address, and all safe areas of conversation.

Then they dressed in fresh things—a plain gown for Betz and a rather stunning blue one for Cherry, who grinned with delight at it in spite of her nerves.

They presented themselves at the dining room at the appointed one o'clock hour.

The room was aglow. Soft afternoon sunlight fell through the twining vine stained glass. There were tables of varying sizes scattered about the room, and dozens of guests were arriving from several doors opening to the veranda.

The air of aristocratic decorum in the room was unnerving. If *she* was concerned about making the right moves, Betz thought, how nervous Cherry must be.

Halfway across the dining room, thinking that Cherry was at her heels, Betz noticed that each table had hand-lettered placecards tucked into miniature china ducks. Turning to glance at the names at the nearest table, she noticed Cherry furtively checking placecards at other tables as well. Looking mischievous, Cherry finally signaled that she had found their places.

Betz kept Cherry from seating herself, whispering, "Stand quietly behind the chair until I can determine who is hostess, or until everyone else sits down."

As the room filled, there seemed to be some confusion about the names. To Betz's dismay, she saw that the placecard at the head of her table read, Mr. Teague. Her chest constricted and she knew she couldn't wait to see his face again. At the same time, she dreaded the encounter. Would he again make some improper invitation, or cause her face to redden and her heart to flutter? She was altogether too old for such foolishness, but she seemed unable to shake off her growing excitement.

Startling Betz, a handsome man of medium height in his late thirties grasped the back of the chair across from her. The rings on his hands glinted with diamonds. With a penetrating gaze, he smiled at her in an especially predatory way.

"Good afternoon, ladies." His voice was curiously smooth. "I'm Leon Howard, in case you don't already know." His somewhat eastern accent made Betz suspect he, too, had once been a "city" man.

"I'm happy to make your acquaintance, Mr. Howard. I had the pleasure of meeting your wife a short time ago," Betz said, noticing the woman coming into the dining room.

Mr. Howard's wife paused at their table, saw that her name was not on any of the placecards and narrowed her eyes. Without a word, she turned away, finding her place nearby.

"Perhaps we should move," Betz offered.

"Nonsense, ladies. We're often shuffled about, like pawns." He winked at Cherry.

Another man, the piano teacher Betz had seen the day before, looked anxiously for his placecard. Finally he seemed relieved to find it and grasped his chair back with long white fingers. He looked disconcerted to find Mr. Howard gazing at him with lifted brows. Then he glanced at Betz and remembered to smile.

"How is it that you're at my table today, Macklin?" Mr. Howard inquired with a smirk.

"I'm sure I don't know, sir," the piano teacher said, stepping back. "I can't sit elsewhere if..." He looked around and saw that Mrs. Howard and their young daughter were seated nearby, scowling. Mr. Howard's teenaged son and daughter were at still another table, obviously pleased to be out from under their parents' scrutiny.

"Oh, go ahead and sit with us," Mr. Howard said, waving his hand. "I don't give a damn where you sit. Pardon my language, ladies. There seems to be a lot of intrigue going on when it comes to seating arrangements in this hotel. I hear the waiters make a veritable fortune in bribes by switching around the placecards that our formidable Mrs. Ellison takes such pains to arrange according to rank. I hope *you* don't mind sitting with *me,* Miss Witherspoon. I find your face ever so refreshingly pink."

Thoroughly taken aback by Mr. Howard's boldness, Betz turned her attention to the more genial piano teacher.

Mr. Macklin had dark, neatly trimmed chin whiskers and gentle eyes. He combed his hair to conceal its thinning on top. She gave him a weak smile, because Mr. Howard had been so rude to him.

One of the elderly Hobble sisters, Millie, arrived then. Finding her placecard, she sat without ceremony.

"So distressing—Do sit, gentlemen. Don't wait on me." As her sister sat elsewhere the two frowned at one another, obviously suspicious.

They had taken their seats when Mr. Teague approached. Spying his card, he said, "Ah, I should have guessed. Afternoon, Howard. Who could have accomplished such an interesting mix at this table?"

Betz was immediately engulfed in an overwhelming sense of selfconsciousness. Was Adam looking at her? Would he speak to her, and if so, what would he say? Whatever had been on her mind seconds before was now gone!

Cherry, looking alarmed, concealed a stray placecard in the folds of her skirt. She had plucked it from the table moments before. It dropped to the floor. It clearly read Gettie Hobble, but no one saw it.

Waiters carrying steaming platters fanned between the tables. A gangling lad, frowning with concentration, placed two dishes on their table, and then stepped back, gazing at Cherry. His cheeks went red before he turned away, stumbled over his feet and headed for the door to the pantry.

"You may begin passing, Mr. Macklin," Miss Hobble said to the piano teacher. Pleased to find herself presiding at the table, she saw to all necessary introductions.

Everyone listened attentively as Miss Hobble extolled Mr. Macklin's virtues. Betz was finally able to gather that Nolan Macklin was the Howards' tutor, versed in everything from piano and violin to Latin and arithmetic.

Betz nodded and murmured casually, subtly showing Cherry which utensil to use, but when she realized that Mr. Teague was indeed watching her, color rose alarmingly from her neck to her forehead. She suddenly felt that she couldn't think and felt an awkward smile spread on her face. Oh, why did he have to be sitting at her table?

Noticing her lack of composure, he chuckled softly behind his napkin. Cherry watched with silent delight and nearly giggled. At that moment, the elderly Miss Hobble stopped speaking. She gave Betz a withering look.

"What are you smiling at, Miss Witherspoon?"

"E-excuse me?" Betz sputtered. She had no idea what Miss Hobble meant.

"You were all sniggering about something. Have I gotten a spot of soup on my chin?" The frail old woman looked wounded and angry. She looked about for her sister, who was watching with cold eyes nearby. "I wish I knew who separated us," she said distractedly. "My sister looks quite angry with me."

Betz patted the old woman's trembling hand, and murmured, "We certainly weren't—"

Cherry came to the rescue, lying with astonishing eloquence. "I kicked Miss Witherspoon under the table. A private joke."

At that moment the waiter returned to remove the plates. A small square of paper lay where Mr. Teague's plate had been.

"What's that, Mr. Teague?" Cherry asked.

Mr. Howard leaned closer to Adam, one brow cocked.

"What have we here, Adam? Love notes?"

Adam unfolded the note and read the message in a single glance.

"I doubt this was meant for me." He looked pointedly at Betz and then Cherry. "This isn't my usual seat. Who was sitting here yesterday, Leon, do you remember?"

"Are you implying that I arranged to sit next to you?" Betz demanded, not thinking how such a response would sound.

Mr. Teague lifted his hands, palms up, in a gesture of innocence.

"It is my pleasure, I assure you, Miss Witherspoon."

Leon Howard smirked as Adam refolded the note and tucked it into his breast pocket.

"It must be a tip on tomorrow's races at Saratoga then. I may have sat there yesterday." His mouth stretched into a crooked, knowing grin.

"No," Millie said loudly. "My sister and I were here yesterday. So if someone left a note beneath your plate, Mr. Teague, it was surely meant for Gettie. I insist that you give it to her—or me. I'll see that she gets—"

"It's nothing really, Miss Millie," Adam said with a gentle sincerity that made Betz admire his sensitivity. And his voice was so deliciously warm.

Millie's words were cut short as a shrill voice of anger rose above the general din of conversation. Gettie Hobble had the gangling waiter who had been stumbling around Cherry during the meal by his sleeve.

"This boy just slipped my spoon into his pocket. He takes a spoon from our table every day. Search him, and you'll see," she said to a mustachioed gentleman seated across from her. The man looked quite ill at ease. The waiter looked terrified.

"Oh, what'll they do to him?" Cherry moaned.

Betz nudged the girl with her foot. "Sh-h-h. It's none of our business."

"I'll turn out my pockets right here!" the trembling youth said loudly.

The headwaiter arrived from the pantry to quell the commotion. He silenced the lad in midsentence and marched him away to face the majordomo.

Six

Cordelia Finds Mischief

"That was quite a maneuver," Adam Teague said as Betz dragged Cherry from the dining room a few moments later.

"I beg your pardon?" Betz lost her hold on Cherry's arm and the girl scampered back through the dining room toward the swinging doors leading into the pantry. She was going after the waiter. "If you'll please excuse me, Mr. Teague, I can't let Cherry run off—"

"I hope we can sit together again tomorrow, Miss Witherspoon. I find your company very enjoyable." He was grinning, oblivious to her concern over Cherry's behavior. Under more favorable circumstances, Betz might have realized he was teasing.

Betz halted, and fixed him with a stern eye. "You do think that I arranged to—Don't be absurd, Mr. Teague. I have to be going—" That awful color was coming back to her cheeks. What could she do to stop feeling so self-conscious in front of Mr. Teague?

"My invitation to Newport still stands, Miss Witherspoon. Or might I call you Betz, now that we've shared a meal? Very cleverly done, too, I might add. I wouldn't have thought you so…inventive."

Appalled, she spun on her heel to retrieve Cherry from whatever disaster she might be inviting in the kitchen. But she plunged headlong into Mr. Howard's tobacco-smelling coat front.

"Excuse me—" she said with a gasp, about to rush on.

Mr. Howard laughed softly as he moved aside for her.

"The pleasure was certainly mine, Miss Witherspoon, but don't rush off on my account." It took several minutes to convince him to leave her alone. Finally, tense and alarmed, she hurried to the kitchen. Startled, muttering waiters fell silent as she rushed in to the huge steamy room. Cherry was nowhere to be seen.

"Oh, dear…" Betz exited the hotel through the servants' entrance in the rear of the kitchen and emerged onto a gravel path leading to the enclosed lawn, where the children were just finishing a noisy meal beneath striped red-and-white awnings. The black-clad nannies and maids were all in attendance, and the unpretentious scene appealed to Betz so much that she wished she might never have to endure another meal in the dining room.

The Reinhold nanny came across the lawn toward Betz. She was covered with strawberry jam, and seething. She pointed back behind the hotel where the meadow rose steeply away from the bay. "Miss Witherspoon, is that who you're looking for?"

Turning, Betz saw the small white figure of a girl chasing a youth still wearing his waiter's uniform. Her heart sank.

"Oh, Cherry," she whispered. "No."

"You'd best stop her. Mrs. Fitch and my mistress, Mrs. Reinhold, have had nothing good to say about Cordelia since this morning." She turned back toward the Reinhold girls who were squealing and pulling one another's curls. "Heathens! Stop at once. Your mother will be along at any moment!" Heaving an exasperated sigh, she marched away.

Hesitantly, Lyddie Fitch-Harve approached Betz from beneath the awnings, whispering, "Miss Witherspoon, you might take a buggy. There's a cart path where you can meet Cordelia and the waiter. We used to go berry-picking up that way."

Momentarily, Betz felt at a loss. What was the use? Cherry had just ruined everything. Lady Agatha would likely not pay her, and Cherry would never make her debut in society.

"Miss Witherspoon, would you like me to go along with you? It wouldn't do to go alone—Oh, damnation, here comes my mother. I won't be able to go now. Don't leave them alone any longer than necessary."

Betz nodded her silent thanks to the young "widow" and

started at once toward the stables.

If they were forced to leave Summersea to avoid gossip, where might they go? Since Agatha had already left on her world tour, Betz assumed that Cyrus Wood had been closed for the summer.

Hadn't Agatha realized how difficult it would be for Cherry to conform to strict social rules? Why had she thrust Cherry into this setting unprepared? Betz felt utterly inept to change the girl, and now it seemed already too late. No quality family would ever allow a son to court her.

The corset was useless, but necessary for the observance of propriety, Cherry thought as it cut into her ribs. She sat atop some smooth gray boulders a distance behind Summersea, where she and the waiter could see all of the sparkling bay. Their run had been halted by an eight-foot wall of boulders which tumbled into the berry field from the hills behind them.

"If you were innocent, why didn't you turn out your pockets?" Cherry asked Teddy.

"It's an insult." He pitched a stone across the rocks into the grass. "I shouldn't have to. I'm no thief. I hate working here, but if I complain I'll get the sack. And my family needs the money."

Being alone with this young man reminded Cherry of times when she had sat with some of the boys from the hat factory near where she lived in the city. It seemed strange now to miss those drab, hungry days, but at times she did. She had felt so uncomfortable at dinner just now she would have welcomed any distraction.

"That pinch-faced old hag…of all the so-called ladies at Summersea, she's the very worst. The others, they're careful what they say. But not that one. She likes embarrassing people. It's like she's got no heart. I guess it's because she's so old."

Cherry felt a momentary pinch of guilt. She was no longer one of the lower classes. She didn't actually feel any different, but she knew that she was. Her father and grandmother made her different.

Now, instead of being a street urchin, she was an heiress. She could no longer scuff her heels and grumble about her lot in life like the mill boys and the factory lads, and like this gangling youth.

Feeling peculiar, not wanting to be part of Gettie Hobble's and Felicia Ellison's world, not wanting to lose her own, Cherry jumped up suddenly and flounced her skirts.

"The way she embarrassed you…it just made me so mad!"

"And now look what you've done," he said, his eyes dull. "You know what they'll all say about you. I'll probably have to marry you next week."

Cherry gaped at him.

"Don't be silly!"

He didn't look at all like he was teasing.

"You don't seem to know the rules, Miss Cordelia."

She gritted her teeth.

"I hate that name! Is this what it means to be compromised?"

"I'm afraid so. I don't see your chaperone any place around. You shouldn't have followed me. I would've come back. I need the job. Sit down before you fall, and use my kerchief to keep the sun off your face."

Cherry dropped undecorously back down beside him. She accepted his white kerchief which she draped over her face like a mask.

"I was once poor like you. I think it was easier, then. Nobody cared about my reputation. I wasn't important. Now you'd think I was glass, all fancy dresses and hair bows, and a chaperone of my very own." Through the coarse cotton weave of the kerchief she could see the faint blue of the sky. "Kiss me," she teased, "so my ruination will be complete!" She was giggling, remembering the factory boys in the city. They would have only scoffed at this, and punched her arm.

Teddy didn't answer, and he didn't punch her arm.

She snatched away the kerchief, looked into his astonished reddening face and then with a burst of daring, she pressed her lips against his mouth.

"There! I don't give a tinker's damn what those old crows think of me."

She supposed that she should feel better, more like herself now that she had rebelled, and yet she didn't. She just felt awkward. And she realized that Teddy was taking her kiss more seriously than she had intended.

He seized her shoulders and turned her toward him. "I think I love you!"

"Don't be silly. We've only just met." She giggled.

"You're different from all the others. Can I kiss you back now?"

She squirmed, remembering Al, the gardener's assistant back at her grandmother's house and the to-do kissing him had caused.

"You'd better not. Here comes Betz, and I think she'll be cross. I'll meet you later, anywhere you say! Put a message under the door." That would quiet him a while, she thought, sorry now that she had followed him.

Teddy stood behind her. They watched the one-horse buggy approaching.

"Are you sure, Miss Cordel—"

"Cherry! My name is Cherry!" she cried, scrambling down the rocks away from the cause of her confusion.

"Betz, scold me and get it over with!" Cherry cried, looking flushed and frightened.

Betz shook the buggy lines and turned back toward the main road. Her tone was brisk, betraying her efforts to control her anger.

"I have nothing to say until we see what is said about you when we get back."

"I don't care what they all think. I want to know what you think," Cherry pleaded, tugging at Betz's sleeve. "Did you see me kiss him?"

Betz felt her stomach drop, and she rolled her eyes.

"Mercy, no."

"Well, I won't get a baby from that, if that's what you're worried about," Cherry said explosively, her cheeks darkening. "I know that's what unmarried ladies think, but my mother told me long ago that that isn't enough. I wouldn't do the rest." She nodded her head emphatically.

"Oh, Cherry! you embarrass me," Betz muttered. "If you must know, I understand your sympathy for the waiter, but he's not the right sort for you. I'm sure he's a fine young man, but he's in no position to look after an heiress's—"

"Holy jumping mother of—"

"Cherry, hush!" Betz gasped, appalled.

"I don't want to *marry* Teddy. I'm only fifteen years old! Who wants babies and laundry tubs and bill collectors? I was just afraid of what he might do. That was so embarrassing, being accused of stealing in front of everyone. He might have run off, poor thing. He might have…"

"As an heiress, you will certainly never see a laundry tub or bill collector. Now, let's try to stay out of trouble for a few hours, and let's talk about something else. What about that young gentleman Mrs. Ellison mentioned yesterday. Did he sound interesting to you?" If you have any chance with him now, she thought.

Cherry slumped back into the buggy seat. "He's probably as boring as that piano teacher who stared at you all through dinner. Yech!"

"Mr. Macklin seemed nice enough!" Betz said, glancing at Cherry's rebellious pout.

"Of course you would think so. He was drooling in his soup plate for you."

Betz found herself speechless. Finally she had to laugh.

"I'm afraid I'm going to have to insist that we stay in our suite this evening. There was supposed to be some sort of poetry reading in the reception parlor, but I think we should avoid the gossips tonight."

"Hang the gossips."

Betz held her tongue and turned the buggy in toward the stables. No frowning matrons were waiting for them. She breathed a sigh of relief, wondering if it was at all possible that this escapade would go unnoticed.

Later, while Cherry perfected her penmanship in her room, Betz wandered through the hotel, listening on the fringes of several conversations. Whenever she came near she received wan smiles and veiled looks. She could not imagine that Felicia and her friends had failed to notice Cherry's dash after the waiter, but nothing was said about it.

No one took Betz aside to advise her that they ought to consider leaving quietly. It was all very puzzling, and Betz's nerves were raw by evening.

She and Cherry had a simple meal in their suite that night. Afterward, Betz read from a book on female etiquette, on the subject of male callers. Cherry listened with uncustomary patience, and went off to bed at nine, docile and subdued, like a proper young lady.

Cherry seemed preoccupied. Perhaps she was only beginning to comprehend the complexity of being an heiress. Betz hoped so, and prayed that Cherry would do nothing further to jeopardize her chances of being accepted at Summersea.

Miss Witherspoon Finds Mischief

Betz woke feeling restless, finding the humid night-air suffocating. When she peeked from the half-open French doors and saw that no one was about at that hour, she stepped onto the balcony where the air was a bit more refreshing.

Restless, she longed for a walk along the beach, alone. Tending Cherry was not as taxing as looking after four half-grown children, she thought, but she longed to be by herself for just a while. Since arriving at Summersea, she had felt on display. She suspected that she was going to grow very tired of behaving perfectly long before the summer's end.

There was a soft murmur of voices coming from the veranda below her balcony. Golden light fell in soft squares across the front lawns from the parlor windows, and a whiff of tobacco smoke was in the air.

Betz sighed. There was no proper way for a woman to slip out for a midnight walk without running the gauntlet of late-night gentleman smokers and talkers below. Sometimes, being a woman was as confining as being a child.

Cherry appeared to be sleeping soundly. She had her covers pulled over her head. Wondering how she could stand such heat Betz tiptoed into the room to adjust her covers.

When she pulled back the covers, Betz's veins flooded with alarm. Beneath the covers were several pillows bunched together to resemble a sleeping body.

"How can you keep doing this?" Betz cried softly, whirling, feeling panic rising. The girl must be deliberately trying to ruin herself. The stress of trying to conform must be too great.

Where had she gone? Betz wondered, rushing to dress and chase after her. If Cherry was seen out after hours, they would have no choice but to leave as early as possible the following morning.

Shaking with anger, Betz tiptoed out into the dim corridor. A shadow at the end of hall caught her attention. She froze, listening. Someone was standing there, she thought. Could it be Cherry?

Hurrying in that direction, Betz paused suddenly at the door leading to the servants' stairs. She smelled tobacco smoke. Some man was nearby.

What if Cherry had already encountered someone? Frightened, Betz turned back toward the door to their suite. How could she find Cherry? Where would she look?

In the middle of the hall, she froze. She must go on looking for Cherry! If the child had surprised someone prowling the halls…In full panic, Betz dashed back to the servants' stairs and opened the door. "Cherry? Are you in here?" The dark stairwell echoed her call. She slipped inside and listened as the door closed behind her with a soft click.

Disoriented in the complete darkness, with no idea where the landing fell off the first step, she groped for a handrail. Her fingers grazed the warm softness of a muslin shirt. At the next instant before her gasp could turn into a scream of alarm, a shadowed man struck a safety match, bringing a familiar handsome face and wavy hair into sharp relief.

"Mercy, Mr. Teague!" Betz cried. "You frightened me."

Adam cocked his head in inquiry. "Have you lost your young lady again, Miss Witherspoon?"

An outline of the stairs was burned into her memory as he shook out the match, plunging them back into darkness.

"Have you seen her?" Betz whispered, backing, toward the place where she'd briefly observed the handrail. Of all the people, she would have to run into Mr. Teague.

His voice hushed, "No," he said.

"Thank you," she said, starting gingerly down into the blackness. "I would be grateful if—"

"No need to instruct me, Miss Witherspoon. I know how to hold my tongue. Careful there."

Step by step she found the mid-landing and turned, searching for the edge of the step with her slippered foot. He made no move to follow, and said nothing more as she felt for the door at the base of the steps and slipped out into the deserted servants' hall.

Finding her way to the rear exit from the kitchen, Betz prowled the back lawns, slipping from shadow to shadow like a thief. Her fury and panic made her ill. Finally she stopped, determined to make herself think straight.

There was really nothing to be gained by prowling about in the dark. Still, she couldn't resist making at least one circuit of the hotel in hopes that Cherry was meeting the boy nearby. The hotel was irregular enough, with a dozen shadowed alçoves and nooks, that two people might hide themselves quite easily from strolling gentlemen out for the night air.

She found she couldn't walk past the front veranda. Several gentlemen were still there talking. Just turning back, she saw another shadowed man emerge from the darkness behind her. She gave a deep sigh of exasperation and started toward him.

Thinking it was Adam Teague, she said, "I simply don't know

what to do about—"

The dim light from the front of the hotel highlighted Leon Howard's cocked brows.

"Is there something I can do for you, dear?"

"Oh, I—uh, excuse me, please—" There was something about this man that she definitely disliked. How could she have mistaken his slim silhouette for Adam's broad-shouldered one?

"Don't rush off, dear. I'd be pleased for some company." He blocked her flight and backed her against the side of the building. She felt the rough weather-beaten cladding pressing into her shoulder blades.

"Mr. Howard, I have no desire to be caught talking with you here in the dark like this. Do let me pass!" She was trembling like a frightened child.

He leaned so close that she could smell brandy on his breath. As he ducked his head to steal a kiss, she pushed with both hands, sending him stumbling backward, and he chuckled with amusement.

She dashed back toward the kitchen. To save herself from attack, she might have to seek refuge on the front veranda after all, where everyone would see her and know she'd been about. What a horrid mess this was turning out to be!

He caught up to her easily, grabbed her and spun her around in the darkness. There was a brief struggle in which she felt his hands fumbling at her breasts. Her mind reeled. To think this was happening, when so short a time ago she had been peacefully sleeping in her room. She slapped him.

"Mr. Howard, I would not hesitate to expose this assault!"

"Then why haven't you screamed?" he whispered, still sounding amused.

A deep voice came from the darkness nearby.

"Because she's trying to spare herself from the gossips."

A fist shot past her, landing squarely against the side of Leon Howard's cheek. Leon gave a grunt of pain and staggered back, clutching his jaw.

Betz was jerked aside then, and pulled along toward the

darkened kitchen.

"Get back inside, Miss Witherspoon, before you incite a riot." Mr. Teague shoved her gracelessly into the large silent room.

"I don't know how to thank you, Mr. Teague," she whispered, shaken. "He would have—"

"I think we're definitely on a first name basis now, don't you, Betz? Go upstairs, quickly. I'll look around for your little flirt and send her back to you safe and sound. Go on now. You're a menace."

Wounded by his amused tone she whirled, ready to lash out with the most vehement words she could muster, but as she stumbled into the pantry and saw his face illuminated in the pale light, she saw that he was concerned. Strangely, in spite of her anger and embarrassment, she knew she could trust Adam Teague to find and bring Cherry safely back.

Miss Ryburn's Folly

Teddy's eager lips covered Cherry's. And the way he held her, arching against her, was very alarming.

"Teddy...Teddy! Please," she gasped, twisting her face away. He was frightening her now. "Can't we just talk?"

The dim light from a window fell across the stable yard where they huddled in a corner against the building. Teddy's breathing was ragged now, and his touch had taken on an urgent quality. He didn't seem capable of speech any longer. He simply groped at her like a young man starving for touch.

She hated the childish quiver in her knees, and couldn't stop herself from noticeably trembling. She felt light-headed suddenly, and couldn't get enough breath into her lungs.

"Oh, please!" she wept suddenly. "This is too much! I don't like it!"

"Don't cry, Cherry," he whispered hotly against her neck.

Angrily she pushed him away. He wasn't like her old pals at all. She was afraid, horribly, that he was deliberately trying to compromise her. Was he one of those fortune hunters she was going to have to watch out for?

"I have to go back. I think I see someone coming this way. Let me go! Oh, please, let me go!" She tore free, wanting to slap Teddy, but she couldn't. She was as guilty as he.

She flung herself out into the darkness, and ran across the rear yard toward the kitchen door. She was half way inside before she realized that a broad-shouldered man was standing nearby and was now slipping in behind her.

"You're not hurt?" he whispered. "You're sure?" His hand pressed softly against her half scream.

She shook her head. Salty tears sprang from her eyes and spilled in huge drops along the edge of his fingers. She welcomed his comforting embrace like a father's and melted against him. I am so stupid, she thought.

"Don't do this again, Miss Ryburn," Mr. Teague whispered, guiding her gently toward the servants' stairs. "You don't know what you might encounter. Summersea is not the safe place it appears to be."

She looked up into his shadowed face, admiring the way his wavy hair caught the meager light.

"Does Miss—"

"She's been looking for you. Hurry, now. Don't be a little fool."

Shaken and weary, Cherry climbed the dark stairs and found her way along the dim corridor to her suite. What had she been thinking, sneaking out? Was the effort of pretending to be an heiress so great that she had to try openly to ruin it all? Could she bear it if she disappointed her grandmother?

As she eased open the door, she wished she could find her Miss Witherspoon asleep in her bed, but Betz was standing at the balcony door. She whirled the moment Cherry crept in from the corridor.

She started toward Cherry, her hands out, blurting, "Cherry, whatever—"

Cherry ducked and shielded her face, blindly waiting for her chaperone's wrath.

"Please...Don't!" She felt so wretched suddenly, so confused, so alone.

When she felt no blows and heard no slurred, scalding words like those of her mother, she peeked, and found Betz staring at her with a look of astonishment.

Quickly, Betz locked the door, and then she turned back to envelop Cherry in comforting, trembling arms.

"Darling, are you hurt at all? In any way?"

"I-I'm all right," Cherry said, hiccuping, hating herself suddenly for what she had done. "Aren't you furious with me?"

"Oh—" Betz held Cherry away and looked deeply into her eyes. "Mercy, yes, I'm furious. I could just shake you, but—You're sure you're all right? You look very peculiar."

Cherry could not believe her ears. The woman did care. It was more than she could bear. Her mother would have been very severe. As Betz led her to bed where the covers were thrown back to reveal her silly attempt to disguise her absence, Cherry sank into deeper, racking sobs. She had really wanted to throw it all away!

"What is it?" Betz whispered. "Tell me!"

Cherry couldn't find the words. They were dammed up inside her somewhere. All she wanted was to feel Betz's arms around her, and she clung to her like a lost child.

After a few moments, she felt the terrible tension inside her subside, and she drew away from her chaperone, feeling foolish and exposed.

"I'm s-sorry," she said, mopping her face with her sleeve.

Betz offered a hankie; she was watching Cherry. Her expression thoughtful, she asked, "Did you think I was going to strike you, Cherry?"

"No, I—"

Betz looked at her with unsettling perception, then seemed to shake off her curiosity.

"Well, never mind, darling. What can I say or do to make you see that you mustn't ever do anything like this again?" Betz shuddered visibly, as if she had been the one Teddy was pawing.

Cherry's eyes brimmed again. Looking at her chaperone's creased forehead and anxious eyes, thinking that she never wanted to displease her again, she promised softly, "I'll be good." Her tone was convincing.

"We'll talk more tomorrow," Betz said, drawing the cover up to Cherry's neck and tucking in the edges.

Cherry relished the feel of the woman's gentle hands. "Don't go, Miss Witherspoon, please. Tell me a story."

Betz paused, looked down at Cherry, and her anxious expression softened to something resembling pity.

"You dear little thing. Let me tell you about Beauty and the Beast…"

Miss Witherspoon Ponders

Asleep, Cherry looked to Betz like a small, helpless child—not so different from George's cherubic Sally, who would be nine in the fall. She rose from the edge of Cherry's bed and tucked the quilt securely beneath Cherry's chin. She felt convinced that the girl wouldn't be sneaking out again any time soon.

Still shaken, however, Betz went to the balcony to settle her nerves. She had recognized Cherry's protective gestures only too well, the cringe, the throwing up of her arms to protect her face. Betz had learned to do that with her husband.

Betz's heart ached to think that such a precious child had endured enough abuse to learn that reaction. Who had abused her? Her mother when she had been drinking? Betz put trembling fingertips to her lips. No wonder Cherry was such a wild little creature. No wonder she had believed that Betz would strike her. And how desperate she must be for genuine affection.

She had not expected to be so moved by Cherry, Betz thought while gazing across the dark beach toward the softly surging breakers. She had grown so attached to George's children, only to be asked to leave. She had hoped not to become involved emotionally with any young person she was hired to look after. A few months in Agatha Dunwitty's employ, then some other, and another, until she knew what to do with the rest of her life…

She had not wanted to care about anyone deeply, and here she was inextricably entwined with Cherry. Did she dare go on? In the morning they might be forced to pack and go away. If not, was there even a shred of hope left of making Cherry fit into a "stuffed shirt" society? Was that something Betz really wanted to see happen?

Finally she went back to her bed, fully clothed. Her thoughts strayed to those brief, panic-filled moments when Mr. Howard's hands fumbled against her breasts. It had been so long since she was touched in that way. Though horrifying, everything at Summersea seemed to put her in mind of herself as a woman. All her womanly needs seemed to be surfacing from some dark sea within.

Almost at once, she thought of Adam Teague and the sense of safety she'd found near him. And she thought of his attractive face, his rugged physique and the tingling, aroused feeling she had whenever he was near.

Of all the things she had wanted to avoid this summer, the most important had been any sort of interest in men. But in spite of all her efforts to silence the thoughts, and to drive away the spark of attraction she felt whenever his name came to mind, she couldn't erase what she felt about Adam Teague.

Adam Teague was already in her blood. She wanted to flee Summersea far more because of him than because Cherry might ruin their reputations. Could she hope to spend even one more day at Summersea without finding herself caught in an emotional undertow she could not escape?

Seven

The Second Week at Summersea

Friday, June 7, 1889

The breeze from the bay felt soft on Betz's cheeks. Cherry sat some distance away on the beach, frowning at her sketchpad. She was trying to draw Summersea as it looked in the morning light, dreamlike and unapproachable.

Betz was idly sketching Cherry, whose tendrils of blond hair were wafting on the breeze. Her sun hat wove delicate shadows across her flushed cheeks. Cherry tucked her tongue in the corner of her mouth, made another line and then heaved an exasperated sigh.

"I'll never get this right!"

"You'll get better with practice," Betz said calmly. "Try a bit longer, and then we'll go in. Frankly, I can't bear going back any sooner than necessary."

Cherry said nothing, but a quick nod showed she agreed with Betz. Their first week had been difficult. Cherry had fumbled her way through dinner each day. Her conversations tended to be too animated, and she often had to break off in the middle of a story, for fear of revealing something untoward from her past.

Though no one had spoken of the night Cherry had gone out to meet the waiter, Betz half suspected the gossips were humoring them—pretending ignorance and courtesy when they really felt contempt.

To her consternation, Betz had to endure attentions from nearly every available gentleman in the dining room. Each day they vied for a seat at her table; the confusion over placecards was becoming a daily source of amusement. The attention was ever so gratifying, if unexpected, but it only served to make Betz the object of more gossip.

Thankfully, Mr. Howard had kept his distance, but still Betz felt ill at ease whenever he was near. Adam Teague, of all people, displayed little interest in her. Why, she wondered, wasn't he one of the ones slipping greenbacks to the waiters so that he could sit beside her?

"I can't keep my mind on this!" Cherry blurted, squinting into the brilliance of the morning. "I hate sketching!" She began watching some activity on Summersea's lawn. Finally she cast down her sketchpad and stood, flouncing away to the edge of the waves lapping on the sand.

Betz noticed a girl in a bright pink dress sashaying around the rear door leading to the kitchen.

"I promised you I'd be good," Cherry wailed, "but I'm so bored. Now look at that—Marietta Howard just gets on my nerves the way she acts. Am I really supposed to be like her? Why don't they gossip about her?"

"They do, if you remember. Gettie Hobble tore her reputation to shreds day before yesterday."

"I hope *she* never sits at our table again. I don't like her, either."

Betz tucked her sketching leads into her pocket. She leaned back rather gracelessly on her elbows, feeling the sun-warmed sand give beneath her. She was hard put to decide which woman she liked less, Felicia Ellison or Gettie Hobble. At least Felicia had a mere fawning malice. The elder Miss Hobble was just bitter to the soles of her size-three feet.

Cherry collapsed in a childlike heap of skirts and flashing petticoats, and began scooping handfuls of moist sand into the shape of castle. She looked like a beautiful overgrown child. The breeze caught her sun hat and bent back the brim, exposing her nose and cheeks to the freckling sun.

"You should keep your face in the shade," Betz said automatically, forgetting how quickly Cherry could take offense at any correction.

Cherry had been behaving beautifully now for days, but Betz sensed tension building. Cherry found all of the arts boring. Sketching was proving a trial. She actively resisted lessons in piano. No amount of coaxing could make her sing a note. There seemed to be nothing the girl was suited to.

Just as Betz had feared, Cherry resented her correction. She took off her sun hat. And her scowl deepened. Suddenly she scrambled to the opposite side of her growing sand castle, dirtying the knees of her white dress. She scooped out a deep moat and then breached the sandy wall, allowing a foamy wave to surge in and eat away at the shapes she had made.

"I know I'm supposed to be polite to those boys Mrs. Ellison introduced me to at tea yesterday, and I know I'm supposed to join in at croquet, but…"

"You feel terribly awkward," Betz said for her. "And you don't know what to say. It all seems rather forced and…artificial."

Cherry lifted her face, her expression one of surprise.

"Betz, if you know how it feels, why do you make me do these *ghastly* things?" She emphasized ghastly so dramatically that Betz couldn't help but chuckle.

"Because one must learn to get along in the real world, Cherry. We've been over this time and again, darling. Sometimes one must grapple with hard facts—"

"Like my mama getting run over, and you taking care of your mama until you were too old to get married," Cherry put in.

Betz took a moment to gather her thoughts.

"Yes, looking after my mother who was ill for so many years was a very real challenge. I was not able to get out as much as I would have liked. There was no hope for more education. I couldn't leave her for even a few hours, darling."

"And then you had to move in with your brother. You don't get along with him. I can tell." Cherry abandoned the sand castle and came to sit by Betz. "I love it when you call me darling." She leaned against Betz's shoulder. "I always wished—" She stopped herself and instead looked at the sketch Betz had made of her. "You make me look pretty."

"But you are!" Betz said. "Don't you feel pretty?"

Cherry looked away and finally shook her head.

"Mama was prettier. Everyone always said so."

"Who said so?" Betz asked.

"Her...gentlemen callers."

Betz sat up and put her arm around the girl's shoulder.

"You dear thing. No wonder you feel awkward. Let's get off the irritating subject of my brother. You are correct to assume that he doesn't approve of me. Now, lets see what we can do that will make you a bit happier. Perhaps you would like lessons on the harp? I know your grandmother would find that a suitable instrument—"

"Oh, no, I couldn't stand it! I want to swim! I-I want to ride horses! I want to climb mountains and see the world. I want to be free!" She clutched at her corset-encased torso and gave a cry of frustration. "I hate being an heiress. I think I'd rather be working in the shirt factory. At least that was real. Summersea is all pretend! Don't you think so? Everyone is pretending to be more than they are. You. Me. Marietta and Miss Hobble, and that ghastly Mrs. Ellison. I'm so tired of it all I don't think I can stand another week!"

"I'm afraid your grandmother did not give me leave to take you anywhere else. We'll simply have to endure."

"I'm supposed to think about finding the right beau, aren't I? But all the boys here are so stuffy, like their fathers. Yesterday Mrs. Ellison said no one here now is good enough for a great heiress, that they're only good enough to be distractions until Drew Whitgift arrives in July. She treats people like grades of beefsteak. I don't want to be like that."

Betz had to agree, but she said nothing.

"Drew Whitgift is probably as boring as all the rest, tea in his veins instead of human blood." She sprang up and whirled around. "I didn't have these problems when I lived with Mama! I was too busy—"

"Being frightened?" prompted Betz.

Cherry's face clouded. She glanced guiltily at Betz and

started away.

"I did whatever I pleased. I went anywhere. I had lots of friends, and folks liked me. I-I know I can never go back. That's the worst of it. Since finding Grandmother, I'm changed forever. I can never again sit on the stoop and talk with my old friends. I'm an heiress. I don't belong here, and I don't belong there. Sometimes I wish Grandmother had never found me." She plucked at the underarms of her bodice. "I'm going in. I'm all damp. You can stay, if you like."

"I can't leave you alone, especially when you're working yourself into a melancholy mood. I'll see about riding lessons for you. Would you like that?"

"Yes! And you must come along with me…and we'll invite Mr. Teague. Oh, yes, we will! You know it's a good idea!"

Betz couldn't hide her secret smile. The child was a romantic genius. To distract her she changed the subject. "About Monday's benefit dance…"

Cherry groaned. In a falsetto she said, "Morning treks to the spring, dinner in the dining room, afternoon promenades through town…now this! I don't want to dance with anyone! I-I don't know how."

"We'll begin practicing tonight," Betz said.

"We don't even need to bother. I won't go without you. I think Mrs. Ellison is just plain mean not to invite you…or Mr. Macklin or even Mr. Woodley."

"Nor has Mr. Bonaventure's nurse been invited," Betz said, secretly pleased that the young woman she had seen talking quietly with Adam the day before would not be there to dance with him. "It's only for…" She fell silent.

"*Real* guests," Cherry said with disgust. "Mrs. Ellison is a snob."

"Felicia did organize the benefit for her favorite charity, and she has the right to invite whomever she desires. It is rather expensive. And remember, a lot of guests from the nearby hotels have been invited. You might meet someone very nice."

"I don't expect to," Cherry said, her nose in the air.

"Now who is the snob?" Betz queried softly.

"I suppose I will go, but only to please Grandmother."

Betz smiled and hugged the girl.

"Think of that wonderful gown that your grandmother had delivered from the dressmaker yesterday. Can you resist such lovely things?"

Cherry's expression brightened and she admitted, "Sometimes it's fun to be rich. But I do wish Grandmother was here. It's hard to please her when she's on the other side of the world."

"I'm not much use sometimes, am I?" Betz said.

"Oh," Cherry said in a pretentious haughty voice, "you'll do, for a while." And then she giggled, rushing ahead in a kind of impromptu waltz. "At least Summersea is pretty to look at. Our rooms are very nice, and the food is all right." Then she lowered her voice. "But I feel like an impostor. They're going to find me out and laugh."

"I know just how you feel," Betz said, sighing. "And all we can do about it is keep trying until we no longer feel so strange. Your grandmother loves you. Let's try to please her." Suddenly she sobered. "Oh, look, the Marshes are leaving."

"Those people Mrs. Ellison said couldn't pay their bills? Why did they come here if it was too expensive?"

"For the status," Betz said.

She knew the entire story about this unfortunate family. Felicia had gleefully whispered the details over tea the afternoon before. Mr. Marsh had claimed that there were simply a mix-up at this bank, but his hopes of stepping up a rung on the social ladder had been dashed when he couldn't afford the expense.

Now his young wife sat in one of the hotel carriages with her round-eyed children ready to depart for home in disgrace.

"I must say good-bye to her," Betz said. "They must feel dreadful. Wait for me in the suite."

Hurrying forward, Betz called to young Mrs. Marsh.

"It was so nice meeting you, Maggie. Such a shame that you had to cut your summer short. I hope your mother is soon feeling better."

Betz was well aware of the excuse Maggie had made up to save face. Maggie's eyes brimmed and she tried to smile. Her husband climbed into the carriage and ordered the driver to pull away.

Backing away from the carriage dust, Betz felt sad. Would she and Cherry leave in a similar manner when they failed to live up to standard at Summersea?

At dinner that afternoon Adam was not at any of the tables. Betz felt annoyed with herself as she slyly looked for him.

Nurse Tully brought the consumptive Mr. Bonaventure to Betz's table and tucked him securely across from Cherry. As she took a seat beside him she, too, noticed Adam Teague's absence. She cast Betz a blank look, but Betz was not misled. Nurse Tully liked Adam, too.

Even before the first course, a commotion began at the far table. Felicia Ellison was sitting with her usual circle of friends, "the Gossips," as Betz secretly thought of them. Myrtle Fitch and Mrs. Reinhold and the Hobble sisters all watched with interest as Felicia stood up suddenly, knocking over her chair.

Felicia's gasp was heard across the dining room, and everyone turned to watch her. She was staring in horror at the latest copy of *Society Topics.*

She was reading aloud breathlessly, but her words were too rushed and muddled to understand.

"I can't believe this!" was all Betz could make out from across the dining room, and "How could he do this to me?"

"What's wrong with Mrs. Ellison?" Cherry whispered, tugging at Betz's sleeve.

"I can't imagine—"

Felicia lifted her face and looked across the watching guests with unseeing eyes. When Myrtle Fitch tried to take the scandal sheet from her trembling fists, Felicia snatched it away and crushed it to her ample bosom. She staggered back two steps, looking around her wildly.

"You'd better help her," Cherry whispered to the uniformed

nurse watching from her seat next to bright-eyed Mr. Bonaventure. Betz thought the words had been whispered to her, and quickly crossed the dining room and grasped Felicia's arm without saying a word. It took no effort to lead the woman between the tables and through the doors to the staircase.

"I'll help you to your room," Betz said softly. She felt transported back in time to her mother's house, where anxiety attacks had often rendered her mother almost feebleminded. With each stair-step, Felicia's breathing became deeper and more ragged, until she was gasping just as Betz's mother had during her attacks.

"How could he do this to me, after all I've given him? I made him what he is. I've never held a thing back..."

"You're going to be all right," Betz said soothingly.

A steward rushed ahead leading the way to Felicia's suite and opened the door.

"Send for Mrs. Ellison's personal maid," Betz whispered as she helped Felicia sit on the edge of the mattress. "Perhaps you should fetch a doctor—"

"No!" Felicia spat out, jerking free of Betz's solicitous touch. "Get out! Leave me alone! Get out!" She turned blazing eyes on Betz. "Get out, I say!"

"If you need me—"

"Out!"

Betz backed through the door and the frightened steward yanked the door closed. Seconds later, the key turned in the lock and something shattered on the other side of the door.

The steward, a man in his mid-twenties, called over his shoulder, "I'll send for a doctor!" He disappeared into the servant's stairwell.

Betz was left alone in the corridor, at a loss to explain Felicia's bizarre reaction to the scandal sheet. What could be in it that would cause the woman such anguish?

Betz returned to the dining room. With a casual nod, she assured everyone that all was perfectly fine with Felicia.

She had just seated herself and indicated that Cherry must not question her, when Mr. Howard's acerbic, amused whisper cut through the quiet.

"The ever-resourceful scandal sheet seems to have uncovered yet another well-kept secret," he said, and chuckled. "But not kept well enough, apparently."

Betz wondered if the insufferable man would continue.

"Let me see," someone from across the room said, referring to another copy of *Society Topics*.

Betz's hands curled into fists.

"What are they reading?" Cherry whispered.

Betz shook her head.

"Oh, my," someone murmured. "Flouting his affair in public, the poor woman…" It was Millie Hobble, reading over her sister's shoulder. "What a horrid way to find out."

"Don't be stupid, sister. Of course she knew," Gettie said. "I say she deserves—"

Betz found herself on her feet, silencing Gettie Hobble by her abrupt movement.

Trembling, Betz tried to make herself turn away from Gettie's upturned face. Women like this had once made her status as a divorcée nearly unbearable, and she had retreated to her brother's house, hiding behind her duties for six long years. Women—gossips—like Gettie had robbed her of so much…

The old woman was staring at Betz now, daring her to speak in Felicia's defense. Felicia's *faux pas* was that she had lost her head in public.

The entire assemblage of guests was looking at Betz now. She put her napkin across her plate, her hand steady.

Her mind was suddenly clear. She was furious with herself for letting these snobs rule her. Gossip alone could not have relegated Betz Witherspoon to her brother's back stairs and nursery. She had allowed it to happen. Betz turned to the elderly woman.

"Miss Hobble, you are by far the best qualified among us to cast the first stone."

There was a soft gasp from Millie Hobble as Betz turned away, and Cherry followed Betz from the dining room. They went up the stairs without a word. Betz was rigid with anger, and Cherry looked awestruck.

"Why are you so angry, Betz? Mrs. Ellison isn't even nice to you most of the time," Cherry whispered. "Why would you defend her?"

"I'm not defending Felicia Ellison," Betz said, exhilarated by her anger. "I'm standing in defense of myself at last!"

•

Waves of Despair

Betz couldn't sleep. The night air was humid and heavy. Even on the balcony she could not get a refreshing breath. Cherry seemed to be sleeping soundly. Betz was quite certain that the girl would not be sneaking off into the night again. Since the incident with Teddy, Cherry had stayed close by her side.

Now it was Betz who longed to slip down the back steps. She did not hear any men talking or smell any tobacco smoke. If ever she might find a few minutes alone, it would have to be now.

Not bothering with a corset or petticoats, she slipped into a shirtwaist and skirt. After checking Cherry, she went into the corridor and listened, straining with all her senses to be sure no one was about.

She heard a murmur of voices near the central stair, and momentarily thought of abandoning her venture. Then she heard someone bid the doctor good night, and thank him for coming. After a moment of complete silence inside the hotel, with the faint sounds of the doctor's buggy disappearing down the road, Betz started for the back stairs.

Adam Teague was not lurking on the landing this time, ready to light her way. But now the stairwell was familiar, even in the dark and she had no trouble getting to the bottom.

The moment she was outside she felt a weight lift from her shoulders. Trying to live up to Summersea's standards was making her weary. Once Cherry was successfully navigated through the summer, she would find a job without annoying pretense. She would find a simple middle-class family needing a live-in governess…

Her fists curled tightly. Why couldn't she go back to college, she wondered, or learn to type on one of those newfangled machines… or do just about anything except hide in someone's nursery, subject to someone else's commands?

Was she living in a prison of her own making, with invisible walls a lifetime thick? She was screaming to be set free, but would she ever be able to break through those walls? Could she free herself of the confining roles of chaperone or leftover woman in a world where most women only wanted marriage? She might have to go against every social convention she had ever known. Did she have the mettle for that?

She had started across the lawn, heading for the beach where Mr. Woodley most often did his painting, when she heard a door on the veranda slap shut behind her.

Whirling in the darkness, Betz saw a white-clad figure stagger across the front veranda and stumble down the steps. Betz could not imagine what woman staying at the hotel would be so bold as to venture out at night by way of the front door in her undergarments.

Not wanting to be seen, Betz started for the dense darkness of the trees skirting the lawn. Then a peculiar sound caught her attention. The woman in white was sobbing softly. She sounded intoxicated. Her cries were heartrending. As she found her way to the wide sweep of marble steps leading down to the sand, Betz felt certain that the woman would surely fall.

Betz would not have been able to see the woman if she had not been wearing white. Gasping, she watched the woman teeter drunkenly on the steps safely reach the bottom, then keep walking straight toward the lapping waves twenty feet away.

Pausing, Betz felt a sudden sense of dread. Without knowing why, she started after the woman. She lifted her skirts, glad to be free of her corset; in it she couldn't have run a step.

Still sobbing, the woman waded into the water. She was in it up to her hips by the time Betz came panting up behind her.

"Wait—" Betz whispered loudly, splashing a few steps into the foamy waves.

The buxom woman—her graying hair askew, her hourglass corset partially unlaced, her soaked petticoats already weighing her down—did not falter. She would soon reach the abrupt drop-off of the deep bay water.

"Is that you, Mrs. Ellison?" Betz whispered, more loudly. "Felicia, you're in danger! Come back."

Felicia Ellison, sobbing even louder, staggered farther and farther into the water. Clutching her sodden petticoats, she fell headlong into the water twice, gained her footing, and plunged on.

"Felicia! Felicia, please, what can you be thinking? Are you going to drown yourself? Over some foolish words in a scandal sheet? Surely you are made of sterner stuff than that."

Frantically, Betz wondered if she would be able to reach the woman and overpower her. Was she strong enough to drag her back to safety, particularly when she had no experience in deep water? She couldn't swim a stroke. She would certainly try, if she had to.

Silent, Felicia stopped moving forward.

"Am I right to understand that your husband has humiliated you?" Betz asked, hoping to engage the woman in distracting conversation.

The woman's sobs increased.

"It happens to so many women, doesn't it? But most husbands are discreet enough to keep their mistresses safely out of sight."

A sound of deep grief broke from Felicia's throat. She growled out an agonized, "Yes!" in the darkness. "I wish I was dead!"

"Certainly you might wish that in such a place as this, where people feast on the misfortunes of others. You, yourself, have done it, thinking scandal would never touch someone of your standing."

The woman whirled around, holding up her heavy petticoats. It was too dark to see her face, but Betz knew she had touched a nerve.

Betz stepped back from the lapping waves at her feet. Her heart drumming, she added, "In the morning your body will wash ashore. You'll look so pathetic with your face bloated, and your clothes torn away by the fishes."

Felicia paused again.

"Everyone will cluck their tongues and say what a useless end you came to. Your husband will go on about his business, and in time perhaps he'll even move his little hussy into your home. Think what will be written about you and your family."

Felicia turned to look at Betz.

"But you...you, Felicia, you will be dead. And they'll talk about you for weeks to come, discussing how your body looked in the morning heat, and how the gray showed so plainly as your hair was washed about on the sand. At every meal I'll have to listen to them whispering about the weakness of your character, and the damnation of your eternal soul."

With a scream of fury, Felicia started back toward the sand. Struggling with the sodden weight of her petticoats, she fell twice again into the waves. Betz stayed at the water's edge just long enough to make sure Felicia was out of danger before scrambling back toward the marble steps.

By then she noticed several lights burning in front windows, and the silhouettes of onlookers. Longing to curse them all, she turned to Felicia, who was plodding after her, raving loudly and incoherently.

Betz suddenly realized that Felicia, in her demented state of mind, had now mistaken her for her husband's mistress.

"You...harlot...hussy," Felicia bellowed, strength beginning to flood her voice. She was nearly upon Betz now, her face a mask of rage, her hands clutching up sandy fistfuls of her clinging petticoats.

She stormed up the marble steps into a wash of yellow light now falling from the opened front doors. Several of the gentlemen guests in various states of hasty dress and in postures of extreme discomfiture were waiting on the veranda—muttering theories as to what should be done with her.

A steward was dispatched to fetch the doctor back, and the sound of pounding hooves faded into the darkness.

Felicia's curses brought more windows alight.

Betz backed toward the hotel. Keeping herself just out of Felicia's reach, she wondered if even a dozen gentlemen could contain the wild-eyed woman.

Drenched, her hair straggling across her plump shoulders, her face swollen from hours of weeping, the woman paused to gather up her sandy wet petticoats. As Betz stumbled backwards up the stairs into someone's strong grasp. Felicia started up with murder in her eyes.

"I'll handle this," Mr. Howard said, stepping forward grandly. He had on an un-collared shirt, and his suspenders were down over his hips. Though the black eye that Adam had given him the week before had healed, he still looked common and somewhat battered. As he reached out to subdue Felicia she whirled, swing with her fist, and punched him solidly in the jaw.

Leon Howard fell backwards, taking several chortling men with him. Being thrust gently aside, Betz wasn't really surprised to find that Adam Teague had once again come to her rescue. He was still wearing his hat and coat, as if he'd just returned from the city.

He stepped into Felicia's path, expertly deflecting another punch with his forearm. She abandoned herself to her grief and collapsed forward into his arms. Adam staggered but remained steady under her weight, grunting, "If one or two of you gentlemen will help me—"

Felicia seemed to lose her strength now. She was content to swoon in their arms, wailing out her anguish to the entire Eastern Seaboard.

No longer needed, Betz edged out of the way and watched the men struggle up the staircase back to Felicia's room. She was still sitting there, on the top step, when Adam came out a few moments later. Looking at her thoughtfully, he sat beside her. His gaze was so intense with interest that Betz finally had to look away.

"That was a very courageous thing you did tonight, Miss Witherspoon."

"Formality again, Mr. Teague?" she asked with a weary but teasing note.

"What prompted you to help her? I can't recall that she was much of a friend."

"Could I have stood there and watched her go down? Could I

have eased my conscience later by saying to myself that she was a snob and a gossip, and therefore I didn't have to help her?"

"But now everyone knows you were out after hours, and dressed very...casually, shall we say."

His warm gaze went over her. A flutter of arousal went through her. Suddenly aware that she was not encased in whalebone stays, that her breasts were softly free beneath the pliant fabric of her blouse, and that she was sitting not unlike Cherry did when she forgot her manners, Betz straightened just a bit. She clasped her knees, feeling her cheeks grow hot like a girl's. It was ever so annoying to feel like a schoolgirl whenever Adam was near. And yet...she felt very, very alive.

"I don't care what everyone knows about me," she said. "I have a right to walk about in the dark."

"And Mrs. Ellison was kind enough to punch Mr. Howard, so that I would not have to do it later."

Betz was about to make a curt retort, but suddenly she was laughing.

"Yes, indeed!"

Tentatively, Adam circled her shoulder with his arm and hugged her ever so slightly. The moment she met his eyes she felt a deep kinship with him, as if they were already close friends.

But how absurd, she thought. Her eyes locked with his, wanting never to look away, she grew acutely self-aware, and knew that in a moment she would have to look away, stand and flee from him. They weren't friends, only acquaintances. They had nothing in common!

Yet something in the way he looked at her convinced her that this moment belonged to just them, that whatever pretenses they might play at during the day, at this moment they were free. She suddenly wanted to kiss him very much.

A wash of alarm went through her. His soft smile told her that he sensed her reaction. She did stand, then. She said something like, "I had best go in," and then she did flee. But she knew was fleeing herself.

Something had been unleashed within her. She feared it could not be contained.

Eight

In the Aftermath of Scandal

Saturday, June 8, 1889

Felicia had locked herself in her suite with strict orders to the stewards and chambermaids to stay away. But at one o'clock the following morning she appeared in the doorway of Summersea's dining room, dressed as if expecting to meet the Vanderbilts.

Her hair was perfectly coiffed, her gown nothing less than stunning. She took her place at her usual table as if nothing was amiss. She ignored the quick surreptitious changing around of placecards (she had not been expected, and had been left out of the seating arrangements) until all was as it should be.

With hauteur, she greeted the Fitches and Reinholds, and then she asked loudly after dear Lyddie's health. Every person in the dining room strained to hear the formal conversation that ensued.

After only a few moments, it became clear that Felicia Ellison, wronged and humiliated wife of Mr. Randolph T. Ellison of Ellison Steel Manufacturing, had fully recovered from her despair of the night before. And that she intended that not another word be whispered about her.

Stunned, Betz had to express her admiration, whispering, "She's much stronger than I suspected."

Mr. Teague murmured, "Yes, she's changeable, all right."

Cherry leaned across the table, her eyes aglow.

"Then you did hear what she tried to do last night, Mr. Teague! I slept through it all!"

Betz shushed the girl, deciding the best way to distract Cherry was to focus attention on Adam's recent absence. "We all missed you at dinner yesterday, Mr. Teague," she said.

Adam's eyes were as warm on her as they had been the evening before. He gave her a nod of acknowledgment but said nothing.

"Yes, Teague, where were you?" Mr. Bonaventure said. "It seems my attendant is taken with you. She asks to sit at this table every day." He coughed delicately. "She pined all the evening long and made me quite tired."

"I hope you'll forgive me, Nurse Tully, but I went into the city," said Adam, looking amused.

The nurse gave him a blatantly seductive look.

Quietly seething, Betz thought the nurse looked as common as a streetwalker. It galled her to think that Adam would speak to her.

Cherry plunged merrily on.

"I noticed you have a new hat, Mr. Teague. Did you get it to please Mrs. Ellison? Remember what she said last week? I saw you wearing it this morning on the beach. It's ever so flattering. Didn't you think so, Miss Witherspoon?"

Betz stared at her plate, hoping Cherry would not see how her feelings openly showed. She was amused even though Cherry blithely ignored her instructions about correct dinner table conversation.

"I lost my other hat during a game of baseball," said Adam. "The Giants were playing. Have you heard of this new game, ladies? It's quite popular in New York City."

Mr. Bonaventure expressed an interest. The conversation turned in that direction. Incredibly, nothing further was said about Mrs. Ellison's behavior of the night before.

After the meal, while leftover vanilla macaroons were being cleared away, Betz noticed Teddy giving Cherry a secret wink. Relieved, she saw the child pointedly ignore him. Felicia Ellison exited the dining room like visiting royalty.

"I'll be along in a moment, Cherry," Betz whispered, rising quickly from her seat. "Since I'm not really interested in staying for the recital, we'll go for a walk if you like. But I want to speak to Felicia first, to assure myself she's all right."

"She looks as stuffy as ever," Cherry muttered, squirming about to see in which direction Adam was going.

Silently agreeing, Betz followed Felicia to the parlor. Everyone was gathering there to hear an impromptu three o'clock recital by the Howard children. Mr. Macklin, looking oddly as if he had just been given a severe scolding, was standing at attention beside the box piano.

Leon Howard was walking just ahead of Betz and turned to watch Felicia pass into the parlor. He looked the woman up and down, and rubbed his jaw where she had struck him the night before. Then he said snidely, "It looks like the old battle-ax has recovered."

Betz paused to give him a scathing look. She felt revolted to be so near to him.

Drawing himself to his full height and raking her person with mocking eyes, he added, "I've heard that her husband's had mistresses for at least the last twenty years—some of them as prominent as the wives of congressmen. But our dear Felicia doesn't think to throw herself into the briny deep until the news appears in *Society Topics.*"

"A man like yourself wouldn't understand," Betz said with contempt.

"No, you're quite correct, Miss Witherspoon. Hypocrisy does seem to be over my head. I am what I am, and, I dare say, so are you." He leaned closed and tweaked her nose. She reared back, loathe to have him touch her. "Have you read about your own sweet self in those same scandal sheets that so vexed our high and mighty Mrs. Ellison?"

Betz went cold.

"Ah, I see that you have not. A pity. It would open your eyes, and serve to warn you. Someone here at Summersea has a keen interest in all you do, in all of us, to be sure. I hear the job pays very well, indeed." He gave a mock start of surprise, and struck a thoughtful pose. "Could it be that you are the *Topics'* spy?" He seemed to be baiting her.

"Whatever do you mean?" she cried.

"Are you the very asp in society's bosom, gathering secrets and selling them to the unscrupulous editors?" He lowered his gaze as if encouraging her to confess. "You can tell Leon. Are you an enterprising woman, wandering about hotels after hours in various stages of half-dress in search of gossip items?" His brow arched.

"I can't imagine what you're talking about. I was looking for—"

"Tut, tut, Miss Witherspoon. Don't think that I failed to note your presence at Madame Ellison's most convincing performance last night. You were wandering about again. What were you doing?" His tone was mocking, as if he knew better.

"Wha—It's none of your business what I was doing!"

"What I'm really wondering, dear, is why you got her to come out of the water. Surely Summersea would not miss her."

At Betz's blanched cheeks, he laughed openly, and sidled into the parlor, where his daughter Tippy was positioning herself on the piano stool. She tossed back her perfect corkscrew curls, and arched her tiny fingers over the ivory keys. Betz wondered how such a pretty child could spring from such an odious man.

Stiffly, Betz made her way across the parlor. The piano recital was about to begin, and she began to sit in the chair next to Felicia. Felicia turned to her cooly, as if they had never before met, and said, "I beg your pardon..."

Taken aback, Betz stammered, "I-I'm so glad to see you're feeling better, Feli—Mrs. Ellison."

The ladies surrounding Felicia looked at Betz as if she had made an unforgivable social error. Was she supposed to pretend nothing had happened? Were they going to? Was Felicia immune from their judgement? Betz couldn't imagine that anyone was. Felicia herself looked as if she was being annoyed by a servant.

"I've saved this seat for a friend, Miss Witherspoon, if you don't mind."

Blinking, Betz straightened and backed off a step. She tried to understand the meaning behind this public snubbing.

"I see," Betz said.

An ominous silence settled over the parlor as everyone waited for Betz to move away so that four-year-old Tippy Howard could begin playing her piano piece.

Bo Howard, the child's handsome eighteen-year-old half brother, sauntered in just then, leading Cherry by the hand. Cherry looked confused. This was one of the lads Felicia Ellison had said was worthy of her time, but only as a distraction. Seeing Betz, Cherry shrugged in a bewildered way and allowed herself to be seated among the frowning upper crust.

Betz was not at all sure she approved of Bo Howard as a friend for Cherry, and debated with herself as to whether she should hasten Cherry away to safer pursuits. But she could not bring herself to add fuel to this embarrassing scene. So, prickling with indignation, Betz made her way from the parlor and headed for the veranda. Escape was all she could think about.

She should not take their snubs personally, she reminded herself. It was the nature of the rich to judge and exclude. But Felicia's behavior puzzled her. Was there something more going on with the woman? Had she been suicidal because of her husband's faithlessness, or because the news had reached the scandal sheet?

Betz marched across the grass toward the lonely stretch of beach leading toward the steps going up to the pavilion. Perhaps she had merely stepped too close to Felicia, a woman who valued position far more than friendship.

At the far end of the beach, Betz made the one hundred twelve steps easily. Alone at last in the pavilion, she stripped off her suffocating jacket, unfurled her hair and began to cry.

She should not care at all what anyone thought of her, but Felicia Ellison's snub and the judgmental stares of the woman's friends had reminded Betz of what it felt like to be without society's approval. What if she did not have the courage to oppose what society decreed? If she didn't, she was doomed to be a chaperone, companion, or nanny to nieces and nephews.

She still didn't want to be married. She did not want a cozy cottage or children of her own. Her chances for that had passed in any case.

Fearful, she bemoaned the social chains binding her, knowing that in a while she would hasten back so as to not be out so late at night. She could not remember when she had felt more miserable. Then, her thoughts turned to Adam Teague. If he were near, she would not care about anything but his smile.

Mr. Teague Finds Mischief

Adam stood in the rear of the parlor listening to the lilting strains of a piano piece played by the Howard child, who was so small her feet couldn't reach the pedals. They were all present, "the Grand Assortment," he liked to call them, as boring a bunch of snobs as he had ever met.

Mrs. Fitch was seated next to her pensive daughter Lyddie, who was dressed all in black even though she was no widow. Adam had heard the Fitch maid whispering that Lyddie was expecting. Suppressing a smile, he wondered how or if they would hide that small detail from the curious "assortment."

Mr. Fitch, with his long, fuzzy mustaches, was nodding onto his chest, bored by the recital. The Fitches weren't ones for ostentatious jewelry, but Adam suspected that the man had a sizable amount of cash in his room.

Leon Howard was smoking a cheroot, much to the distaste of the ladies nearest him, and leisurely blowing smoke rings while his youngest daughter played.

When Tippy at last curtsied, giving rise to the hope that the recital was at an end, Leon clapped loudly, a diamond-and gold ring flashing on his left hand.

Then, as his elder daughter, Marietta, sauntered to the piano stool, looking for all the world like she was going to play something amazing, Leon consulted a gold watch from his pocket. It was typical of the vulgarly expensive trinkets the *nouveau riche* enjoyed flaunting.

Leon's wife, Lillian, her sun blond hair done up with diamond stickpins, and her throat glistening with several thousand dollars' worth of gems, was not to be overlooked, by any means. Her ears and fingers were dripping with costly little baubles, which she tossed and flashed like secret winks and kisses. It was a rather gaudy display for so early in the day, and definitely one to attract thieves.

Her wandering eye caught sight of Adam, now, which she did almost as often as Leon mentally undressed Betz Witherspoon.

Adam searched the backs of the heads in the parlor, looking for Betz's auburn hair. Frowning, he skirted the rear of the parlor to see if she was standing in the lobby. She was nowhere.

Saucy little Cordelia Ryburn was seated next to Howard's son Bo. Like his father, Bo seemed to mentally undress whatever hapless female was in his sight. Adam had thought Cordelia was infatuated with the waiter. Of course, that wasn't done. She was an heiress, for all her awkward, unrefined (and refreshing) behavior. But she was just an adolescent, prone to crushes of brief duration.

The Reinholds were grouped around Mrs. Ellison in a very suspicious, unconvincing display of support. Mr. Charles Bonaventure was looking suitably pale and attentive from his wicker wheelchair.

Nurse Tully began to give Adam the eye. She was the kind of self-serving female that Adam disliked most, but he raised his brow at her, feigning interest. She would likely be camped on his doorstep by midnight. At other times, in other places, he could have looked forward to bedding her; if the bar was open and the drink was free, Adam had been known to indulge. But the presence of Betz Witherspoon, someone of a very different cut, put a damper on his thirst for the easy delights being offered by the woman he was supposed to cultivate.

No one seemed at all concerned that Betz was absent. The eccentric old artist might have been, but he was not present. He would not have bothered with such as this in any case. He was a truly free man whom Adam admired.

Adam threaded his way between the parlor chairs, and bent to whisper in Cordelia's ear, "Where's your chaperone?"

There were disgruntled murmurs of irritation all around at his uncouth interruption, but because he was a mere "businessman" from Chicago, it hardly mattered. He was of no consequence, just an object of curiosity to distract the "Assortment" when nothing better served. He could not be expected to know that one did not move about nor whisper during a recital.

Cordelia shrugged. He would have to warn her about Bo Howard, he thought, and ambled away through the doors into the lobby, feeling rather pleased with himself for having disturbed the excruciatingly dull recital. He still wondered where Betz had gone, though, and whether he should walk the beach in search of her. Then he decided against it. Much as he might have liked striking up something more that an acquaintance with Betz, he had more serious concerns.

He took the opportunity to slip up to the second floor to the end of the corridor where he found Bonaventure's room. Picking the lock with ease, he let himself inside.

Closing the door, he paused a moment to note what he could before going through the drawers and wardrobe. The room was tidy, of course, thanks to the hotel maids. There were no books or other personal item lying about that might suggest what the man did in his idle hours.

Adam found nothing out of the ordinary in the drawers, just an assortment of laundered items of considerable quality. Bonaventure didn't act like a man of privilege, but a box in his nearly empty valise contained several expensive pairs of cufflinks. Gifts? Adam thought, a sour taste in his mouth.

He checked beneath the mattress of Bonaventure's bed, looked behind each picture hanging from long wires from the picture rail high on the wall. There was nothing useful to be learned in this room, he thought with irritation, and he had waited nearly two weeks to find a moment alone in here.

Frustrated, he scanned the floor behind a chair and small table, under the bed, on the far side of the wardrobe, but either the maid was especially conscientious or Charles Bonaventure simply left nothing for even a keen-witted man to find.

All that remained was to search the nurse's room on the third floor. That could be quite easy, given her character. But he preferred to search it in private, and that would require yet another wait.

Slipping out, he made his way quickly to his third floor cubicle. Lighting a candle, he removed his jacket and shirt. Suspenders dangling at his hips, he sat at the tiny desk and wrote in a small notebook for several minutes.

Sweat was rolling down his back almost at once, as the room had no ventilation. But he wasn't about to write to ask for funds to finance a more comfortable room.

He was certain that his time at Summersea would prove to be a complete waste, anyway. And his evening in the city had further served to frustrate him, because there were events afoot there that he wanted a part in. While here at Summersea, pursuing an obligation he had taken on freely, he could not hope to become involved there.

It seemed his entire summer would go to waste here while he waited for matters to come to a head.

Almost suffocating, irritated, reluctantly hungry for an easing of his physical needs, he began pacing. Was there anything he could do to move events along? Did he even dare consider engaging the very respectable Miss Witherspoon in anything more than proper conversation? Would that be fair?

Soon he realized that the piano playing had ended, and the hotel was taking on the late afternoon hush that he relished.

After supper that night he would be able to stroll about virtually undetected. He would watch as Lillian Howard crossed from her suite to an unbooked room, from which Powel Reinhold would later emerge, adjusting his cravat and trousers. He would listen at doors to all manner of interesting gossip. Last, he would find himself lingering on the servants' stair, in hopes that Miss Witherspoon might again be in search of the capricious Cordelia.

Mopping himself with a towel, and then rinsing his head and face in the tin basin—the third floor did not merit porcelain—he paused when he heard footsteps scamper along the narrow hall. A folded square of paper slipped beneath his door.

Straightening, he smiled. If nothing else, these people enjoyed their intrigues.

Meet me at the pavilion during the benefit.

Studying the neatly penned, unsigned note, Adam sank to the edge of his ungiving bed. Nurse Althea Tully? No, her penmanship would never match this. Lillian Howard? He doubted she would resort to unsigned notes. Her sort would beckon with an arched brow.

He chuckled. No, this had the distinct air of authentic romance about it. He sniffed the paper and smiled.

He ruled out all the maids and nannies.

Someone might want his advice. It had happened in the past; he had been mistaken for a gentleman eager to act the brotherly part.

Sniffing again, he thought of Marietta Howard. The girl was certainly the type for this, but he was far too old for her. She had the entire male staff to pick from. His prowess could not match that of the wagon driver, who stood several inches taller and was a dozen years his junior.

There seemed to be no likely author of this fragrant, pretty note other than Miss Witherspoon. He fanned himself with the note, breathing in the scent, and thought about the direct way she always looked at him.

And he *had* suggested they spend some time together if she was not required to attend the benefit, he reminded himself.

Grinning, he tucked the note beneath his pillow, tossed on a fresh shirt and waited to set out on his nightly rounds.

A Letter from George

Monday, June 10, 1889

Two days later as she and Cherry were headed out of the hotel, Betz found letters waiting for them in the cubbyholes behind the main desk.

"Your grandmother has written to us both," Betz said, noting the postmarks and then tucking her two letters into her skirt pocket.

"Who's your other one from?" Cherry asked, trying to pluck the second letter away from Betz.

"My brother," Betz said, giving a quiet sigh. "I don't look forward to opening it."

"What do you suppose Grandmother has to say to both of us—look, there's a copy of *Society Topics.*" She pointed to a table in the corner of the lobby. "Can we take it? I want to know what upset Mrs. Ellison the other day."

Remembering the warning she had received from Mr. Howard, Betz discouraged Cherry from taking the sheet. "It's really none of our business. We don't want to stoop to reading gossip—"

But before she could stop Cherry, the girl had snatched up the single fold of paper and was dashing away.

Adam was just coming down the stairs to the lobby. His face was red, and he looked overwarm.

"Morning, Betz."

"I noticed a letter in your box," Betz said, wanting to engage him in conversation, but concerned about Cherry running off.

He raised his brows and glanced toward the desk, but didn't appear very interested in his mail.

"I didn't see you at the recital the other afternoon, Betz. Nor at dinner yesterday." He had a disconcerting twinkle in his eye that emptied her mind of all concerns.

"Cordelia and I went to chapel yesterday and stayed late for a walk in the village," she said. She didn't want to explain how she had felt after Felicia snubbed her, so she edged away in the direction the girl had taken. "You'll have to excuse me, Mr. Teague—"

He clucked his tongue reprovingly.

"We're back to formality? A pity."

She forced herself to ignore his remark. She had almost forgotten her place, but she must remember that she was a chaperone. She must not entertain romantic thoughts.

"Cordelia has just run off with a copy of that scandal sheet. Someone warned me that there was something in it about…me."

Amusement crinkled the corners of Adam's eyes. "It's hard

to keep out of that thing. There's probably a spy staying at every resort along the Eastern Seaboard. Some provide information for the money, others do it for the power. Think of the silent revenge one would get leaking a confidence for public consumption."

"Gossip," Betz said with contempt.

"Yes, and some will pay quite a premium to keep certain things out of the paper. You'll find the oddest people owning 'stock' or taking out 'advertising' in the news sheet. I believe such investments are more rightly called 'hush money'. And true to form, not all payment is in cash. Inside information has its own unique value."

"Now you sound like Mr. Howard," Betz said, cooling to Adam's bitter tone.

"Forgive me. Do you have a secret that you hope has not found its way into the paper?"

"Certainly not," she said, genuinely confused. "I was even accused of being one of those spies!"

"Ah..." He looked as if he understood. Fishing a folded square from his breast pocket, he handed it to her.

A simple sentence scrawled across the page read: *We're on to you, spy.*

Betz blinked in surprise.

"They suspect you as well?"

"Perhaps. Or it might be part of a carefully played game to throw suspicion away from the true source. If I know I am not the one feeding juicy tidbits to the editors, and you know you're not, I'd say we were safe with one another. What is your secret, Miss Witherspoon?" His tone was teasing but his gaze was as warm as the sun.

Suddenly breathless, Betz moved away.

"Good morning, Mr. Teague."

Trembling, she escaped before he could lure her into saying something she might regret. After several steps she had to stop to remember where she was going. How odd, she thought, to feel so self-conscious when looking into Adam's direct brown eyes. How odd to feel the presence of him as a man, and find it so...arousing.

How…wonderful!

How terrifying.

At last she remembered she was in search of Cherry who had the scandal sheet, and could be at that moment reading something upsetting about her. Checking their suite she found only a young maid changing their linens and muttering as she punched the pillows. Betz rushed back down the stairs to look along the beach.

A good quarter mile from Summersea, Betz found Cherry, holding up her skirts and wading barefoot in the waves.

"You've run me quite a chase," Betz said, exhausted and irritated. "Are you all right?"

Cherry made no reply.

Panting, Betz collapsed into the sand, certain no one would come along to observe their disarray, and scold them. She saw the scandal sheet lying a few feet away, weighted by two handfuls of damp sand. She decided not to press the issue just then. She would read her letters and then see if she might take up the scandal sheet without undue fuss.

"Dear Miss Witherspoon," Agatha Dunwitty had written in an unlovely script, "I trust you and Cordelia are getting along famously…"

Betz read on with interest, while watching Cherry from the corner of her eye. Further instructions, which she had expected in the letter, were absent, giving her the feeling that Agatha Dunwitty had entrusted her far too much with Cherry's care.

She wondered if Cherry's grandmother had actually not expected much to come of the summer. Perhaps, she secretly thought that Cherry could not be cultivated into anything more than a weed.

The close of the letter left her feeling irritated and lost, for she didn't know—beyond the original instructions to introduce Cherry to various lessons of refinement—what Agatha expected to find upon her return.

Still reluctant to open George's letter, she edged across the sand and plucked up the scandal sheet and shook it clean. Skimming the closely printed words, she came to the third paragraph of a column titled "Tidbits" and read:

> "The silver-haired gentleman can be seen nightly with his raven-haired beauty, she a mere thirty years his junior. While his stately wife vacations with her goodly friends, unaware of the blatant overtures of affection being publicly squandered on this most unworthy of young strumpets, this gentleman of steely proportions steadfastly tests his mettle. We can only say, take heed, madam, for your marriage is in jeopardy. Nay, we fear it is at an end, for when so respectable a man takes his paramour to the very seats fit only for a wife, it is suspected that he is bound for the courts. Dare we mention the odious word, divorce?"

Betz wanted to wad up the sheet and throw it into the sea. To think that in this day and age there were still creatures who feasted on the heartaches of others…

She brushed off the paper and read on.

> "It is on good authority that we hear the increasingly interesting stories of a young heiress so new upon the scene as to arouse the most dull-witted to curiosity. Not only do we find the questions, where did she spring from, and who was her mother, flooding the mind, but one cannot help but wonder what she is doing prowling at night, particularly in the company of low persons of the menial class."

So, the escapade had not gone unnoticed.

Betz gnashed her teeth, wondering if she would be able to control her temper after reading such foolishness. Then her eyes wandered farther down the page.

> "What is even more surprising is that one hired to perform certain custodial functions, who can also be seen prowling about at hours unbecoming a respectable woman, which certainly rouses suspicion as to the quality of character in

one of the servant class. Can we have two such spoiled fruit among our gentry without causing the entire scene to degenerate into a mass of sordid episodes unworthy of even the lowest of the low?"

Betz felt stung just as if she had been slapped. When she folded the paper and pushed it into her pocket, she looked up to see Cherry watching her. The only people who knew she had been out that night were Adam, Mr. Howard and Cherry. Who would they have told? Why would anyone have bothered to give that information to the tabloid?

"It was talking about us," Cherry said matter of factly.

"Not necessarily," Betz said, rigid with anger.

Cherry stomped through the water, soaking her hem. "You know it was! Grandmother will be furious with me."

Betz was at a loss for an answer. "What can we expect of these people? And…" she added, wanting and needing to voice her feelings, "look at the way Felicia Ellison snubbed me during the recital."

Cherry rushed to Betz's side and dropped to her knees in the sand.

"She snubbed you? Tell me!"

Betz was unable to avoid describing the scene, but finally got off the subject by making Cherry open her letter from her grandmother. It, too, proved to be benignly encouraging, and lacking specifics.

"What am I supposed to do, Betz? Does she really want me to be like those people? Must I be like Marietta, and go around with my nose in the air?" She struck a pose, and then scrambled to her feet. Strutting about, she held herself in an only slightly exaggerated imitation of the way Felicia had held herself since her venture into the bay. "I'm better than everybody. I have blue blood. *La-dee-da-dee-da.*"

"If you want to hear something that will truly raise your hackles, I'll read you my brother's letter."

"Why did you live with your brother so long?" Cherry asked,

dropping her haughty expression and returning to Betz's side.

Betz tensed. "I felt I had no choice. I'd made such a mess of my life on my own. And when I left George's house not so long ago, I was frightened, because I feared I was not suited to much. You're so fortunate. Agatha will provide you with an education…"

"I suppose I am," Cherry said, sighing.

"Well, let's read this. We'll have a good laugh, and then go back inside to prepare for the benefit. I think you'll make an excellent showing tonight. Not a one of the girls will be wearing a gown more elegant than yours."

Nine

The Afternoon of the Summer Benefit

Betz read only a few lines of her brother's letter. She couldn't go on.

"You get the general idea of George's attitude," she said to Cherry, abruptly, angrily folding the letter with trembling hands.

Cherry stopped her from pushing the papers into her pocket. "You must read me the rest!"

Sighing, Betz decided to comply. Better to get it over with than brood about it the rest of the day. "Dear Sister," her elder brother had written. "Imagine my profound relief after receiving your recent letter. Cynthia and I had certainly given you up for dead, for when we received no word from you in all the days since you left us, we could not imagine where you had gone or what you were doing with yourself. I had even driven the buggy over to Mother's house, expecting to find you there, sulking in your usual manner—"

"Sulking? You, Betz?"

Betz tried to laugh off her growing fury. "Anything short of complete agreement seems like sulking to my brother."

"Well, I don't like him at all. Read on." Cherry nodded her head.

Amused somewhat, by Cherry's brash invasion of her privacy, Betz continued. "…but the place was closed up tight, as always. And, it was my shame to notice, it looked decidedly neglected. I will forever be mystified by your refusal to deed Mother's house to me. I am the responsible member of our small family. You, my dear sister, cannot be expected to keep up the place yourself, nor properly supervise that incompetent caretaker. It's just too much to expect.

"But past grievances aside, I must say I am completely baffled by your decision to not live at Mother's, in view of the fact that you will not allow myself to live there as owner. Of course, it remains unthinkable that I should live there when the place remains in your name. Why, then, do you not choose to live there, but to labor in this disgraceful fashion, for strangers?

"Are you so wounded by Cynthia's desire to assume control over my children that you must shame us by working as a common woman? I see I must concede to your fit of temper. I relent, and humbly suggest that you return to us, your family, at once. You may be reinstated in our household, not as a working member in charge of the children, but as a guest."

Betz's voice was shaking as she paused to draw a breath.

"If he thinks I'm going to sit around and do nothing for the rest of my life…"

"He sounds ever so pleasant," Cherry said, her cheeks aflame. "Why, then, do I feel like scratching out his eyes?" She made an amusing catlike face.

"I have often wondered that very thing myself. He would have me without property or means. I've told him time and again that he may take his family to Mother's house any time he wished, and he may live there as long as he likes."

"Then why doesn't he?"

"Mother left the house to me. In the event George died and failed to provide for me, as she was afraid that he might, I was to have something of my own to live in or sell as I saw fit. It was Mother's last and only wish. I gave her my solemn word that I would never deed the house to George. She didn't want me to be dependent, as she was. George, of course, cannot understand this." Betz flexed her fists and tried again to retain her humor. "Listen to me, getting all upset by a foolish letter. Let's go inside now. I have a need to lose myself fashioning your hair into something beautiful."

"No, you must read on to the end. He must want something from you, or he wouldn't have written."

"How wise you are, Cherry," Betz said, astounded by the girl's wisdom. "Very well."

"Upon your immediate return, dear sister, you and I shall have a serious discussion. You shall see the foolish selfishness of your decision to keep Mother's house empty and in disrepair. We shall deed it to me, and then remove there, forthwith. There, we shall all be most comfortable.

"And so I must instruct you to immediately give your notice to this person you refer to as your employer. You must disentangle yourself from those people residing at the hotel, and forget at once all your foolish notions of becoming an independent female. You must realize, dear, that as an unmarried woman you cannot hope to retain your impeccable reputation in such a place, for surely you realize that you yourself require a chaperone of the most sterling character. You must understand and learn to accept the limitations of your sex, dear. If you require further convincing, may I remind you of the last time you attempted to make a decision on your own? It was quite a disaster, and took six prudent years with me as your guardian to live down those most regrettable mistakes."

Betz leapt to her feet. Throwing the letter into the beach grass, she snapped, "The fool! It was he who insisted that I marry that so-called man! Where was his brotherly duty and concern then? He wanted only to get me out from underfoot."

Cherry gathered up the pages of the letter. "He has the nerve to sign this, 'Your loving brother,' I don't like him at all. Why must the world have people like this?"

"Give me the letter. I intend to burn it. As to why, there is no answer. It remains that there are people like this, and we must learn to live among them."

Mrs. Ellison Finds Mischief

Felicia Ellison strained to hear if Myrtle Fitch was coming out. From her chair on the veranda she could hear the woman's hushed voice in the lobby. She was likely talking to Lyddie, who wanted only to stay in her room.

Anxiously, Felicia straightened the pleats of her voluminous skirt. Or were they discussing her? She was almost beside herself because she couldn't seem to stop the gossip about her. She couldn't be everywhere at once! What more could she do to silence the wagging tongues? She had been such a fool! Even suicide was now denied her!

How had that miserable information come to print? She wanted to throttle the editor! What was the point of going on with their agreement now? He had betrayed her!

Myrtle emerged unexpectedly from the doors as the steward brought around her two yapping dogs.

"You will join me here in the shade soon, won't you, Myrtle?" Felicia asked in her sweetest voice. She gave the woman a smile that belied any and all rumors about her sanity being off.

Myrtle gave her a thin smile and adjusted her kid gloves before accepting her dogs' leashes. She and Emma had rallied around her at first, but as the gossip continued they had withdrawn somewhat. "I really should see to it that my doggies have some time with me. You understand, dear, I'm sure."

And off she strolled, leashes in one hand, parasol in the other, down around the lawn to the tennis pavilion where a few attractive yet inferior gentlemen were playing. She was obviously shopping for a new son-in-law.

Felicia understood only too well, and her hurt and disappointment immediately vaporized into fury.

In an instant she had forgotten wanting to be accepted again. She decided to arrange an elaborate, enviable party that would have them all panting to be included. Somehow she must face the damage done to her reputation and put an end to all the gossip…or she would simply die! And now she could see how useless even *that* was—just as that horrid little Witherspoon thing had suggested, if she did die the gossips would only pick her bones. The party could be her answer.

Jarred from her frantic thoughts, she twisted around in her

chair as that common nurse creature wheeled the ever so handsome Mr. Bonaventure onto the veranda.

"Forgive me, madam, I don't wish to disturb your thoughts," he said, removing his hat.

"It's quite all right," she said, appraising him. He looked particularly wan this morning as he indicated that he would like to be parked next to her chair. He gave a nod to the nurse, who disappeared back inside.

Felicia was stricken, suddenly, with the fear that he would begin asking her awkward questions. How could she prevent that without hurting the feelings of an invalid? And he was her inferior. Should she be seen with him?

He sighed, lifted a limp-wristed hand and drew it across his brow.

"I believe," he said softly, "that I am growing weaker. But perhaps it's only the heat."

What could she say to that, she wondered. Then blessedly, her old curiosity welled, and she became once again the expert inquisitor she had always been.

"Tell me more about it," she urged in her gentlest tone. "I am terribly concerned about you."

Weakly, he waved his hand, as if his condition and feelings were not worthy of note.

"I wouldn't think to trouble you, dear. You are too kind to ask."

The endearment electrified her. How long had it been since Randolph called her dear…She went on urging Mr. Bonaventure to speak, and at length he consented to tell her a bit about his condition.

"In place of the treatment, I have been urged to take the sea air, and a very kind friend was dear enough to book my room here for the summer. It was all she could manage, sweet generous creature. The treatment, of course, is ever so much more expensive than a mere three months at a hotel like this." He had been talking without looking directly at Felicia, but now he turned to her, fixing her with eyes so dark and sweet she found herself riveted. "I have to ask why a woman of your stature is staying at this rather second-rate hotel."

"Not second-rate, surely, Mr. Bonaventure! Not so fine as Cape May or Saratoga perhaps, but quite adequate."

"Granted, some rather fine people like yourself are staying here. But I can tell by your demeanor, and your extraordinary poise under duress that you are several cuts above everyone here. And I see how you so grandly allow others imagine that they are above you. It takes a truly great woman of character to be so generous to one's underlings."

She felt speechless. He understood her own conviction that she was far superior to everyone around her. They were all fools and pretenders, while she had the inborn greatness of a lady. That was why Randolph's preference for a tramp so mystified and pained her, and why she had gone to such lengths to keep his behavior out of the scandal sheet.

Why, this poor invalid man—who might otherwise be prancing about on the tennis pavilion and was instead bound to his wheeled chair by impending death of lung fever—why, he understood her quality! What could she tell him, the truth?

"I couldn't bear to be among my real friends this summer," she confessed, and to a degree, that was part of the truth. "Under the circumstances..."

"Say no more, madam, for I would not think to discuss anything that would pain so kind a lady as yourself."

"You must tell me more of this treatment you can't afford," Felicia said, leaning close to him. "Who was this person who financed this summer by the sea for you?"

"Ah, she was so kind, a lady not unlike yourself, but not so wealthy, of course. I have never had the honor of sitting near, much less talking with, the wife of so renown a man as—"

"Never mind my husband!"

"Certainly—*certainly,* he is not your equal, but what I was trying to say..."

He went on and on, and she lapped up his words like the thickest of cream. She might have taken his hand, in a motherly fashion, of course, had he not turned to her with such a personal look that she was taken aback.

"My former friend..." he said, with his handsome cheeks coloring unexpectedly, "found my condition somewhat...frightening. She and I were never, shall we say, close, though it was my fondest desire to have her as my..." He lifted his eyes which were moist with emotion. "Am I embarrassing you, my dear Mrs. Ellison?"

She was tingling with amazement. He was...interested in her, and suddenly she wished they were alone somewhere instead of on a veranda where anyone might happen along. "Call me Felicia," she whispered.

"Without the treatment, I shall surely die within a year, and I do understand her inability to do anything further for me," he rushed on. "It's just that, dear woman that she was, she was only willing to give me what she could in terms of money. I, unfortunately, would have been willing to settle for a far, far greater...final gift." He lowered his face and contemplated his folded, graceful white hands. They seemed to be shaking imperceptibly.

"And that would have been..." Felicia's querying voice was shaking, too.

"She feared contagion." He seemed wounded to the core. "I assured her, but she denied me, giving me money when all I wanted from her was...love." His last word was softly spoken.

Felicia nearly swooned with surprise. She would have leapt to her feet and gathered him into her arms, but at that moment Betz Witherspoon and the wicked little heiress came along from the beach, their clothes sandy and in disarray.

Felicia drew back, still shamed that Betz had witnessed her night of weakness. What might Witherspoon say about it to those who would ask for money? Felicia's eyes raked the two young women, her mind racing with thoughts. She nodded when Betz looked at her, and then allowed herself to turn away, snubbing the young woman. Betz must be made to understand that one word about Felicia's lapse of control would bring disaster to herself. Felicia still had that kind of power.

From the corner of her eye Felicia watched Mr. Bonaventure

to see if he looked at Betz or Cordelia in the same way that he had looked at her during their astonishing conversation. His eyes remained fixed on her. How was she going to manage any type of association with this man without attracting unwanted attention?

Swelling with confidence that she could control the direction gossip might take in the coming weeks at Summersea, she waited until the veranda was again deserted, leaving her alone with this remarkable, perceptive man.

"What may I call you, Mr. Bonaventure?" she whispered.

"Charles," he answered, equally softly. She settled back in her chair.

"Tell me more of this expensive treatment, Charles. Then, if your nurse hasn't returned, I shall wheel you back to your suite myself. She shouldn't leave you alone for such extended periods, a man in your delicate condition."

"Ah, but I instructed her to take herself away—so that I might be alone with you...Felicia. I've longed to talk with you, from the first moment I saw you. You've been in my most intimate thoughts."

Her breathing quickened and she nearly swooned. "Oh, dear, dear Charles!"

The Rendezvous

Cherry's gown was of white tulle. Gathered in sheer folds down the bodice to its narrow waist, it was garnished with pink silk roses that tumbled from her right shoulder to the floor. The sides of the gown's skirt were drawn back in complicated gathers that took almost half hour to properly arrange. Her slippers were satin, trimmed with pink roses on the toes, and her white kid gloves were the thinnest and most finely stitched that Betz had ever seen.

When Cherry turned from the dressing table, Betz pinned a pink rose in her blond hair, which was drawn up in front into a pile of perfectly arranged curls but tumbled about her shoulders in back in a froth of ringlets that had taken the better part of the afternoon to crimp with a stove-warmed iron rod. Cherry stared at her reflection.

"I don't recognize myself. What would Mama say if she could see me?"

"She would be proud. I know that you're going to have a very enjoyable time tonight. Do you remember what you're supposed to talk about?"

Cherry gave her a sidelong look, answering, "Bo Howard never talks about the right sort of things."

"Well, take extra care with him. I don't trust him. I half suspect that his father may be that tabloid spy everyone is so frightened about. Try to behave the way you will when Drew Whitgift arrives. And if you can, pretend that your grandmother is watching from nearby. You'll want to make her proud."

"I'll try," Cherry said, stealing peeks at herself in the looking glass. "I can't believe that's me. Is this a dream?"

"You're going to have a wonderful time. I'll be waiting for you here, the moment you grow weary of all the dancing."

Faint strains of a waltz were drifting up from the ballroom. Moments later someone tapped. Betz opened the door to discover Mr. Fitch brushing back his white mustache with a knuckle.

His thin cheeks were pale, his hooded eyes looking rather bored until he spied Cherry cringing behind Betz.

"My, my, uh, my wife and daughter asked that I escort you to the ballroom, my dear Miss Ryburn." He offered his elbow to Cherry, he was wearing an especially grand black tailcoat.

Cherry took his elbow and maneuvered her enormous tulle-draped bustle through the door. She swished softly away down the corridor, leaving Betz feeling pleased yet faintly sad.

The music grew more lively during the course of the evening. The lights shone yellow across the darkened lawn below the balcony, and Betz could see the shadows of the dancers moving through the light. Several times she thought about slipping downstairs to look in on Cherry, but she couldn't think where she might peek from. She tried to occupy herself in her room.

Toward midnight she heard footsteps come along the hall and stop at her door, and she wondered if Cherry had tired of the dancing. About to open the door, she saw a folded square of paper. Picking it up, she read a hasty scrawl: *I'll be waiting at the pavilion.*

At once her pulse was racing. Flinging open the door, she looked left and right to see if she could tell who might have left the note for Cherry.

Would Teddy or Bo Howard be waiting at the pavilion? There didn't seem to much hope for the rest of the summer if Cherry defied convention again and openly risked her reputation. But luckily, she had intercepted this note. Now she could slip away to the pavilion herself. She would see to it that the young man, whoever he might be, would be summarily discouraged.

Betz put on a pair of low shoes and left the hotel by the back way, hurrying along the trees at the far edge of the lawn until she was on the sand.

As far as she could see, there was no one ahead, nor anyone climbing the steps to the pavilion overlooking the bay.

Her thoughts were in turmoil as she mounted the steps. The night was cool and quiet except for the faint music drifting on the air. Behind her, Summersea looked far different, lit like a grand wonderful, place where one ought to be proud to stay.

As she hurried along, Betz suddenly thought of the portion of Agatha's letter that she hadn't told Cherry about. It seemed that Cherry's grandmother had sent her solicitor in search of Cherry's father. What would the old woman's reaction be if she learned Cherry's father was dead, as Cherry feared? And what would Cherry think if her father did reappear, after so long an absence? Would she be delighted or angry?

And what might have happened if Cherry had received this note and come to the pavilion? If Agatha had learned of all Cherry was doing, Betz would be fired and Cherry returned to the streets, disowned and disinherited. Betz must prevent that.

Sighing, feeling anxious and angry, Betz topped the last step and paused. There was a faint breeze off the bay. She had been there in the dark before, and had felt so safe away from Summersea's prying eyes. Now she felt apprehensive as she crossed to the circular pavilion and began pacing before it.

Then, at the sound of a footstep, she whirled. A man stood some distance away, his silhouette made more noticeable because he was wearing white trousers and a white shirt. He tipped his boater and stepped forward. From his broad-shouldered frame, she knew him at once.

"Mr. Teague!" she gasped, backing away and encountering the post at the entrance to the pavilion. "Whatever are you doing arranging to meet Cherry here, of all places? And you, of all people!"

"I didn't arrange anything of the sort, Betz," he said and chuckled. "A very pretty note was slipped under my door last evening. I knew it was from you. You can dispense with the surprise and formalities now. You asked me to meet you here. What can I do for you?"

"I did no such thing!" she cried with embarrassment. "A note was slipped beneath my door, too! Just a few minutes ago. Look!"

Producing the notes they had found, they approached each other to compare messages. Adam began to laugh, then. It was too dark for Betz to see him clearly, but being alone with him, even for these few moments...she found herself laughing, too. She felt giddy and nervous and was suddenly flooded with the awareness of him as a man—standing so near.

"It would seem," Adam said softly, "that someone has gone to a bit of trouble to bring us together tonight. Alone."

"Cherry!" Betz breathed in amazement. "She's behind this!"

"A clever child," he said, and chuckled softly.

Reeling, Betz started toward the steps, blurting, "I hope you'll forgive Cherry, Mr. Teague. I'll certainly box her ears."

"I hope you don't Betz. I think both of us have wanted a few minutes like this. Let's take the opportunity to talk. Stay a few minutes, and please, call me Adam. I admit to being a bit lonely here at Summersea."

"All right...Adam." She shivered with pleasure at saying his name aloud. "But I don't believe for a moment that you're lonely. You're the sort of man who fits in wherever he goes."

"In that, you're mistaken. Come and sit, please."

She stood at the top of the long curve of rustic steps, wondering if she dared spend another moment with him. Her composure was in chaos. She felt silly, like a school girl, and was grateful for the dark so that he couldn't see her flushed cheeks.

After a moment she was able to turn as if it was perfectly acceptable for her to spend a few moments alone with an attractive man. She felt his eyes on her. She was aware of herself as a woman, aware of how she had fixed her hair, and of the clothes she was wearing. She felt the presence of him acutely as she entered the small pavilion and took a place on one of the benches.

When he sat next to her, turned toward her with his arm resting on the railing behind her back, she felt like a candle flame burning so brightly that surely no one in the world could fail to see or sense her excitement.

This could not be happening, she thought, her chest constricted and her throat tight. She had promised herself that she would never again surrender to the wiles of an attractive man. Men weren't to be trusted! If she dared give Adam even a moment of her time, she might be lost again to those feeling she had vowed six years ago to forget.

But in spite of the warnings in her head, her heart was dancing in her breast. They were alone together, and he was sitting very near, as if he found her just as attractive as she did him. It all seemed too incredible.

"What did you want to talk about?" she whispered.

"You."

Ten

Miss Witherspoon and Mr. Teague Find Mischief

Betz was completely flustered. The focus of his attention was too intense. She wanted to escape him and reassemble her composure in some safe place.

But he was there, sitting so near that he might touch her if he wanted. She felt breathlessly aware of herself, afraid she would not be able to speak or act sanely.

He was so near now that she could smell the clean fresh scent of the night air on him. Her stomach fluttered, and her breath began to come in noticeable gasps. Must he lean so close?

She found herself standing. Abruptly, she moved away, and as she did, she cast about in her mind for something to say.

"Why are you afraid to be alone with me, Betz?" His voice was so hushed and intimate that her skin tingled.

Turning, she stared into the shadow at his face. As he stood she felt she was losing herself. The world seemed to come to a halt as his hands closed on her shoulders. Now she couldn't breathe without audibly gasping. She wanted to bolt! What was he doing? He wasn't going to…

She could no more have moved than she could have hoped to fly. Something in her rooted her to the spot, keeping her face upturned so that if the impossible might happen…

Her heart was pounding now, her senses reeling. He had touched her before, the night Felicia came in from the bay. But that had been the sort of touch anyone might bestow to keep her from stumbling down the steps.

This was different. This was the two of them alone, locked in this endless moment that would forever belong to them alone. Her awareness heightened. For one spine-tingling moment she was just a woman, and he was just a man holding her firmly before him. She felt small and young and inexperienced, yet very aware of what her feelings meant—what he might expect. Incredibly, she was responding. This was a special man. This was a man she could want, did want.

Surrendering to her instinct, she tilted back her head, yielding to the command of his hands on her shoulders.

"Aren't you pretending?" he whispered.

"I don't know what you mean."

"Are you sure you didn't send the note so that I would be here..." He left off, searching her face with those dark, penetrating eyes.

Then, incredibly, he was drawing her closer, his fingers firm on her shoulders. The blood started pounding in her ears. She watched his face come so near that his breath brushed her cheek. When his lips closed over her mouth, softly, warmly, an explosion of surprise and intense, overwhelming desire flooded through her body.

She was yielding with no conscious thought to the touch of his moist, possessive lips. She felt the firm, warm pressure of his chest against her breasts, and the sure clutch of his hands spread across her back.

The moment was vivid and seemingly endless, wrenched from time and held in suspension while the fire coursed through her, erasing all thought. For that delicious moment, she was lost to her body, possessed by her womanliness that craved something she had successfully kept hidden, had even blocked from her own thoughts, for most of her life.

The sensations filling her chest were so intense and arousing that she was suddenly cast into the darkness of shock. Tearing herself away, drawing a breath that sounded ragged and primitive, she stumbled backwards.

He reached to prevent her from tumbling down the steps, and now his touch was sharp.

"Careful!" he said, yanking her way from the edge.

She pulled free, her mind in a complete whirl. What was this that she was feeling? She was too old for it, too... "Don't—" was all she could choke out as she stumbled back to the bench and sat down heavily.

He remained at a distance some minutes and then joined her. His presence in the small pavilion was too much, now. She wanted to jump up and flee.

He leaned down to peer at her. Propping his right foot on the bench beside her, he said, "Forgive me for not acting like a gentleman just now. I can see I've upset you."

She sat stunned, more because of her reactions than because he had kissed her. When she lifted her gaze, she was not really able to make out his features in the darkness. But feeling him so close that she might reach out and caress his cheek, she gave a shudder. Dear heaven, she thought. He had pierced the armor of her heart. She wanted another kiss.

But to remain respectable, she must somehow get away from him. She must now avoid his gaze whenever they should meet in the dining room or in the lobby. She would have to make her position quite clear...

His warm hand curved along her jaw, slipping back to her knotted hair. As if expert in seduction, he spread his fingers into the knot, loosening all the pins. Several dropped softly to the bench behind her, and the auburn waves began tumbling, like her composure and her reserve.

When he sat beside her and circled her back with his arm, all thought vanished. She could not bring herself to discourage him. She could not speak nor move out of reach. Her senses strained to memorize every breath of this moment, to etch it deep into her heart so that she might have it always to dream upon. For surely there would not be another night like this in all her life, this first fluttering moment when he leaned close again, tipped back her head and kissed her throat.

She gave a soft "ah" of surprise, and waves of desire rippled through her as if she had been waiting for just this night to know the fullness of her being as a woman.

Then he was holding her face, guiding her lips to meet his, and when she felt the first tentative touch on her mouth, she strained forward, meeting his kiss with her own.

She could not have stopped herself if she had wanted to. Her body was in command, demanding the quenching of a thirst she had not known existed so deeply and secretly within. His kiss probed into her mouth, filling her with the most extraordinary explosion of desire; it was almost satisfaction itself.

Overwhelmed, astonished, she pulled back, feeling her hair tangled in his embrace, and she whispered, "Adam…Adam, you must let me go!"

"You don't want to be let go."

"But Teddy…or someone…"

"Betz, don't be frightened of me. A few kisses…"

She managed to stand again. Her legs were weak and shaky. She was trembling like a frightened fawn. It wasn't a matter of few kisses, she thought in a panic. Perhaps it was only that to him. For her, it was everything. These kisses could mean only one end, an end her body was, at this moment, demanding with the most primitive, unrelenting yearning for fulfillment. She had been married. She knew the kissing would not stop.

She tried to gather up her hair. He sat watching her a moment. Then he stood, suddenly seeming to tower over her, closing her yet again into an embrace she could not move from. She lifted her face for yet another kiss, and drowned in it, afraid not for herself, but of herself.

She had, in this one moment in time, fallen in love with Mr. Adam Teague, and she wanted all that love implied.

Adam was physically reeling. He could not remember when he had held in his experienced arms a more responsive, exciting woman!

He knew she had once been married, but she was quivering like a virgin now. And yet she was the most intensely sensuous woman he could remember.

How had she managed to save herself, and he knew she had, while being so vital and alive? It couldn't be, surely, that she was coming to life because of his touch. The thought staggered him.

He released her for only an instant, but it was long enough for her to escape him. She fled to the entrance of the pavilion. He could see her silhouette, and marveled that society should dictate that a woman with such long, luxurious hair must keep it pinned up at all times.

She was like a girl, suddenly, darting to the uppermost step, pausing before her soundless flight from him. He felt like a...No, not a masher. He felt like a man. His arousal would take some minutes to abate.

Yet she was not a girl, but a woman with more within her to give than any other he had ever known. His desire to possess her was overwhelming. He wanted to go after her. But he had not come to Summersea to satisfy a fleeting...Betz was not that sort, he knew.

Balling his fists, he leaned back against the pavilion's railing, drawing careful breaths until the urgency of his need eased. He was not unaccustomed to feeling arousal for an attractive woman, but he could not remember the last time it made him want to forget his purpose. He had long held the opinion that entanglements, for him, could not be of the lasting kind.

Chuckling, he raked back his hair with both hands, and heaved a ragged sigh. Such thoughts! He forced himself to his feet. Whatever made him think that a woman like Betz Witherspoon wanted anything permanent in her life, much less with his sort? That wasn't it. He had simply frightened a woman lacking experience. He had taken advantage.

But he couldn't forget the moment he first drew her close. Something in him had kindled, something familiar long, long ago when he was terribly young—back before he first learned about life in the west as a marshall, and then as a Wells Fargo guard.

Pacing, waiting impatiently for his thoughts of Betz to subside, he thought of the women in his past—the good ones and the less good ones who had entertained, wanted, and sometimes loved him. When, when was the last time he had felt the keen, driving need to possess like this? What had he done to himself by kissing Betz Witherspoon?

He muttered a curse. Back at his suffocating cubicle he would probably find Nurse Althea Tully, waiting to ease this sudden, annoying craving. He started down the steps.

As he crossed the sand he could see Betz ahead, just disappearing around the back of the hotel. He wondered just how aloof she would be by morning. Would he laugh then, and mentally dismiss her as a foolish, unfulfilled female? Or when she gave him the flashing freeze of her eyes, as he was convinced that she would, would he feel…

He balled his fists again. He was worried. He could not remember the last time an expression on a woman's face had been worthy of such concern.

Avoiding the few guests still milling around the lobby, Adam hurried up the stairs. When he reached the third floor corridor, it was dark and suffocating. As he had expected, Althea edged from the overwarm shadows and into his arms without the slightest hesitation. Still aroused, he paused when her firm little mouth pressed hard against his lips with calculated ardor.

"You've kept me waiting a long time," she purred.

"Won't your employer be concerned about your whereabouts?" he murmured when she freed his lips.

"He doesn't need to know about this," she said, pressing herself against him.

He couldn't help but respond. It could be an easy seduction. He should indulge then talk to her afterward and learn all she knew.

But the arousal, to his growing irritation, was not the same. Only moments before with Betz he had felt something well up from so deep in him that he had not known it existed. It had been far too long since he had learned anything new about himself. He had thought his life neatly in order; all corners of himself explored and no new territory to be found.

Suddenly he felt new, and unsure of himself. This was so strange and engrossing that he found the thought of bedding the nurse akin to eating a cold, unappetizing meal.

Betz's vibrant kiss came back to him with blinding clarity. He had not known kissing could be such an electrifying experience. He wanted her lips again.

Althea must be brushed aside. He captured her wandering hands, kissed her knuckles in a practiced gesture. Then put her away from him, with "I wouldn't dream of jeopardizing your position with Mr. Bonaventure." Tempted to add that if she needed accommodation her employer might serve, he resisted indulging in that bit of sarcasm.

He unlocked his door deftly and went inside, turning when Althea attempted to follow and blocking her way. His purpose at Summersea could be threatened if he did not follow through with the flirtations he had been tossing the nurse's way, but suddenly she was beneath his concern. He didn't care to indulge in stale, dry bread when a banquet that had been in his grasp was now only a short distance away.

How, he wondered as he gently closed the door to the startled Althea, might he go about being alone with the very proper Miss Witherspoon again. He must taste her kisses again. He began to hope they were only for him.

Cherry had just gone into her room when she heard Betz come in from the corridor. Heart leaping, she stood still and listened. Then when she heard nothing, she crept to the door.

Betz was standing motionless, her head cocked, her auburn waves tumbling down her back, her gaze apparently fixed on some spot on the wall opposite her.

She stood like that so long Cherry was tempted to giggle, but the air fairly crackled around Betz. The feeling of her intense secret emotions was filling the rooms with wonder. Cherry could scarcely contain her curiosity.

Cherry was sure that her Miss Witherspoon and Mr. Teague had found each other tonight. But what if they had argued? Or worse, what if they had met and parted, saying nothing more? Oh, she couldn't bear it!

"Betz? Are you all right?"

Betz didn't answer. After another few moments, she drifted aimlessly across the room toward the doors leading to the balcony of her own room. Facing the hinges, she bent and pulled at her high-button shoes until enough buttons were undone and she could drag them off. She let each shoe fall and then stood, half bent, as if frozen in thought.

Mystified, Cherry crossed the sitting room and stood in the doorway to Betz's room watching this peculiar performance.

Then Betz fumbled with the door to the balcony and went out onto it. She circled herself with her hands as if chilled, as if holding herself together. She looked up at the dark sky, then beyond to the bay. When a door slapped closed below, she started. Turning, she moved back into the room, still holding herself. Then she saw Cherry.

"Oh," she said sweetly, blushing scarlet.

Her heart thudding with a mixture of excitement and guilt, Cherry ducked her head with a hope-filled little grin. Maybe her ploy hadn't been too worthy of punishment.

"Are you cross with me, Betz?" she asked, employing all her innocent, girlish charm.

Betz came closer. Her face a mask of wonder, she asked, "Did you arrange that—"

Cherry nodded in tiny little movements. Her curls dancing on her shoulders, she suddenly thought of Bo's groping hand at her breast as they parted in the corridor so few moments ago. If Betz hadn't come along when she did, driving Cherry into the suite seconds ahead of her, Cherry might still be there with him, tasting the frightening kisses of a distracting, very lewd young man.

"Oh, well..." Betz breathed heavily, as if she could not think, and looked away. Almost at once she took on that distracted look again, and stood out of touch with the moment.

What was she thinking, Cherry wondered, her spine beginning to tingle. Was it possible that the very exciting Mr. Teague had kissed her Miss Witherspoon?

Now Cherry wanted to squeal for joy!

"What happened?" Cherry whispered.

Betz drew a shuddering breath and turned away. Sighing, she laughed nervously, raising one hand in a half-formed gesture that indicated her thoughts were chaotic.

"I, uh...I'm very tired, I think. I'll be going to bed now. Uh, how was the...benefit?"

Cherry didn't want to say she had been terrified most of the evening because Bo had tried to fondle her at every opportunity, and she had been afraid someone would notice. Nor did she want to admit what a heady thing it was to be the prettiest girl there, wearing the prettiest gown, granddaughter of a woman whose fortune would one day be her own...if she was prudent.

She had felt watched and awkward. Toward the end she had been thinking of Betz alone on the pavilion with Mr. Teague. Had he...

Betz licked her lips, and sank to the edge of her bed, saying vaguely, "That's nice," as if Cherry had just recited her thoughts aloud.

Cherry spun in a circle. He *had* kissed her!

Betz lay staring at the ceiling, in the blackness of her room. She wanted only to sleep, she told herself. She did not want to think of Adam or the feel of his lips. But such thoughts returned, nevertheless. She felt tormented by them, unable to sleep.

Stiffly she turned on her side, trying to shut out the memories crowding into her mind. Then she turned over, finding the warm night air and the clinging linens almost too much to bear.

Finally she got out of bed and went out onto the balcony. How would she get through the night, she wondered.

Seeing that the horizon was beginning to glow softly with the first hint of dawn, she thought of the day to come. How would she get through it? What would she do when she saw him?

She took a chair onto the balcony and watched the sunrise. Her thoughts wandered to times when she was a girl, reading far into the night. Then, too, she would watch the dawn and fall into bed, exhausted. It seemed that she had passed far too many nights this way, alone—waiting for the morning, waiting for her needs, desires, yearnings to yield to yet another day.

She hadn't been acutely unhappy all these years, she thought. She had been resigned, not expecting her life to become any different or better. From an early age she had known her mother would require years of care. She had taken care of her gladly, but their life had borne the stamp of her father's somber personality, and the solemn pace of his grim profession.

After her mother's death, Betz had been quite undone. She hadn't known what to do with herself. Everyone from her friend Otila Watkins to her brother George had insisted that she must marry. She'd chosen Gordon Carlyle because he had seemed so dashing, and he had made her feel young and wanted. She had succumbed far too easily.

But Adam Teague was not dashing. He was intense. He frightened her. She couldn't imagine what she might have in common with him. For that matter, she knew next to nothing about him. The attraction was purely physical. And she had to admit it was a strong one.

She tossed her head, as if to dismiss a feeling so beneath her. Just as quickly as she did, though, the sound of his voice filled her mind. The press of his mouth against hers had quickened her body. This physical response could not be ignored. How could it be a shallow, fleeting emotion when it sprang from someplace so deep?

A Meeting of the Minds

Tuesday, June 11, 1889

Cherry was playing C scales. Betz and Cherry had the piano reserved for ten each morning. Outside the sky was low and white, promising rain. Most of the ladies were on their daily trek to take the waters. Mr. Woodley had left moments before with fresh canvas, and there was the sound of tableware being laid in the dining room across the lobby.

Cherry played with a heavy hand, banging out notes like a butcher pounding beef.

"Let me show you," Betz said, and Cherry gratefully stood from the stool.

Betz began to play a Haydn minuet. Her thoughts were caught up in memories of the night before, but at the back of her mind she heard her father's sternly scolding voice say, *Elizabeth Jane Witherspoon, you must stop this foolishness at once!* For the first time in years, she felt young. Her fingers stumbled over a difficult portion of the piece. She practiced the section several times until she began playing again, tenderly.

Then suddenly she knew Adam was standing in the reception parlor doorway, watching her. What did he think of her for kissing him the night before? Did he think her a fool?

Finally she met his eyes. He didn't speak or move. He was not smirking. He was just standing with his shoulder against the door frame, his muscular arms crossed.

She couldn't look away. To anyone watching, he gave no indication that anything unusual had passed between them. Then his brows lifted. He uncrossed his arms and straightened.

Felicia Ellison came blustering into the lobby. Adam turned abruptly and walked into the dining room.

Seeing Betz staring after him, Felicia gave a sniff and flicked her huge skirt to the side and stalked away.

"Let's go for a walk," Betz said to Cherry.

"I'll see what direction Mr. Teague took," Cherry whispered in a conspiratorial way, like a schoolgirl.

Betz tried to protest, but the girl darted across the lobby and disappeared into the dining room. It didn't matter, Betz thought, trying to stifle a secret smile. She wanted to know where he'd gone, too.

Eleven

Cordelia's Enviable Opportunity

The engraved invitation arrived later that morning by private messenger. By the feel of the expensive paper, Betz could tell the sender was someone of import.

"Who is it from?" Cherry asked breathlessly as another knock came at the door. A now familiar drayman stood there with two more trunks.

"Agatha's dressmaker must be working night and day," Betz said and laughed. "Just put them over there, please."

While Cherry tore open the invitation, Betz unlocked the nearest trunk. Within tissue paper lay a confection of pink gauze-like silk, shimmering with silvery beadwork. Cherry tugged at her sleeve.

"Should I be impressed?" she asked. She held out the invitation. "Have you heard of these people? What do they want with me?"

The pleasure of Miss Cordelia Ryburn's company
is requested
Friday, June 21, 1889
at
House at the Bay
K.R. Thorndike Pratt and Xylina
Newport, Rhode Island
8:00 p.m.
RSVP

"What kind of name is Xylina?" Betz asked with a smile.

Cherry looked anxiously at the gown, asking, "Do you think Grandmother knew I'd be invited there, and that's why she sent this?"

"If she knew, she either arranged the invitation or possessed second sight. By my calculations she's been in England for days, and is due to sail for India at any time. She would have had to order these things weeks ago." She fingered the beautiful gown. "I wonder if K.R. Thorndike Pratt is worthy of this. I'm tempted to save it for the Summer's End Ball when the Whitgifts are here."

Cherry began to pout.

"Well, we needn't make up our minds for now. This occasion isn't for another few days. We can ask about the Pratts at the desk. Someone may recognize the name. They're probably just old friends of your grandmother's."

Betz finished dressing in a particularly attractive white ensemble that was tailor-cut and had complicated pleating down the bodice front. The skirt was full and wide, trimmed with tucks in patterns of three around the hem. She knew it was a bit girlish for her, but it had been included for her in one of the trunks sent the week before, and Betz wanted to look especially nice at dinner that day.

Cherry gazed at her own new gown as if she couldn't believe she would someday wear anything so incredibly lovely.

Felicia found the parlor particularly stuffy. Mr. Bonaventure—Charles—hadn't yet come down. All she could think about was how she was going to justify her association with him—her social inferior. She could hardly believe how desperately she wanted his attention and his kind words.

She had a small clip of money which she was going to offer him today, as a token of her affection and her assurance that he would not have to do without his treatment if he chose to be her friend. She would offer more, of course, when the opportunity arose. He had only to ask.

Though worried about him, she could not go in search of him.

Myrtle Fitch or Emma Reinhold might notice her inordinate interest in him. They had just better be careful what they said about her, Felicia thought. She could easily reveal any number of things she knew about them in order to remove attention from herself.

Betz Witherspoon and the heiress started down the stairs just then.

"Witherspoon dresses as if she thinks she's a guest," Felicia whispered.

"I can't say that I like her," Myrtle said, nodding agreement.

"She doesn't know her place," Emma put in with a sniff of disgust.

Betz approached the desk clerk, asking, "Can you tell us who R.K. Thorndike Pratt is?"

Emma and Myrtle fell silent, mouths open.

Pratt? Felicia thought with a shudder of horror. Not *the* Pratt's! What could Witherspoon want with those people?

The clerk murmured something.

"Then you wouldn't know who Xylina might be, either," Betz said with a sigh.

He shook his head.

Both Myrtle and Emma rose now. Ignoring Felicia, they moved with grace into the lobby.

"Miss Witherspoon, you look lovely this afternoon," Emma said. Cocking her head to admire Cherry's highly fashionable striped afternoon-dress, she added, "And you always look divine, Cordelia dear."

Myrtle guided them both into the dining room, urging, "Won't you both join us for dinner today? And we couldn't help overhearing…"

Trembling, Felicia watched Myrtle rearranging placecards. It was too much! She stood, her head whirling. Didn't they understand that Witherspoon and the heiress were beneath them? What difference did a bit of name-dropping make?

Felicia hastened to join them, and that's when she saw the engraved invitation they were all admiring. The Pratt dinner party…

Not possible! Not one of them had been invited to it!

Feeling suddenly ill, Felicia noticed her placecard lying on a nearby table, face down. She stood a moment longer, waiting for her friends to ask her to take her usual place, but Myrtle and Emma were acting as if she was not there.

Turning her back on them all suddenly, Felicia stalked from the dining room. They would be very sorry about this.

"K. R. Thorndike Pratt has a delightful cottage in Newport," Emma was saying in a flat, unimpressed tone. "He has some connections in gold mining in the west, and yes, I believe there is some connection with the Hunts, as well, but I can't be sure. Cordelia will surely have a very pleasant time at their summer home. I dare say I do not know too many people who have been fortunate enough to be invited there."

Cherry looked bewildered.

"Xylina is his wife," Emma went on. "some thirty-five years his junior. From the South, or perhaps Virginia. I've forgotten. Fine people. Quite wealthy."

Betz listened with care as the ladies went on to describe someone they said belonged to the envied Four Hundred of the current Social Register.

It was all rather annoying to Betz that a mere piece of paper had gotten Cherry a place at the head table. She could misbehave all she wanted to, evidently, so long as she had "connections."

The dining room was more quiet than usual that day. Adam was absent, and for Betz the meal was tasteless.

"You must borrow our carriage, of course," Myrtle was saying. "The drive to Narragansett is very pleasant, and you should enjoy the ferry ride immensely. Will you require our driver, Miss Witherspoon? You don't have one of your own. . .if I recall."

Betz shook herself from her reverie long enough to realize there was quite a lot to arrange if Cherry was going to the Pratt's party in appropriate style.

"Oh, no, I wouldn't dream of inconveniencing you," she said. She didn't want to be involved with these two-faced socialites any more than necessary.

Myrtle acquiesced gracefully, but her eyes glittered as she said, "As you wish." Betz wondered if accepting Myrtle's offer might improve Cherry's position at Summersea. As everyone rose to leave after the tables had been cleared, she said, "On second thought, Mrs. Fitch, I do think we'll be glad use your carriage after all."

Myrtle raised her brows as if an important gambit had just succeeded. "Fine. I'm afraid you'll have to drive yourself, though. I just recalled that our driver is off that day."

"I don't mind," Betz put in. Then she mentally kicked herself. Chaperones shouldn't drive! Cherry must arrive in proper style.

They were on their way out of the dining room when Leon Howard rose from his place and joined Betz. Myrtle and Emma gave him withering looks and drew Cherry away, chattering to her as if they considered her an equal.

"Quite a coup, Miss Witherspoon," Mr. Howard began. "Your darling Cordelia has gained by mere accident of birth, all that my money could not."

"I don't know what you mean, and I don't care to talk to you," Betz said, wanting only to be away from him. She knew exactly what he meant, and he was correct.

"Come, come, dear. We all know the value of connections."

"If you'll excuse me, Mr. Howard, I have a great deal to arrange."

"I should say." He lit a cigar. "If I could buy my son's or daughter's way to that party, I would. It could be worth a lot to the right person." His smile was sly.

Pausing, Betz looked up at him. "I'm not sure I understand what you're getting at, Mr. Howard."

"You'll figure it out, I'm sure. You're probably well paid, but a working woman can always afford to squirrel away a bit more. No one here need know you've taken along a couple of passengers to the Pratts. I can arrange to have Bo and Marietta waiting along the road."

Betz went cold.

"We received only one invitation."

"A small impediment. A clever woman could show it to me, and I could have it copied. It's done all the time. I'm amazed Mrs. Fitch didn't ask that Lyddie go along."

Betz marched away but Mr. Howard stayed close. As she went out and crossed the veranda, she hissed, "Are you suggesting that I accept money from you to allow you to forge invitations, so that I can smuggle your son and daughter to the Pratt party? Are you suggesting the Fitches would resort to such a thing?"

"My dear Miss Witherspoon, the Fitches would do just about anything to weasel their way into a party where the Vanderbilts and Hunts might appear. You are apparently ignorant of the company your Miss Ryburn will be keeping that night. I would be happy to pay five hundred—"

"Good day, Mr. Howard! I must find Cher—"

"Don't worry about that young lady. She knows how to take care of herself, I dare say. She's probably off somewhere cuddling with that waiter. She seems to prefer his company to a boy of my son's caliber…"

"If you are any indication of his caliber—"

He laughed loudly.

"I have enough money to make my son just about anything he wants to be. You could help, and as I said, I'd be grateful. And you should warn your charge to stay away from the riffraff. My son doesn't mind second goods, but the Whitgifts surely will." At Betz's sputtering indignation he struck an indifferent pose. "I'm only giving advice where it's sorely needed."

Shaking with rage, Betz hissed, "I'll thank you to keep your obscene remarks to yourself. I can still report your behavior—"

He laughed loudly again.

"Anything you do after hours is at your own peril, Miss Witherspoon. Getting rubbed against the wall in the middle of the night is no embarrassment to me, but it would certainly be for you."

"You're a horrid, vulgar man!"

"Perhaps, but if I choose to come to your room some night

and accost you, you will suffer consequences more lasting than I. A woman of already questionable connections can only lose her virtue once. I, my dear, need no reputation. I need only money. I trust that you'll remember my offer. Just don't wait too long to take me up on it."

Betz found herself at the end of the veranda, staring down at Mr. Bonaventure seated in his chair. He and the nurse were watching her.

"Oh, good day, Mr. Bonaventure," Mr. Howard said, grinning. "Your nurse looks particularly sullen this afternoon. Don't you pay her well enough, or do you abuse her behind our backs?"

Betz's drew her breath in sharply.

Mr. Bonaventure didn't dignify the remark with a reply.

Nurse Tully met Leon Howard's hard little laughing eyes with her own brand of smouldering malice, and did not look away for almost a minute.

"Perhaps we should remove ourselves from here," Mr. Bonaventure said as if embarrassed by all he'd overheard Mr. Howard say. He and the nurse began the painstaking maneuvers to get him down the side steps onto the lawn.

Leon Howard exhaled a huge smoke ring. He sneered and he said, "That son of a bitch is as healthy as I am, and he's taking his medicine from that wench nightly. I'd bet money on it."

Betz felt her cheeks flame.

"Oh, Miss Witherspoon, It's a pleasure to watch your face turn scarlet." He made a sweeping bow. "You're so suited to your position. Upright, priggish and virginal to the core. Yet you might prove to be a delightful romp if you didn't always look at me like you had just eaten lemons. Take care the next time you go slinking away for a late-night visit to the promontory. With field glasses an idle gentleman observing the stars can easily see the pavilion. And you might take more care coming back to the hotel. If I saw you return last night with your hair tumbling to your waist, others surely did, too. What amusing reading that would make. Ta-ta!"

Watching him depart, Betz shivered.

Twelve

Preparing for Newport and A New Guest Arrives

Wednesday, June 12, 1889

The youngsters, presenting a serene picture of refinement, were playing croquet. The girls were wearing calf-length white dresses and sporting big white bows in their plaited hair. The boys were in shirtsleeves, suspenders and knickers.

Guests sat about the lawn on scattered chairs, the gentlemen dozing and the ladies gossiping beneath pools of shade cast by ruffled silk parasols.

Betz was always struck by Summersea's picturesque beauty. The colors were so dreamlike, the atmosphere so luxurious. Thoughtfully she approached the steps leading up to the veranda. She and Cherry were coming from a walk along the beach, where they had discussed arrangements for getting to the Pratt party.

"There's Mr. Teague!" Cherry whispered excitedly. "I think it's a good idea to ask him to come along with us. We can't get lost or in trouble with him along."

"I wouldn't dream of inconveniencing him!" Betz gasped, feeling herself go warm.

"But it's such a good idea! Think how fun it will be!"

Adam was lounging at the parlor door—looking wonderful, she thought. When he saw her, he smiled.

"Go ahead, ask him. Please!" Cherry cried, and giggled.

"Well, I have to admit it would be nice to have a man along," Betz said. Having Adam with them might prevent any unpleasant scenes along the way.

But now she could hardly bring herself to speak to Adam. She felt so self-conscious. He would surely think she was trying to spend some time alone with him again. It was already bad enough that he thought she'd arranged to meet him on the pavilion!

"Ask him!" Cherry prodded, poking Betz in the ribs.

"Later, when I can explain why we need his help," Betz whispered, hoping to steer Cherry toward the stairs. "It's too public here!"

With a huff of exasperation, Cherry rushed ahead and seized Adam's sleeve. On tiptoe, the child whispered in Adam's ear while pointing eagerly toward Betz.

Mortified, Betz gathered her courage and approached Adam. His eyes were dancing darkly as he listened attentively to Cherry. When he gave her a wink, Betz couldn't help but bless Cherry for her audacity.

With Cherry hanging on his arm, Adam gave a slight bow. He said to Betz with an expectant expression, "I heard of the impressive invitation, Miss Witherspoon. You have 'The Assortment' steaming with jealousy."

Confused, Betz asked, "What do you mean by 'The Assortment'?"

He waved his hand as if to say his comment meant nothing.

"Never mind. I'd be happy to accompany you and Miss Ryburn to Newport."

A top buggy with the hood folded back suddenly rolled to a stop before the veranda. Adam paused to squint through the dark screen cloth of the main doors, and then his brows lifted.

A sensibly dressed woman of perhaps forty climbed down from the buggy. As she removed her plain hat, she revealed graying-brown hair and a suntan on her face. Glowing with robust good health, she smiled at all the pale-faced ladies who gaped at her from veranda rocking chairs. Betz had never seen a tanned woman before!

The woman pulled a jacketed tennis racket and a sheathed rifle from the buggy floor and turned to look up at Summersea with appraising blue eyes. A bicycle was strapped to the rear of her buggy and equipment of all sorts was heaped on the seat. The lobby clerk rushed to greet this new guest and directed one of the stewards to unload the bicycle.

"I think you should tell the Fitches you can't use their carriage," he said, "I know of a closed coach for hire in Huntington Station with a driver and six-horse rig. You don't want Cordelia windblown by the time she arrives in Newport. There'll be two ferry rides, remember, and it could storm. Have you decided when you want to leave?"

Betz stammered something as the athletic-looking new arrival marched purposefully into the lobby, nodding matter-of-factly to everyone, calling out, "Good morning! Delightful day, don't you think?"

Behind her came a bellman carrying her walking stick, stout hiking boots, binoculars and several golf clubs.

"I shall want to reserve a horse each afternoon—oh, no regular riding accommodations? But I was assured...well, never mind. I'll simply bicycle over to the Huntington. Dear man, don't choke. I chose Summersea for the promised quiet. I shan't leave unless accosted by rowdies. May I see my room now?"

Carrying some of her own equipment she followed the bellman and stewards up the stairs, and the excitement was over as quickly as it had begun.

Adam turned back to Betz with his full attention, saying, "I don't suppose you know how long you'll be in Newport. As I said once before, I know of some amusements there. I assume you'll be going in with Cordelia?"

"Oh, I...Well, I hadn't thought about it. The invitation was for Cherry, only. I assumed she would be assigned a maid..."

For all her maturity, Betz hadn't the faintest idea what was expected of her on this occasion. If she was chaperone, it seemed logical that she might be expected to go to the party to look after her charge. But wouldn't she then have been included in the invitation?

Adam chucked Cherry beneath her chin. "From what I hear, the Pratts are shoulder to shoulder with Mrs. Astor. After this,

Summersea will worship at your feet. Not even the Reinholds received an invitation. My hat's off to you." He doffed an invisible hat, and Cherry giggled.

An Evening Among the Elite Elite

Friday, June 21, 1889

The weather turned sullen by Friday, and Betz decided to leave for Newport early in the morning. Their trip would comprise a pleasant coach ride to Narragansett where they would board a ferry to the island at the mouth of the Bay and finally cross into Newport on another ferry. The Pratt's cottage wasn't far from there.

Cherry was packed into the hired coach like a princess, her silk gown safely folded into her finest trunk. She was wearing her most costly and elaborate traveling costume, and would change into the gown after a brief rest at the Pratts'.

Betz wore a well-made but understated traveling gown that she hoped would be suitable attire in which to present Cherry to the Pratts.

Adam arrived on the veranda steps wearing a dashing tailored tweed frock coat that clearly marked him as a city man. In spite of herself, Betz couldn't stop herself from smiling as he gave the driver instructions and then gallantly handed her up into the coach.

"After you, Miss Witherspoon," he said, a pleasantly teasing note in his voice.

She didn't care what he wore so long as he kept smiling at her, she thought as she took a seat on the far side of the coach across from Cherry. She hoped to keep her feelings in check during the trip, but memories of his kisses reddened her cheeks.

And when Adam sat across from her, next to Cherry, Betz could not look away from his smiling face. She was hopelessly in love, she thought. How would she endure these next few hours so close to him?

• • •

The trip had been delightful, thought Cherry. She had watched Miss Witherspoon blush and act foolish, and Mr. Teague teasing and baiting like a schoolboy. It was just too wonderful!

But now as their coach tolled from the ferry to the platform and away into Newport, she tried to imagine what was ahead. Would she remember how to address everyone properly? Would she remember how to behave, to eat, to dance, to smile, to walk?

Betz noticed the sudden pallor of Cherry's cheeks and reached across to pat her hand, but seconds later her eyes turned back to Mr. Teague's grinning face. She seemed to be only dimly aware of what Cherry was facing.

A wave of fury welled inside Cherry. Miss Witherspoon was acting just like her Mama, who had always been preoccupied with her own needs—her men and her jug—and Cherry felt frightened and angry. Tears swelled in her eyes. She turned away, fixing her unseeing gaze on the passing streets.

How was she, a child raised to think she'd someday work in a factory, going to manage at a party to which even the grand, stuck-up Mrs. Fitch had not been invited?

Now the coach turned onto a wide street skirting the shore, where breakers crashed beneath an increasingly leaden sky. Cherry wanted to jump out and run.

"This can't be the right street," Betz said. The driver slowed the coach, and the three of them looked out of the little coach window.

Before them sat a house of such incredible magnificence that it reminded Cherry of palaces she'd seen in books Betz had found for her in the Huntington Station library.

Mr. Teague leaned back, smiling with amusement, as if he had known all along what Betz and Cherry were getting into here.

"Mrs. Fitch called this place a cottage," Cherry whispered, suddenly petrified with fear. "I can't go in there alone!"

The coach stopped and the driver got down. As he opened the door. Betz was about to say that there had been some mistake. Then she saw a brass placard along the base of the iron fence: House at the Bay. The "cottage" looked like a marble mountain.

Cherry couldn't swallow. She shrank into a corner, moaning, "I feel ill."

Betz patted her hand again.

"I'm sure they'll let me go in with you. You'll need me to help you dress, and it'll take hours to redo your hair—" She looked rather pale, herself.

Cherry had just begun to feel a sense of relief when the door of the "cottage" opened and a woman strolled out. Her bustled navy satin gown was trimmed with a froth of white lace on the shoulders, bosom, hips and hem.

She waved and started toward them, calling, "Hello! I'm delighted you're early. Ah, you must be Miss Witherspoon. Agatha has written me all about you. I'm delighted to meet you at last. Agatha has been like a grandmother to me—" The lovely young woman laughed as she extended her white-gloved hand while Betz emerged from the coach. "Forgive me. I'm Xylina Pratt. Everyone calls me Xynnie. You must all stay for luncheon—Ah, who is this very attractive gentlemen? And, of course, this must be the very special Cordelia. Darling!"

"H-how do you do, Mrs. Pratt."

"Do step down and let me have a look at you. Why, you look like a frightened rabbit. I assure you, honey, that none of us bite. Oh, some of them will be perfectly horrid snobs, but some of us still remember that we all pull on our drawers one leg at a time."

"So good of you to invite Che—Cordelia," Betz murmured, bewildered.

"Don't you just adore Agatha?" Xynnie went on. "I could hardly believe my luck when I met her! And here is her very own granddaughter. Darling, it's just too marvelous. Come, come, everyone inside."

Betz was able to wedge in brief introductions while Cherry hung back, wondering why this pretty young woman was so high up on the social ladder that she had the Reinholds, Fitches, Howards and Felicia Ellison herself green with envy.

Mr. Teague gave a slight bow and murmured, "I beg your patience, Mrs. Pratt, but I'm along only as protection. The driver and I will return at whatever hour you require to see Che—Cordelia home."

Mrs. Pratt cried with delight, "But my dear sir, the party will last all night! You can collect Cordelia at noon tomorrow if you have pressing business to keep you away tonight, but you are both most welcome to stay. I insist you stay for luncheon, at least. I assure you, my husband will have amusements. The billiard room is his favorite haunt, Mr. Teague, and you look like a gaming man to me. And Miss Witherspoon—may I call you Betz?"

Betz nodded, bewildered by this woman's easy charm.

"You must make yourself at home here. Come and go as you like. This evening is just a little get-together of friends. So you mustn't feel that you weren't included. Stay, if you like, or have your friend Mr. Teague show you about Newport. I venture to guess, sir, you know this town well."

Adam gave a smile and an attractive shrug.

"We do things differently at House at the Bay. I'm a simple woman who had the grandest fortune to fall in love with a wealthy man. I do whatever I like and so do my friends. Please, include yourselves among them. Do come inside. I insist, Mr. Teague, if only for a while!"

Cherry looked from gaping Betz to reluctant Mr. Teague. She heaved a huge sigh of relief when the two nodded their consent and followed beaming Mrs. Xylina Pratt up the walk.

The inside of Xylina Pratt's house was too splendid to take in all at once. There seemed to be a profusion of Victorian elegance on every surface—gilding and carving and ornamentation of the most complex design. Overcome with astonishment, Cherry burst out laughing.

"It is a monstrosity, isn't it?" Xynnie said, smiling at Cherry. "If you don't tell anyone I said so, I'll confess a little secret. My husband adores showing it off, and he's a dear and I love him. It doesn't matter that I can't stand the place. We're only here in the summer, anyway. You should see our place in New York. And well you might, because I'll surely invite you there during the holidays. I *love* to give parties!"

The woman chattered on, leading them through a maze of truly grand reception chambers into the private portion of the house. Here the rooms were no less ornate, but at least they were smaller.

During lunch Xylina had no trouble monopolizing the conversation. Afterward, she urged Mr. Teague to come and meet her husband who was in the rear garden tending his prized roses.

"He doesn't take lunch," Xynnie said, leading Adam away. "Too stout!"

"I don't know what I'm doing here!" Cherry gasped the moment they were alone. She stared at her plate as though she wanted to scream.

"Do the best you can, darling," Betz said, looking around. She seemed utterly overwhelmed, too, which did not reassure Cherry at all.

In due time Cherry and Betz were taken to a suite of rooms that far outdid anything Cyrus Wood had to offer. There they rested and then reviewed several points of etiquette Betz thought important, in view of their elegant surroundings. Cherry practiced speaking and walking all afternoon, and then they began to prepare for the festivities.

At Cherry's insistence, Betz had decided to let her wear the gauze gown, but Cherry was now a bit doubtful. She thought the small "get-together" sounded too informal for such a confection of ruffles and lace.

"Never mind," Betz said, finally helping her into it. "It'll have to do."

By the time all Cherry's curls were perfect, and an understated but elegant necklace was clasped about her throat, music had begun in some distant portion of the massive "cottage."

Xylina herself fetched Cherry in order to present her to the guests. Seeing Betz not dressed for the affair, she asked, "But aren't you coming along?"

"If Cherry doesn't mind, I think I'll wait here in our room. I didn't expect to attend, and don't feel comfortable intruding. I also have nothing suitable to wear. You will forgive me, I hope."

"I would be pleased to lend you something," Xynnie began.

Betz shook her head emphatically.

Cherry looked terrified suddenly, but Betz felt it was best to let the girl grow used to her peers on her own.

Xylina, who was wearing something astonishingly provocative with ruching and pearl studding appropriate for a coronation, made a light gesture, saying, "But of course, I wouldn't dream of forcing you. Don't look so frightened, Cordelia darling. You're going to have a wonderful time." They started out. "Miss Witherspoon, if you get hungry, just ring. And you're welcome to roam about or join us later, if you change your mind. I believe Mr. Teague is about to leave. You might want to arrange with him what time he'll return with your coach. Such an attractive man," she added, winking.

"He's leaving?" Betz called after her, alarmed.

"He and my dear darling husband found a great deal to talk about in the billiard room, if I may judge by the amount of spirits they consumed after luncheon, and the pall of cigar smoke all about the place. But Mr. Teague, too, has declined to join us for dinner and dancing. Perhaps we are a bit too much for his blood."

"I should speak to him," Betz said anxiously.

"Ring for Lullie and ask her to take you to the entry. You must forgive my curiosity, Miss Witherspoon, but Mr. Teague is just so terribly interesting. I asked him far too many questions just now, and he successfully evaded them all! Such a clever man! What does he do? Thorny was certain he knew him, but couldn't recall where they might have met."

"I believe I heard he's in shipping," Betz said.

Xynnie nodded thoughtfully.

"I hope…you will urge him to stay for another luncheon tomorrow, I did enjoy his wit. If you decide to go out, take care when coming back. I think it's going to storm, and here on the point the wind and rain can become quite alarming."

Smiling farewell, Xynnie led Cherry into the hall.

"Have a wonderful time," Betz said.

Cherry turned back to her hostess, took a deep breath and felt a surge of panic.

Xylina kept up a steady prattle as she led Cherry to the ballroom. When Cherry found herself walking into a huge crowd, she was so overwhelmed she couldn't think.

Some one hundred and fifty of the Four Hundred stood about as if waiting for her. Her gown was clearly in keeping with what everyone was wearing. The ladies dripped jewels and the gentlemen wore the finest black cutaway coats she had ever seen.

A hush fell over the glittering ballroom as Mrs. Pratt introduced Cordelia. Soon afterward everyone started toward the grand dining room where the table seemed to stretch on forever, laid with enough crystal, silver and china to dazzle Cherry into complete silence.

People spoke to her, but she heard not a word and did not know if she replied. Her heart was in her throat, and long after she sat down she couldn't swallow a bite.

Twenty courses and two hours later, everyone adjourned to the ballroom. The music began, and a tall man with whiskers who reeked of bay rum whisked her away in a dizzying waltz. Cherry wasn't sure if Xynnie Pratt had called him a duck or a duke.

Cherry concentrated on keeping her satin slippers from beneath the man's clumsy ones. She was very glad she had not eaten, because she was whirled about like a top for the next several dances. She might have gone on like that for hours if she had not been rescued by Xynnie and drawn aside to meet someone.

"...says he's never seen a prettier young guest," Xynnie gushed. "Everyone is so taken with you, darling. And of course I've found several here who have heard of you. You're the talk of the seaboard this season. One young man in particular is terribly interested in meeting you. Mr. Whitgift, this is Miss Cordelia Ryburn. Cordelia, darling, may I present Mr. Drew Whitgift of New York."

Cherry scarcely heard the introduction. She was so out of

breath that she murmured only a distracted hello. She longed for a place to sit.

"May I get you a bit of refreshment, Miss Ryburn?" came a deep young voice.

Absently Cherry nodded, trying to remember if it was acceptable for her to mop her brow. Deciding against it, she wished herself back at Summersea, in bed.

Conversation swirled around her. Muted laughter and the strains of another lovely waltz gave her the feeling that she was in a dream. Or perhaps it was a nightmare? She was so afraid of making a mistake.

When a tiny glass cup of pink punch was pressed into her trembling gloved hand, she sipped without looking up at the person who had given it to her. It seemed less taxing to pay attention to the dancing couples twirling by.

The throat-stinging punch made her cough with surprise. With watering eyes she looked up into a handsome, grinning young face.

Xynnie had just turned away and was unaware that Cherry had been given a stiffly laced punch.

"Ah, so the young lady deigns at last to look at me. Do you remember my name, Miss Ryburn?" the tall grinning young man said with a mock air.

"At this moment I can hardly remember my own name," she said. Still wanting to cough, she sipped a little more of the punch. Remembering the exhilarating effect the liquid in her mama's jug had once had on her, she heaved a sigh. "Thank you, indeed. I needed this."

"You looked it. Come, we'll sit on the terrace until you've gathered your wits. They tell me you have appeared from nowhere, that you're very precocious because you've lived in the wild parts of Borneo or some such savage place. Oh yes, there's been a good deal of talk about you and I among the old dragons who would like to see one such as myself married off this season. But don't get any ideas, Miss Ryburn. I am a free man. I have no intention of marrying anyone, not even someone as pretty and fresh and exciting as yourself."

As they edged away from the press of the crowd, Cherry finished her punch and felt immeasurably better. Now she had a moment to carefully scrutinize Mr. Drew Whitgift. What had he been jabbering about?

He had a plain but attractive aristocratic look about him, his brown hair brushed perfectly to the side and his ears a bit prominent. Only twenty-one years old, he promised to be a very distinguished looking man one day.

"I wonder if you could get me some more of that punch," Cherry said, her body going warm with the effects of the alcohol. She felt much better.

Drew lifted his brows with a casual smile of approval, and excused himself.

Xynnie was instantly at Cherry's side.

"What do you think, dear? Isn't he simply too adorable for words? The most eligible bachelor this season. Your grandmother insisted that I must introduce you two, and I can see you're a perfect match. Won't it be simply wonderful when he and his grandmother arrive at Summersea? You'll both be acquainted, and not in the least uncomfortable. I'm convinced that a fine friendship is going to spring up between you two delightful young people. And look there, he's coming back. I just knew you'd get on famously!"

Cherry accepted the punch from Drew, longing to gulp it down. She didn't sip it though, until Xynnie moved away to dance with a portly, bearded man.

Cherry took a gulp. The warmth of the spiked punch lent her increasing courage.

"Now that you're looking a little better, Miss Ryburn, would you like to dance?"

She nodded and stood, tingling with a special awareness as he took her in his arms. She seemed to be floating on air as they whirled about the ballroom. No longer was she afraid of the wealthy guests eyeing her. She felt pretty and safe.

Drew skillfully outmaneuvered all gentlemen wishing to cut

in. More and more Cherry realized how delightfully attentive and possessive he was being, and her thoughts began to focus. She looked up into his handsome young face and suddenly she laughed.

"Why…you're…him! You're the young gentleman I'm supposed to—" Before saying too much, she was able to cut short her words.

"Impress?" he offered to complete her sentence. "Yes, indeed, Miss Ryburn, I would expect you have heard as much about me as I have of you. I'd like a bit more punch myself. Would you? I suspect we won't be missed if we go out onto the terrace again. Want to come?"

By then Cherry was so excited, bewildered and tipsy she was willing to do anything. She looked up into the cultured smile of this handsome young gentleman and realized in a rush that he was asking her, Cherry Rose Nesbit from the slums, to go walking on the terrace.

He was not Teddy the waiter. He was not Bo Howard, the lewd son of an upstart. He was the very eligible Mr. Drew Whitgift, son of wealth and culture. He was as close to American nobility as she might ever hope to get.

Dizzy and giddy, she tucked her gloved hand into the crook of his offered elbow and let him lead her away into the darkness.

Mr. Whitgift Intends Mischief

Drew poured another healthy dollop of brandy into Cordelia's glass cup. She smiled up at him, fragrant and flushed and as pretty a girl as he had ever seen. When she pressed the cup to her pink lips, his body quickened. He had never felt anything quite like this before.

Twirling around, Cordelia scampered to the edge of the terrace where steps led down into a shadowed garden, where the light spilling from the ballroom's big windows didn't reach. When she disappeared into that darkness, he found himself following.

Only a few hundred yards away the garden ended abruptly at

the rocky shoreline. There the high tide was lapping hungrily at the land as if trying to devour it. Drew knew that some of the shore was treacherous, because his father constantly bemoaned the erosion at their own cottage down the way.

"Don't go too far," he called, seeing her carefully set her cup on a rock, gather up her skirts until he could clearly see her white stockinged legs. Then she started tiptoeing to the very water's edge.

Tucking his flask into his breast pocket he dropped his own cup and ran after her. "Miss Ryburn, take care!"

She had chosen a dangerous path to the water, and stood now ahead of him, poised on a boulder while the ocean surged on three sides, splashing her hem a little.

As he caught up to her he couldn't stop himself from circling her waist with his hands. If she fell, she would surely hit her head on a rock.

"Aren't you afraid," she sighed, fragrant with brandy, "I like this!"

He felt guilty now for thinking she would be a boring tease like all the others. She turned in the circle of his arms until she was pressed breast to chest with him. Her eyes in the darkness were black, glinting ever so faintly. She was warm and vibrant, and he wanted to kiss her, but then her reputation would be ruined.

She had been gossiped about by so many—even his own mother—as a chance child dredged up from the nether regions of Lady Agatha Ryburn's son's past. Now he realized how easily he had fallen into the same damnable attitude as his parents, whom he so despised. He had judged and condemned her unfairly, and had taken it upon himself to embarrass her with the spiked punch. Now look how she gazed up at him in innocent wonderment.

Her lips were only inches from his now. Suddenly nothing else mattered. If this darling was already in ruin, he might as well tell her in this way that he was sorry, because suddenly he cared very much about what he had done.

As he closed his lips over her sweet mouth, he whispered her name. He felt her kindle in his arms, and then squirm.

"Call me Cherry," she whispered as she snuggled against him.

A wave crashed around them, soaking his shoes and pantlegs. He drew her tightly against him, savoring the feel of a girl he believed would not toy with his heart nor flatter him only because of his inheritance. This one was special.

"Cherry," he murmured, losing himself in her lips. "Cherry!"

Thirteen

Miss Witherspoon Courts Mischief

The fog moved in, enveloping Adam and Betz as they crossed the street from the casino in Newport, and headed for the hired coach which they had left standing a block away.

"My mother and I were living in a boardinghouse with my little brother Henry when the fire broke out," Adam was saying, referring to the Great Chicago Fire of 1871. "We were driven across the river with thousands of others, carrying only the few things we'd grabbed when we realized the fire was coming our way. I'll never forget that night we spent standing at the edge of Lake Michigan up to our waists in water, watching what seemed like the end of the world."

Betz was glad to be out of the casino and on her way back to the Pratt's house. From the moment she had left the house she had felt uneasy. This was what it felt like to be an unencumbered woman, she told herself while listening to Adam. It was a frightening amount of freedom.

"It must've been terrifying to watch the city burn," she said.

"I don't remember feeling afraid," he said, thoughtful. The fog made it difficult to see him as he handed her into the coach and climbed in beside her. "I remember feeling angry."

"Why angry?"

He tapped, indicating to the driver that they should proceed. The coach lurched ahead cautiously, the way lit by the feeble coach lanterns.

"If I tell you the story of my life, you must tell me yours," he said with a hint of a chuckle. Betz sensed that the subject held some pain for him.

"Fair enough," she said, not sure at all that she would tell him a thing.

It was enthralling to listen to him, though, she thought, fascinated by the many changes in his expression. She was always delighted when his gaze fastened upon her face for a breathless moment.

He seemed to find her fascinating, too. They had spent a good two hours in the casino, playing at cards briefly and finally having a drink; she had sherry and he had bourbon.

Later they had watched what could only be called a seductive dance at the burlesque theater by a woman with provocative, liquid body movements. The dance, the most astonishing thing Betz had ever witnessed, was still having an extraordinary effect on her senses. She was quite glad to have Adam dominating the conversation, because she was having a difficult time with her urgent feelings of desire for him.

Sighing as if it was suddenly difficult to assemble his thoughts, Adam went on, "My father was the sheriff of a small farming town southeast of Chicago. My mother had just completed her schooling and was taking in sewing when she fell in love with him. For years I was told that she was widowed, and we moved to Chicago after I was born because she couldn't support me on the small amount of money she could make with homework where we had lived. When I was about fifteen I asked her why she hadn't stayed with her parents, as widows often do."

When his silence grew long Betz asked, "And what did she say?"

"She refused to discuss it. Then she met a man…" His tone deepened. "…a man I respected. When she told me, though, that she was going to stay with him in the boardinghouse where we lived, unmarried, I couldn't understand. Though I had never known my father, I had believed she held his memory sacred. That's when she told me she was carrying my halfbrother. I was so stunned and angry that she finally admitted why she had to leave home before I was born, and why we lived in Chicago, why she now longed to have someone of her own, after so long. She said she was lonely..."

Betz waited, tingling, until he continued.

"My father had been killed three days before he and my mother were to marry."

"How sad," Betz said. What a heartbreak for his poor mother, she thought. What a tragedy.

"I grew up believing my father had died shortly after their marriage. Her family had not accepted the fact that she had not waited for marriage to...love him. She had to leave them. Fiercely loyal to my father's memory, she endured a hard life...I realize now that my mother did the best she could. But at that age I judged her harshly, too, just as my grandparents had."

"How has it been since then?" Betz asked gently.

"After Mother's gentleman friend moved in following the fire, I sought my fortune in the west." He grinned broadly, as if making sport of his venture. "For a time I tried my hand at...various jobs in a small Montana town. And then one day, while riding a Wells Fargo stagecoach..." His expression changed suddenly and he frowned, turning away toward the window. "This fog is deadly. I hope the driver doesn't take us into the sea."

Betz sensed he was troubled, and she thought it was touching that such a self-assured man should feel some things so keenly. She hoped he would tell her what was bothering him.

He glanced back at her. His attention captured by her thoughtful expression, he assured, "Why do you look at me like that, Betz?"

"I'm comparing you to my brother, who seems to have no feelings whatsoever."

He gave a shrug and nodded. His melancholy lifting, he said, "It's your turn to reveal your past, Miss Witherspoon." He emphasized Miss teasingly.

"First you must tell me what was so troubling about being on a Well Fargo stage," Betz said softly.

He thought for a moment, then said softly, "Someone I cared for very much was killed. I might have prevented it, if I had had quicker wits."

"I'm so sorry," she said softly. "And so eventually you returned to Chicago and your mother, I take it?"

He nodded, closing his hand over hers in an intimate gesture that told her he appreciated her sympathy.

"Yes. She and I get on very well now. I can even tolerate her gentleman friend. And my brother Henry is a nice enough lad—doing well in his studies. They talk of sending him to an eastern school to become a lawyer." He chuckled. "I never had such hopes."

"You went into trade instead," Betz put in for him, wishing he would tell her more about his work.

Unlike other gentlemen at Summersea, Adam never talked business. Perhaps it was true that his trade was not on the same level as that of the other men at Summersea, but…

"I think trade is a far more respectable than what some men do," she said.

Adam looked pointedly at her as if he wished to tell her something, but instead he nodded, saying, "Trade. Well, one can tell you have a plebeian background. I think that's nice."

What an odd thing to say, she thought, feeling slightly foolish. When the silence grew long, Betz said, with a sigh, "I suppose it's my turn now."

He nodded, watching her in the pale light falling from the interior lantern.

"I had an unremarkable childhood…" she began. "It was very proper of course, and very dull. My brother George, who is four years older than I, married when I was seventeen, leaving me alone to care for our mother."

"And your father?"

"He died when I was twelve. We could afford no servants. I also had a younger sister Ellen, who died as a child. My mother never recovered after her death."

Adam looked saddened.

"I tried going to a small women's college a year after George's marriage, but Mother went into a decline, and so I went home, resigned to caring for her. She had had a somewhat dismal life when

Papa was alive, so I tried to brighten it for her, but toward the end she wanted only to stay in her room. She died when I was almost twenty-seven." Involuntarily she shivered, remembering those long empty years.

"And during that time you remained as pure as the driven snow."

His mocking words cut through her, and she cried, "Adam Teague, what a cruel thing to say! I had time for few friends. Mother received almost no visitors. When would there have been time for courting, even if I could have considered it? And besides, I saw what the institution of marriage had done to my mother. She had once been full of life. I know because I've read her diaries. Father had been very stern, and took all that from her with his dismal propriety. I had no desire to allow a man to take what small spark of life I had left in me after ten years in that house. I'm hurt, Adam. I said nothing cruel to you when you told me about your life."

He took her hand and held it tightly.

"I was trying to lighten the mood by teasing you. Forgive me. I thought you had your past life well in hand, but I see you've lied to yourself. You didn't choose not to marry. You were afraid to."

"You're wrong." She twisted away.

"Betz, you mustn't be so somber all the time. I know there's life in you. I've…felt it." He began to lean closer.

She stiffened, still wounded.

"There is a very good reason that I sometimes act… overly formal."

"It's all right to tell me, Betz." he said softly. "I know you were once married, and I know you've been divorced. Cherry has told me all that. I'm not the sort of man who cares about such things." Abruptly he pulled away. "Maybe you'd rather discuss something else."

Though the coach had been rolling along slowly, they had almost reached the Pratt house, and Betz was tempted to agree that they should drop the subject of her past. But in spite of the painful memories he was dredging up, she wanted to cling to the closeness she felt when talking to him.

"My marriage and divorce are but a small part of the reason I act so stuffy sometimes," she said softly. "I grew up with something that has overshadowed all I've ever known. It's as if my life has been shrouded in crepe, and now that I've finally gotten away from my brother's guardianship, I have the hope of casting off the gloom forever."

He was silent for a moment, and she went on.

"What troubles me is that sometimes I can't cast off my past completely. One would think I could in a place as distracting as Summersea. But I feel haunted, unable to figure out how to live what my best friend Otila jokingly called my new life as a free female." She hesitated, hoping to hold off the grim confession a little longer.

"I promise I won't make light of your feelings this time," Adam said, sincerity ringing in his voice.

"You may think what I'm about to say is foolish," she finally said. "Perhaps I'm making more of it than it necessary. But when I was a young girl it seemed very important. It kept away all beaus, even early prospects in short pants." She paused, summoning her courage. "My father was an undertaker. So is George."

Adam was silent for so long that Betz was suddenly afraid she had just ruined whatever hope she might have had of keeping his interest. What man could want the daughter and sister of men who tended the dead? What man ever had, except the one who had wanted her inheritance?

Then Adam was sputtering, and a laugh erupted that he could not control, and he blurted, "Forgive me!" circling her shoulder with his arms and pulling her close. "Are you telling me that you've led a solitary life because of that?"

"How many friends do you think I had as a child? Who could tolerate the smell of our house, or the thought of what he did in the cellar? Oh, Adam, you can't know!" She could not understand his laughter. Were her feelings about her papa's profession truly foolish?

"Oh, my dear Betz. It's all behind you now. Rise up from your funeral parlor and kiss me, darling!"

Stunned by his words and his mirth and his easy acceptance of what she always kept hidden, she felt his lips close over hers. A flood of arousal swept through her body. Her desires rushed through her and blotted out all that had kept her stiffly composed.

She began to return Adam's kiss with an urgency she had no intention of curbing. If they had not just rocked to a stop before the brightly lit Pratt house, she might have abandoned herself altogether.

A Provocative Couple

The "get-together" still filled the magnificent "cottage" with the sounds of lilting music and laughter. With the greatest reluctance, Betz left Adam at the door and made her way toward the private rooms Xynnie Pratt had provided earlier that day. She did not expect to see Cherry until dawn.

With a maid leading the way through the maze of corridors, Betz was soon closed in the ornate guest room, still trembling from her moments in the coach with Adam. It was nearly midnight. She marveled at how these people, so much higher up on the social scale than those at Summersea, could tolerate her going out alone with Adam. Where were the nosy gossips like Felicia Ellison and Gettie Hobble who condemned her every move?

She went to the window to gaze out at the rugged shadow that was the shoreline behind the great house. The fog was moving out as quickly as it had rolled in, giving her the feeling that she was waking from a dream. How quickly she would have given herself to Adam if circumstances had been different, she thought.

What could she do but endure the madness of her yearning for him, and escape Summersea as quickly as she could?

She stood at the window, wondering suddenly why Adam was at the hotel for the summer. He wasn't one of the idle rich, nor was he in the market for a bride. He wasn't there for his health, and did not seem particularly enthralled to be near the sea. He did not appear to need a rest from the daily strain of his trade, whatever it was. He was just mysteriously there…not an adventurer, she hoped.

If he was, he had nothing to gain by seducing her. He must realize that, surely!

It was then that she noticed a young woman dashing along the edge of the lawn, her gauzy gown billowing around her legs. Someone tall and lanky followed at an easy pace. Momentarily, the girl whirled and ran back into his arms. They danced to the music drifting on the night wind. Wisps of fog still swirled on the edge of the crashing surf.

Now a crack of thunder made the couple pause. On tiptoe, the girl kissed the young man's mouth and made a dash toward the house. He followed more quickly, as if to restrain her. They were out of sight beneath the window by the time Betz realized she was watching her own Cherry.

She gripped the windowsill with trembling fingers. The little fool! Rain began to patter against the windowglass. Numb with shock, Betz wondered if such behavior could possibly go unnoticed this time. It was no longer only a question of Cherry's endangered reputation, Betz was beginning to question the girl's character.

She didn't have long to brood about it. There was a quick tap at her door, followed by shushing and giggles.

"Cherry!" Betz whispered, dashing to open the door. The girl's face was flushed and her fog-dampened curls were hanging in limp coils about her shoulders. "Come it at once! What have you been doing? Hush your giggling!" The young man standing behind Cherry was grinning as if nothing was amiss.

"I'm afraid I've gotten her a bit tipsy, ma'am, so I thought it best to bring her inside before she attracted attention. I assure you, Miss Witherspoon, Cordelia is not at all harmed, and she will suffer no consequences because of our delightful evening together. If anyone asks, I'll simply explain that she decided to retire, that our company was too much for her. Our hostess will think nothing of it. Guests have a great deal of freedom here. Mrs. Pratt is a remarkable lady and my good friend."

And then he was gone before Betz could even demand his name. Closing the door and locking it, she turned back to Cherry.

The foolish child was not tipsy! She was three sheets to the wind! She staggered across the suite and fell onto her bed in a giggling heap! "Oh, Miss Witherspoon, wasn't he *wonderful*?"

Betz was too shocked to find even a shred of humor in the scene. She wished she could whisk the girl away from the house at once, that there was some way to contact Adam so that they might quietly slip away.

"Have you lost all your senses?" Betz muttered, helping the giggling Cherry out of the ruined gauze gown. "How could you get yourself into a mess like this? I don't believe for a moment that no one will hear about this. At the very least, that young man can't think much of you for this kind of behavior and young men do talk among themselves. You can be sure of that!"

She felt overwhelmed with fury. The gown, ruined. Such waste! She could only imagine what Xynnie Pratt's maid would think when she packed the trunk in the morning. She had better do it herself, hiding all evidence of this fiasco.

Cherry's slippers were waterlogged, her expensive stockings torn and beyond repair. Betz might have lived a year on what the gown alone cost. What had made her think she could control this little tomboy and school her to the refined behavior of a debutante?

"Cherry! Cherry!" Betz moaned, shaking her. "What happened with that young man? Did you…Who was he? Did you even ask his name?"

Cherry didn't answer. Grinning, she collapsed back onto the pillows, dead to the world.

Betz was appalled by her fears that the girl had been compromised by that handsome, grinning young gentleman. Agatha would be beside herself.

Tucking the snoring girl beneath the coverlet, Betz began pacing, trying to decide what to do. She berated herself for allowing Cherry to attend the party without constant supervision. She should have sat during the entire party with the other matrons, relegated to the ballroom sidelines. What difference would it have made if she had a nice time or was even comfortable? She should have watched

Cherry's every move.

But she had thought only of her chance to be alone with Adam. Cherry's welfare had truly been the last thing on her mind.

And this was her reward. Her little charge had behaved as wildly as any creature brought up among savages.

And to think she had gone out with Adam, alone in the coach, knowing full well that he might kiss her. Leaving Cherry to face society alone...even *she* had been too intimidated to attend!

Tortured by guilt, Betz undressed and climbed into bed. Unable to sleep for hours, she lay trying to assess the damage that must have been done this night. Clearly, she must end her association with Mr. Teague and devote her entire being to Cherry's refinement.

If she could not fulfill this assignment, what hope was there for her in any future positions? Failure with Cherry might very well mean a poor reference, or none. Then all that would remain would be to return to the house that still smelled faintly of embalming fluid. In such a case, she might as well be dead.

The Envied Return

Saturday, June 22, 1889

The return to Summersea was shrouded in silence. When it was time to join their hostess for luncheon the afternoon following the party, Betz had been forced to lie. She said Cherry was ill from having indulged in too much excitement the evening before. Xynnie appeared to believe her. Betz had explained to Adam that they must leave as soon as possible. He had bid his host good-bye, and seemed rather glad to do so.

"He was asking too many questions," was all Adam would say.

Cherry was too hungover to pay much attention to the silence surrounding her in the coach during the seemingly endless return trip. If she was aware of the depth of her disgrace or Betz's anger, she didn't show it.

When at last they arrived at Summersea, the fog had rolled in again, enclosing everything in a sheer, eerie blanket of white. Cherry climbed down and started up the veranda steps, under the sharp appraisal of the Hobble sisters, who sat in twin rockers near the door.

Adam put his hand on Betz's arm to detain her, asking softly. "Can we talk privately later? I'd like to know more about what happened. I feel partly responsible."

She shook her head. She wanted to squeeze him from her heart and regain her composure.

"The responsibility was entirely mine," she said rather curtly, knowing she must let him know that their indulgence had gone as far as she would allow.

She climbed down, half hoping for some word of entreaty from him but behind her was only silence. As she climbed the stairs, having cut him off, her heart began to sink. Oh, not to feel his lips again! Could she bear it?

"Miss Witherspoon, how are the Pratts?" Millie asked innocently, speaking, Betz knew, for her flint-eyed gossip sister. "I suppose Cordelia was up late, dear thing. She looked so tired as she went inside. She's not unwell, I hope?"

Betz smiled, her casual stance perfect, explaining, "The food was rather rich. I'm afraid she's feeling a bit off…all the dancing, you know. She had a wonderful time. If you ladies will excuse me…"

Adam emerged from the coach now. He took care of directing the driver back to town, assuring him that his pay would be arranged through Miss Witherspoon's employer. Then he briefly greeted the two keen-eyed old ladies, whose expressions clearly showed their avid interest in the threesome.

As he moved through the doors into the lobby, Gettie sniffed and muttered, "Agatha will find this most interesting, I'm sure. Did you see that child's eyes? She's been weeping. I mean to get to the bottom of this."

An Unexpected Visitor

Felicia had risen at dawn to dress in her most youthful gown and to have her maid arrange her hair. By six she was waiting in the lobby for Mr. Bonaventure; they were going out to take the waters at the spring, before everyone else.

It would be their first time alone, and she had been beside herself with excitement, when Charles suggested it two days ago.

She refused to let herself brood about that little heiress and the Pratts as she waited for him. Myrtle and Emma might fawn over the child now that she had been "received" in Newport by the Pratts, but young Miss Cordelia Ryburn still had Summersea and Felicia Ellison to reckon with.

Morning light streamed into the dining room through the reception parlor windows. Out on the lawn, the dew sparkled like diamonds on each blade of grass.

At the sound of footsteps on the stairs, Felicia turned, a thrill of excitement cutting through her almost painfully. For so many years she had lived within the boundaries of respectability. She felt the hope of something different now, something better, and that hope spread across her face in what she earnestly hoped was a pretty smile.

The new guest, a widow calling herself Julia Lyon, was coming down the stairs. She was wearing what Felicia thought a perfectly ghastly brown bicycling costume—a fitted bodice and plain dark skirt. Looking very collegiate though she was surely forty, the woman nodded good morning and went out to where a steward was waiting with her bicycle.

Appalled to think she and Charles might encounter this woman out at the spring, Felicia was suddenly seized with a fit of fury. How dare this creature interfere with her one last hope of romance. Dear Mr. Bonaventure—dear, dear Charles—had made it clear from the very first that he craved her love. Now that they had arranged to be alone…

At last Felicia heard the creak of his wicker chair, but she wasn't able to turn and greet him, because her expression was still twisted with frustration. The nurse said something, and then he sighed delicately as he rose from the chair and made his way painfully down each step to the lobby.

The chair rattled and bounced as the nurse brought it down without a shred of consideration for the quiet hour. Felicia stood waiting with baited breath, wondering how she might warn him that an interloper might intrude on their time together at the spring.

She heard him get settled in the chair, and still she couldn't turn. The nurse swished by, going out the doors onto the veranda to see about the buggy he had said he would arrange for. Feeling the nurse's scorn, she wondered if she could manage to have the woman replaced.

A deep voice coming from the parlor broke into Felicia's thoughts. "My dear…" She whirled, thinking she had surely gone mad. She had heard Randolph's voice, though she longed to hear Charles' soft, silky murmurs.

Randolph stood in the reception parlor doorway, derby in hand. He looked stout but impeccable in a double-breasted gray suit, and sported a white carnation in his lapel. How had she failed to smell his cigar, she wondered, going cold all over. She felt caught in the very act of infidelity, her thoughts and hopes naked for everyone to see and laugh at.

But as quickly as that feeling arose, it was drowned by her anger. Suddenly she could think of nothing but his infidelities and his blatant flaunting of his cheap harlot companions. The rage over his cheap behavior and the editor's betrayal that had sent her into the bay so many endless nights before suddenly exploded in her breast.

With a grunt of anguish she flung herself at him, pummeling his chest. Briefly aware of his astonished expression, she slapped him soundly once, and then again.

Startled by her own rage, she backed away. It was the first time in twenty years that she had expressed her indignation over his behavior.

Shocked, he carefully removed the broken cigar from his

mouth. For once he was speechless.

"What are you doing here?" she demanded, made strong by her anger, and she turned away to deny him the opportunity to answer. Now she realized Mr. Bonaventure had made a silent exit from the scene, and suddenly that was all that mattered to her.

To her husband, she flung back over her shoulder, "You'll never get a divorce!"

"Felicia, dear, I cannot imagine where that stupid editor got his information, but I assure you I've never—"

"Oh, don't patronize me, you fool! I know about your exploits. If only you knew what I've been through to keep them secret…you have not made it easy by any means! How much did you pay him to print that filth? I've been a laughing stock ever since. And divorce? Never! Never, do you hear? Never!"

She started grandly for the stairs, making it quite clear that she had no intention of dignifying Randolph's presence with any further display of emotion.

"I don't know where he got the information. But if you've been paying for his silence, dear, as I have been, then there must be someone very eager indeed to embarrass us."

Felicia paused on the step, her body going cold. Who would have paid more than she? If all she provided to the *Topics* editor wasn't enough to assure his discretion, what more could she do? And if Randolph had been paying as well…

With one hand on the banister, she twisted to look back down at the man she had married thirty years before. The only coherent word in her mind was, "disgrace."

Feeling utterly helpless, she felt her eyelids droop. The world turned black as it spun around her, and she felt herself falling backward into nothingness.

Fourteen

Disaster Overtakes Mrs. Ellison

Randolph looked suitably alarmed, Felicia thought as she lay in her room, the bump on the back of her head throbbing. Through slitted eyes she watched him pacing at the foot of her bed, puffing on another vile cigar, his face revealing his age.

"Randy," she whispered softly, as if just rousing from her faint. "Randy, dear, are you there?"

He paused, tore the cigar from between his lips and turned to scowl at her, "I'd forgotten what an unpleasant woman you are to be around, Felicia. That bit of theatrics isn't going to work this time. I've decided that I do want a divorce. I'm done paying for that damnable editor's silence. Your suicide attempt cost me a small fortune!"

"How do you think I felt when you didn't come in my hour of need?"

He began to turn purple; in a moment they would be screaming at each other, like always.

"Oh, never mind," she said, "We must decide how best to silence the talk."

"I don't care any longer, I tell you, Felicia. I came here today thinking to go on with the pretense, but your direct words have been a breath of fresh air. Let's stop fooling ourselves. We haven't had a marriage in years. I don't relish your company any longer, and I dare say you don't want mine. I'll provide for you. You know that."

The feigned weakness left Felicia replaced by genuine impotence. She could not lift even her hand to silence him. Divorce?

Unthinkable! She couldn't go on alone, unconnected to anyone. Her parents would turn in their graves! She didn't even have a child to soothe her grief. There were only her fickle friends…

As she lay helplessly listening to her husband reason with her, she felt like a silently screaming, trapped animal. Surely something horrific would happen to stop him. But he went on talking so reasonably, she felt trapped in a nightmare.

At length he saw that she was going to make no reply. Not knowing that she was incapacitated, he gave an eloquent shrug.

"If you're going to say nothing more on the subject, Felicia, then I'll go. For whatever reason, we have been exposed. I'm glad now, and in time I'm sure you will be, too. Good-bye, dear." And with that he walked out, leaving her on the precipice of madness. He *couldn't* have just gone, she thought, unable to bear it.

There was not enough money in the world to silence that editor when it came to divorce, she knew, not on the heels of what had already transpired this summer. She could feel the world bearing down on her, laughing. And if anyone ever found out that she had been a spy, she might as well disappear into oblivion.

How could she forestall this disaster? What could she do to repair the damage? Nothing came to mind. She needed comfort. She needed understanding. She needed a kind word and a smile and a fragment of hope that her life was not over while she still lay breathing.

After a moment her maid tiptoed in, whispering, "Can I get you anything, madam?" The girl looked truly frightened. Felicia wanted to slap her.

"I must see Char—Mr. Bonaventure. Send for him, immediately. Does my hair still look all right?" Her voice held a tremor of intense control.

"Yes'm," the girl said, slipping out, her eyes veiled.

As she waited, Felicia's thoughts came erratically. She must concentrate…she would think about Charles. She would not let this turn of events derange her. She must get her wits together so that she could formulate some kind of plan…

After a moment she struggled out of bed and crossed to the window. The surf was pounding against the beach like the blood in her head. She couldn't think. That editor...That editor!

The information she had provided over the years had kept her reputation safe. Who had managed to break up the express agreement between herself and one Mr. James Hampton, editor of the famed, feared *Topics*? Who wanted Randolph's affairs public? Who wanted him ruined?

With a shudder she realized that any number of her friends might be delighted to see her name raked through the mud. Had someone guessed that she was the spy? Had they all? She'd been so careful. She'd even left notes, casting suspicion on those who were more likely spies. Surely no one had ever suspected her!

Oh, why did Randolph have to be a philanderer? She wished he was dead! Other marriages survived mistresses, but those husbands always kept them out of sight, affording the wife her duly respectable position in society. Why was it not so for her? How could she go on?

Her maid came back into the room, her expression one of discomfort to the point of fear.

"He—Mr. Bonaventure asked me to tell you—He said he... couldn't come." The girl ducked back, looking as if she was ready to bolt if Felicia decided to throw something at her.

Felicia mouthed the words, "couldn't come" and felt as if she would sag to the floor once again. So Charles, too, had turned against her. Why? Why?

"Very well," Felicia heard herself say coldly.

What remained to be done? she asked herself as the door closed. She couldn't kill herself. She lacked the ingenuity to kill Randolph or to have him killed. She might travel...

Momentarily she felt a flicker of hope. If she was abroad, Randolph couldn't divorce her.

There came a tap at her door and her hopes soared. Her dear Charles had changed his mind!

"Come in," she whispered.

"Felicia, they said you fell down the stairs. Are you all right?" It was the very annoying Betz Witherspoon, standing in her doorway looking so kind and concerned. She had just returned from taking that heiress creature to Newport. Not Witherspoon again! Felicia would have none of her pity!

"A mere misstep," she said frostily. "I don't require anything of you. Go. Go away! You have no standing! What makes you think I would accept the friendship of an inferior?"

Betz Witherspoon's face went very white.

"I thought perhaps I could help…because I understand how you're feeling."

"Oh, you do, do you? How presumptuous you are."

"I heard that your h-husband, Mr. Ellison, was seen leaving…" Her words trailed off as Felicia's eyes sharpened to dagger points and she sat down in a chair.

"I'll not be pitied! Get out of here. Leave me alone!"

"I'm sorry for you, Felicia," Betz said, softly, starting out. "There will come a time when you will be a very lonely old woman."

And then blessedly, she was gone.

Felicia's eyes narrowed until the room before her was blur. There was pain somewhere deep inside her, the pain of loneliness, of the horrible truth in Betz Witherspoon's words. She blocked it all out. She knew enough about everyone at the hotel to make them all squirm for the rest of the summer. And as for Mr. Charles Bonaventure…she would find out all there was to know about him. When she put it to him in the proper framework, he would belong to her, and not a person would be able to touch them. She would someday rule them all.

Miss Ryburn is Contrite

Betz marched into her suite, where she had left Cherry to undress from their return from Newport moments before. She was seething, baffled by Felicia's behavior. How could a woman be so blind and so stupid?

She was about to blurt out her feelings when she saw Cherry standing at the chest of drawers looking puzzled.

"What is it?" Betz asked, grateful for a distraction from her anger.

"My reticule. I left it there in this top drawer. Someone has taken Mama's brooch. What would anyone want with it? It wasn't even pretty."

"I can't imagine—Cherry, darling, I've just had the most unpleasant encounter with Mrs. Ellison. I don't know why I bother with the woman, but I thought—Never mind. I know you're very tired and probably not feeling very well just now…I don't feel very well myself."

Cherry turned, her face ashen, and said softly, "I'm sorry about last night, Betz. I don't know what got into me. I guess I was so scared by all those people at the party. They were so…grand! And really, he was being very nice to me. He offered the punch and I had no idea that he had laced it with brandy until after I tasted it. And then it helped me feel ever so much better. I couldn't help myself. Please don't hate me. I'll do anything you say. I'll stand in a corner for a week…"

Betz sank to the bed. Motioning for Cherry to join her, she said, "I'm not angry, darling, not now. I won't stand you in a corner, but I'm going to ask that you take a nap now and have your dinner here alone in the suite. I must have a bit of time alone, to sort through my thoughts."

Shuddering at the ominous "he", Betz felt certain that Cherry's reputation was now in ruins. What sort of young gentleman would compromise Cherry that way? Surely not anyone worthy of the girl.

"You're not leaving me!" Cherry looked terrified.

"No, no, not at all," Betz assured her. "I just need to be alone a while, to think, to try to make sense of my feelings. You might as well know. I am…quite taken with Mr. Teague. This isn't a proper time or place for romantic notions, but I'm having them, and so must deal with them. I can't believe that ignoring my feelings will do me any good, in the long term. Yet I must not let those feelings make me forget my duty to you."

Cherry hung her head.

"I should not have left you alone last night with all those frightening strangers. I hope you can forgive me. My neglect may have very well ruined your reputation. I cannot see how this will go unnoticed. Within a matter of hours, everyone will be talking. You mustn't be alarmed, because the fault lies entirely with me. You understand that, don't you?"

Cherry's eyes were very round. She didn't appear to understand anything.

"Well, darling, in any case, I would like some time alone, and you need rest. I'll leave instructions that you're not to be disturbed. If you should need me, I'll probably go up to the pavilion. By the looks of the weather, I won't be long. You'll be good?"

Cherry nodded. When she had finished undressing, she climbed into her bed and lay there very stiffly with the cover pulled up to her chin.

The sky was very gray indeed as Betz topped the last step and crossed to the windswept pavilion. A storm seemed to be boiling up on the horizon. The thunderheads were dark and ominous.

She wouldn't be able to stay long, she thought, sinking onto the bench. What was she going to do about her feelings? She didn't want to care so much about Adam Teague. Involvement would thoroughly complicate her life.

Oh, but the yearning she felt. How was she going to master the desire she felt for this man? It was improper for her to think the scandalous things that kept her awake all hours.

She should never have let him kiss her…but the moment she thought of his kisses in the coach the evening before, she remembered in such stunning detail the feel of his mouth on hers. Could she ever recover from the warmth he brought to her; from the surging of life in her veins, from the awakened need?

Abruptly, she stood. The rising wind annoyed her, because she wanted to stay long enough to sort out her thoughts. Then hearing voices, she realized someone was coming up the steps and would soon join her at the pavilion. How could she explain what she was doing there alone?

Looking around, she decided she could skirt the pavilion and slip out of sight along the bluff. It looked rugged, but she would at least be alone while she waited for the intruders to go back to the hotel.

By the time Betz had clambered over some boulders and hidden herself among the trees and bushes clinging to the bluff, she could hear the voices behind her more clearly. One of the intruders was the new guest, Julia Lyon. The other must surely be Lyddie Fitch-Harve. And there was a murmur now of male voices as well, the cultured tones of Nolan Macklin, the Howard's tutor, and…the nervous bachelor Mr. Quarles!

Well, they would not stay too long, she thought, beginning to shiver.

Lightning split the sky over the sea suddenly, and the wind picked up. Betz's hair came loose of the pins and began tumbling about her shoulders. She began to doubt the wisdom of her desire to remain alone.

The way ahead seemed truly treacherous. Dare she go on, or would it be wiser and safer to return the way she had come, suffer the curiosity of the foursome on the pavilion, and go back to the hotel?

As she turned herself slowly around from her precarious perch between some boulders, more lightning split the quiet. She started, lost her footing and slid hurtfully onto her side.

Now rain came, suddenly lashing at her. The sky turned dark and the sheets of water turned the air gray. All her handholds were slippery and cold now. Feeling foolish and alarmed, she started making her way back.

Now she couldn't seem to find her footing. Her shoes slipped often, and she stumbled again and again.

Just as she had almost reached the trees where she would

have handholds on branches and roots, the wind and rain attacked, leaving her blinded and huddling to protect herself.

Shivering, she was struggling in crablike movements along the bluff when she felt the earth beneath her feet beginning to give. The soil was turning quickly to mud. She was sliding dangerously close to the edge of the bluff overlooking the beach forty feet below.

There was a brief moment of panic in which she thought of crying out, and she felt herself falling. Desperate for any kind of handhold, she grabbed an exposed root and found herself dangling for one astonishing moment with her face and body pressed against the bluff, her feet swinging freely over the sand below.

With a blinding flash, a tree exploded a hundred yards away, sending splinters into the air. The earth trembled from the force of the lightning strike. From nearby came a scream and some shouts. Had they seen her falling, Betz wondered, eyes clamped shut to keep out the rain and mud?

Then the whole of the overhang gave way, with one ominous rumble. For an instant Betz was clutching at air, feeling all around her move. Then she was rolling and tumbling, then engulfed and silenced.

From his tiny circular window, Adam watched the storm advance from the ocean. It galled him to think there was such a fierce fresh wind outside and he could get none of it into his room.

Spurning a jacket, he stormed out into the corridor in his shirt sleeves and down the stairs to the lobby. Everyone was standing anxiously at the door, concerned about guests who had gone out a short time before.

He pushed past the group and onto the veranda where the air was tart with salt spray. The air was dark with rain; the surf crashed angrily against the beach. The bay looked wild and dangerous. Adam breathed it all in, wishing himself anywhere but on the porch of this stuffy, staid place.

He almost regretted promising his mother he would come here "for as long it takes." How could he have known his promise would devour an entire summer? If not for Betz's lips…and the slight but increasing hope that she would throw off her crippling sense of convention and make love with him…he would be mad with boredom.

From the direction of the pavilion came four figures, one striding in front at the head of this parade, the other three grouped together as if against the onslaught of the driving rain.

Soon the new guest stepped briskly up onto the veranda with a healthy sigh of satisfaction, declaring, "Very bracing!" She shook back her soaked hair but seemed unconcerned with her drenched walking costume.

Moments later Lyddie Fitch-Harve, huddling white-faced beneath the offered coats of Macklin and Quarles, ran for the steps and dashed inside, looking frightened and mortified over her dishabille.

Macklin smoothed his thin hair across his wet scalp and marched inside, and Quarles followed, looking quite exhilarated.

Adam chuckled to himself, thinking he would like to walk in the rain, too—if it wasn't quite so fierce, and if it offered hope of getting stranded somewhere dry, dark and romantic with Betz Witherspoon.

Had it not been for the Pratts' damnable proximity to the casino the night before, he might have…why hadn't he ordered the coachman to take the long way around, or paid the man to drive them all over Newport?

The storm settled over them all with gloomy determination. The stewards were scurrying about, lighting lamps and candlesticks against the midday dark. Almost everyone was at the windows, commenting on hurricanes and speculating as to whether the barometer was low enough to warrant one. Adam wanted a drink.

He was on his way back up to his airless cubicle when he saw Cherry poke her head out of her suite door.

"Feeling at bit better?" he called teasingly. Betz had told him the girl had gotten herself drunk. She nodded demurely.

"Have you seen Betz? She went out a while ago and hasn't come back."

"Out? In this storm?" He felt a tingle of alarm.

"It was before…I'm a little worried. Would you…" Cherry gave him a playful smile.

"You know I'd be happy to check on Betz. I didn't see her below in the lobby."

Cherry mentioned Betz's fondness for the lonely pavilion. Adam thanked her and continued on to his room, where he fetched a half-filled flask. He remembered that pavilion only too well.

Taking a stinging gulp, he grabbed a rain slicker from his wardrobe. He threw it over his head and started down, tucking the flask securely in his hip pocket.

Then he paused. Bonaventure, with his nurse, Althea, had been in the reception parlor playing checkers with some old gentleman. Now was the perfect time to search her room. He took a step back in the direction of the nurse's room. Then he thought of Betz out in the rain, alone.

Resisting the urge to hurry or to indicate alarm in any way, he went down the steps, giving the impression that he was going walking in the storm. No one cared what he intended to do. He knew, though, that if the opportunity arose, he was going to do more than simply find Miss Witherspoon.

Fifteen

Miss Witherspoon is Rescued

Betz was trapped. Her arms and legs were immobilized by the weight of the earth around her. She could scarcely draw a breath because of the sinking weight on her chest. Able to move only her head, Betz struggled briefly. When she felt the earth settled damp around her, she froze in terror. Who might find her here?

"Help me!" she called weakly, hearing thunder all around. Everything was dark gray, and the rain was running in her face and causing mud to run down her neck.

She lay on her back amid the earth and sand of the collapsed overhang of the bluff. Forcing herself to remain calm, she called out again.

Certain that she would suffocate or drown in a few hours, Betz did her best to figure out how she might save herself.

The storm raged on over her head, soon beginning to turn the earth around her to slop. After a struggle, she was able to move one arm free, but she was so dirty she couldn't wipe her eyes without getting more dirt in them.

"Help!" she called, waving her arm. "Help!" Who would even know she was missing, until Cherry woke from her nap later?

She was trapped in the fallen earth, with most of her body encased and her upper torso lying in a kind of depression that was rapidly filling with rain water.

All at once, she felt something warm and sure clasp her hand, heard a voice demanding, "Betz, lie still and I'll dig you out!"

Adam!

Opening her eyes to the driving rain, she saw the shadow of a man, heard his voice, and then she burst into sobs. She was safe at last to cry out her terror.

"Be still," he said again, and she froze.

She was still sobbing as she felt his hands scraping at her sides, pushing away rocks and shoving double handfuls of earth away from her body. Then he lifted her by the arms, dragging her until she rolled inert onto the cold wet sand. The rain drummed against her numbed body, washing away some of the mud. He was gathering her against his body and saying soft words she couldn't concentrate on.

He had pulled her out of the crushing weight. Adam. Suddenly this entrapment seemed symbolic of her life. He had freed her. When he drew back, about to speak, she captured his mouth with hers and kissed him as she had never before dared, except in her most secret yearnings.

His instantaneous response was all she craved. His mouth became urgent and demanding. He held her as he had not done before, possessively. She was yielding to him even as she clutched him close.

This was life, she told herself. Nothing else mattered. All the rules of convention could be damned, for all she cared. She was a living, breathing woman and she wanted this man to fulfill her.

"Betz, Betz," he panted, drawing away for a moment. "Are you hurt? Is anything broken?"

He helped her to stand. The rain was lashing and cold, giving them no respite from the fury of the storm. She tried to concentrate. Wouldn't it be amazing to think she was making love when an arm or leg might be broken?

"I-I'm all right," she said, laughing a little. "What will they all say to this, I wonder. What would Summersea have to talk about without Cherry and me?"

"To hell with them. Let's find some shelter. I know of a cove where we might get away from some of this wind and rain for a while…unless you want to try to get back to the hotel."

She shook her head. She knew what she wanted, and she would not find it at the hotel.

They made their way along the beach to the cove. Behind the shelter of some rocks, they settled down together under his rain slicker to wait out the storm. Adam offered her his flask and she took several gulps that made her eyes sting. Gradually she began to feel warmer.

For a while, Betz was content to huddle against Adam. When the rain subsided, they went to the water's edge to rinse off.

"You might want to wade out a few feet and rinse your hair and clothes," he said, grinning down at her. "You're covered with mud."

The turbulent sky lightened slightly. Betz looked at the waves beating wildly against the sand and shivered admitting, "I can't swim."

"I'll go with you," he said, taking her hand.

She let him pull off her shoes and together they waded into the waves. She felt the water pulling and pushing at her, and she was afraid, but she clung tightly to Adam's hand, and then his arm, and finally she threw herself against him, frightened by the power of the water and her desire for him.

When she felt ready, she immersed herself in the waves and savored the feel of the water as it rinsed her hair and clothes and body clean.

When they emerged from the cove, her clothes felt clammy and clinging. She was shivering as they returned to the protection of the rocks and the slicker. They drained the flask and then huddled there, drawing warmth from one another. Betz finally turned her face toward Adam. He was looking down at her, his dark eyes piercing, his expression serious and faintly troubled.

His wet hair was curling against his brow and along his neck. His mouth was soft, curving finally into a very endearing, arousing smile. As he leaned close for a kiss, she felt her body kindle with desire. When his hand brushed across her breast beneath the cover of the slicker, she arched involuntarily, craving his touch.

As he kissed her again, his hand closed on her breast and then moved swiftly to cup the other. The fabric covering her was cold. Adam plucked at the hooks of her bodice front, convincing himself that he wanted only to free her of the chilling clothes.

But his true purpose became quickly apparent as he found his way by instinct past each layer of protection, and his arousal grew.

This was how he wanted her, he thought, so warm and pliant in his arms. At last the corset cover was untied and pushed back and he was able to spread his palm over her cool skin and erect nipples. She was moaning ever so slightly, as if his touch was exquisite torture.

He wanted to look at her body, but because of the slicker he could only explore by touch the mounds and valleys of her body, now flaming at his touch. She was breathing raggedly almost at once, alarming him as much as fueling his need. It was not a virginal response, but one of a woman long and cruelly denied her rights as a beautiful, sensuous creature.

Her hands were as quick and hungry on his body as his were on hers. She held his shoulders, and then spread her hands down across his chest. The linen was cold on him, too, and he was suddenly tearing his shirt off, pressing himself against her warm soft breasts.

And then he ceased thinking. He was only feeling, memorizing the way she opened to him, receiving him with the most incredible yearning.

Betz lay still beneath him a moment, quivering as she savored the intensity of his power within her. She was a tiny pinpoint of flame, focused with all her awareness on this moment. He was there for her, giving her all she craved, but it was more than mere physical union. It was forever special, never again to be equalled, because this was not just any man, but this one man.

Her hands curved across his broad warm back. She was still afraid to move, afraid that all too soon it would end. But then the need began to build and they were moving together, joined and one, melded into a single point of light that began to glow brighter and hotter until there was only the exploding, pulsing, engulfing light.

Betz did not even realize at first that she was weeping. She pressed her face into his neck to quell the quiet, grateful sobs, but she felt him tense and draw back.

"What is it?" he whispered.

She could scarcely choke out the words, "It was wonderful!" and then she was kissing him, hoping somehow to tell him what he had done for her without risking the foolishness of words.

"You're so beautiful, Betz," he whispered, holding her tightly, moved to his soul that he could bring a woman to this peak of emotion. He was afraid, very suddenly, that he loved her, and that meant only danger, a terrible risk, a threat of disappointment he had thought would never touch him.

He held her then for himself. His former worries—over the expressions on her face or her words—had grown to true fear that he might not be able to keep her.

There was only this stolen moment. He could not bring himself to let her go and knew he was going to have to have her again now, and again later. Where they could be together in the future, he didn't know, but someone like this did not come along more than once.

Adam folded her against his chest, as if he could make her a part of himself. The need for her grew quickly again, and with all his being he showed her that he loved her. He had not known he was capable of tears, but when they came he was glad.

The rain was subsiding and the fierce wind had driven off some of the clouds. The air was briskly sweet and fresh and exhilarating as Betz allowed Adam to lift the slicker from over her head. He helped her stand, and then they stood righting their clothes, faces reddened and smiles lurking on their lips and in their eyes.

At last she dared to look into his eyes and the warmth she saw there kindled her all over again. She was in love, she thought with a sense of wonder. Suddenly the world was washed as clean as this day. All colors had taken on a new brightness. Even the smell of the bay was more intensely wonderful.

She stood looking up at Adam and her heart was soaring. She

could feel the air going in and out of her lungs, and she felt free and naked. Her skin tingled, she felt weak and languid in the most wonderful, erotic way. She wondered how she could possibly yearn for still more satisfaction.

"We'll cause quite a stir when we go back," Adam said, looking her over.

Her clothes were ruined, sodden and still quite muddy, and she had hooked her bodice crookedly!

Chuckling, he helped her rehook the hooks, and then they started back toward the hotel. As they passed the great muddy gash in the side of the bluff where she had fallen, she shuddered and took Adam's arm.

"I might have been smothered," she whispered.

He circled her shoulder with his arm and hugged her. She saw the strain about his mouth and reached to smooth away the wrinkles. "Thank you, Adam, for saving me."

Pulling her close, he held her. Her thoughts churned as she debated whether she should tell him of her love. Perhaps Adam already knew the depth of her feelings for him. She had given him herself, and that was everything she had to offer.

She noticed him swallowing with emotion as he pulled away and they started on again, back to the hotel.

"How much longer do you think you'll be staying at Summersea?" she asked.

"Why do you want to know?" His voice was suddenly guarded.

"I have this unreasonable fear that you're going to disappear from my life. Forgive me. I must sound like a clinging fool."

He paused, squinting out at the surging waves and the break in the clouds that was letting streaks of sunlight down to the sea. Then he said, "I will always try to be as honest with you as I can, Betz. I won't disappear without a word. When I go into the city, I'll tell you. I hope you can trust me."

She nodded, thinking it a rather guarded speech for a man who appeared to have nothing to hide. She wondered again if he did.

He kissed her forehead then, and they walked on. When they

were close to the hotel, he advised that their starry eyes might be overlooked if he carried her inside. Protesting, Betz finally allowed Adam to lift her into his arms. He carried her easily the remainder of the way visible from the veranda. There was the expected furor of concern and alarm over her mishap when they arrived, but it seemed indeed that no one guessed what had really gone on during the storm.

Melancholy Reverie

What had made her marry Gordie Carlyle, Betz wondered, as she lay on her bed in the evening shadows. It had been years since she had allowed herself to think about Gordie. Always before, she had only wanted to erase the memory of her fiasco with this young man. But now she felt ready to explore what had made her do what she had done, to understand how it could have been so wrong. Certainly with Gordie she had never even approached the intimacy she had known with Adam.

She was just twenty-seven when her mother died in her sleep.

There had followed the horrid conflict with George about whether he would tend to their mother's funeral or allow another undertaker to handle things. In the end Betz had prevailed.

Then had come the reading of the will, and her mother's explicit instructions that under no circumstances were her possessions to pass automatically to her male heir George. The house and furnishings were to be Betz's, regardless of any future marriage.

George had fought the provisions of the will, but after a time his first wife miscarried their fifth child and became bedridden. The matter of the house was temporarily forgotten.

Alone for the first time in her life, Betz began to socialize as never before. It was difficult to begin her life at such an advanced age, but with the help of her best and only friend Otila, who lived down the street, Betz made a beginning.

She had been managing the household accounts for some time,

so making do on a monthly allowance from her mother's estate wasn't too difficult. But when the property taxes became overdue, she found herself in the gloomy parlor facing two rather frightening young gentlemen from the tax assessor's office.

One of the men had been a spade-faced simpleton whose only concern was to intimidate a young woman on her own. The other man had been Gordie Carlyle, a lawyer along to assist.

Betz was never able to determine afterward if it was by guile or coincidence that Gordie was there. That day, she only knew that he was young and attractive, and seemed sincerely interested in helping her.

When the matter of the tax was cleared away, to the satisfaction of the assessor, and to the annoyance of George, who had had to be called in to advise her, Gordie Carlyle came one afternoon to call. Tall and slender, he had a ready smile and a glib tongue.

"Your pretty smile has haunted me, Miss Witherspoon," he had said, turning her head as no man had ever done before.

Gordie wore his boater at a dashing slant, and his suits were always the finest. He was new in town, he claimed. Because he knew so few people, he said, he was forced to sidestep convention and pursue her without an introduction. She was completely captivated by his charm.

Later she was to realize he had no idea that there were special provisions to her inheritance of her mother's house. She appeared to have money because she had the estate. Gordie had seen an opportunity to turn a quick profit by marriage. And perhaps he had also relished the challenge of seducing a spinster.

He had taken her for buggy rides in the park, and stopped by with candy and flowers. He was so full of zest, Betz was completely taken in, and soon she believed that she might previously have led a normal life, if only she had tried. Gordie convinced her that she was perfectly normal and desirable in every way, and that he was utterly smitten by her.

When he asked for her hand she accepted, partly because her brother George made her feel her actions were sheer, perverse rebelliousness. She would not wait to receive George's blessing, although she expected her engagement to this near-stranger to cause an uproar.

George surprised her, saying calmly, "Of course you must do whatever you think is best." She still did not know, lying here at Summersea, if he had meant what he said, or had been trying to discourage her.

Within three months she and Gordie were married. They took a wedding trip to Boston. There in a hotel a room, Betz had rather unceremoniously forfeited her long-cherished virginity.

Gordie quickly abandoned his efforts to be charming.

He had run up a exorbitant tab by the time they checked out of the hotel a week later, and claimed he had been bilked and robbed and was short on funds. Betz had been forced to settle the account.

She thought no more about the incident until other bills began to flood in, a month later. Gordie had started going out in the evenings to his club, and of course he was gone all day, handling cases.

Lying there in the darkness now, she remembered clearly the afternoon when he came home and she confronted him with the bills charged to her accounts. He had stood in the doorway to the parlor, looking at her as if she was beneath his contempt. Then he had turned on his heel and left, leaving her to wonder when or if she would ever see him again. He had not said a word.

Beside herself with worry, she had waited until the next day for Gordie to return.

"Tell me why you're charging on my accounts, and we'll settle this, darling!" she had said, frightened by the change in him but determined not to be treated badly. If the marriage didn't work, she would have to face George, and George Witherspoon seemed a far more intimidating foe than Gordie Carlyle.

"What's yours is mine now," Gordie had said.

"I'm afraid you've made some incorrect assumptions," Betz had said, suddenly afraid she might have married a fortune hunter.

She had explained her financial position, all the while watching Gordie's reactions. He'd given her no further indication that he was upset by the arrangements. It had simply been a mistake on his part. He would surely right the accounts.

When she climbed the stairs to their bedchamber that night, Gordie was quite drunk. He undressed before her, displaying his prowess proudly, and then he took her.

She had submitted, as she had on her wedding night and every night since. The excitement she had felt when he was courting her had long since vanished. It was as if she had truly married a stranger.

Holding her in his arms that night, he had whispered softly that she would have to make arrangements to pay the accounts from her own funds, and that as a lawyer it would be an easy matter for him to properly title the house and accounts to his name. He had made it sound like the most reasonable request, and for a brief moment Betz had considered complying.

But as she hesitated, he couldn't sustain his charm. He'd drunk too much. His greed and impatience took over, making him demanding and increasingly angry.

"What kind of marriage is it when the wife withholds from her husband! I could divorce you for this!"

The threat did its work. Betz was so afraid of what George would say that she agreed at once to pay the accounts.

The following month, the bills doubled and she could not pay them from her monthly allowance. Gordie convinced her she was not competent to handle the accounts, and arranged with the bank to increase the allowance.

By the third month Betz had lost all touch with her own finances. When a very worried family friend called one afternoon to ask why she had withdrawn all her funds from a bank that served her family well for thirty years...Betz had been stunned.

"What have you done with my money?" she had asked the moment Gordie returned from his club that evening.

He had been drinking again, and she was mortified by what followed. He had all but raped her in his effort to cow her. Afterward he said he would next want the house transferred into his name. He even suggested he might sell it and move them to another town where he might prefer to practice.

The following day a strange man called on Gordie early, and there were hushed words in the parlor between them. Gordie demanded all her household money, and went off, leaving her to wonder what kind of trouble he was in.

She was so frightened about what her brother would think that she was immobilized. She sat rigidly in her mother's parlor, dreading the sound of Gordie's first step on the porch, yet fearing he might never return, thereby shaming her with abandonment.

Many times afterwards she wished that was what he had done. But he returned, and she dared to ask what was wrong. In the very room where she had grown up reciting verses for her sober-faced papa in his death dark black suit, where everything had been so proper and perfect, Gordie had slapped her to the floor.

Stunned, incredulous, frightened beyond words, Betz had fought Gordie there on the carpet, been raped for her trouble and then beaten soundly.

"I am your husband and you will do as I say!" Gordie had yelled, straddling her battered body. "Is that clear?"

It had been intensely clear at that moment, Betz recalled now, shuddering and weeping. She had been seduced by a swindler, and there had been only one recourse.

Never in all her days would she forget what it felt like making her way to George's house that night. She had half feared he would not defend her in spite of her bruises.

His expression as he stood in the doorway was clearly etched in her memory, too. At first, there in his kitchen, she let her brother believe she had been attacked and raped by a stranger. His anger had been complete. When she confessed her attacker was her own husband, he had settled back, lifting his whiskered chin. The cold breath of "I told you so," chilled her to the marrow.

"Can I stay here tonight?" she had asked, trying not to whimper. He had nodded and then sent for the police.

It was unnecessary, though for them to evict Gordon Carlyle from her mother's house. He was packed and gone by the time they arrived. With him he had taken every silver candlestick and all the silverware. Every valuable that he could carry and later sell had been stripped from the house. And for good measure he had slit the feather mattress on their marriage bed, and every chair cushion in the house.

In spite of it all, she had had difficulty convincing the judge that she was entitled to a divorce. Finally she was freed of her mistake, and compelled to take up residence in George's house. Her estate was gone, and she could not bear to live where she had endured such disgrace. She tended George's dear wife Bess until she died. Then she filled her hours with the needs of the household and the four motherless children.

For six years she watched her life pass by quietly, and she had been grateful. The shame of her marriage had rendered her small and meek.

As Betz lay in her bed at Summersea that night, her body still tinglingly aware of Adam's lovemaking, she knew that her brief infatuation for Gordie could never compare with her feelings for Adam.

She had married him to rebel against a life she had secretly hated, against a brother who had always envied her and treated her like a child. She had plunged headlong into a marriage she could not have known would end in disaster.

What could she do now to keep herself from making another tragic, regrettable mistake? She must use caution and restraint. She was still employed, obligated to do her best for Cherry. How difficult would her job be now that she was in love? She was to be tested when the weather cleared. A picnic luncheon on a nearby farm was the next event.

Betz turned on her side, hoping to sleep, but there in her memory was Adam's dear face, his dark penetrating eyes, his knowing smile…and the sense of mystery that did indeed surround him. Was she headed for disaster again, this time with her heart at stake?

Sixteen

Mrs. Ellison Plans Revenge

Friday, June 28, 1889

"Mrs. Ellison, how g-good of you to receive me," the little weasel said, slinking into her suite and taking the chair she indicated on the far side of the table. He had shifty eyes and, she had always thought, the intelligence of an ant. She had planned it so that he would be blinded by the morning sunlight streaming in her window.

"I trust Mr. Hampton is well," she said, her voice icy.

"A regrettable mistake, letting that information about you find its way into the paper," he said, squinting and smiling uncertainly.

"Quite regrettable," Felicia said, offering a thick envelope. Then, just as the little man reached for it, she drew it back a few inches. "I wouldn't want Mr. Hampton to misinterpret my continued generosity," she said softly.

"He asked me to assure you that nothing more about you or Mr. Ellison would ever reach print. You have his word."

"I had it before, and he failed me," Felicia said, her mouth thinning to a grim line. "This letter contains some very interesting information gathered from my most trusted sources. The information comes at quite an expense to me. Should I become divorced I would be quite unable to pay…and I might be forced to reveal certain confidences that Mr. Hampton has been assured I would never give out. I hear…" she said in her sweetest falsetto, "that certain rival papers might be interested to know his tactics and…his sources. I'm told they pay awfully well, but of course my loyalty was always with my dear friend…Mr. Hampton."

The weasel had the wit to look uncomfortable.

"Mr. Hampton apologizes for any distress he may have caused you. He wishes to assure you that your recent incapacity shall never be revealed. And in addition to his personal protection, he has indicated he would like to pay his respects to you…in cash. Are you interested, Mrs. Ellison?"

Felicia smiled ever so haughtily. She extended the envelope and allowed Mr. Hampton's "assistant" to take it. He opened the envelope and began scanning her hastily penned words. She watched with satisfaction as a smile spread across his face.

"She's a divorcée? But how did you find out?"

"Dear man, do you not know how poorly paid some dressmakers are? And look there, the mother killed outside a beer hall. Some mothers, and grandmothers, will be glad to learn of that fact. But those things are trifles compared to this. Look, here are the lies being spread to cover an illegitimate pregnancy, right under this very roof."

He read quickly, his little eyes skipping back and forth across the lines.

"And an affair of old money and new…how delicious. Mrs. Ellison, you've outdone yourself. Mr. Hampton is going to be extremely grateful. You are so kind to forgive the mistake—"

"I expect something else in return, my good man," she said in a silky tone. "I expect to be told who encouraged Mr. Hampton to betray me."

"But dear lady, it was purely a mistake! Mr. Hampton was ill that week, you see, and we were forced to go to press without his approval. One of the other assistants stumbled across…" He went pale.

"Do you mean to tell me there are files?" Felicia breathed. Her eyes narrowed. "I hope, for Mr. Hampton's sake, that you convey my fury. Those files must be destroyed or *Society Topics* will fold. I have already been approached by your rivals," she lied, "make that utterly clear to Mr. Hampton."

"Indeed, I will," he said, quivering.

"You may go now, and this time don't forget the hatboxes. I will not have anyone wondering what you were doing here."

He scurried from the suite, four hatboxes in hand, and thumped noisily down the corridor to the stairs.

The insufferable little toady, Felicia thought, sinking to a chair after she had locked the door. Let this be the end of it all, she wished. Let them all squirm beneath the lash of James Hampton's barbed words in "Tidbits" and then dare to suggest that she should not cultivate Charles Bonaventure's friendship.

All that remained was to lure Charles back. The unpleasantness between herself and Randolph in the lobby that day had surely driven him off. She needed only to see him privately as soon as possible, and assure him that their friendship need not be affected by Randolph's posturing. Then she would be free to enjoy his company all she wished.

An Eminent Guest is Expected

Betz and Cherry had begun to pass their mornings along a stretch of beach south of Summersea. In an hour they would return to the hotel to dress for the picnic, but for now they savored the peace and tranquility of the still morning away from the gossiping guests in the dining room.

Cherry was sketching the sea again, growing more and more confident of her ability. Her true talent still seemed to be with dramatics, but Betz didn't have the energy to organize any sort of tableau or dramatic reading to show off the girl's natural abilities.

Betz had arranged with Julia Lyon the day before to have some cycling lessons for Cherry, and soon they would all go over to the Huntington Club for some riding lessons. Cherry seemed excited by that.

But Betz's thoughts were all on Adam now, and Cherry, too, had seemed somewhat distracted and dreamy since her visit with the Pratts. When Mr. Woodley came along with a new canvas under his arm, Betz called to him, "Is it a good day for painting, Mr. Woodley?"

"Any day is good for that, dear," the man called back, not bothering to pause for politeness's sake. He continued past them, squinting through his little spectacles to find the spot he would paint from this day. "I would sleep out here if it weren't for the fact that I can't abide sand in my drawers."

Cherry looked up from her sketch and asked teasingly, "Have you seen our Mr. Teague this morning, Mr. Woodley? Miss Witherspoon is ever so taken with him, you know."

Betz's mouth dropped open in embarrassment. Cherry flushed but grinned.

"Pay no attention to her, Mr. Woodley," Betz said, trying to keep her voice light. He lifted his spectacles to regard Cherry. Then he looked surprised, as if he had just noticed her sketching.

"Ah, where did this sand flea come from?" He strode over to Cherry, scowled at her sketch pad and then tweaked her nose. "You're quite talented, my dear, but loosen your wrist. You are sketching, not carving in marble. A good day to you ladies," he said, moving away.

"At least it's not so windy this morning," Betz said. He paused then, laughing silently at a private joke.

"Speaking of a great wind, I have just come from the dining room, where everyone is in the most irritating tizzy. It seems that the indomitable dowager Whitgift is expected by next week. Earlier than expected. I met her only once. A veritable locomotive of a woman. Makes our unbalanced Mrs. Ellison seem as harmless as a gnat."

"Oh, my," Betz said, looking over at Cherry. "This is quite unexpected. I'm glad you came along to tell us."

Plucking off his spectacles and then polishing them with his shirttail, he said, "I'm glad to see you've recovered from your misadventure during last week's storm, Miss Witherspoon. Quite the luck to have our Mr. Teague out there to bring you safely in."

"Thank you, Mr. Woodley," Betz murmured, flushing. Few people had failed to speak to her on the subject and each time Betz had scarcely been able to stammer out her replies. She was convinced everyone could tell by her flaming cheeks that she had experienced the forbidden joys of love during that storm.

Cherry giggled, asking, "It was ever so romantic, don't you think?" He nodded, squinting into the sun.

"Indeed. You've caused quite a stir. But I wonder, whatever possessed you to go out in such weather? An old fool like myself might to capture a mood with paint but you, dear, have no such excuse."

Betz answered without thinking, "My room was stuffy."

"Ah, well, I can understand that. Summersea has taken on an especially unpleasant atmosphere of late. Our dear Mrs. Ellison is trying to outdo Mrs. Fitch and Mrs. Reinhold…One wonders where it will all end. Most tedious. Bad for my digestion."

"I haven't found her company very good for me, either," Betz said.

"If you have trouble dealing with such females, my dear, I would advise you to stay away from Mrs. Whitgift. She possesses a viper's tongue and cares not whom she stings. Cordelia should be especially careful. A word from Victoria Whitgift could leave Ryburn Department Stores quite empty of moneyed customers."

"Thank you for the warning, Mr. Woodley." Betz felt a chill run along her back.

"I've been meaning to ask, dear, what do you think of my friend Adam? I believe that he has a great deal of regard for you." He grinned, the broken front tooth like a wink in his smile, as Betz stammered something.

"Yes, well never mind. I thought as much. Good day, ladies. Enjoy the picnic, I shall not bother with it. I have much to do if I'm to leave before the ironclad standard of society arrives."

"We shall miss you," Betz said as he ambled away, waving briefly over his shoulder.

Cherry whispered, "Do you suppose Drew will be coming with his grandmother?" Her cheeks were quite red.

"You mustn't be so familiar with a young man's given name before you've been introduced, darling," Betz said.

Cherry opened her mouth, then looked quickly away. Whatever she had been about to say, she had thought better of it.

"I know, dear, this is the ordeal we've been waiting for. I had hoped to have more time to prepare you. We had best get back and practice—"

Cherry dropped her sketch pad into the sand, jerked off her shoes suddenly and started for the lapping waves, yelling, "I don't want to go back. I want to go bathing! I want to get right in the water the way we saw everyone doing at the public beaches along Narragansett last week."

"No, Cherry! Not even Marietta Howard has dared such a thing!"

"I don't give a tinker's damn what Marietta does or doesn't do. Getting wet can't do any more harm to my reputation than wetting my whistle at the Pratts'."

Startled, Betz laughed.

"Perhaps not, but we must be on our best behavior from now on. You have been far too fortunate. In any case, you have no costume for bathing," Betz said, unable to forget the exhilaration and terror of standing in the sea during the storm. She couldn't blame the girl for wanting to experience that.

"Order one from town! If you don't, some night I'll go out in my chemise and drawers."

"I thought we had agreed to behave," Betz said, terrified that the reckless girl just might. Cherry wasn't being as contrite as Betz had hoped. In fact, with each of her escapades, the girl's daring had seemed to double.

Cherry had waded so far out that each surging wave was wetting the lace of her long drawers. Fully half her leg was exposed.

"Come back now, Cherry," Betz called, keeping her voice calm.

Frowning, Cherry obeyed, but nothing could induce her to continue her lesson in sketching. There was nothing left to do but return to the hotel and dress for the picnic. Betz had a feeling the afternoon would not be uneventful.

A Formal Picnic

The parade of wagons and buggies, loaded with guests dressed to the hilt, had cut deep muddy ruts across the meadow. The fragrance of grass and earth was so pure that Betz couldn't resist relaxing against the hard back of the wagon seat.

Cherry was beside her, wearing a charming afternoon dress of pink bombazine. Her hair was done up in a complicated style of ringlets and a narrow plaits. Betz was wearing her usual lawn blouse and a very plain gray skirt. If she didn't feel like a proper chaperone, she had decided to at least act and dress the part.

Still, she could not avoid thinking that today she would be near Adam for several hours. How she would manage her feelings about him, she didn't know. Everyone would surely be able to see she was in love. Thinking about it, her stomach became a mass of butterflies.

Early that morning some hired workmen from town had erected a platform near the trees at the edge of the meadow. A quartet was seated on it now, playing a Mozart minuet.

The hotel staff and extra hired help from town had arrived later that morning to set up tables and lay them with snowy linen and glinting tableware.

As all the wagons and buggies arrived, Betz thought the meadow looked as if the finest hotel dining room had been transported there. The breeze was mild, tugging gently on the draped table linens. The violin music curled about, undulating like the deep grasses, and the warmth of the sun made everything feel like a dream.

Betz looked everywhere for Adam. She hadn't seen him all morning and now was hungry for just the sight of his face. It had been nearly a week now since the storm, and they had exercised the most severe propriety whenever they passed in the dining room or sat talking on the veranda. Though she had done all she could to overcome her intense desire for Adam, each time she had seen him her heart raced. She felt as reckless and unpredictable as Cherry.

Felicia Ellison had gathered quite a crowd at the center table. Nearby were the Fitches and Reinholds, looking as untouchable as their "old" money.

As they moved toward the tables, Felicia averted her eyes from Betz's curious gaze, indicating that Betz and Cherry were not welcome to approach.

"Miss Witherspoon, Cordelia dear, won't you both sit with us? We've saved places for you," Mrs. Fitch called loudly.

"Must we?" Cherry muttered to Betz.

"I believe it would be to our advantage," Betz whispered, smiling her reluctant acceptance.

Betz took a place beside Lyddie, who was looking more wan than usual, asking, "How are you feeling?" She had guessed, along with nearly everyone else, that the young "widow" was pregnant.

"It's a very hot today," Lyddie said breathlessly, patting her upper lip with a lace-edged hankie. "Where's your Mr. Teague this afternoon?"

"He's not mine!" Betz whispered hastily.

Lyddie smiled as if she knew better.

Flustered, Betz wondered just how much talk there was about her and Mr. Teague. Then she wondered suddenly what she might do if she found herself pregnant. Sickened to the point of nausea, she became acutely aware that pregnancy was, indeed, a possibility. How could she have been so reckless? "I-I haven't seen Mr. Teague today."

"He may not have been invited," Lyddie said, casting her gaze toward Felicia Ellison's table. "I'm really quite surprised she invited you. She's been insufferable since—"

"We shouldn't speak ill of Felicia," Lyddie's mother Myrtle said in a hushed whisper. "But you know, Miss Witherspoon, Felicia has been asking the most unusual questions about you. And about Cordelia."

"Thank you for telling me," Betz said. "I think it might be nice to walk over to that pond before luncheon begins. There's a boat there. Perhaps later one of the gentlemen can take us rowing." She got up from the table before the gossip could continue.

"The old bat," Cherry muttered when they were out of earshot. "She's as bad as Felicia."

"Sometimes I feel we're being used as pawns."

"Did I hear someone say Mr. Teague won't be here today? The picnic must be ruined for you," said Cherry.

Betz felt her heart sink. Then she chuckled, and admitted, "I'm afraid you're right. The day will be quite tedious."

They dawdled beside the pond as long as possible, and then went back to take their seats. A number of newcomers had joined them, and introductions were made all around. Betz scarcely paid any of the people her full attention.

After the twelve-course meal, with the languid afternoon stretching before them, a gentleman approached Betz after she and Cherry got up from the table. Smiling, he announced, "I was sitting near you just now. Apparently you didn't notice me. I was beginning to think I was invisible."

Looking up into attractive blue eyes, Betz thought immediately of Adam's dark brown ones. She felt quite distracted.

"Miss Witherspoon, I'll only take a moment of your time. My name is Brandon Shane. I'm staying at Cape Helen Hotel for the next week. Might I call on you?"

Blinking with surprise, Betz managed to focus her attention on his smiling blue eyes again. He was wearing a very nice white afternoon jacket and white trousers. Was he younger than herself, she wondered, and was he asking to call on her…as a suitor?

"You realize I'm a chaperone, not a guest at Summersea, don't you, Mr. Shane?" she asked, sounding suddenly priggish. Unable to bear such a trait in herself, she softened her expression with a smile. "What I'm trying to say is, well…" She flushed and chuckled. "I thought you might not be aware…is this the reverse of snobbery?"

"I am fully aware that you are an extremely attractive woman, and I would like to know you better." He offered his right elbow to Betz and his left to Cherry. "Miss Ryburn…if you and your companion would allow me, I would be honored to row you about the pond. I saw you on the bank before luncheon and promised myself to offer."

Mr. Shane Intrudes

"Of course, you realize why the rich are such horrid people sometimes," Brandon said to Betz as he rowed slowly across the pond, which was proving far larger than they had realized. "They're bored. They have too much of everything. Whatever strikes their fancy, they can buy. Even people. But someone like you, or this charming young lady, they can't buy, and it is terribly distressing to them."

Betz watched him talking, his cheeks flushed from the effort of trying to impress her; and she suddenly found herself wondering what this man's connections were. Should she be spending her time with him?

If she could have had her wish, he would have been instantly transformed into Adam.

"The tittle-tattle of high society bored me long ago," Brandon went on with what he appeared to think was droll humor. "Suits by Pool's of London, gowns by Worth in Paris, all so pretentious. Don't you agree, Miss Witherspoon?"

Betz sighed. Mr. Shane was trying too hard to bring himself to her level, and that was a kind of snobbery, too. She listened to him with growing irritation, and began squirming about on her seat at the bow of their little row boat.

"...I find lawn tennis quite interesting," he was saying. "How do you find the game, Miss Witherspoon? Would you care to join me for a match some afternoon this week?"

Betz was not so sure that she should discourage this man, even if she was not particularly interested in him. Perhaps spending a little time with him would help her keep her head about Adam.

"I haven't had much time to cultivate my skill in the game of tennis," she said, still sounding stuffy. She gave up trying to sound like herself. Brandon made her feel self-conscious.

"Or perhaps you would enjoy parlor skating? There is a very fine rink in Newport. I could take you to my favorite restaurant afterwards."

Betz made an effort to look agreeably interested, but Cherry's expression of disbelief had her quite concerned. Was the girl going to make a fuss?

Not to be daunted, Mr. Shane tried yet again. "I'm also fond of yacht races. My uncle has a rather fine little boat I would be proud to show you. To appreciate the yacht, of course, one must sail to Cape Cod. That might be a pleasant way for me to conclude my vacation before I return to my practice."

"Are you a doctor?" Betz asked, relieved to seize some less threatening topic of conversation.

"A lawyer," he said, smiling with a pleasant degree of modesty.

Cherry's mouth was set in a grim line. Her eyes darted first to Mr. Shane's grinning face and then to Betz's pleasantly pink cheeks. It was just too much. After all the pains she had taken to bring her Miss Witherspoon and Mr. Teague together, she couldn't believe that Betz would flirt with this man. Gripping the sides of the boat, Cherry knew that something had to be done!

"Can I switch places with you, Miss Witherspoon?" Cherry asked, standing abruptly.

"Miss Ryburn, don't rock the boat!" Mr. Shane cried, letting go of the oars.

As he did, he stood and turned toward the bow to save Cherry from falling out. Cherry watched in a kind of fascination as she crouched, deftly avoiding his helpful reach. She grasped the sides firmly again, threw her weight to one side as if losing her own balance...and with a yelp of surprise, Mr. Shane keeled over the side into the water like a tenpin.

"What if he can't swim?" Betz looked stricken.

Mr. Shane bobbed to the surface. Blinking water from his eyes, his hair streaming onto his forehead, he asked, "Are you ladies all right?"

Cherry huddled in the bow and nodded. The moment Mr.

Shane began to laugh, Cherry felt a wave of remorse.

"Miss Witherspoon," he sputtered, grabbing onto the side of the boat and grinning drippingly up at her startled, concerned face, "I wouldn't dream of asking you to help me back into the boat. We would all get drenched, and I couldn't allow that. I'll swim back and arrange for help. The two of you please sit very still and don't lift a finger to help yourselves, or you shall surely ruin your pretty dresses. Promise me."

"I won't move," Betz said, lifting her eyes to glare at Cherry. "I can't swim."

Cherry averted her eyes. Pouting, and on the verge of tears, she frowned down at the ripples in the water and wished with all her might that Adam had been invited to the picnic.

Seventeen

Mr. Teague Withdraws

Sunday, July 7, 1889

Adam's weekly trip into the city had taken two nights instead of one. Now he sat feeling the gentle rocking rhythm of the train speeding back toward Summersea, thinking of Betz. They had arranged to meet the evening before on the pavilion, and he had not been able to get back.

Sighing, he fixed his gaze on a woman in a flowered hat, several seats forward, and thought over the events since the afternoon of the picnic. While everyone else had been away lunching "on the green," he had had ample time to search nurse Tully's room. He'd found nothing he could use as evidence against either her or her employer.

With so little to go on, making no progress whatsoever in his investigation, Adam had decided to call in some help. That help was now sitting in that forward seat, wearing that amazingly ugly flowered hat. If she did not incite Charles Bonaventure into revealing his true bent, Adam would have to consider abandoning his efforts.

Now he hoped that events would soon begin to move along. As the train slowed, his assistant in the flowered hat turned to cast him a flirtatious glance. Then she debarked from the forward platform of the coach car.

Impatiently brushing lint from his sleeve, Adam wished he could race to Summersea and explain to Betz why he hadn't been able to meet her on the pavilion as they had planned. Surely she would understand.

But would she? Could he afford to reveal his true purpose at

Summersea, just when everything might begin coming together? As he left the coach from the rear platform, he gnashed his teeth. He had not wanted to get involved with anyone!

At the rear of the train two passengers were stepping down from a private car. Adam pretended to glance at his pocket watch while observing them, his face immobile. That was surely Mrs. Victoria Whitgift and her young blade of a grandson, followed by their retinue of servants. Well, things were certainly looking up!

Starting away, he remembered the day Betz and Cherry arrived. Betz had been so reserved he hadn't given her a second thought, and now all he wanted was to be with her. Something had to be done about this, he thought.

His head told him to give her up, to continue avoiding her as he had been since she'd started receiving so much attention from that Cape Helen man. His heart, however, drove him to remember her sweet urgent kisses, as fresh and exciting as a girl's yet deep and sensual. How could he go on resisting her when she filled his dreams, even though she now distracted him from his work?

He thought of begging a ride in the Whitgift carriage, but decided he needed to walk. He wasn't thinking clearly. An important investigation was at stake, one he'd taken on for his mother, so there was more than duty and justice hanging on what he accomplished. He was mending a relationship that had, at one time, been nearly dead.

What would Betz think now that he'd stood her up, he wondered again. And would Brandon Shane still be hanging around? Every time he had seen him, candybox or flowers in hand, Adam had reacted like a jealous schoolboy. Adam smiled now. He was remembering Thursday. He had cornered Betz after dinner and said with more feeling than he had wanted to, "I think we had better talk."

With a hurt, questioning expression, Betz had stared up into his face. It had been a whole two weeks since their romantic encounter on the beach. He had successfully avoided being alone with her all that time, too afraid of what he was feeling. When he looked into her eyes, he knew he was still hopelessly smitten. What had he done about it? He had gone into the city as usual, and he had gotten himself royally drunk.

"We can talk whenever you like, Adam," she had said softly. "You've seemed very busy and…rather distant…lately."

"I have to be in the city tomorrow, but I'd like to see you Saturday evening after I get back. Would you meet me at the pavilion? We can talk privately there."

"I could try." She had looked unsure.

Now he paused on the road to Summersea. The Whitgift carriage passed by without slowing to offer a ride. Betz surely must believe that he had, indeed, stood her up. She could not know that he had missed the train.

Then again, she might have decided not to meet him last night. If he had been able to get back on time, would he have had to wait all night alone?

Startled by a sick feeling in his stomach, he plodded on. Shane had paid attention to Betz as a true suitor should. What had Adam done to show Betz she was more special to him than any woman he had ever known? He had avoided her. He had scarcely acknowledged her presence at dinner each afternoon. He had instead hung about Nurse Tully, hoping to make her trust him enough to reveal her employer's plans. Betz must surely think him a cad. She could not know that since making love with her during the storm, he no longer even cared about his usual investigations in the city. A dozen men might be mimicking London's ripper, and he would still find himself drawn back to Summersea…to Betz.

Finally Adam vaulted over a low fence and sat beneath a tree for a while. Regardless if Betz had gone to the pavilion or not, he had to decide what to do about her.

If he kept his head a bit longer, he might get over her. There was no room for her in the kind of life he led. He loved her. There was no question of that. But he couldn't settle down. He had made his life choices long ago.

Supposing he allowed her to believe that he had purposely stood her up? To protect herself from further hurt, she would avoid him. In due time he would be on his way. She would forget him. It would be far better in the long run. For her, at least.

Burying his face in his hands, he tried to imagine the look on her face when he made it clear that what they had had so briefly on the beach during the storm was all there would ever be. He had not known he could feel such dread.

The Dowager Arrives

As usual, Felicia was on hand in the lobby to observe new arrivals. A wistful looking pretty woman in a flowered hat gave her name to the clerk as Mrs. Evalee Grayson of Charleston, offering "I'm here for a rest," but no further information. She did not have a reservation.

Mr. Bonaventure was sitting in the reception parlor, talking quietly to a gentleman from Maine. He paused in his conversation to stare at the woman. If Felicia had not known better; she would have thought he was appraising her with pleasure.

Since the scene with Randolph, Felicia had not been able to rekindle Charles's interest to her own satisfaction. He had been shy with her, and quite evasive. It was driving her mad.

But last evening after a rather fine poetry reading, she had been able to corner him out on the lawn and they had talked of his treatments. She had offered the small sum she'd been thinking about giving him.

"No, no, dear Felicia. I cannot accept it, not when you have… forgive me, fallen on hard times." Charles had looked terribly uncomfortable about discussing such a private matter.

"Nonsense, dear Charles. Anything you may have overheard between my husband and myself had no significance. I am still interested in your…welfare, and you must accept this as a token of my concern for you. I will make it my business to see that you receive your treatments."

And the dear man had finally, reluctantly, accepted her gift… and kissed her hand. Felicia watched him now, gazing at the new woman named Grayson. When he noticed her, he smiled ever so lovingly at Felicia.

Ah, her gift had endeared her to him! Men could be easily pleased sometimes, when they were wise enough to understand what a woman wanted. Elated, Felicia turned back toward the door. Then, seeing another carriage arrive, she felt the breath go out of her lungs.

The grand dame herself, seventy-five year old Victoria Ardelle Whitgift, known to most as "The Standard" of her social circle, was just stepping down from her Victoria carriage.

Summersea was beneath the Whitgift family, but Mrs. Whitgift bestowed her grand presence at a number of these lesser resorts throughout the summer. Her sole purpose for years had been to look over the debutantes for her very polished-looking grandson, Drew, now helping her solicitously to the drive.

It was often whispered that Victoria, for all her grand manners, was a real shrew when it came to the treatment of hotel staff. Felicia believed she stayed at various resorts because wherever she went she was quick to wear out her welcome.

If Felicia could learn one tiny juicy detail about Victoria for the scandal sheet, her position would be unassailable. She hastened to the veranda and extended her hand in greeting. Victoria Whitgift looked up at her with chilling superiority. Then she contemplated the steps with casual loathing.

"*Good* afternoon, my *dear* Mrs. Whitgift," Felicia said in her most solicitous manner.

"I am not your dear," Victoria intoned without looking up. Leaning on Drew's elbow, she gathered her heavy skirts and started up the steps. For all her indomitable vigor, Victoria was clearly tired.

Puffing, lifting her keen eyes, Mrs. Whitgift surveyed all around her with contempt. She stood taller than Felicia and most of the women staying at Summersea, and taller than some of the men. Her massive shoulders would have served a drayman proud. But she clung to Drew's arm as if ready to fall.

Her pearl gray satin gown was a massive work of art, covered over with intricate ruching and pleats so complicated not even those on Cordelia Ryburn's frocks could compare.

"The Standard" wore long matched pearls at midday, and her gloved wrists and fingers were encrusted with a dazzling array of diamonds no one could hope to rival south of New York.

But most noticeable about Victoria Whitgift were her heavy jowl, her mannish chin, her pursed disapproving mouth, and last but not least, her eyes. The irritation and contempt she seemed to feel for all she surveyed was concentrated in twin indigo beams. She fixed Felicia with a belligerent unwavering stare.

Felicia wilted, asking, "May I help you inside, Mrs. Whitgift?"

"If you're the hotel hostess, you're overdressed and impertinent. If you're a guest, get out of my way," the woman said, slashing Felicia's self-confidence.

Oh, to learn one shred of scandal about this woman…

"I'm Felicia Ellison. If I may speak on behalf of all the guests, we are honored by your arrival."

Victoria huffed an impatient sigh.

"Do I *know* you?"

"We met briefly at a party given by the late Alyce Connelly, a very dear and old friend of mine. It was in New York during the summer of…"

Giving off the aura of a gathering electrical storm, Mrs. Whitgift fished a long-handled lorgnette from her fringed reticule and regarded Felicia more closely through the twin lenses. She did not appear to be impressed.

"Humph. Alyce Connelly. She was my cousin twice removed. I don't recall you, or even your name."

Rigid, Felicia summoned the stupid little clerk who was quaking in his shoes nearby. Through the lorgnette, Victoria scrutinized each person unfortunate enough to be in the lobby at that moment.

"Who is that person in the wheeled chair?" Victoria asked, lifting her nose in the direction of the reception parlor.

"A very kind and intelligent invalid," Felicia said, "my dear friend, Charles Bonaventure."

"Would you like to sit down, Grandmother?" Drew asked,

sagging as his grandmother clung to his arm.

"Of course not. Do shut up, dear boy. I'm not ill."

Ignoring her, he searched the faces staring appreciatively up at him as if he was looking for someone. His lips curled into a faint smile of anticipation.

As Victoria's things were carried up the stairs, her army of servants followed in rank, from social secretary to personal maid and hairdresser. In a distracted tone, she said, "Inform Emma and Myrtle that I've arrived. I'll expect them in my suite at four."

She moved away; clinging ever more heavily to her grandson's elbow, she started up the stairs.

Had the woman left that order with her? Felicia wondered indignantly. She would never be reduced to delivering messages! Let her so-called friends fail to appear.

A Fine Catch

One of the stewards tapped at the door, and Cherry jumped to answer it. She took the offered note and whirled crying, "He's here!" dashing to Betz's side. "He wants to see me! Look! A note from Drew Whitgift himself. Won't Grandmother be pleased?"

Betz had been sitting, listless, in a chair by the balcony. Looking for a moment at Cherry, she couldn't focus her thoughts. Finally she read the note and frowned.

"How is it that young Mr. Whitgift is inviting you to join him at the concert tonight? Surely the invitation should come from his grandmother. You don't know him, do you?"

Cherry flushed an alarming shade of red which made Betz immediately suspicious and nodded, admitting, "At the Pratts' party."

"Not the young man who..."

Cherry gave another small nod, practically whispering, "He brought me back to the room, tipsy. But he meant no harm, and we had such a wonderful time! I wanted to tell you who he was, but...I was afraid."

Groaning, Betz laid the note aside. What could the young man be thinking of poor, reckless Cherry? Could he have any respect left for her? Had he any to begin with? Was Cherry safe in his company or was she at the young man's mercy?

"I know you're not feeling well, Betz, so you needn't come along to the concert tonight," Cherry said quickly, unable to meet Betz's eyes. Her face fell into a pretty pout, and she sank to the edge of the bed. "Our Mr. Teague has been perfectly horrid to you all week! It's not your fault that Mr. Shane came over every day. I did all I could to get rid of him."

Betz muttered, "You certainly did," and smiled.

"I just wish you had told Mr. Teague that your friendship with Mr. Shane didn't mean a thing to you." She shrugged. "You didn't like Mr. Shane very much, did you? You said he was just a distraction."

"He was a very nice young man, but no, I wasn't taken with him." She managed another weak smile. "And yet I'll miss him. He was terribly sorry when I refused to join him on his uncle's yacht."

"Well, you wouldn't have gone in any case, would you have? I certainly wouldn't have gone along to look after you." Cherry giggled. "I'll speak to Mr. Teague on your behalf—"

"You'll do no such thing!" Betz cried, seizing the girl's arm. "Promise me! It's better this way, truly. I-I'm trying to forget him. He asked me to meet him on the pavilion last night. Then he wasn't there. I went off again, leaving you alone in order to be with him. It's all too clear to me that I'm too involved emotionally, and he is not. For some reason he didn't wish to see me, after all. I-I just can't go on like this with my head in a muddle."

"You could ask him why he wasn't there!" Cherry stamped her foot.

"No, my duty lies with you, Cherry. Let's see about what you'll wear to the concert. And I shall certainly stay at your side all the night long. No more escapades for you. Especially not with Drew Whitgift."

Cherry was weary of having all her meals in the suite. Now she sat cross-legged on her bed, wondering what she might do to save

Betz's romance with the wonderful, illusive Mr. Teague.

Plucking a chocolate from one of Betz's six gift candy boxes, Cherry nibbled, eyes narrowed. Finally she slipped off the bed and discovered poor Betz, who had not been sleeping well for a week, asleep on her bed fully clothed.

Without a backward glance, Cherry tiptoed from the room and dashed down to the lobby, where she found the dull evening crowd milling about. The ladies were drifting toward the parlor, and the gentlemen were smoking and relaxing on the veranda.

Idle and bored, knowing that for a short time she would be free to slink about the corridors unseen, she ran up to the gloomy, stuffy third floor.

Tapping at Mr. Teague's door, Cherry waited breathlessly until finally the door opened a crack. He looked out and then smiled. He was in his shirtsleeves, with his suspenders down.

"Miss Ryburn, what brings you up here?"

"I need to talk to you."

Adam stepped into the hall and pulled the door closed behind him.

"What's wrong? You look upset. Is Miss Witherspoon all right?"

"You-you weren't…you didn't…my Miss Witherspoon is…" She began shaking. "She was only being polite to Mr. Shane! She didn't like him. Not at all. And now…why didn't you meet her like you said you would?"

"Cherry," he said softly, shushing her. "I don't think Miss Witherspoon would like it if she knew you were here talking to me like this. Can't you trust me? I had good reasons, and at the first opportunity I shall explain myself to Miss Witherspoon. I promise."

Cherry could not get over how embarrassed she was. It had been so much easier to switch about placecards and slip perfumed notes beneath his door. Facing this handsome wonderful man now, she realized she was toying with Miss Witherspoon's romance, and her own audacity frightened her.

"You do believe me, don't you, Cherry?" Mr. Teague whispered, smiling so nicely down at her.

Before she lost control and began to cry, Cherry darted away down the hall. She should have left well enough alone, she told herself in despair. She was a fool, and now Miss Witherspoon would hate her forever for interfering.

A Mysterious Woman

When Cherry disappeared down the stairs, Adam heaved a sigh of relief and slipped back into his room.

"An admirer?" Evalee asked, plucking idly at the flowers on the hat she held in her lap.

"I was just getting to that," he said, closing the door. "A problem has developed. I could use your advice..."

Evalee smiled, dimpling prettily. In her most practiced Southern accent she said, "I don't believe I have ever known you to need advice from anyone. I suppose I should have guessed that something was afoot when you failed to succumb to my charms last evening. You displayed quite a fondness for whiskey, however, and it has been my experience, honey, that when a man drinks that heavily, his world is toppling. Can I guess? Is it this Miss Witherspoon you were whispering about? Such a delicious name."

Adam nodded and then sat down.

"Then maybe you don't really need my help with this assignment. You're just muddled. Poor darling. Let Evalee rub your head—"

"No, I do need you," he chuckled. "I can't think of a way to get at this man who sits in a chair and stares out to sea all day. How can a man live that way by choice? It could go on all summer. I need you to dazzle him with your wealth. Felicia Ellison may be his next victim, but I can't get to him through her. She's...no use to me."

"Then dazzle him I will, and I'm charmed that you thought of me. You're ever so fortunate that I was available on such short notice, too. Now, darling, tell me of this female you find so distracting. Is she worthy of you? You and I have been friends a very long time. I have no intention of losing gracefully to some round-heeled hussy."

Adam let her rub the tension from his neck and the words began to flow—"It began when she looked into my eyes. It was as if she somehow connected with me in a way that no one else ever had. I began sensing something different about her…"

"Dear me," Evalee mused, her fingers kneading his neck. "This sounds most serious."

Drew was just coming out of his grandmother's suite. He was wearing a wonderful suit much like the one he'd worn at the Pratts' party. Racing back toward her own suite, Cherry crashed into him and nearly screamed with surprise.

"You're in a terrible hurry to meet me," he said, chuckling and giving her shoulders a quick hug. "I would have collected you—Are you all right, Cherry? What is it?"

"I can't bear this place another moment! I wish I could get away." She struggled to make sense of her thoughts. "I don't know how to behave. I do such stupid things!"

Drew captured her fists and held them gently, cautioning, "Try not to let Grandmother hear you. Go change into a proper dress and I'll collect you in a few minutes. We'll slip away during the concert and talk. I want you to tell me everything that has happened to you since we were last together."

She gazed up at him in wonder. Was this how Miss Witherspoon felt when she looked at Mr. Teague? Wanting to squeal with excitement, she said, low, "Oh, I'm sorry! I am ever so glad to see you again!"

"Hurry, before someone sees us," Drew whispered.

Standing on tiptoe to peck his cheek, Cherry giggled nervously and then darted away.

Miss Witherspoon Advances

A distinctly tense feeling prevailed among the Summersea guests collecting on the tennis lawn that evening.

At the far end of the lawn sat musicians who had arrived from Boston only an hour before. With paper lanterns aglow around the perimeter of the lawn, and small flickering footlights illuminating the makeshift stage, everything had a dreamlike glow.

But the tension increased as Victoria Whitgift plodded toward the first row of folding white chairs and selected one. Immediately, the hierarchy of guests assembled around her like courtiers: the old-money Reinholds and Fitches to her immediate right and left, Felicia rushing to take her place before Leon Howard could seat his smirking, bejeweled wife…and on down through the ranks until almost everyone was settled.

Betz had taken a chair to the side, feeling like an old washerwoman relegated to the shadows, so that she could observe Cherry's pale face as she approached the chairs on Drew's arm. Sitting with the girl seemed to be an impossibility now that she was with the young man. To try extracting Cherry would only cause a scene.

Now the girl clung to Drew's arm while he seemed undecided about where to seat her. At last they chose places in the last row. Betz was immediately on alert. They were going to slip away as soon as the darkness of the evening was complete! She stood, intending to take a place close enough to discourage any mischief.

Not seeing Adam anywhere, Betz was seized suddenly with a pang of longing. She wasn't sure she could remain. Someone might notice the sheen of tears in her eyes.

It was better this way, she reminded herself. She dared not love a man who would reveal so little about himself. And since his return from the city she had glimpsed him walking arm and arm with a woman in a flowered hat. And he had made no attempt to communicate with her.

Suddenly overwhelmed by her emotions, she marched back to the veranda as if she had forgotten something important. She mustn't be seen weeping!

The nurse was whispering something to Mr. Bonaventure, who was parked along the edge of the assembly. The woman in the flowered hat appeared at that moment, looked Betz up and down as if she knew her. Then she seated herself next to Mr. Bonaventure, asking, "Do you have any idea what they'll be playing this evening?" in a soft Southern accent.

Mr. Bonaventure scarcely had time to reply before the woman in the hat launched into a recital about her own health. "My dear daddy has done all he can to place me in health-giving surroundings. He spends so much on me, but one can't buy health, can one, Mr. Bonaventure?"

"My dear Mrs. Grayson," he replied in a tone bordering on devotion, "one certainly cannot. But one simply feels better to look at such a lovely person as yourself."

Betz decided against hiding in her suite and veered suddenly, skirting the veranda to walk alone in the dark along the south wing. She knew she was not behaving sensibly but couldn't help herself.

Everything had seemed so wonderful after the storm, she thought. She had been in love, hopelessly! The feeling was still so intense she sometimes felt as if she might burst. She had wanted so to talk with Adam, but he had been avoiding her, to the point of taking his meals in his room. Then he asked to meet her on the pavilion, and never came…

She had not wept then. She had kept herself rigidly detached and calm, certain that anything might have detained him. She had believed that the moment he returned he would explain. He had not.

Tears spilling, Betz made her way to the far side of the hotel. What was it about him she sensed? He seemed filled with purpose, his mind always churning behind his penetrating eyes, his body exuding restlessness and suppressed energy. He had not been open with information about his past, but not his present. What was he hiding?

Holding herself, she marched on around to the deserted, dark servants' lawn. In the outbuildings were the hushed sounds of laughing maids and stewards, and the chatter of the kitchen help. Now the concert had begun, and the lilting strains of a Beethoven concerto drifted on the cool night air.

Shivering, she paused, asking herself what she was doing and where she was going. There was really only one place she wanted to be. The desire to see Adam and talk to him was obliterating all her reason.

How might she see him? She could send a note, detain him at dinner the next day…engage in conversation while walking along the beach…

The very thought of waiting another moment to know if he had ever cared at all was too much to contemplate. She wanted to talk to him, and talk she would.

All thoughts of propriety vanished; she walked mindlessly back around to the veranda and stood in shadow staring up at the face of the hotel. While riding to Narragansett Adam had described the small circular window in his room. She saw it now, lit and tantalizing.

An irresistible force drew her up the steps and into the deserted lobby. She didn't think to look to see if Cherry and Drew were still in the last row. She had only one thought—Adam.

For almost five minutes Betz stood immobilized in the third floor corridor, her hand in midair, ready to rap Adam's door. Her reason screamed that she should reconsider. The consequences of her rash actions might be far-reaching indeed.

But the fear of ruining her own reputation by being seen going into Adam's room melted away when she thought of seeing his face, his eyes again. Failing to set a proper example for Cherry seemed unimportant in the face of losing Adam's affection.

She wanted his hands on her again. She wanted his lips. Cherry's needs seemed paltry in comparison. In any event, it did seem to be a hopeless effort to groom Cherry for acceptance by Summersea's uppercrust.

With effort, Betz broke through her fear of what Adam would say, and tapped softly. He answered almost at once, as if he'd been expecting her. Taken aback, she stood before him, tongue-tied, tears still on her cheeks.

"Oh, Betz…come in. What's wrong?" Looking concerned, he ushered her into his suffocating little room. He glanced out into the dark deserted corridor and then closed the door.

She saw his jacket draped over the back of a desk chair, a small notebook cluttered with scrawly writing open on the desk. The bed was rumpled, as if he had napped, as she had all afternoon. There was a supper tray on the floor by the nightstand.

"Have you talked to Cherry?" he asked, his eyes tight with concern.

Frowning, Betz shook her head.

"I left her at the concert with Drew Whitgift. Adam, I—"

He took her hands and drew her close. She resisted, afraid to allow herself to be cajoled when her hurt was surfacing so keenly. At length, he let her hands drop. He sank back onto the edge of his mattress, asking, "Would you sit beside me while I explain why I couldn't meet you?"

"You don't have to," she said, though she did need his explanation. Why did she smell roses?

When he said nothing more she edged closer, so hungry to sit next to him that she couldn't help it.

His silence grew so long that she feared at first he had no explanation. Then she expected him to explain gently that what passed between them during the storm was just a momentary coupling, that she should not take it so seriously.

He would tell her that he couldn't allow himself to become involved. He would have a number of convincing reasons…and she had thought of them all already.

"I got drunk," he said.

Torn from her thoughts, she blurted, "I beg your pardon?"

"I got drunk and missed the last train. I was struggling with myself about whether to…" He paused and sighed, gripping the edge of the mattress with wide tanned hands. His head was bowed as he gathered his thoughts. "I don't think you should stay here long."

"Why?" she asked softly, provocatively, and then was aghast. Was she there to seduce him? Suddenly she wanted to bolt.

He looked at her from the corner of his eye. His thoughts were turbulent accentuating the dark brown, making him appear quite dangerous and exciting.

Betz's breath caught. Suddenly she was melting with desire, casting aside all caution. She knew that her feelings were naked in her eyes.

When his arm stole around her shoulder, she knew the delicious satisfaction of feeling his touch. She yielded against him, tipping up her face. Just as he closed his eyes and leaned closer, she knew he was abandoning his caution as well. Whatever their reasons for wanting to remain free of one another, their need to get close was clearly far stronger.

His mouth closed over hers, filling her with a constellation of shimmering feelings that made her fall back on the bed. His hand closed on her breast as he kissed her, and he leaned hard against her. Their breathing was suddenly labored, their hearts racing with excitement.

When he stood and stripped off his shirt, her eyes widened in appreciation. His chest was broad and heavily covered with fine dark hair. He crossed to turn the key in the door lock, and then he turned back to her.

Betz drank in the rugged beauty of his body. Sitting up, suffocating from the heat in the room and her own desire, she began plucking at the buttons of her blouse. She wanted his eyes on her, she wanted again to feel her breasts against his chest.

When she had managed, with shaking hands, to uncover herself, he came to her quickly, scooping her into his arms in an embrace more fierce than tender.

"Betz!" he growled hungrily against her neck. "Oh, Betz!" He kissed her neck and throat, all the while crushing her against him. Then he loosened his hold to duck his head and suck at each of her nipples.

She could hardly stand as he helped her unfasten her skirt. Stepping out of it and her plain petticoat, she shivered with expectant delight as he swiftly drew down her lace-edged drawers, baring her to his eyes and hands.

Then he pushed her back, freed himself of his trousers and entered her swiftly, thrusting as if starving, and then unexpectedly became very still.

She could think only that he was inside her, filling her with passion, easing the need that had awakened when they first met. Never had the need been so intense, so demanding, so overpowering. She kept her eyes locked with his, drowning in the awareness that they were together like this, that he wanted her as much as she wanted him.

In the short moment that she watched his mouth open as he leaned over her for a kiss, she felt her passion building, enveloping her, consuming her. He moved in her, making the exquisite utterly unbearable, and then she was crying out, clutching at him, weeping and holding him as if she would never let him go.

She felt him tense against her, arch suddenly and crush her in his powerful embrace. He cried out, too, as if it had never been so keen for him. And then they lay still together panting, molded to one another, glistening, tingling, reeling.

How could she fight this? she wondered, still clinging to him. How could she go on without knowing she would have this with him forever?

Eighteen

Miss Witherspoon Withdraws

"Betz, please go before the concert is over," Adam said almost at once. "We can't be found like this." He looked down at her, his arms around her beautifully curving body, and he wanted nothing more than to fall asleep with her there.

"I came to talk," she said, her voice unsteady.

"And we will, but now isn't a good time. Please…"

He rolled away and lay on his side, watching her sit up as if unsure of how to move her body. Her shoulders were so pretty and rounded, her back slim, her waist whittled small by many years in a corset.

As she struggled to put on her clothes over her sweat-drenched skin, he long to tell her everything about himself, but the timing was very bad now. He listened intently to every sound, amazed to think that he could forget so much when holding Betz in his arms.

Then as he had feared, there was a tap at the door. Betz went rigid. She turned to him with wide, horrified eyes, whispering, "Who could it be?"

He waved her quiet and climbed noisily from the bed. Groaning and yawning as if he had been asleep, he called, "Who is it?" going to the door and unlocking it. Edging it open, he peeked out, his backside as tantalizing as anything Betz had ever imagined. "I can't see you just now." His tone was urgent and intimate, as if the person knew him well…and had been expected.

Betz remained frozen on the mattress, half dressed, her

thoughts racing to explain the caller.

When at last Adam closed and relocked the door, and turned to face her, his expression clearly showed that he knew an explanation was required. She knew somehow, though, that he was not going to explain.

She stood, adjusting her clothes. If she was lucky, she'd be able to get to her suite unnoticed, and explain later that she had been taken ill during the concert.

It seemed amazing, in the face of things, that she could suddenly feel so composed. But she seemed to be relying on instinct now. She had just lain with Adam, trusting all that she was to his passionate touch. If she had been a fool, then so be it. She chose to believe that those moments between them were true and real, and that there was a reason he couldn't tell her who had just tapped at his door.

"I'll be going now," she whispered. "And I'm not going to ask who was just here." She looked deeply into his eyes, savoring what might be their last moments together.

Her heart was screaming for her to trust him. Then in the blink of an eye, she crossed from being a frightened, inexperienced woman of thirty-five to being strong and mature, in the grip of something timeless.

"Adam, I love you," she said, knowing somehow that might have to be enough.

His guarded expression softened. His brows drew together in an expression of yearning. He wanted to tell her, she knew. She cupped his hard jaw and kissed his cheek.

"Thank you," she breathed close to his face. "You have given me so much. When you're ready to talk, I'll be waiting. Mr. Shane meant nothing to me. I was only trying not to love you, and I couldn't stop myself. I do love you, and I'm not sorry."

His mouth tightened. He cautioned her as he turned and unlocked the door, opening it and looking out to see if there was anyone nearby. Motioning her to slip out, he whispered, "Trust me, Betz." And oddly, she thought, she did.

Betz knew she could not love a man without that trust at the root of her love. She didn't know who he was, but she did know what he was—a man who had touched her as deeply as was possible. She would cling to that as long as she could, and caution be damned.

Drew pulled Cherry around to the stables, his hand fast and warm around hers. Giggling, she tripped after him, clutching up a handful of her voluminous skirts and feeling wickedly happy. Oh, if he could be as adventurous as this when his stuffy old grandmother was so near, what a delight he would always be!

"Sh-h-h," he said, creeping softly into the stable. "Here she is, my pride and joy." He led the way to a stall where a beautiful chestnut thoroughbred stood watching with soulful eyes. "We had her sent over only yesterday. Have you ever gone riding?" he whispered. He opened the door to the stall and coaxed his horse out into the throughway.

Cherry shook her head.

"I'm supposed to have lessons soon."

"Her name is Sheba," he said, "and she is as swift as the wind." He stroked the horse's flanks, whispering to her so sweetly, Cherry felt momentarily jealous. Then he cupped his hands so that Cherry could mount the mare.

Terrified by the height of the sleek, breathing animal between her thighs, Cherry thrilled when Drew flung himself up behind her and clutched her about her waist.

They rode quietly out of the stable and down toward the beach. Along the way they encountered a shadowy pair of waiters smoking among the trees. Cherry ducked her head, hoping not to be recognized. Moments later Drew made a clucking sound and the mare began to gallop down the beach.

It took all Cherry's strength to grip the mare with her knees and cling for life to her flying mane. Behind her Drew leaned close, holding her tightly, his breath hot on her neck. Her heart was pounding and she thought that if he stopped and tried to kiss her she might not try to stop him at all. When Drew turned Sheba into the waves, sending sprays of water up to dampen her gown, Cherry was breathless with excitement.

After a while he slowed the horse and walked her along the waves in the darkness. Cherry felt a thrill of anticipation.

And when Drew slipped off the horse from behind her and held up his arms to her, Cherry edged down into his embrace, her body tight against his.

"Now you must tell me everything about yourself," he whispered, his smile just visible in the darkness. "Leave nothing out."

Suddenly she was afraid. He wouldn't want her when he knew where she'd grown up. She would have to lie, but she couldn't remember the story her grandmother had invented for everyone at Summersea.

Squirming, she tried to get away from Drew, but he held her fast, his breathing becoming heavier, his hold tightening. When he bent to kiss her, she was overwhelmed by her body's response. This was nothing like what she'd felt with Teddy or Bo. She welcomed this!

Instantly, though she knew where the kissing was leading. She knew he wouldn't respect her if she gave in, and so she struggled still harder.

"My mother worked in a beer hall!" she blurted, determined to make him abandon his efforts to seduce her. "She met my father one night when he was drunk. That's what she told me later. I saw him occasionally when he came to town, but he never stayed...he never stayed." Her voice had dropped to a plaintive whimper because she was going to lose Drew, too. She would end up back at the streets she knew so well.

"My parents weren't married, and my mother, she had friends... and she tipped the jug too much, and didn't pay her bills. I've never been anywhere pretty like this. I'm nothing! I'm a nobody! I know my grandmother won't leave me her money because I don't deserve it. Look at me, here in the dark alone with you while my Miss Witherspoon is back at the hotel fretting over me. And she's never as cross with me as I deserve. I can't go on being an heiress, but now

I'm not the same anymore. I like my pretty gowns and my soft bed and the ribbons in my hair! I like having whatever I want…except… except that I'm afraid of the people. They know what I am, and I can't help it!"

She spun away from him, waving her fists and beginning to weep. Now he caught her and pulled her close again, whispering, "Cherry, Cherry, my sweet thank you for being just who you are. I would not have you any other way!"

Could this be true? she wondered, relaxing slightly.

That was when he kissed her and she knew that she was lost to him. She wanted him to kiss her forever.

An Unwanted Visitor

Monday, July 8, 1889

Betz had been in the suite when Cherry returned. Each of them was lost in their thoughts and unwilling to ask what the other had done that evening during the concert.

It was late morning. They were through with their usual walk along the beach. There was nothing left to do but wait for the mail and then dress for dinner at one o'clock.

It was quiet in the lobby at that hour, and still too early for the staff to lay tables in the dining room. The Hobble sisters were playing Twenty Questions with a number of other elderly ladies in the reception parlor. They all seemed rather quiet, though, and Betz felt watched.

The mail had already come, and Betz took it from their box—another letter from George, and one from her friend back home, Otila!

Cherry tugged at her sleeve.

"I see Mr. Teague coming up from the beach. Let's wait and talk to him."

Betz was not sure she trusted herself to look at Adam without her cheeks flaming, but she turned to greet him…and froze.

There was a man sitting in the parlor, off by himself near the windows where the brilliant morning sunlight cast him into a sinister silhouette.

How, after so long, could she recognize the shape of that head, that particular slant of the shoulders, the cocky air with which he sat, legs carelessly crossed? Was that man engraved in her memory?

The doors from the veranda opened. When she felt a touch on her shoulder, she flinched and whirled.

"Sorry I startled you…" Adam said, puzzled by her reaction.

She twisted back, still disbelieving. The man was approaching now, moving from shadow into a shaft of sunlight that glinted off his brushed blond head. She shuddered and took a step back.

Adam's keen dark eyes followed the direction of Betz's wide-eyed gaze, as he whispered, "Who is that man?"

She shuddered again. Urgently, she hissed, "Take Cherry… somewhere. Please!"

But Adam didn't move.

And Betz was forced to go on looking at a man she had hoped she would never see again—Gordon Carlyle, her former husband.

Gordie didn't even realize that it was she standing there, gaping. He had apparently risen to check the tall clock in the lobby. When he recognized her, a cocky grin stretched his lean face into familiar lines.

Betz was forced to take a stand. What did he want? How could she talk to him with all those old ladies looking on?

She was not even aware of Adam or Cherry as they retreated to observe in silence her strange performance. Betz was only aware of a knot in her chest, of her dry mouth and trembling hands.

"What are you doing here? How did you find me?" Her voice was hushed with panic.

Gordie looked Betz over with some secret amusement but eventually the expression wilted. His mouth tightened and he began to look disappointed.

"Staying in a place like this, I expected you to be wearing some fancy get-up. You look older, Betty. Out on your own working now,

I see. George throw you out?"

His words struck like his fists once had. She almost threw up her hands to protect herself. He would not dare to touch her here, and she had nothing left for him to steal.

"Why are you here? If you think I have any money, I don't. I have nothing."

"I can see that. The wages for a chaperone must be meager." He strolled to the front door and let that odd statement settle into silence before turning and regarding her with amusement once again. "Whatever you've done, my sweet, you can confess it to me. Someone is having you investigated, and the questions have reached as far as your devoted former husband."

"You must be mistaken." Betz wanted to pace, but found she couldn't move. She felt faint.

"I don't think so. In the past few days a wormy little man with jittery eyes has been by to ask me about you, about our marriage. He wanted to know if I'd seen you lately. Of course I lied and said we were the closest of friends."

Incredulous, she advanced a step.

"Why would you lie—Never mind. I don't care. I don't care! Just go away. If someone is investigating me, it's merely for references…"

But even as she summoned the reason from thin air, she knew that if Agatha had wanted to check her references, she would have done so long before hiring her. And besides, her references had not included Gordie. Never Gordie!

Gordie strolled closer, looking her up and down as if he still fancied that he owned her. He pulled out a hundred-dollar note and fluttered it before her face, saying with sneer, "He was willing to pay, so I gave the weasel good measure."

She whirled, afraid of what she might say or do. There was nothing to be done. That's when she saw Adam. A frown of concern on his face, he motioned for Cherry to stay put and then started toward Betz. After only a few steps, Cherry scampered after him, the expression on her face showing clearly that she had guessed who Betz was talking to.

"Introduce me to your caller," Adam said, his voice ringing with undeniable authority.

Betz couldn't remember ever hearing him sound more intimidating.

Gordie pocketed the hundred-dollar note and strolled toward the stairs.

"Thought I'd stay a night or two. It might be nice to know what you're up to now that you're on your own. If you get lonely later…" He grinned and wiggled his eyebrows. "Don't bother introducing me to your gentleman friend, Betty. I won't stay around long enough to make friends with him."

Clapping his hat on his head, Gordie gave Adam a cursory nod and started to climb the stairs.

"One moment," Adam said coldly. "Might I have a word?" His tone was courteous but commanding.

When Gordie didn't pause, Adam started up after him. Near the top of the stairs, he put his hand on Gordie's shoulder. Then he looked pointedly at Betz.

"Miss Witherspoon seems to be in some distress over your appearance at Summersea. State your business to me, sir."

Gordie stuck out his chin.

"I don't have to, unless you're the law."

"I've spent some time in places where law wasn't needed. Let's step outside." Adam smiled coldly.

"I've got no quarrel with you!" Gordie complained, glancing back at Betz. "Got him trained, I see."

Adam's hand closed on the fabric of Gordie's coat and he was hauled back to the foot of the stairs.

"I seem to have *forgotten* this man's name," he said to Betz.

"Gordon Carlyle," she whispered, sick with disgust over seeing him again. "My former husband…who robbed me of everything."

"Oh, yes," Adam said with a mocking air. "Mr. Carlyle just remembered an important engagement, elsewhere, didn't you, sir? Let me assist your memory…"

Gordie Carlyle was summarily hustled onto the veranda, and

after a few whispered words from Adam, he took off up the road, headed back toward the village.

"He's going now," Cherry exclaimed from the door. "I wonder what Mr. Teague said to him. Mr. Teague, what did you say? Did you say you'd thrash him? Did you? Oh, he did look like a fortune hunter and swindler. Mr. Teague, hurry. My Miss Witherspoon looks faint!"

Adam came quickly back to Betz and subtly supported her; they all started up the stairs. The ladies in the reception parlor turned back to whisper among themselves, and once again silence reigned in Summersea's lobby.

Betz began to sag as they reached the door to their suite. Adam assisted her inside and saw that she was settled safely in a chair by an open window.

"Are you going to be all right?" he asked, motioning for Cherry to fetch a fan.

Cherry snatched one from the bureau and began flapping it before Betz's ashen face.

Blinking, Betz looked down at the two letters clutched in her fist. Ignoring Adam's concerned look, completely unaware that it was highly improper for him to be in her suite even if the door was standing open, she tore into her friend's letter and read a few lines.

Dropping the letter to the floor, Betz looked ready to cry.

"She thinks someone is investigating me, too," Betz whispered. "Gordie came all this way to taunt me. Now Otila writes of a man asking questions..." She looked up into Adam's frowning brown eyes. "Why?"

Adam could only shrug.

"Summersea will find this entertaining gossip," she moaned bitterly.

"To hell with Summersea, Betz!"

But she could not feel that way. She had Cherry to think of... She looked up at the poor child looking so alarmed, and remembered how easily she had abandoned her duty, again, the night before.

Clutching her head, she shook it, wishing she could drive out her feelings for Adam as easily as he had marched Gordie out the door.

"Please, Adam, you had best leave us alone a while. I must try to think, and I cannot think when you're near."

His mouth tightened. Then he murmured with understanding, "If you need me…" Then quickly he was gone and Betz covered her eyes with her hand. "I never thought I'd have to see Gordie again. It makes me all the more determined to do a better job as your chaperone than I have."

Cherry just looked at her with wide eyes.

"It must've been awful for you."

Betz shuddered and drew a ragged breath.

"It was."

Nineteen

Miss Ryburn and Mr. Whitgift Find New Mischief

Tuesday, July 9, 1889

Setting out from the Huntington riding stables, Julia Lyon led the way on a stunning black thoroughbred. Behind her Cherry rode sidesaddle on a smaller roan mare. None too sure of herself, Betz brought up the rear on a chestnut gelding. They were on the trail to the spring, hoping to arrive late and miss the usual people from Summersea.

Julia had suggested the ride the day before during dinner, and Cherry had leapt at the chance. True to form now as they rode, Cherry was asking rather improperly, "Is it true that Mr. Macklin has been paying attention to you?"

Julia slowed her mount so that she could ride alongside Cherry. She smiled and answered, "Though it is none of your business, Cordelia dear, yes, it's true. He seems to have some interest in me. Do you realize you're gossiping when you ask such a thing?"

Cherry flushed.

"I don't like gossip, Mrs. Lyon."

"Nor do I. Because you're inexperienced, I know you meant no harm. I'm your friend, so I will forgive it if you ask impertinent questions."

Betz had been so busy trying to stay atop the horse she scarcely heard Julia. When she realized Cherry was being admonished, she said, alarmed, "I hope we're not annoying you. We both seem to have a lot to learn about social deportment."

"Nonsense. You're two of the most refreshing women I have

yet to meet. You, Betz, seem to be very preoccupied of late. Is everything all right with you?"

"I suppose not, but there doesn't seem to be much I can do about it."

"She's very taken with Mr. Teague," Cherry piped in.

"You mean the attractive gentleman from Chicago, whom Mrs. Ellison refers to as suspicious? Mrs. Ellison has a great deal to say about him, and everyone. You, for instance."

"I shouldn't wonder," Betz said. "I seem to be of great interest to a number of people."

"Mrs. Ellison claims you're a divorcée. She's convinced Cherry is an impostor, among other things…" She cleared her throat and smiled, indicating she didn't believe a word. "She claims you're both trying to swindle Agatha Ryburn out of her millions."

Betz nearly toppled headfirst off her horse. Steadying herself, she stammered, "Well, I am divorced, b-but did she say it in just that way?"

"Yes. We were all rather aghast. She seems to be a very troubled person."

"I hope Victoria Whitgift wasn't there to hear it."

"Well, I couldn't say what the woman has said to that old dragon, but she was quite vocal on the subject to the elderly sisters. I heard it all as they were pouring over the latest copy of that scandal sheet. Isn't it amusing what some people consider important?"

"At Summersea that scandal sheet seems all important," Betz sighed.

"Of course you realize it's all nonsense. Only those with skeletons to hide can possibly fear such exposure. A mature person admits improprieties if they occur. A wise person, of course, avoids such unpleasantness. That's what I find most tiresome about staying at resorts like Summersea. There's an unhealthy mix of social and moral tone. One cannot lose sight of what is important in life."

"No," Betz said without the slightest notion any longer of what was important. "Cherry," she said absently, "why not ride ahead? Julia and I will catch up to you in a moment."

"Are you going to talk about me?" Cherry said, looking rebellious.

Julia laughed. "My dear child, surely you are used to being discussed by adults. If Miss Witherspoon wishes to confide in me privately, you must show her the courtesy of making yourself scarce. As you yourself pointed out, your chaperone has concerns besides you."

Disgruntled, Cherry rode on ahead while Betz and Julia stopped riding and dismounted.

"Cherry is a quaint nickname," Julia said. "I like it." Her smile wilted, however, when she saw that Betz was truly troubled. "What is it, dear?"

"I'm utterly lost," she said, and began to talk at length about the problems she and Cherry had encountered since coming to Summersea. Then, remembering George's most recent letter, she added, "I can't imagine why, but someone seems to want me to fail at my job as chaperone. My former husband appears like a ghost from my past. Someone is questioning my friend Otila and my brother, as well. Now my brother writes to say that if I don't come home at once, he'll fetch me." She laughed softly. "He wouldn't dare. I'm a grown woman, after all."

"You're not, so long as you're under the influence of a male," Julia said matter-of-factly. "If it's any comfort to you, a number of extremely delicate secrets have found their way into the light of day, thanks to that scandal sheet. You may feel that you're the only one under attack, but from my vantage I see almost everyone at Summersea being exposed."

"Nevertheless, I must decide what to do. I mustn't fail with Cherry. I cannot bear the thought of returning to George's house. I will be forever lost there."

"As a widowed and independent woman who believes in freedom and suffrage for women, I know how repressed and childlike our female sex is. We must demand our rights as individuals. We must not let men dominate us. We have only one life to live. I sense there is still more troubling you."

"I long to trust you, Julia. I must be able to talk and know that my words won't be printed next week."

"I'll most likely leave at week's end. You shall not see me again. Sometimes it's easier to talk to a stranger. In any case, I would not betray your confidence. I am concerned about you. You're like I was many years ago."

"I'm thinking of taking Cherry away. My feelings for Mr. Teague are jeopardizing her future, because someone will surely discover… that we have been lovers. I can't be responsible for her ruin."

"I see. And I can tell by the torment in your eyes that you cannot bring yourself to leave this Mr. Teague. Such a dilemma for you, dear. If you can go, when will you?"

"I'll need to contact Agatha's housekeeper to see if the house can be opened when she's abroad. It seems the only way for me to fulfill my obligation to Cherry."

"It's not my place to advise you, Betz, but…is it wise to teach Cherry that the only victory for a girl is in defeat? If your brother comes for you, you need only refuse to obey him. Agatha Dunwitty pays you, after all, not he. It is the typical female reaction to run and hide. Can we not learn to stand strong? You must surely be a fine person for Lady Ryburn to have hired you. Do you want Cherry to run and hide all the rest of her days? Teach her strength."

Victory by defeat, Betz thought, shivering. Though she felt fear, she murmured thoughtfully, "The easy way to avoid unpleasantness is apparently the cowardly way. If we want to succeed, we must try a bit harder."

"Bravo!" Julia said, and mounted her horse. "Let's press on now before Cherry gets lost. To be an independent woman requires traveling a road never traveled before. It can be frightening, but freedom is the reward. And…" she smiled with a knowing light in her eye, "there is much along the way that those too afraid to travel with us will never experience."

Betz sensed that Julia was talking about love, and suddenly she smiled. Mounting her horse, she said, "Thank you for your kind ear. I need a friend, and I'm sorry you'll soon be leaving. I would have liked to know you better."

"Well, who's to say we won't meet again later, by chance or because we want to? We all have much to learn from one another."

Behind them came the muffled thunder of hoofbeats and they both turned. Drew Whitgift galloped past on his thoroughbred, waving his cap and shouting, "I found you!" Reining, he looked for Cherry. Then he plunged on. "Hello, Cherry! Hello!"

"Do I gather by your alarmed expression that we had better hurry after the girl?" Julia said.

Betz nodded and urged her horse forward.

Cherry wished she had not been sent on ahead, because she was not sure which way to go. Now, rounding a turn, she saw the spring and all the ladies from Summersea sitting on the benches by the rocks, sipping spring water from little tin cups.

The children were restless, wanting to start back. As always, the gossip bubbled as freely as the water.

Not sure how to dismount, Cherry attempted to make her horse walk in a circle. Marietta Howard kept looking up at her and smirking.

Victoria Whitgift lifted her long-handled lorgnette. Regarding Cherry, she asked loftily, "Who is that girl on the horse?"

Someone whispered Cherry's name.

"Come over here where I can have a closer look at you," Victoria commanded. "I hear far more about you than your slight stature warrants."

Marietta giggled.

Teeth together, Cherry urged the horse closer to the ladies on the benches, enduring their scrutinizing stares. Her black velvet riding costume was spanking new and of the latest European style. Her hair was smoothed back into a chignon and topped by a velvet riding hat with a trailing white veil. Cherry wondered if the squinting woman would notice all this through her funny-looking eyeglasses.

"How old are you?"

"Fifteen," Cherry said, adding, "ma'am."

"And I've never seen nor heard of you before, not in any social circle?"

"No, ma'am."

"There is much speculation on the subject of your mother. Tell us. Who was she?"

"Peggy Norbit," Cherry said, beginning to tremble. She wanted to bolt, but loathed giving them all the satisfaction, especially keen-eyed Felicia who sat nearby.

"I've never heard of her."

Suddenly reckless, Cherry blurted, "She never heard of you, either." And she turned the horse sharply and started away, ignoring Marietta's grin. As added show of her feelings, Cherry stuck out her tongue, angrily heeling her mount. He bolted, and she could barely hang on as he raced away.

At that moment Drew came riding into the clearing. Seeing that Cherry was being carried off, he started after her.

"Drew, you're stirring up dust!" his grandmother said, coughing with annoyance. "Oh, I knew it was a bad idea to come here. The moment that headstrong boy is back, I shall take him away. Summersea holds no further interest for us this season." Ignoring her, Drew spurred his mount.

Felicia straightened, exclaiming with alarm, "You're not thinking of leaving us!"

"Indeed I am, my dear Mrs. Ellison. I will not allow my grandson to be polluted by young temptresses. He must be protected from his natural urges. Drew, Drew!" she called, as Drew disappeared down the path leading back to Summersea.

"My dear Mrs. Whitgift," Felicia began plaintively, "I had expected to have you as my very honored guest at the Summer's End Ball!"

"Then you had best make hasty arrangement for something else, because I see that I have already stayed too long at Summersea."

Cherry's horse had raced wildly as far as the turn in the road where the hotel wagon waited and she was barely able to keep her seat. She was very grateful when Drew came alongside her and seized the reins, steadying her nervous mount.

"Did you hear, Cherry?" he said, flushed and breathless. "My grandmother thinks she can keep us apart by taking me away."

"But she mustn't!"

"Fear not, fair damsel. For all her indomitable power, Grandmother does dote on me. I'll convince her to stay simply because I want to. And you are very eligible, in spite of everything. Grandmother is a practical person. An alliance with your grandmother's wealth could not be unwelcome."

Was he talking about marriage? Cherry began to feel faint. She certainly wasn't sure about that, not yet anyway. But the thought of being parted from him when they had only just found one another made her blurt, "I think my Miss Witherspoon is thinking of taking me away, too!"

"Then we must outsmart them." Drew laughed outrageously, helping to rein her horse as they rode on toward the beach. "We'll disappear all afternoon and not return until after dark. By then Grandmother will have forgotten all about leaving and will be ordering the champagne for our wedding."

"Oh, Drew," Cherry giggled. "You don't mean it."

"My sweet, I know my way around these old peahens. What do you say to an afternoon of bathing in the surf? Are you game?"

Cherry felt afraid, but when she looked into Drew's grinning face she was ready to do anything for him. She tore off her hat then flung it high and away, shouting, "Yes, yes!"

Twenty

Mr. Teague's Uneasy Sleep

Adam lay in a drenching sweat, tossing and turning as a dream surged through his mind. He was riding shotgun on the Wells Fargo stage, the rifle cradled in his lap. The rutted road ahead was steep and muddy. And out of the pouring rain rode the masked highwaymen. He lifted the rifle and aimed, bringing down the bandit to the left. Always, in the dream, there seemed to be many of them. In fact, there had been only four.

Beside him had been his best friend, Joe Ranger, a leather-faced old coot who had joked and cussed his way into Adam's heart back when he was a rangy, idealistic youth sowing his wild oats in the west.

In the dream, Joe's laugh was big and loud. So was his shout of pain when the bandit in the glossy rain slicker fired, blasting open his chest.

Adam never experienced the dream in the way the real events happened. He was just pulling off a second shot when Joe got killed. He always hoped in the dream that slowing everything down would enable him to bring down Joe's killer before Joe took the slug. Sometimes, too, Adam tried with all his might to get in front of Joe to protect him.

But always Joe died. Always Adam could do nothing to change what happened.

The grief was always overwhelming, leaving him shouting out his rage over losing someone so close and dear. Then he would turn to his friend, slumped dead against his shoulder, and push back the hat from his face. Instead of Joe's leathery old face, however, Adam always saw a faceless stranger lolling on his arm.

Soon after he began to have the dream, Adam had realized who this faceless stranger was. He was his father, shot dead long before he was born.

Now Adam bolted upright on the bed, in panic. Without comprehending, he heard knocking at his door.

He hated the dream. It came to him when he was troubled, or facing a dangerous situation. But nothing like that was going on here at Summersea, he reminded himself. Wiping his drenched brow, he heaved a ragged sigh.

The knock came again, soft and urgent. He swung his legs over the edge of the hard mattress, trying to recall the day and time. It seemed to be early afternoon, from the brightness of the light falling through the circular window.

Stumbling to the door, he peeked out. Evalee pressed in and closed the door, saying impatiently, "I waited for you at dinner."

"Did I miss it?" he asked, raking back his hair. His head was pounding now from his unplanned nap. He couldn't think clearly.

"While you were sleeping, Adam, a lot has been going on. All the talk has been about that young girl, Cordelia, riding away with the old dowager's grandson. Your Miss Witherspoon is distraught."

"There's trouble? Maybe I should go to her."

"You would do well to concentrate on the business at hand. If you had been there you would have heard that the old Whitgift woman is thinking of leaving, and Felicia Ellison is running around like a chicken with a wrung neck, trying to put together a grand ball for this Friday. This Friday, Adam! I don't think that leaves us much time. If I know our quarry, he'll strike and be gone. I don't believe he's going for the monetary gift this time, not from Ellison and not from me. He's just not responding. I think he's tired of this place. You're right. He's bored."

Mouth tight, Adam frowned at her. He felt the power of his purpose and energy returning. Crossing to his washstand, he soaked his head and then combed back his hair.

"So where is everyone now? Dinner's done, I take it."

"Witherspoon is wandering around outside waiting for the girl to come back. Most of the old hens are lined up on the veranda to watch the show. That bastard Howard started following me around and tried for another kiss. I gave him something to think about. He's probably doubled over in his suite right now."

Adam chuckled and asked, "And Bonaventure?"

"Wheeled away by our very attentive Mrs. Ellison. They were talking about some very expensive-sounding spas in France."

Meeting her gaze, Adam raised his brows and commented, "Interesting."

"It's good to see that you're finally awake. All I can say, Adam, is that this place is dreary. No wonder you wanted to move things along."

Grinning, Adam pulled up his suspenders and fastened his cuffs.

"Let me button you collar on straight, darling," she said in a teasing tone. "Then I must be going. I hear that a mesmerist is giving a lecture and demonstration in the parlor tonight. I think I'll ask to speak to my dear departed grandmama and ask her where she left the family diamonds. If that doesn't do the trick with Bonaventure, I think I'll take my leave. You don't pay me enough to stay, dear. There, you look positively dashing."

He kissed her forehead and sent her out into the corridor with a pat on her bustle. What was Cherry up to now, he wondered. Then he dismissed that minor concern from his mind and grabbed his jacket.

Coming down from the third floor to the second floor landing Adam heard the clatter and bump of the wheel chair being dragged up from the lobby. Felicia called in a falsetto down to Bonaventure, who laboriously made his way up each step as if it might be his last.

From the corner, Adam watched Bonaventure gain the top of the stairs, and teeter long enough to make Felicia throw her arms around him. Then together they got his slim body settled into the chair once again. Adam shook his head wryly. In spite of this convincing sham, Bonaventure was no invalid.

Ducking back out of the way, and then following at a safe distance, Adam chuckled softly to himself as Felicia struggled to push Bonaventure along the hall and into his room. She went in after him and closed the door. Adam slipped up quickly and pressed his ear to the door panel.

"You mustn't argue with me, dear Charles. I insist that you accept my gift and have the treatments you require. If the finest doctor is in France, then I shall take you there myself. We can leave as soon as the ball is over, if you like."

"Of course, dear. If it pleases you. Could you go now, dear? I'm terribly tired."

There was a pause. Adam wondered, amazed, if they were kissing. Then he supposed that she was helping him onto the bed.

"Are you sure we can leave by Saturday?" Bonaventure asked in a weak voice.

"But surely, dear. I'll have my attorney bring the funds and we shall be off, away from this miserable place. Oh, we're going to have such a grand time. And you, my dear Charles, will have far more than you have ever dared to dream. I will give you your last gift with all of my heart, and then miraculously you shall see for yourself that it is not to be the last, but the first of…but I can see you're terribly weary. I'll go now. Rest. Rest, dear, dear Charles. We're going to be so terribly happy in France."

Adam slipped quickly to the nearby servants' stairwell. He managed to be out of sight as Felicia, humming huskily, glided from Bonaventure's room.

Then she began to march, muttering a list of things to do. Becoming more excited, she called, "Steward, steward, you there! Fetch the majordomo, if you will. I have many plans for Friday, and there's not much time. Do hurry!"

Adam returned to the hall, his mind racing with all he, too, would need to do by Friday.

Mr. Woodley Departs

Betz was beside herself. Cherry had not come back. She and Julia had been forced to return the horses to the Huntington's stables without knowing where Drew and Cherry had gone.

They had missed dinner at one. Now it was dusk, and everyone was lined up on the veranda, waiting and watching the sky darken along with Cherry's reputation. Betz dared not pace, for she didn't want anyone to realize she was concerned. If she appeared to think that Cherry's behavior was all right, perhaps the ladies would assume that Agatha had given her blessing.

At any rate, Betz wished she could make them all think that!

As Cherry's chaperone, she was supposed to be livid with disapproval, but she couldn't pretend that she shared the socialites' rigid views.

She was torn now, more so than ever. She wanted to treat Cherry with love and concern, and guide her gently toward a rewarding future. To do that it seemed best to overlook her innocent rebellions and her rash behavior.

To please those in power at Summersea, however, she should condemn Cherry for her every flight of fancy. She should be sending scathing reports to Agatha, threatening dire consequences. And perhaps she should even be keeping the girl under lock and key.

Yet her heart wasn't in punishment and threats. She herself was longing to break free of the suffocating restrictions reigning at Summersea.

She had no business being responsible for the reputation of an heiress. Cherry was being ruined beneath her very nose, and she couldn't stop it. She did not believe in the prevailing moral code that said a young girl could not ride astride, could not bathe in the sea, could not go riding or walking alone with a young gentleman—could not, could not, could not!

It was the same as saying the young girl could not live.

Cherry was young and beautifully vibrant. Society would snuff out her vitality, given half a chance. Could Betz stand to watch the sparkle leave Cherry's eyes if the girl accepted the constraints of high society? Could she be a party to the crushing of the girl's boundless spirit?

Betz knew in her own sinking heart how inextricably a woman could be bound by convention. A respectable unmarried woman had to sit home under the protection of a male relative.

She hid her fists in her skirts. No! She would not settle for that!

She moved toward the steps to head out onto the beach where she wouldn't have to listen to the nerve-wracking creak of the rockers and the hushed voices of Emma, Gettie, Myrtle, Millie and the insufferable Victoria.

Evalee Grayson came out onto the veranda and looked around. Looking the elegant Southern belle in a lovely peach-colored India silk walking costume, she murmured polite nothings to the ladies and started down for the lawn. Betz hated her suddenly, because Adam had been paying her so much attention.

As Mrs. Grayson drifted away, the matrons resumed their inexhaustible speculation about her, Millie Hobble concluding that the poor woman must be recovering from a heartbreaking love affair.

Seconds later a half dozen stewards filed out the door and down the steps to await a hotel wagon just arriving from the stables in the rear. Each steward carried a paper-encased canvas and stacked it in the wagon bed. Mr. Woodley emerged from inside the hotel, polishing his spectacles. The stewards went back inside to fetch the easel and his carpetbag.

"You're not leaving," Betz found herself saying.

"Yes, dear. You've been a pleasure to know." He put on his spectacles and then regarded her with his broken-toothed smile. "I hear there's mischief afoot."

"I'm afraid so. Cherry has run off, and this time everyone saw her do it. This makes us look bad indeed."

He took her hand and shook it. He smiled warmly and said softly, closing his other hand over hers and giving her a reassuring squeeze, "Don't you see, dear, none of it matters, because they don't like you or Cherry anyway. You, my fair Miss Witherspoon, completely surpass them in beauty and intelligence. You are all they long to be."

Overcome with surprise, almost weeping, Betz exclaimed, "Why, Mr. Woodley, how kind of you!"

"Not kind, dear. Truthful. I paint what I see. And you I can see very clearly, as a free spirit about to cast off the chains. Go with your heart, dear. Life is precious and short. Don't waste a breath of it. What does their opinion matter, in any case? Will you be a better woman or friend because they nod their heads and say well done?"

"I-I don't know," Betz stammered.

"God gave you a mind, dear. He gave them mush. Think, dear. Be what you are, like me." He grinned broadly, his broken tooth revealed like a bit of defiance. "I don't give a damn about anyone. Consequently, I'm very happy indeed. Now, I shall be happier because I've found an excuse to move on. Think, dear. Your keen mind is what I liked about you. And so, good day."

He strode away, leaving Betz stunned. He simply didn't understand! He was a man, after all. Men were allowed eccentricity. She and Cherry were women, subject to…

Hurrying out onto the veranda as if he had been following Mr. Woodley, Adam called, "Sir, wait!" He bounded down the stairs and shook the old artist's hand enthusiastically.

Betz was so lost in thought she didn't hear what they said to one another, but it was clear that Adam appeared to be losing a friend he valued.

At length, Mr. Woodley climbed onto the wagon seat and rode away, his lenses flashing in the afternoon sunlight. Adam stood for some minutes with his hands in his pockets.

Betz let herself study him, surprised to feel afresh her attraction to him. She yearned for him to turn and see her standing there.

As quickly as she felt that, she turned away. She must try to forget him. She had to. Whatever they had known in his room during the concert was gone now. She had agreed to trust, and it had come to nothing. She would not be toyed with, lured into another tryst which would tempt her to abandon all that she had ever been brought up to believe.

Nevertheless, she couldn't stop herself from turning back for another brief look at him. A bolt of surprise went through her. He was staring directly at her. Was he, too, trying to remind himself that they did not belong together?

"Adam," she heard herself say, and a wash of horror went through her. "M-Mr. Teague, h-have you seen Che—Cordelia this afternoon?" Her voice was tremulous and weak. She needn't have spoken, she told herself, but she was so very alarmed for Cherry.

He approached the veranda where she stood at the railing, saying softly, "No, I haven't, but I'll watch for her. I'm sure she's safe." His voice was low and comforting even at that distance.

"Perhaps she's safe with Drew," Betz whispered. "But she won't be here, when she gets back. My efforts are in a shambles—"

"Betz," he interrupted, "I can't talk. I hear there's a lecture tonight. We'll talk then." His expression was a mixture of distraction and pleading. He wanted her to understand.

She didn't. She couldn't! He was rebuffing her in public. Turning away now and scanning the lawn, he made no effort to disguise the fact that he sought the Grayson woman. The moment he spied her out on the beach he started after her, at a trot, hailing her as soon as his shoes sank into the sand.

Betz steadied herself. She loved him desperately. Seeing him approaching the Grayson woman tore at her heart. Yet she could not reveal a shred of her feelings to the hungry-eyed gossips rocking nearby.

"He has altogether too much interest in women," Betz heard Gettie mutter.

She forced herself not to turn and scald the woman with well-earned insults.

"Dear Miss Witherspoon," Felicia said just behind Betz, causing Betz to start. "You really mustn't encourage that man."

Betz whirled, scathing words on the tip of her tongue. She managed to say only, "I-I beg your pardon?"

Felicia drew Betz away toward the far end of the veranda where they had a scrap of privacy, whispering, "I have it on very good authority that our Mr. Teague is not at all what he seems."

"I see," Betz said, eyes narrowing. "How is it you know this?"

"Oh, it's important for someone like myself to look into these things. I can assure you that from what I have heard, there is no such man as Adam Teague known to anyone of importance in Chicago. Or anywhere, for that matter. The man does not exist."

Hardly able to contain herself, Betz demanded, "Where did you hear this?"

"Goodness, I have friends all over, and they've assured me that Adam—"

Betz bit her lips together. Willing herself to keep back the words threatening to burst forth, she asked, "What do your friends say about me, or Cordelia?"

Felicia's smile turned to ice.

"Can you be challenging my information?"

"I'd just like to know where you get it all."

"You're quite impertinent for a hired person of no rank."

"Don't throw that my face, Felicia. I'm as good as anyone here, and so is Cordelia. You'd do anything to make me forget what happened here last month, when you walked into the sea. But I won't forget. Your friends are the ones who talk behind your back about you. Everything is backwards here! I-I…"

With a shudder of horror, Betz realized that she had lost her head. Stiffening, she closed her mouth and turned away.

"I dare say you've insulted me for the last time," Felicia breathed.

"If I insulted you by saving your life, I am truly sorry. If you might accept a word of advice from an 'inferior', Felicia, you might think to have Mr. Bonaventure investigated. If you think no one has noticed your inordinate interest in him, you are only fooling yourself. He is after your money, I'll wager, and I seem to be the only one who cares."

Felicia lifted her head and moved away, her rigid smile cemented into place.

Betz pitied the woman, and longed suddenly to be as far from

Summersea as she might get. But wherever she went she would find women like Felicia. She felt herself drowning, and there was no one to talk her back from the sea.

She fixed her gaze at last on the bay where the water looked milky gray and serene. Her mind stopped whirling. She thought of Mr. Woodley's warm smile and Adam's pleading eyes. There was nothing left to do but wait for Cherry's return. Whether or not they were ostracized from now on, Betz still had to look after Cherry.

Millie Hobble stood from her chair. Tottering, her voice petulant, she whined, "I don't care! I just don't, sister. I-I'm overheated, and I want to go inside."

Gettie called for a steward to escort Millie up to their rooms, but Millie appeared to be having one of her unpredictable fits of pique and resisted.

"I'll go myself." And, looking frail and bent, she went inside.

Betz wondered if the vultures would sit and rock until Cherry came back…*if* she came back. Her stomach knotted. What might be going on between Cherry and Drew?

Miss Hobble Finds Mischief

Millie pulled herself up the stairs, step by step. She didn't know why she felt so upset with her sister. Sometimes it was so distressing to be around Gettie.

What difference did it make to any of them if the little heiress had ruined herself? It wasn't anyone's business, but Gettie seemed to think that everything was her business, and that she had a sworn duty to keep up the standards of propriety.

Standing a moment at the top of the landing, Millie wondered what she was doing there. Oh, yes—she hadn't wanted to sit all afternoon in the heat like a hanging judge, waiting for a foolish girl and a very charming young man to come back to a veranda of frowns.

Sister Gettie had once been rather impetuous, but the young

blade who had jilted her had left her with a heart of ice. Millie had never been so fortunate as to know love, but she imagined that if she had been so blessed she would have been enriched, not embittered, by the experience.

She made her way down the corridor, unsure of which direction to take and that made her a bit peevish. Sometimes she felt so like an elderly child that she wanted to throw a tantrum.

Oh, well, she would find her room eventually. And even if she didn't, someone would come along to direct her to it. Gettie wasn't going to order her about all the time. No, indeed!

Pausing, she decided she truly didn't know where her room had gone off to, so she opened the next door she saw.

It was rather startling to discover that this door opened onto a dark service closet where linens were kept on rows of shelves.

Standing right in the middle of the closet with his suspenders and drawers down was a tall man. His thinning hair was all mussed.

Attached to him in the most peculiar contortion was a young girl with her skirts bunched about her waist, and her…her limbs… completely naked.

Staring open-mouthed at Millie, they grew very red-faced. Millie wanted to beg their pardon, but it was ever so disconcerting the way the two were standing together. The girl seemed to be trying to climb up the man, for her leg was curled around his hip, and he was crouched in a very peculiar way as if trying to get under her.

"What are you *doing,* Mr. Macklin?" Millie asked, trying to understand.

Marietta began pushing at Mr. Macklin and trying to get her skirts down. She was unbuttoned, too, her pert young breasts popping out from the front of her bodice. When they uncoupled, Millie saw for a brief moment the very first erection of her sheltered sixty-one years.

"Would you just close the door?" Marietta snapped.

Mr. Macklin turned away and did something hastily to the front of his clothes. Then he bolted past Millie and raced down the stairs. The screen door to the veranda slapped and someone called to him, but apparently he just kept on running.

Marietta snatched up something from the floor of the closet. Then glaring at Millie, she hissed, "If you say one word about this to my father, I'll…"

Millie, in a full swoon, collapsed in a powdery heap.

Twenty-One

Miss Ryburn and Mr. Whitgift Court Disaster

As the wind shifted, Cherry felt goose bumps all over her skin. Laughing and shivering, she splashed one last time out into the bay and let the next wave knock her face first into the salty water.

When she came up sputtering and giggling, knowing that their time was growing short, Drew was wading closer in his soaked, skin-tight silk shirt and long drawers. She could see the springy dark curls of his pubic hair and the soft tantalizing curve of his manhood outlined by the wet fabric.

Looking down at herself, she could see her breasts pressing eagerly against her dripping camisole. She ducked down into the water, suddenly aware that all afternoon they had been playing at a dangerous game, as if the game would never end.

Now as the cool night was approaching, she knew that somehow they must face what they had kindled in one another. If she succumbed, she might become pregnant and destroy her chances to become part of the life her grandmother wanted for her.

If she denied Drew he might walk from her forever. There might never be another young man like him to love her.

"Are you ready to dry off?" he asked, reaching out to her.

She took his hand and let him draw her to the beach, squealing, "Oh, it's too cold!" She was frightened by the heat in his eyes as he gazed at her body, so clearly revealed by her wet underthings.

"I'll build a fire," he said, going off to gather dry grass and driftwood.

She had been clever enough to remove her dress and petticoats so they wouldn't get ruined by the water, but now she didn't know whether to wait for her underthings to dry on her body or take them off and put on her dress without them. What she would do about her hair she didn't know.

When the fire was snapping in the breeze, Drew pulled her down beside him on the sand and enveloped her in his warm arms. For a time she relaxed against him, thinking that never again would she feel so close to someone.

But as he turned her face and leaned close to kiss her, she felt a rush of emotion too intense to bear, and whispered, "Oh, Drew, I'm afraid!" She began to weep.

"You can't be afraid when you're near me," he whispered, exploring her lips with his.

"What will become of us when we go back? Surely you don't think your grandmother will let us get married after this? I-I can't believe it will happen like that!"

"But it must, because we've been alone all day, like this, and now…" He eased her back against the sand and leaned against her, partly covering her body with his.

She tried to surrender to the powerful urgency of her feelings, but her terror was too great. He might love her with all his heart, but if she became pregnant and his grandmother or parents prevented their marriage…

"Drew, if you care about me, you must understand. I just can't!" she whispered, holding him back with both her trembling hands. "I think we'd better go back to Summersea and what damage we've done. I feel too guilty about this, and I don't want guilt to spoil my happiness with you."

"I will marry you, Cherry," he whispered, his voice convincingly sincere. "No one can stop me."

"You just don't know," she said softly, squirming from his hold. Standing at last, she put her dress on, over her damp, sandy underthings. "You've never lost anything in your life. From the day you were born, your family has given all you asked for."

"And they will let me have you," he said grinning in the fading dusk. Half his face was illuminated by the snapping beach fire, the other half was already in dark shadow.

"But first you want me, and I don't believe they'll let you marry me afterwards. I can't take that chance."

Drew's smile wilted. Propped on one elbow, he watched her struggle into her gown. His expression turned thoughtful. Finally he sat up looking a bit dejected, sitting cross-legged on the sand like a bewildered young boy.

Strangely, Cherry felt very old. Her impetuous act of the morning was now ashes in her mouth. Hungry and frightened, she fastened the last hook on her snug bodice and thought how everything would look to all the snoops at Summersea.

They would all believe that Drew had made love to her. She was compromised whether she let him love her or not. Her reputation was gone, and she felt a great sense of regret. If only she had tried a bit harder to be a quality person…

Drew stood and went in search of his trousers and shirt. Sheba was nibbling beach grass high on the beach, and now it was dark and almost sinister as the waves surged against the sand, crashing harder and harder as clouds gathered on the horizon.

When he was dressed, he took her hand and led her to his horse. Helping her up onto the saddle, he stood several minutes frowning at the bay.

"I want to marry you anyway, Cherry," he said. "I wasn't trying to trick you with empty promises."

She wanted to assure him that she hadn't thought that, but it would have been a lie. Suddenly she was awash with love for him, swelling inside to think that he was not the selfish, spoiled rich young man she imagined, but a gentleman.

He swung up behind her and circled her body with his arms, saying softly, "I will prove my sincerity," clucking to the horse and leading hers by the reins.

But he already had, she thought.

A Lecture on the Powers of Truth

Dr. Melchesidec Chamless had a full beard streaked with white, and lank iron gray hair that fell in broad strands across his brow. He had a biting way of looking at a person, and as he entered the lobby, the first person he saw was Felicia Ellison.

"How good of you to join us this evening," Felicia said, noting that the stewards were lighting the parlor lamps. Some hotel guests already finished with supper were taking seats in preparation for the lecture. "Have you taken supper, Doctor?"

"Indeed, I have, madam. If you will be so good as to show me to a small quiet room where I might meditate before beginning..."

"But certainly, Doctor. You must forgive me, it's been a trying day. There has been an escapade with two young people, and now one of our elderly guests has been taken quite ill. I fear that your audience may be somewhat distracted."

"I am used to resistance to my advanced ideas, madam. Perhaps the good people of...uh, Summersea, yes, would find it enlightening if I was to heal the elderly guest before their very eyes. I assure you the results are quite authentic and lasting, and your friend shall not be in any discomfort." He spread large, long-fingered hands before himself. "These hands bear the gift of Anton Mesmer himself. For one hundred years the powers of truth and magnetism have been available to mankind for the purposes of healing. I am but one of many spreading the word..."

Felicia's eyes began to glow, and she asked, "Can you heal more than one person at a time?"

"Oh, surely, my good woman. Bring them to me, your sick of heart and sick of soul. The ills of the body are but trifles to me."

Felicia directed him to a small storeroom that connected the rear parlor with the servants' hall, where the agreeable man swirled off his cloak like an opera star.

With all the dignity she could muster in her elated frame of mind, Felicia dashed for the stairs. Once on the second floor, she rapped at Charles's door, panting and scarcely able to speak.

She thought she heard a scrambling of footsteps on the other side of the door. Wondering if he was having some difficulty with his chair, she called, "Don't bother answering, dear, I'll just come in…" His door was locked. "Charles, dear, the mesmerist is here, and he says he can heal you! Do open the door. I insist that you come down at once and avail yourself of his powers while they are fresh."

"I…uh, yes, I'll be right down. I'm dressing and…will you come back for me in a few moments?" His voice sounded peculiar.

She wondered if he was having some sort of attack.

"Are you all right, dear Charles?"

"Quite. Go away now. Go away…" He began coughing. She turned to see Betz Witherspoon at the top of the stairs. She almost laughed, thinking of the scandalous trouble the insulting woman was in, now that Cordelia had shown her true stripes.

Felicia rushed to the Hobble suite to inform Gettie that there was a doctor who could remove that blank look from her sister's eyes. As she hurried along her mind raced ahead to the crossing to France—if dear Charles were healed by then they could tour the grand resorts as a healthy couple. She felt years younger, deliciously happy…

In due course, the parlor filled with the usual crowd. Felicia helped Charles Bonaventure to a seat in front while Gettie assisted her bewildered, speechless sister to a place nearby.

"What's the matter with the old lady?" Tippy Howard chirped from her seat between her half sister and stepmother.

"She's had a stroke or something," Leon Howard muttered, leaning back and blowing smoke rings. "This should prove amusing." He noted his eldest daughter's pale face and sullen expression. "You are a trial, Marietta," he said. "Perk up, girl, or I will tell Lillian to give you castor oil."

Marietta rose to leave, but a sharp look from her father made her sit back down.

"I said, you're going to stay right here by my side until you tell me what you said to make Macklin run off like he did this afternoon.

I paid well for that tutor, and all the others. I'd like to know what pleasure you get driving them off."

From his seat on the far side next to his father, Bo Howard snapped, "It's her ugly face."

"Shut up, son. I was talking with your sister." He turned his attention to the mesmerist approaching the podium. "Saints preserve us, he looks like God himself."

One of the guests overhead his remark and looked back at him with a withering expression of disapproval. Leon shrugged and fell silent.

The lecture began quite tediously, affording Leon the opportunity to note who was in attendance. Betz Witherspoon came down the stairs into the lobby—he could see her from where he sat, puffing on his cigar. She was very obviously upset, he thought with a smirk. That delightful little heiress was keeping all of them so splendidly amused with her escapades.

Betz went out onto the veranda for a while. When she came back in, her expression haggard, she took a seat by the parlor door. Leon winked at her but she failed to notice.

It was plain that Felicia wanted the mesmerist to lay his hand on the consumptive Mr. Bonaventure. But the bearded old faker seemed far more interested in the feeble Miss Millie Hobble. It was whispered that just a few hours ago she had fainted in the upper stair hall. She was probably at death's door, but the audience didn't seem to care. They wanted a convincing show.

The Grayson woman came in, looking timid and pale. Leon eyed her. When he'd attempted a bit of light conversation with her that afternoon, she's summarily kneed him. To say he was surprised was an understatement. He was more interested in her now than ever.

The mesmerist began:

"My dear…what did you say her name was? Millie, listen to the sound of my voice. You're quite well, and when you feel the touch of my hand on your head you will have back all your vision and hearing and memory. You're going to go back in your mind to this afternoon. When you feel yourself fully healed, you will begin to speak to me."

The doctor repeated himself a full three times. Then—with a marvelous show of theatrics—he placed the palm of his hand on the old woman's forehead and nearly pushed her head from her shoulders.

"Speak, Millie!" he exclaimed in a booming voice that took the audience aback. "Be healed by the powers of magnetism and truth!"

Mrs. Grayson sprang to her feet, calling out, "Oh, Doctor, can you help me, too? I am ever so distressed. I have lost a great treasure worth a fortune, and you alone can contact my grandmama, so that I might learn where it has gone. Do help me, Doctor!"

"Silence, please," the doctor muttered.

Very quietly, without any interesting dramatics, Millie opened her eyes beneath the doctor's trembling, powerful hand and said, "What were they doing?"

"I beg your pardon?" the doctor said, crouching before the old woman. "What did you say?" She began whispering very fast, and the doctor's eyes began to widen.

"She was standing *how,* in relation to the man?" he asked, blinking. "Ladies and gentlemen, I do believe my powers have released a dream in this dear old woman—"

"No! I saw them! In the closet! She was…he was…" She locked her mottled hands together. "Was it…intercourse, Doctor?"

The audience gasped and shuddered in astonishment. Emma Reinhold stood immediately and directed her daughters to file out of the reception parlor and back up the stairs. A number of other families left almost as quickly, as everyone else buzzed with whispers. Leon's children and wife were snickering, and the lovely Evalee Grayson was speechless. With a peculiar look of annoyance, she looked around, wondering where Teague was. Finally she sat down with a huff of disgust.

"She's delirious!" Gettie gasped, her face so red that Leon began to laugh out loud.

"Mr. Macklin and Marietta were in that closet, I tell you, and he—"

The doctor gently covered the old woman's mouth with his hand. The entire assemblage was turning toward Leon and his family.

Marietta? And Macklin? Son of a bitch! For an instant Leon felt the heat of shame burning in him. Then he quickly turned to look at Marietta whose eyes, wide with terror, was leaning against her stepmother.

"He made me, Papa," she whispered.

Leon knew it was a lie. He'd picked Macklin because he was such a sop. Standing woodenly, he motioned for his family to exit. Rage was curling through him. His fist was iron hard and ready to strike. Had he nearly killed himself all his life to have his efforts to come to this, over a sop and a tramp? Now they'd have to move to California!

As Leon followed his humiliated family out of the parlor, he caught a glimpse of Gettie Hobble's face, and she looked positively apoplectic. He wished he could enjoy it, but his family's reputation was in sudden, irrevocable ruin, and there was only one thing left for him to do about it.

The lecture dissolved into chaos. The doctor straightened before what remained of his audience, intoning, "I do believe the powers of truth have reigned here this night. I retire—"

"But what about this man?" Felicia said, tearing her eyes from the parlor door to look at the doctor beseechingly.

The doctor held up his hands.

"I cannot do more here, good lady. The truth in this place is all powerful. You and he must carry on without me. I must go!"

It was blessedly quiet on the veranda after the doctor clattered away in his top buggy. Betz sat huddled in a shawl, wondering if this day would ever end. Adam had missed the disaster in the parlor. Where he had gone, she couldn't imagine. But once again he had failed to meet her as he had said he would, and still she waited for Cherry and Drew to return.

After dressing for the lecture, Betz had begun to pack. She didn't want to leave in defeat, but she couldn't prolong her misery at Summersea. What Julia Lyon had said early that morning had made a great deal of sense. Now, though Cherry was ruined, and it did seem wise again to remove her from the scene as quickly as possible.

Tears threatened now. Whatever and whoever Adam was, she loved him, but she was going to have to go on somehow without him.

All of a sudden Betz heard the crunch of footsteps approaching on the road from town. She tried not to hope that it was Adam returning, but couldn't stop herself.

Adam climbed the stairs, obviously tired from a long walk. He stood a long moment in his shirt sleeves, his coat thrown carelessly over his shoulder. Finally he asked, "Did I miss the lecture?"

"It ended abruptly," Betz said, not wanting to speak of such scandalous happenings, but Adam's strange silence prompted her to fill the void between them with something. So she told him all that had happened, while he looked suitably amazed.

"Macklin and the Howard girl?"

Betz nodded. Suddenly very tired, took she asked wearily, "Should I send for the police to search for Cherry? It's growing so very late."

Adam didn't have time to answer. At that moment there was a volley of shouts from somewhere in the hotel. A ringing silence followed.

"The Howards?" Adam asked softly.

"They've been arguing since the lecture broke up. Oh, can't we get out of here for just a few minutes? I need to talk to you. Where have you been?"

He sighed deeply and shook his head as if where he had been was unimportant.

"Forgive me, Betz, is it definite about the Midsummer Ball on Friday?"

"I suppose. Why?" Trying to understand why Adam didn't seem very concerned about Cherry, she clutched at her hair, mussing it. "I don't know why I'm so worried. These people at Summersea aren't worthy to judge Cherry."

Adam reached for her hand, agreeing, "In that you are very correct." He fell silent a long time but his hand was warm and firmly holding hers as if he did not want to let go. "I may have to leave suddenly."

She let that information sink into her heart and found herself growing chilled in spite of the shawl. Suddenly Cherry's whereabouts were not important to her, either.

"When?" she whispered.

"Soon. If I find it necessary to go, and I have no time to say good-bye…try to understand that it had nothing to do with you. Later, perhaps, I can contact you."

"I don't understand."

"I know, and yet I must ask you to try. I…haven't been entirely honest with you. There's more to me than meets the eye. It's not that I've lied, Betz. I've just left out some of the truth. Can you try to make do with that?"

She wanted to say no, but there was a huge aching knot in her throat that kept her from speaking, and she knew that in spite of everything, she did love him. If that meant giving him up because he asked her to, then she must. Her love was very deep in her heart now, so deep that even the absence of him would not diminish it.

He let go of her hand finally, then straightened in preparation for going into the hotel as if it was an ordeal.

"This won't be the last time we speak, Betz, but I doubt we'll have time for anything more than light conversation."

His tone was so final that she wanted to jump to her feet and hold him. It was one thing to tell herself that she must give him up, quite another to hear that same conviction in his words.

They would soon be parted and nothing she could do would stop it.

"Thank you," she heard herself whisper. She remained rigidly in the rocker, aching inside.

He paused and looked down at her, something very touching in his dark brown eyes. She knew in that brief moment that Adam loved her, too. There was great comfort in that.

When he had gone in, she sat a long while rocking and staring out at the bay, oblivious to all concerns. Her heart was full of love. She had never known anything so fulfilling.

The Mischievous Pair Return

Adam was stationed in the servants' stairwell when Leon Howard came out his suite that night, carrying a valise. There wasn't enough time to get out of sight as the man burst through the door. Leon was halfway down the stairs when he realized that he had been seen. Looking back, his face twisted with bitterness, Leon said, "You're lucky you're not an ambitious man, Teague."

"Leaving?"

"Wouldn't you, if your daughter had been caught in the act in a linen closet with her piano teacher? The little bitch."

"No love lost between the two of you, I see," Adam said, feeling just a bit sorry for a girl. She came by her character honestly, it was obvious.

Leon made a disgusted noise and went on his way. Moments later Lillian followed, looking as if she had dressed hastily. Her hat was askew, a veil pulled down to cover her face. Most of her disheveled hair was hanging down her back. She was carrying a small carpetbag with a few lacy items trailing from the opening.

Feeling a bit alarmed, Adam stepped into the second floor corridor in time to see Tippy running from the Howard suite, silent terror etched on her face. He held the door to the stairwell for her and felt sorry as she hurried down after her parents.

That left Bo and Marietta. Adam started for the open suite door where the lamp light from within fell in a yellow oblong across the dim corridor. Just as he reached the door, Bo came out, a bitter smirk on his face. His hair a mess, he looked as if they all had been in a fistfight.

Startled to see Adam, Bo momentarily lost his bravado, but he was as quick as his father. Recovering almost instantly, he asked, "Want some?" and jerked his head toward the suite. And then he was gone, too.

Adam looked into the suite. There were clothes all over the floor and flung about on the furniture. Marietta sat on the edge of a window seat overlooking the side garden. She was sobbing eerily, without making a sound.

He felt a chill go down his back, for he had the powerful impression that he was present at the beginning of a young whore's career. Her father and family had deserted her. She was in disgrace, and would likely be disowned.

As perhaps never before, he understood what it meant to be a member of a family. He had always felt he had missed something by growing up alone with his mother, but now he could see that a family was only as good as its members. Here before his eyes was a girl unloved and unforgiven. He felt enormous pity for her.

"Marietta, can I do anything for you?"

She looked up at him, a half-hopeful look in her eyes. Then she turned bitter. Reaching for the nearest oil lamp, she was about to throw it at him.

"Sorry!" he called. "I'll leave you to your misery!" And stepped away from the door. If she threw the lamp there would likely be a fire. He wondered if he dared leave her alone, feeling as she did. But Marietta didn't throw anything.

As he waited in the corridor, wondering what she was going to do, he saw Powell Reinhold sneaking from his suite not far away. It must be just past two, he thought, watching the man cross to the stairs and tiptoe up them. Powell would not find an attractive wife of another man to please him this night, Adam thought.

He was about to turn away when he heard Marietta walking across the suite. She emerged in the corridor, her face swelling with bruises. Brushing past him, she started for the main stairs and went down them as if she had nothing to hide. Watching her, Adam admired her fortitude. She would survive. Her kind always did.

He made his usual rounds of the third floor, where very little ever happened. At three he was waiting as Powell came out of the unbooked suite looking quite distressed. He turned pale when he saw Adam leaning against the wall, his arms crossed over his chest.

"She'd gone," Adam said. "They all are."

Powell paused, his suddenly turbulent thoughts showing only in the workings of his bushy eyebrows. At length, he approached, asking Adam, "How much do you want, Teague?"

"How much for what? She's gone. I just thought you'd rest easier knowing you weren't stood up. I admit, in the face of what happened tonight, you showed a remarkable lack of restraint. Did you think Lillian would still be here at the appointed time, when her family is in disgrace?"

"You'll require something to…assure your…discretion." Powell looked quite disconcerted.

"No, sir, I won't. Go back to your wife. You've been incredibly lucky…this time."

Powell did as he was instructed. Once again Adam had the hotel to himself. He made a circuit of the second-floor wings, finding only silence. He paused at Betz's door, wondering if Cherry had returned while he had been smoking and taking notes in his cubicle.

Finally he tapped. There was no answer. He peeked in and saw that the suite was empty. Mildly concerned, he started down to the lobby when he saw Betz, Cherry and Drew coming in from the veranda.

The "trysting" lovers had chosen a good time to return, Adam thought, as he edged into the shadows to watch.

Cherry's hair was still damp and clinging to her shoulders in a tangled mess. Drew's hair was slicked back and damp as well. Their clothes were rumpled, reminding Adam of the first time he and Betz had been together during the storm. He felt a tightness in his chest that he didn't like. How could he go from her?

"…and you're all right, you're sure?" Betz was whispering as they mounted the stairs.

"Nothing happened," Cherry whispered urgently, holding onto Betz's arm and tugging a little. "Please believe me."

"Sh-h-h! Go on, Drew. Your grandmother must be beside herself by now. It's been a very trying night. Oh, Cherry, look at you..." They rushed away toward their suite. Adam marveled to see Betz's reaction compared to the Howard's.

Why, Adam asked himself, couldn't he just confide in Betz, and claim the love he knew was his for the taking?

Twenty-Two

Mr. Whitgift is Defiant

Wednesday, July 10, 1889

Weak sunlight fell almost timidly on the subdued face of Summersea the next morning. A thin layer of clouds made the morning faintly gloomy.

But a tension that everyone could feel crackled in Summersea's dining room. Victoria Whitgift reigned at the head table, her heavy head and elaborate headdress making her look something like a gargoyle.

Beside her was Drew, sitting exceptionally erect in a suit more appropriate for Sunday morning in a cathedral. He wore an aloof expression that mirrored his grandmother's, and not a soul in the room dared to question the young man's behavior of the day before. Drew and Victoria Whitgift were like the heir apparent and the dowager queen mother; they could do no wrong.

As the waiter placed a fresh bowl of strawberries before Drew's grandmother, Drew began to believe that she was going to let the entire previous day pass without comment. Briefly, he felt smug and pleased.

Carefully stabbing a berry and lifting it to her lips, she said calmly, "I see your little adventuress is not at breakfast this morning." She poked the berry into her mouth.

"I understand she takes breakfast in her suite, Grandmother," he said, stiffening.

"I shouldn't wonder, given her behavior. You realize, of course, that we can no longer consider her a possibility for you. And that is quite regrettable, because an alliance with her grandmother's family would have served you well in the future. In any case, there is no rush for any such alliance with anyone, and I still have much to say about Blythe Blanchard in Hartford. Blythe is quite pretty, and Blanchard Shipping could serve you well."

"I intend to stand by Cherry," Drew said, laying his napkin across his plate.

"I'm very distressed to hear you put it quite that way, Drew dear," Victoria said, brows raised, "but since you have…well, perhaps we should continue to discuss this in private."

"There's nothing to discuss."

"Oh, but indeed there is, dear. I am convinced this entire disaster with the Ryburn girl was manufactured by that person passing herself off as a chaperone. No respectable woman would have allowed what transpired yesterday. It's clearly been a plot to throw you and that unfortunate girl together. And Xynnie Pratt is just as responsible, for introducing you. She just doesn't realize the importance of these matters, regardless of all her husband's money. I'm quite sorry I allowed you to accept the woman's invitation. If I had had any idea what she was up to…I take it that the rumors I heard about you and this Cherry creature drinking together at the party were true, then."

Drew's eyes narrowed to slits.

"Cherry Ryburn is a very decent young lady, and I'm going to marry her."

"Tut, tut, dear. Lower your voice. I blame myself entirely for this unfortunate attitude of yours. I should have warned you. This was your father's duty, and he has always neglected you. If you insist, I will speak bluntly. A girl who has jeopardized her reputation is not worthy of you."

"But she was with me! And nothing happened!"

"Irrelevant! She has been foolish. You are exempted, because you are a Whitgift. Your reputation is beyond reproach. And, dear boy, for all the dew still on your brow, you are a man. Because you are so young you are apparently oblivious to some of your most basic rights and privileges, rights and privileges which I, as a woman, have never possessed. And I can tell you I bitterly resent that."

"You're entitled to all of them."

"Your *naïveté* is charming, but you don't understand. You, as a young man, cannot damage your reputation except in wanton excess, and you would have to work very hard indeed to achieve that. Frankly, I don't think you have what it takes to be a rake. Realize, simply, dear, that Cordelia Ryburn is, beneath her pretty trappings, a little tramp. She chose to be that. You are not responsible for Cordelia Ryburn's moral corruption."

Drew slid back his chair, and his grandmother's next words came out as cold as death.

"Don't get up, dear boy. If you do, I shall see to it that your father cuts off your allowance. Then I personally will have Sheba shipped up to the farm for an indefinite stay. I assure you that I can and will do this. My authority exceeds yours, most assuredly. In spite of the male prerogative and the sexual superiority, the one with controlling financial interest holds the greatest authority of all. I, dear boy, am that person."

"Money and horses hold no temptation for me."

"Really? How delightfully blasé you pretend to be. You and I have never locked horns before, Drew. I dare say it'll not be the last time. Simply ask your father if I'm a formidable enemy. I can be your ally, and would prefer it. But test me, if you will."

His face quite hot, he wanted to leap to his feet and soundly curse the old woman. He remained silent, cursing himself silently, instead.

"I may look ancient and infirm to you, but I am quite up to a fight. Cordelia Ryburn is not the girl for you. Accept that fact, dear. Oh, by all means, enjoy her if it amuses you to do so, but understand that when you speak of marriage you are speaking of a financial and social arrangement of the greatest magnitude. The physical does not enter into it."

Drew had lost his appetite. He knew if he stood he would be at war with his grandmother. If he did not, he would be at war with himself. Suddenly he hated his grandmother, and Cherry, too, for placing him in this position.

But his grandmother's challenge was too great. He stood slowly, keeping his expression bland and controlled. His grandmother's eyes widened only slightly as he nodded and smiled down at her, saying calmly, "Good morning, Grandmother. I hope you enjoy your breakfast."

He strolled to the lobby, feeling more like a man than he had thought he ever could, thinking that Cherry would be proud of him. But as he thought of her, he felt faintly sick. He knew now that in spite of all his good intentions, what his grandmother had said was true. He'd besmirched Cherry's reputation and nothing—nothing—would save it.

He went cold, realizing he was immune from such problems and Cherry would never be. He owed her more than he had realized. She was now his responsibility. If they would not let him marry her, he must provide for her. Always. It seemed an awesome burden, suddenly. He should have shown such a special girl more respect. In his recklessness he had hurt her more deeply than she might ever realize.

He went out onto the veranda and finally down to the lawn and the steps to the beach. It had seemed so romantic, riding away with her like that making wild promises. It had seemed so right, so carefree!

How could they have hoped to escape society's powerful code of behavior? Angrily he kicked at the sand and then bent to pull off his shoes. The sand was warm and giving on his stocking feet. Did Cherry have any inkling of what he'd done to her?

Would she someday grow to hate him?

Unexpected News

Betz stiffened her spine, took a deep breath, and descended the stairs to the lobby. She was wearing her most reserved traveling suit, minus the jacket. In a few hours they would be leaving. If only she felt glad, she thought. Crossing to the desk clerk to arrange transportation to the depot, she asked, "Can I send a telegraph dispatch from here?" As the clerk nodded she noticed a letter in her mail slot. With a sinking feeling she took it, but it was not a letter from George, as she expected. It was a letter from Agatha, postmarked in England.

As she tore into the envelope she became aware of an ominous silence emanating from the dining room. Turning just a little, she could see Gettie Hobble staring directly at her, looking for all the world as if she'd just drunk vinegar for breakfast. Considering what the woman's sister had said the day before, Betz didn't think Gettie had much call for staring. She was learning, though, that those who fancied themselves superior were at their best when deflecting attention from themselves onto others.

Ignoring the rude old lady and her sour expression, Betz found herself being pressed back against the desk clerk's cubby while an army of delivery men trooped in from the veranda, each carrying a five-foot potted palm.

Behind them came a dozen hefty laborers who were being yelled at by a fussy man in a brown suit. Felicia brought up the rear, wearing a hideous purple plumed hat and veil and matching traveling costume that exuded road dust.

As usual she filled the lobby with her falsetto voice. A self-effacing little creature fawned and drawled beside her, describing the theme of *Midsummer Night's Dream* for the coming ball and how it could combine nicely with the Antony and Cleopatra elements of palms, draperies and an orchestra in Roman costume.

Betz heaved a sigh. The woman had no taste, or this caterer didn't. Perhaps he was having sport with her.

Betz watched Felicia strutting about in her fog of self-importance, pausing in the doorway to the dining room for everyone to notice the excitement she was creating and to appraise her new gown.

Suddenly her face fell into an incredulous frown, and she swept into the room.

She was surely looking at Mr. Bonaventure, Betz decided, and he was talking animatedly with Evalee Grayson at the far table.

"Oh, Mr. Bonaventure, are you feeling quite well?" Felicia called sweetly, dashing grandly to his table.

Betz turned away, dismissing Felicia and Summersea and all frustrating concerns from her mind. She and Cherry would soon be gone.

For a moment, as she pulled Agatha's letter from the envelope, she felt a twinge of pain to think she might be leaving before Adam, and that she might never see him again. Could she bear it? Her thoughts turned unbidden to the last time he had held her, and she felt a yearning that was almost overwhelming.

She would have to bear it, she thought, absently beginning to read Agatha's letter. After reading only a few words all her attention was sharply focused.

"...I will be arriving on July 10th. Please meet me at the train..."

Betz reread the letter. She was cutting short her trip! And the arrival date was that day!

"How can I find out if a private railcar is arriving at Huntington Station today?" she asked the clerk.

"The stationmaster can find out for you, ma'am. Shall I send a messenger?"

"If you would, please. If there was such a car, when might it arrive?"

"Next train into Huntington Station from Boston is due at four."

Betz pressed her palm to her forehead, muttering, "I can't think. If she's coming, Cordelia and I can't leave. Can you arrange for a buggy for me to use today?"

"Surely, Miss Witherspoon. When would you like to go out?"

"This morning," she said, knowing that if she did not escape even for a few hours today she'd go mad. "Oh, and please have two box lunches made up." She paused, considering asking Adam to go along, then decided against it. She didn't care to hear him say he'd be too busy.

Back in the suite a few minutes later, Betz sank onto a chair and told Cherry, "We're not leaving after all. We're going on a picnic."

Cherry looked startled, her expression mirroring a dozen questions. Then she gave a hopeful little smile, asking, "Is everything all right after all?"

"About that I wouldn't know." She offered Cherry the letter from Agatha and watched her read it. "All I do know is that we aren't leaving today."

"She's coming here? Today?" Cherry squealed. Then her face fell. "She's coming back because of me, isn't she? She's going to be so cross." Cherry turned very pale.

"We won't know why she's decided to cut her trip short until she gets here, so there's no use worrying. We'll meet her at the train and see what she says. Put on that pretty—"

"But I don't want to see her, not if she's going to be cross! Oh, Betz what's going to become of me? Where will I go? Why didn't I listen to you?"

Sighing, Betz worked at the kinks in her back with shaking fingers.

"I told you before, your behavior was my responsibility. I failed you. If anyone should be afraid to meet your grandmother, it should be me. I am most likely going to be let go."

"I won't let her fire you!"

"Never mind, darling," Betz said, smiling. "We did the best we could under the circumstances, and frankly I'm glad she's on her way back."

"I'm not going to the station with you."

"Very well, I'll go alone, but only if you promise on your most solemn word to stay in your room the *entire* time I'm gone."

"I promise," Cherry said as Betz sighed again.

"Let's have a nice picnic and forget our worries. You can tell me about your adventure yesterday."

Cherry looked alarmed. Then she shrugged.

"It was all so harmless."

"I believe that. Change your clothes now. I want you to have a little time to practice your piano pieces before your grandmother gets here. Perhaps if she thinks you've accomplished a little something, she won't be quite so upset."

Mr. Witherspoon Meets With Resistance

Squinting against the bright sunlight, George Witherspoon stepped down from the train after his wife and family. He placed his flat black hat on his balding head and brushed the sleeves of his black suit.

"Children!" he said sharply to Amanda, Georgie Junior, Sally and Lymon, all wearing matching black outfits relieved only by bits of stark white trim. "No gawking. Cynthia dear, you must keep them in line. Betty would not have allowed this behavior."

His wife took on a hurt, stubborn scowl, and snapped, "In that, dear George, I think you're wrong. Betty allowed all manner of freedoms when you weren't looking. I've done all I can to break the children of these bad habits, but I simply haven't had enough time. If only we could have stayed home, instead of—"

George silenced her with a look.

"I must personally bring my sister to her senses. And if you would please, dear, do not contradict me before my children."

Giggling, the children took the advantage and began tussling, until Lymon was wailing and Sally looked mussed. Amanda, the oldest, stood apart, looking miserable.

A hired carriage pulled up nearby and George herded his family single file to it.

The ride to Summersea was silent, the way George liked it. He was curious to see Betty for himself and discover what lure this work had for her. He would have her head straight in no time, and when he had her back at the house quieting his children the way Cynthia could not seem to, he would have his life back in order.

As the carriage pulled up in front of Summersea a half hour later, he was impressed in spite of himself. The place was so elegant that he was momentarily intimidated by the grandeur. As he climbed down in his usual solemn manner, he could see why Betty might like it here. Perhaps, after all, she was in search of another husband, this time a rich one instead of an adventurer. Chuckling with no outward sign of mirth, he guided his awestruck family into the hotel.

"Papa, look!" Sally squealed, pointing to the palms in the parlor.

George gave his daughter a chilling look. The child shrank down into her collar in silence. Her eyes still wide with curiosity, she whispered, "Did somebody die again, Georgie?"

George found the activity much too hectic for his taste. It seemed as if a hundred men were completely remodeling a large room just beyond the reception parlor. Meanwhile, guests strolled like dignitaries through the lobby and onto the veranda.

There did not seem to be any place where Cynthia and the children could sit down, so he directed them back onto the veranda. He had no sooner turned to the desk clerk to inquire about Betz's whereabouts when he heard Sally and Lymon squealing, "Aunt Betty!"

He stiffened his spine and went out. Sally and Lymon had just raced down the stairs into Betz's arms. Hugging them, she looked up, and it was gratifying to watch her face grow pale. She wasn't beyond his influence by any means, he told himself.

As she pulled off her picture hat, some of her hair came loose, trailing at her temples and nape. George huffed his disapproval. A slim girl in a very fine gown got down from a buggy behind Betz now, and a steward came along to drive the buggy away.

George studied Betz. She looked shockingly casual in a blouse and gore skirt. Flushed, she looked fully ten years younger, and much prettier. Suddenly feeling old, he huffed to himself again.

The young girl pointed to him and he bowed gravely. Betz stood and smoothed her dusty skirt. She had not expected him to come to her, he thought, and it pleased him to see how completely he'd taken her by surprise.

"H-hello, George," she said, coming up the stairs toward him.

"You're looking pale," he said, giving her a light embrace. She scarcely brushed his cheek with a sisterly kiss. "I warned you, Betty, that if you didn't desist in this ridiculous venture I would come and rescue you from yourself."

Looking far less disturbed by his words than he would have liked, Betz said, "This morning you might have convinced me to come home with you, George. This afternoon I can't go. My employer arrives on the afternoon train, I believe...and I must meet her. Cherry, may I present my brother George? George, this is Miss Cordelia Ryburn, heiress to the Ryburn Department Store fortune, a fine house, and a vast collection of *objets d'art* from around the world."

For a brief moment he didn't know what to say. He could see that the little heiress needed a chaperone. She was no older than his Amanda, who was now staring hungrily at the heiress's gown. Well, if the employer was coming that day, it would only be a matter of speaking to the woman. He would be reasonable. He said, "I'll make arrangements to stay for the night," hoping he could afford it.

Amid the sounds of furniture being moved around in the parlor and the general din of activity in the ballroom, plus the annoyed murmurings of guests passing by on the veranda and lawn, Betz and her brother's family stood out in the stark relief.

Betz edged Cherry to the side of the lobby and whispered. "I can't believe he's here!"

Cherry made a face, answering softly, "I don't like him. He smells funny."

Betz could smell it, too, and wanted more than ever to get away from her brother for good. Now it was more imperative than ever that she speak with Agatha. Thank heaven she was on her way. Betz didn't know whether to rejoice at or dread seeing the old woman again, but at least now she was no longer alone.

After she had confirmed that Agatha's railcar was indeed arriving in slightly more than an hour, Betz turned to Cherry once again.

"I want you to stay in our suite and not go out, no matter—"

Adam and Evalee Grayson were just coming down the stairs, arm in arm. Betz saw them and her heart rolled over. Adam was talking in hushed tones to the pretty young woman, who was simpering and fawning on his arm like a strumpet. When he spied Betz, he faltered, making an effort to keep his thoughts from reflecting on his face. Then he went on talking to his companion, as if Betz and her feelings were not important at all.

Then, as if suddenly aware of the entire family clad in black standing in the lobby, Adam paused. Looking back at Betz, he queried with his brow. She knew he was wondering if the thin gloomy-looking man was her brother. When she nodded, his face lit with a mischievous grin. He detached himself from Evalee Grayson's grasp and approached.

"Introduce me," he said under his breath. His wavy hair glistened as if he had just combed it with fragrant oil, and there was an air of tension about him that made Betz alert and rather suspicious. What was going on between him and the Grayson woman? He had certainly never conversed with her that openly.

Betz didn't want to introduce Adam to George. She could see that Adam was going to say or do something that would surely make trouble. The sparkle in his eyes was dangerous.

But when she saw George was looking at her as Adam approached and spoke to her, she knew she could not avoid bringing the two men together. She must be casual. George must not guess that she had fallen in love, or he would surely escalate his efforts to exert authority over her.

"Adam, my brother George Witherspoon," she said, her voice trembling. "George, Adam Teague of Chicago."

As the two men shook hands, Adam grinned and said grandly, "I've heard so much about you, Mr. Witherspoon. Betz has told me how good you've been to her in the past. It's so nice to see you join her here, especially since I hear there is a grand entertainment planned for tomorrow night. You'll be staying, I presume?"

Adam was acting so superior that suddenly Betz wanted to laugh.

"George wouldn't have any interest in—"

"We may stay…an additional night," George said. He looked at her, his intention to silence her clear in his eyes.

Betz kept herself from cautioning George about the cost of Summersea. She wasn't sure of it any case, and a stiff bill would serve him right for coming here and treating her like a child.

Another delivery wagon arrived then and the laborers trooped out to carry in little gilded chairs. They seemed to enjoy getting in the way of the guests and making as much noise as possible.

Nervously, Betz stepped back out of the way to watch Adam nod good afternoon to her brother and start away once again, with Evalee Grayson's hand tucked in the crook of his elbow. Betz forced herself to watch, reminding herself that she had no hold on him.

He seemed to remember that she was there and glanced back, a peculiar smile on his face. It was as if he was pretending to be someone or something that he was not. And though Adam was smiling at something Miss Grayson had said, and was strutting away from the hotel looking for all the world like Leon Howard at his cockiest, his eyes were dark and penetrating.

Betz felt as if Adam was sending her a silent message. His look was brief but it reached deeply into her, further confusing her. She did not understand him, she thought, turning away in vexation.

She wished with all her heart that she did not love him, but she did. And because she did, her life had taken on a thousand new possibilities.

Twenty-Three

Lady Ryburn Returns

Betz started out for the depot, not caring if a top buggy wasn't the elegant reception vehicle Agatha might expect. It seemed at this point that her efforts no longer mattered.

As she drove, she felt strangely free. The rhythm of the horses' hooves in the dust was comforting. She wasn't sure what she was going to say to Agatha with regard to Cherry's behavior. It would all depend on just why Agatha had come back so early and what she'd been told in all those scathing reports.

Soon the train was pulling in, and Betz saw the private car at the end. With her stomach fluttering nervously, Betz waited for Agatha to come out. When no one emerged, not even a servant, Betz began to worry and decided to see for herself what was keeping her employer. She climbed aboard the private car and knocked at the rear door.

"Come in, come in, whoever you are. I shall not rush, so there's no use hurrying me along. I'm old and I'm tired, and I do not have to be polite to any of you. You're all paid well enough to tolerate my fits of temper." Agatha was seated, not even attempting to get up as Betz peeked in. "Ah, Miss Witherspoon, I'm glad it's you."

Betz was at once alarmed. Agatha looked gray and sunken, her hair mussed and her traveling suit in disarray. Her bags and trunks were open, heaped with clothes, and a half-eaten dinner on a tray was still on a nearby table.

"Agatha! Are you ill?" Betz cried.

The old woman chuckled wearily, admitting, "Ah, just very weary. I suppose I should not have gone so far. I underestimated my age and overestimated my strength. How clever of you to be here on time. I was convinced my letter was still on a ship somewhere, and that long after I had died on the way you would be waiting in some station for me. Oh, my, I do feel dreadful. Where is Cordelia?"

"I left her back at Summersea. We elected to have you put in with us. I hope you don't mind. My things are being moved into Cherry's room and you shall have mine. Are you sure that you're quite all right?"

"If I look half dead, it's because Summersea holds no fascination for me. Never has." She seemed to remember herself and cut off her words. "And so tell me about my granddaughter. She has led you a merry chase. I've received a number of letters."

"I was afraid so."

"Gettie Hobble seems to think our Cordelia is one lace short of a born harlot. What do you say, dear? Will I be leaving my husband's estate to a…" She fumbled with a monocle and lifted it to her right eye. "Dear me, don't look so stricken! I'm joking. I give Gettie Hobble's opinion no credence whatsoever. She is a bitter old prune. I married her old beau, don't you know." She chuckled. "I do believe she begrudges me the wealth and travel far more than Cyrus's love. I gave him far more that she ever would have, let me tell you, dear. I was not put off by his masculinity."

"We must talk before we get to Summersea, Agatha. Can I help you tidy up so we can get going?"

"Yes, of course. Do what you will with me. I fired my maid. She treated me like a fool, so you had better not. I suppose in regard to Cordelia that there has been *some* mischief."

Betz hastily stuffed the mounds of clothes into Agatha's trunks and carpetbags and started to tidy the woman's hair. Then she helped her into her suit jacket and pinned on her hat, saying, "Perhaps it might help if you told me what you've heard about Cherry so far. I don't want to trouble you with repetition."

"Whatever the dear child has found to do would certainly

bear repeating. But if you must know, I have received a number of missives from old friends. I let my secretary handle all replies, since I did not want to be privy to gossip. I did not read them. Miss Hawthorn, however, did see fit to warn me that some of the letters were quite disturbing."

Betz wanted to fall on her knees and beg the woman's forgiveness.

"I wish I could assure you that it was all gossip!"

"Nonsense. I expected resistance. No, I'm back because I'm ill. I couldn't manage the travel this time, and do you know why? Because I was always thinking about little Cordelia. What an imbecile I am! I was going to stagger about the bazaars to buy rare treasures for my collections, and here all along I had an irreplaceable treasure of my own…a granddaughter who possessed all the fresh beauty I could hope to enjoy watching…and all for free!"

Betz's heart ached to think how carelessly she had guarded Agatha's treasure.

"I realized that I should be here with Cordelia, watching her face light when she first saw this or that wonder. I had been away and alone for so long that I forgot just what things have true value in this world." She clutched at Betz's sleeve to hold her attention. "Life is short, my dear. One must not pass up a single opportunity. You must not reach my advanced age and be able to say to yourself, I did not live, I did not try, I did not love, I did not see. Listen to me, dear Betz Witherspoon. I speak from the heart!"

Betz looked into the old woman's china blue eyes and felt a chill of wonder go through her body.

"I'm listening," she whispered.

"Very well, then. I will stop waxing poetic and debark the train like a docile old thing, and you may tell me what seems to be troubling you so."

Betz helped her walk out onto the platform. A solicitous conductor was waiting there to help them to the ground.

"I will do my best to tolerate Summersea," Agatha went on, "but if I get so bored that I require a doctor's care, we should perhaps consider going home to Cyrus Wood...unless Cordelia is having too marvelous a time. Then my doctor shall just have to bring himself here."

Wondering if Agatha would want to go home after she told her story, Betz said, "I hardly know where to begin."

Agatha chuckled loudly as they moved slowly toward the hotel buggy and asked, "Has she been that incorrigible? Has she seduced the entire male staff and set all my old friends upon their ears? Is she pregnant? Is she...oh, God forbid, smoking tobacco cigarettes?"

"Surely you're joking!" Betz said, staring incredulously at the woman.

Agatha said soberly, "Her father was an adventurer. Her mother was a street and beer hall whore who drank herself nearly to death. Cherry grew up in a tenement amidst the most appalling squalor imaginable. Her friends were pimps and pickpockets. Her life was a half-dime novel nightmare. Don't fancy that I did not know everything there was to know about her one week after she appeared on my doorstep. I paid the man who brought her to me quite handsomely for his ingenuity. He provided the names to contact. My lawyer did the rest."

Betz was speechless. Whatever had made her think such a woman would not have this kind of worldly power?

Agatha smiled, "I wished you to underestimate me, dear," she said gently. "Now..." she got settled in the buggy. "Tell me all, from the very first day and don't spare a single detail. By the way, you may be surprised to hear that there has been some word on my dear son's whereabouts. I doubt he'll be able to join us here, but soon Cherry will see him again. I think she'll be pleased."

"Yes, indeed."

Betz sank down beside Agatha in the buggy seat and took up the lines. She was trembling from head to toe. Her sense of relief when she began telling Agatha all the mistakes she had made was so great that she wanted to weep.

Agatha seemed strong enough to bear Cherry's mischief and her own guilt over the mistakes made. She even smiled from time to time. And as the story unfolded, Betz soon found herself talking more and more of her own feelings until she was confessing her love for Adam and all that had happened during the storm.

Being honest at last about it all gave her a feeling of satisfaction, but left her wilted and drained. By the time they pulled to a stop before Summersea's deserted veranda, all the day's activities in the parlor had ceased. The dining room windows were bright, and the murmur of voices coming from inside seemed comfortingly routine.

"Perhaps we can slip in without being seen," Agatha said, her tone low and somber, "I *am* tired."

Betz feared suddenly that she'd told too much. The woman was disappointed, surely, and she had said nothing by way of comfort.

She got out of the buggy and helped Agatha down.

They climbed to the veranda and went into the lobby. Betz felt tempted to say that she had warned Agatha not to hire her, but she was too frightened and discouraged now to speak.

She could see beyond the parlor to the ballroom. It had been transformed into a grotesque approximation of a fanciful Egyptian or Roman bath. Groaning inwardly, Betz turned back to Agatha.

"Oh, I forgot to tell you that my brother arrived today," she added. "He came hoping to force me back home with him. He doesn't believe in education for women, nor paid work. I don't intend to go with him, regardless of what you decide to do about me. As you said, life is very short…"

"Betz, dear, let's not talk any more. My old brain cannot absorb another word. Let's not make any decisions or plans until tomorrow or the next day. I've been on one conveyance or another for so many weeks that my feet seem to have wheels. I want to speak briefly to Cordelia, and then I want a real bed. Tomorrow I want to speak to this Drew. The last time I saw him, his mother had him in blue velvet and curls."

Without pausing, Betz helped Agatha up the stairs and along the corridor to their suite. Cherry was waiting in her room, dressed perfectly, her hair plaited like a schoolgirl's. She gave a neat curtsy and forced a smile.

"Well, Cordelia..." Agatha said, looking her over while plucking at her hat. Betz helped her remove the pins and assisted her as she took off her jacket. She cast Cherry an encouraging little smile.

"Hello, Grandmother," Cherry said very formally. Then she stepped closer. "You're ill!" She suddenly looked terrified. "What's wrong?"

Agatha waved off her granddaughter's concern with, "It's nothing. I'm just old. I couldn't get you off my mind, child. I had to come back to you. Will you forgive me for leaving you? It must have seemed selfish, indeed, and it was."

Cherry looked to Betz in disbelief and then back to her grandmother. She burst into tears.

"Now, now, child, you mustn't carry on so. I'm too weary for it just now. Run along like a good little girl, and we'll talk when I've rested. I do not want to see or hear a thing for the next twelve hours."

Miss Ryburn Flees

Though they had taken supper together at nine, her grandmother still hadn't spoken to Cherry specifically about her misbehavior.

Nervous, she stood a long time with her hand on the doorknob. She knew by all that was holy that come morning her grandmother would quietly send her packing. So now, with a small carpetbag in hand, Cherry slipped out into the corridor and down the servants' stairs.

She wished she could say good-bye to Betz, but she hoped Betz would understand why she couldn't. She had decided that afternoon, while her grandmother slept, to go back where she'd come from. There would be people there who had known her mother. They would help her. The future was not so bright there, but with her experience among the rich she might be able to do better now than she would have as an orphan on the streets.

Before running out into the night, Cherry paused to reconsider; thinking of leaving Drew behind. Then quickly she dashed out into the dark. He would be better off without her. That was certain.

She crossed the rear yard, heading for the road that led back to Huntington Station. From there she would take the train or ask for a ride on some passing wagon.

She had just started along the road when she heard the sound of running feet. Alarmed to think that someone might catch her leaving the hotel, she ducked into some bushes, stumbling over Mr. Bonaventure's wheeled chair. He was nowhere around.

"Mr. Bonaventure?" she called softly, trying to understand what she had found. "Is something wrong?"

There was no answer, and everything outside the darkened hotel remained ominously silent.

What was going on, Cherry wondered. Had Mr. Bonaventure been out for air and fallen out of his chair? Had someone waylaid him? Would she find him lying in a ditch nearby?

More timidly she whispered again, "Mr. Bonaventure?"

Then she heard the soft sound of footsteps again, and instinctively ducked out of sight. She was only a few feet from the chair, with only the bushes between it and herself.

From her hiding place in the bushes, Cherry saw two men emerge from the darkness. One was whispering in an urgent tone and pointing toward the hotel. They darted near and crouched close to where the chair was hidden.

"Althea and I will go through the rooms and bring the loot to you. Make sure you're waiting right here, and then wait for us on the beach with the boat. Ten o'clock. You got that?"

There was a murmured question that Cherry could not make out, but then the two men fell silent. Someone moved around the hotel from the rear, slowly, cautiously. Cherry thought she recognized Mr. Teague in the dim light falling from the hotel windows.

The two men remained motionless until the intruder had gone on around to the front of the hotel. Then one scuttled away toward the road, and eventually took off at a run.

The other man stood looking around for a moment and then approached the place where Cherry was hiding, clutching her carpetbag in trembling hands. She was convinced that he had seen her and was now going to expose her. But he simply fished the wheeled chair from where it was hidden and brushed it off. As he started pushing it back toward the walk circling the hotel, Cherry realized with a start that he was Mr. Bonaventure! He was moving like a perfectly healthy man!

A few seconds later a woman emerged from the shadows, dressed in something very dark, her white apron stark in the dim light from the veranda. It was Mr. Bonaventure's nurse.

At a distance Cherry couldn't hear what they were whispering, but again Mr. Bonaventure started pointing toward the hotel and then back to the place where he'd told his accomplice to wait at ten.

Then, to Cherry's utter astonishment, Mr. Bonaventure gathered his nurse into his arms. He kissed her for some minutes. Cherry didn't miss a single move of his hands on the woman's body. She felt electrified by surprise.

At length, Mr. Bonaventure sank into his chair and put the lap robe over his knees. The nurse wheeled him around to the front of the hotel as if nothing unusual had happened.

He was a complete fake!

Were they planning to rob the hotel, Cherry wondered in horror. Standing, trembling, Cherry realized she couldn't leave. If she ran away now, no one would know Mr. Bonaventure's plans.

Whatever might become of her here, she owed Betz and her grandmother too much to let them fall prey to a thief.

Moments later she was slipping back into her suite. She pushed the packed carpetbag beneath her bed and tiptoed to where Betz slept in her bed. It was wonderful having her there, Cherry thought, looking down at her. Betz was almost a mama.

Betz stirred and opened her eyes.

"What is it?" she whispered, sitting up.

Cherry dropped to her knees beside the bed and buried her face in Betz's bosom, whispering, "I was going to run away—But I didn't. I couldn't when I saw…I saw…"

Betz gripped her shoulders.

"Take a deep breath and then tell me where you were."

Cherry pointed toward the wall in the direction of the road leading away from Summersea.

"I saw Mr. Bonaventure and his nurse, and a man talking about loot. Then the man went away and Mr. Bonaventure started kissing and fondling his nurse. After that he got back in his chair and they went on as before. I don't think he's sick at all. I-I think he's a con man!"

"Sh-h-h, keep your voice down. We don't want to wake or alarm your grandmother." Betz pushed back her covers and got up. "I want you to get into bed right now and go right to sleep. Do you hear me?"

Cherry nodded whispered, "I'm sorry about wanting to run away."

"We'll talk about that later. I have a feeling I should tell Mr. Teague about this."

"Yes! He'll know what to do!"

"Stay in bed, and listen for your grandmother. Promise."

"I won't leave her alone."

Betz pulled on her dressing gown and tied the sash, promising, "I'll be gone only a moment. This is not something for us to handle ourselves."

A Secret Alliance Revealed

She tapped lightly on Adam's door. There seemed to be no light under the door, and all was quiet within. Tapping again, Betz hugged her shoulders, frightened more about being there again than about a swindler being among them.

"Adam," she whispered, trying the door. It was unlocked. She crept in and closed the door so that no one who passed could see her.

Only a faint light fell through the small circular window in the gable. His bed was mussed but he wasn't in it. His half-packed carpetbag lay on the floor next to the nightstand. He was getting ready to leave, she thought, her heart twisting.

Suddenly she was assailed by the memory of what they had shared in this room such a short time ago. She felt it had been years since he'd held her and kissed her.

How could she want him so desperately, she wondered, breathing in the fragrance of him which lingered in the air. In a few short hours or days he would be gone from her life.

She wasn't sorry she had loved him, she thought. Oh, no. He had awakened a love she hadn't known she could feel. She would be forever enriched for knowing him. Life would never be quite the same…

Suddenly she was crying, for it seemed so unimportant that Mr. Bonaventure was not so ill as he claimed. There was only one important matter on her mind, and it was Adam and her love for him.

And where, she asked herself as she began feeling ever more distraught, was Adam in the middle of the night? Was he, too, not what he claimed to be? He had already admitted as much.

She sank onto Adam's bed and smoothed her hand across the linen. She would wait, she decided. What else could she do?

Twenty minutes passed. She sat there in the dark, remembering all that had passed between them, trying to put it all in place, to rest.

Suddenly she heard the quiet footsteps outside the door, and before she could even stand Adam swept into the room. Behind him was Evalee Grayson.

At first they didn't see her sitting there. Betz was so stunned, and hurt, she couldn't speak.

"I want you to keep a close watch over Fitch and Reinhold tomorrow night. I'll do what I can for Whitgift and Ellison, but with two of them—"

Evalee stiffened as her eyes adjusted to the darkness. She grabbed Adam's arm, and he looked in the direction of Betz, seated on the bed.

The moment of surprised silenced that followed made Betz ill with dread. What was going on here, she wondered, still stunned by the sight of the Grayson woman in Adam's room.

Adam sent the woman out with a mere nod of his head. When she was gone, Adam went to the desk and took out a small notebook. He lit a candle and then, still remaining silent, he wrote in the notebook for some minutes. Though he was only a foot from Betz, she felt he was on the other side of the world. She decided she had better explain herself or he would surely think that she had been spying on him, waiting to catch him with his new…lover.

"My employer, Agatha Dunwitty arrived this afternoon," she began softly. "And it's likely I'll be dismissed the moment she's up to discussing it with me. Cherry was very upset, I think, and decided to try running away tonight. Apparently she was outside only a short time ago."

He straightened, frowning. "She's all right?"

"Yes. But she saw something out there that upset her even more…Mr. Bonaventure. I didn't get much else from her. Do you suppose you could ask her what she saw? I can't imagine what it means, except that Cherry seems to think he might be a con artist. Considering her background, it is possible that she might be right."

Betz forced herself to her feet. She had delivered the message. Now she could gracefully extract herself from a delicate situation.

"I felt someone should know and…you were the first I thought of." She started for the door.

He caught her hand. It was so warm. She knew she should take herself away from him but she could not move. "I do know what to do," he whispered. "Can I send you back to your suite and tell you not worry…and hope that you will not misinterpret what you saw here just now?"

"There's nothing to misinterpret," she said hastily, aching inside.

"I can see that there is. Please sit down. There's something I want you to read." He looked perturbed.

"You have no need to explain anything to me, Adam," she said, but deep in her heart she knew she was lying. She longed for him to explain why he was paying Evalee Grayson so much attention.

He tugged a letter from a slot in the backing of his notebook.

Handing it to her, he said, "Read this and then I will tell you why I am at Summersea." He stood over her, arms folded. His expression was unreadable and terribly intimidating.

Betz unfolded the worn letter. It was written in a pretty hand in blue ink.

"My dearest Jenny,

"I can no longer go on. In my last letter I told you how desperately I loved my dear Mr. Bradleigh, and how very good he was to me. Dear Charles seemed all I wanted in a man. That he was younger than me seemed unimportant.

"He told me he loved me, and when he asked for the money for his treatments, I gave it to him gladly. But now I must tell you, dearest friend, that Charles Bradleigh is not what he claims to be.

"He has left me. He has taken all that I gave him, and all I had in my safe, my jewels, my bonds, everything. I don't begrudge him my worldly possessions, but now I am alone again.

"You were my dearest friend for years, but I was so unkind to you when you warned me he was a swindler. Now, dear friend, my valuables, my friends, my honor, even my sanity are gone.

"He betrayed me, made me a laughing stock, yet I would do it all again. I would welcome him back with open arms. I would give him more if only he would love me.

"How could I have been so stupid? He never meant a word he said. I can never face my friends again. Forgive me for writing in my darkest hour, but I cannot go on. I can only hope you understand. When they talk of me, Jenny, perhaps you will not laugh too much.

"Charles took my heart. Now I lay down my pen to seek respite from the pain.

Your dear friend,

Veronice"

Betz drew a ragged breath. Though she did not know who had written this letter, she identified with every heartbreaking emotion.

She had once felt that she could not bear the disgrace of being abandoned and divorced. When a woman was swindled, it cut deep into her soul. She looked up at Adam and saw his dark expression; she asked silently with her eyes that he explain.

"Jenny is my mother," he said softly, unfolding his arms. "Veronice was her best friend for as long as I can remember. She was a lovely, intelligent widow, so generous in her heart that not a person who ever met her could help but love her. Last summer she met a younger man who swindled her out of all her money… and her honor. She hung herself, and my mother was the one who found her."

Betz shuddered, refolding the letter.

"I'm terribly sorry."

"Mother asked me to find the man who had swindled her friend. She asked me to do something about it."

A bolt of alarm went through Betz. Mouth open, she stood abruptly, blurting, "Mr. Bonaventure?"

"Yes, he's about to do something here. I can sense it. The time is ripe, and Felicia has offered him money which is to arrive tomorrow. They're planning to go away."

"I thought he was planning to rob the guests at Summersea," Betz said.

"He may be planning that, too."

"But what can you do about it?"

"I'm going to stop him. I know when he moves about the hotel. Where did Cherry see him?"

"Outside, somewhere."

"Then his plans are in motion. I have to ask you to go back to your suite now and say nothing. I can't risk having him escape now. I've invested too many weeks in this. Help me, Betz. Help me bring this man to justice by keeping silent about what you know for one day."

"I'll do anything you ask," she said, meaning every word. "But you mustn't do something dangerous. Could you get hurt?"

He looked at her for a long moment. Then he reached into his half-packed carpetbag and pulled out a Colt revolver.

"Oh, Adam!" Betz wailed, terrified. "Let the police handle this. Don't risk yourself! Your mother wouldn't expect that of you!"

Adam pushed the revolver back into the bag and grabbed her. He covered her mouth with a burning kiss. Then he pushed her from him and urged her toward the door. "Go now, Betz. Say nothing, and don't worry about me. Go on about your business tomorrow as if nothing is going on. Trust me! I have to ask this of you!"

She was about to let him push her out into the corridor, and out of his life one last time. Then the impulse to kiss him again overpowered her and she threw her arms around his neck.

She kissed him so hard she was afraid that she would never be able to let go of him. His neck was warm beneath her hand, his wavy hair so silky against her fingertips. His chest felt hard and solid against her breasts, and as his arms crushed her tightly to him, she felt like she could not let him do what he planned. She must stop him.

His lips were urgent against her mouth, and her desire for him was excruciating, impatient. But he would not let her draw him back toward the bed.

"You must go," he hissed, pulling her arms from around his neck. "I'll be all right. Promise you'll do nothing. I want this man. He destroyed a very kind woman. I want him to pay for what he's done. I won't use the pistol, only to defend myself in case...Oh, Betz, have a little faith in me. I've said that I'll explain when I can."

Again he was asking her to leave, to trust, to give him up, perhaps forever. Heart pounding, she let him thrust her into the corridor and close the door. It seemed that he loved her; she thought, hot tears welling in her eyes. And it seemed that he must trust her very much. She could run straight to the authorities. He believed she wouldn't.

Stiffly she moved away from the door. She thought of the ugly pistol and what might befall the man she loved. Somehow she must endure the next hours, knowing he was going bravely into something very dangerous.

Did she love him enough to let him handle it?

Turning away, she walked softly back to the stairs and down to her own floor. She felt attached to Adam by a powerful invisible bond, one so flexible that when she was a great distance from him she was still a part of him.

They were joined somehow, one in their hearts. She could not explain it, but even the presence of Evalee Grayson in his life could not diminish what she felt for Adam.

She made it to her door and stepped inside. Cherry watched from her bed in the next room, her eyes wide in the darkness, her young face trusting and yet afraid.

Betz went out onto the balcony and stared up at the stars. She didn't know what the coming day and night would bring, but at this moment she felt as close to Adam as if she were still in his arms.

Whatever happened, she had a great love for this man of honor and courage. Whatever else he might be, she didn't care. She loved Adam Teague and that would never change.

Twenty-Four

Anticipating the Worst

"I suppose that I should make an appearance at dinner," Agatha said, sitting up in bed amid a half-dozen pillows. "I suppose the old crows want to speak with me and tell me about all that you both have done behind my back." She chuckled. "I heard all that tapping at the door this morning."

"Felicia sent word that she wanted to speak with you," Betz said. "Victoria asked you to tea."

"Let them wait. It is truly convenient to be old, you know. I don't have to be polite. I can ignore even the most important personages. In any case, I'll see them soon enough, at the ball tonight. Did my trunks arrive from the depot? We'll have to have the maid press our gowns—Now, read these letters while I talk to Cordelia—forgive me, child. Your name is Cherry. Now don't squirm about like a monkey. Sit in the chair as you've been taught, and tell me what you really think of Summersea and all my old friends."

Cherry looked to Betz, her cheeks pale and her eyes round. She hadn't slept well, and she seemed to start at every sudden sound as if listening for someone to tap at their door.

"They're very rich...and proper," Cherry said tentatively.

"And..." Agatha prompted.

"And I...I'm very scared of them all, and some of them tell lies, but—" she rushed on, "Xynnie Pratt wasn't like any of them. She was very real! And Drew! He's not like any of them either. I like him..." Her face darkened to crimson. "And he likes me. But I haven't had the chance to speak with him since..."

"Yes, Miss Witherspoon told me about your afternoon away. I must say you have found a great deal of mischief to get into during your first summer here, and I should think we'll have much to discuss as time goes on. You must forgive me, child, but I am feeling weary suddenly, and if I'm to attend this ghastly event this evening—"

Cherry burst into nervous laughter. She leaped to her feet and began strutting about. Looking for all the world just like Felicia Ellison, she intoned, "Put the palms over there, dear man. No, no, not like a bumpkin. Place them artistically. Imagine, if you will, the ancient Roman palaces where Caesar walked, where the great men of history took their pleasure..."

Listening, Betz knew at once that Cherry had spent some time the afternoon before eavesdropping on the activities downstairs. She had not heard all that by staying obediently in the suite. Agatha laughed until she was weak.

"Do let me breathe, child. I don't think Felicia would really want to entertain on the Roman scale. There's not a lion in sight, nor a single courtesan. Such a tiresome woman. Is she as unstable as I remember? And as truly vicious as she is in her letters?"

"She walked straight into the ocean one night and Miss Witherspoon talked her back. Isn't that wonderful! She was just like a heroine in a novel."

"And have you been reading much fiction? I understand that fiction softens the brain." Agatha chuckled.

"Don't you want me to read, Grandmother?"

"I think in a while, child, you will realize what I want from you, and for you." the old woman smiled. "But I am not quite up to revealing my aspirations for you just now. Can you both excuse me? I want to nap before the ordeal of dressing for Felicia's ball. I shall make a grand entrance on your arm, of course, Cherry. And you shall introduce me to your dear Drew, and Miss Witherspoon will introduce me to the very intriguing Mr. Teague."

Betz put aside Agatha's letters. They were from Gettie, Felicia, Xynnie and two ladies she didn't know, who had been at Xynnie's party. Their descriptions of Cherry's behavior since arriving at Summersea were accurate, though. On paper, Cherry did indeed sound like a little harlot, with no reputation left to sully. She had begun as soiled goods, and had done everything to confirm everyone's opinion that she was socially unfit.

Numbed, feeling a very peculiar, virulent anger simmering just beneath the surface of her mind, Betz asked, "Will it be necessary for me to attend this evening, Miss Agatha?"

"Are we feeling intimidated, dear?" Agatha's eyes were sharp in spite of her weariness.

"To be perfectly frank, Miss Agatha, I simply don't find the company of Summersea's guests much to my liking."

"I suppose I must speak my mind, then. I had hoped to wait. Dear Betz, you seem to be laboring under the impression that I'm about to let you go. And I know that my dear granddaughter here is convinced that I am going to put her out on the street like a mongrel who has wet my floor."

"We have both failed you miserably." Betz swallowed with difficulty.

"I wish that you would give me credit for having a brain, and opinions of my own!" Agatha said rather heatedly. "Since you insist upon thrusting me into a position of authority, I will ask that you and Cherry go on as usual. I have no intention of dismissing you at this time. Should the need ever arise, I assure you, you will not be confused as to my intentions." She pinned her old blue eyes on Cherry's ashen face. "As for you, my mischievous minx, you must come to understand that Agatha Dunwitty does not turn her back on family. You are my granddaughter, today and every day, regardless of your behavior. That is the way of family, and I pity you for not knowing that at your tender age. I will not be putting you out."

Cherry blinked back tears, smiled uncertainly, looked back at Betz with a shine in her eyes that tugged at Betz's heart, and then she threw herself across Agatha's lap.

"Oh, Grandmother!" The old woman stroked Cherry's back.

"There, there, you foolish child. Now, might I have a bit

more sleep?"

"Are you really up to the ball this evening, Agatha?" Betz asked. "Are you sure you don't want me to call the doctor?"

"And cause more gossip? Dear me, don't these old women have enough to talk about without putting me one foot into my grave? I am recovering, thanks to you two dears. Go now. And Betz, I've thought about it...if you don't care to attend this evening, you're perfectly within your rights not to."

A Midsummer's Nightmare

Cherry's gown was a demure off-white, layered with deep lacy ruffles. The bodice was tightly fitted in satin and the sleeves were tiny puffs of lace that accentuated the delicacy of her shoulders and arms.

Agatha had insisted that she wear a choker of large rare pearls and two pearl rings taken from a small chest of jewels that she carried in the false bottom of one of her trunks.

Agatha wore a gown of charcoal gray lace with puffy lace sleeves; its intricate neckline accented her ample bosom and a fitted bodice required a most formidable corset underneath.

The skirt of her gown was a rare silk covered over with more of the dark lace. A full train dragged behind her. "I've worn this gown for kings," Agatha said, panting as Betz fussed with the standup collar. "Oh, this is such a trial. You won't reconsider joining us, Betz?"

Betz shook her head. She intended to keep a close eye on the corridors during the ball. What she could possibly do to protect Adam from a swindler she didn't know, but at least she was not going to go on acting as if there was no danger.

Cherry's hair was done up in neat little coils and curls, and a diamond star-burst was tucked in at the top like the tip of a diadem. Agatha's thinning hair refused to do much, but a somewhat tidy little bun seemed to suit her, so Betz stopped fussing.

At length the two of them started out the door. Struck by how right they looked together, grandmother and granddaughter, Betz said, "Have a wonderful time."

Cherry looked back, an eager little smile on her lips. Betz knew she was thinking of nothing but introducing her grandmother to her beau.

When they had gone, Betz tidied the room and then began pacing. As soon as most of the guests were in the ballroom, she would begin to search for Adam.

As Agatha leaned on Cherry's firm young arm and let the girl help her down the stairs to the lobby, she felt a flutter of anticipation akin to what she had once felt upon entering a new foreign land.

It had been far too long since she had felt real excitement. How glad she was that she had returned to this dear girl and the refreshingly sincere Witherspoon woman. It was going to be an interesting year, after all.

The lobby was crowded already with all the guests in their finest array. Felicia was at the parlor door, personally welcoming everyone as if the hotel were her home, and she, the proud hostess.

Victoria Whitgift was just plodding into the ballroom on the arm of a tall, attractive young man. Cherry became electrified, and she tugged on Agatha's arm.

"Run ahead if you must, child," Agatha said, feeling Felicia's eyes fasten upon her. "I have people to speak to. You don't want to hear what they might have the audacity to say in front of you. Insist that Drew dance with me once, so that I don't feel like an ancient wallflower. Is this Mr. Teague anywhere in sight?"

"I don't see him, Grandmother. He usually doesn't come to these things. He's not like the rest."

"A blessing that must be. Summersea is just as I remember," Agatha said as she reached the bottom of the steps and approached Felicia. "Well, dear," she said, seizing the advantage before Felicia could speak. "You're looking remarkably fit, and younger, too. The sea air must agree with you."

"We're so delighted to have you, Lady Agatha!" Felicia cried in her affected falsetto. "When I heard that you had arrived, and not a one of us had seen you…I had hoped to meet with you before—"

Agatha cut the woman off. "Your observations on Cordelia's behavior have been noted. Can you direct me to this gentleman calling himself Mr. Teague? In my dotage I have acquired a taste for younger men, and find them very satisfying indeed."

Felicia's face reddened alarmingly. Coughing as if she'd swallowed the wrong way, she blurted, "I-I haven't yet seen him. He isn't of our class, you see. I've done what I could to keep out the—"

With aplomb, Agatha caught Victoria's gaze and lifted her hand and her brows as if hailing a dear old friend.

"Oh, do excuse me, dear Felicia. I must say hello to Victoria. The two of us are remarkably preserved, don't you think? Two old mummies here in this…Egyptian paradise. How did you ever think up the theme for this lovely ball? I do think the orchestra looks…charming in togas. How delightful. So creative…Victoria, my dearest. You look quite lovely."

Agatha was secretly laughing uproariously at her own performance. She had not had to do this sort of thing in years, and was finding it quite a lark. She would, however, tire quickly, and she did so want to meet Betz's lover before she dropped from exhaustion. She moved to Victoria, whose expression was cool.

"I'm glad to see you're up to this ball, Agatha. Did you ever see decor more hideous?"

"But Victoria, isn't it often a sign of wealth to squander thousands of dollars on vulgar parties for those who don't appreciate the expense? I have heard much to favor your dear grandson. Might I speak with him? Oh, of course, there he is with my dear little Cherry. Isn't she a treasure?"

Victoria's eyes became hard as glass.

"I understand Cherry and Drew were alone together until after dark only a few days ago?" Agatha inquired with feigned innocence.

Victoria looked pained.

"That is correct."

"Well, don't think that my darling Cherry has any intention of accepting a proposal of marriage from your grandson. She is simply too young, and her education has only just begun. I have in mind for her a terribly handsome young rajah's son. I was going to visit his parents in New Delhi when I was taken ill and had to return to the United States. They have a palace on the side of the mountain and, I assure you, I never saw a finer table set...all in pure gold. It was enough to dazzle me. I decided to fetch Cordelia and take her there. The bride-price alone would have given Cyrus a stroke."

Victoria purpled as if her corset had suddenly crushed her lungs.

"But of course I do want to meet the dear lad who has been so kind to Cordelia during her stay here."

"And what of this nonsense about your granddaughter growing up among savages?" Victoria blurted, suitably insulted to think that some foreign infidel should be preferred over her Drew.

Gettie Hobble had been, all the while, trying to reach them through the crowd. She was wearing a dusty old thing a full generation out of date. She plunged into the conversation without polite formalities, snapping, "Yes, what of these fancies of hers? I say you've been duped, Agatha. Whatever she claims to be, she's clearly a fake. We have scarcely been able to tolerate her presence among us."

Agatha's blood began to boil. No wonder Betz had elected to remain in the suite. "Gettie Hobble," she said sweetly, "you're still as slim as a girl. I was just telling Victoria about the fabulous bride-price that has been offered for Cordelia by an East Indian prince. I am considering it. I appreciate your letters, by the way, but as for Cordelia being a fake, I assure you, she is indeed my son's child."

"But this story of savages..."

Agatha raised her brows, answering cooly, "Well, surely any non-Christian country would seem savage to someone like you, dear. Growing up in a royal court would certainly seem savage to some, and I think that's what dear little Cordelia meant when she mentioned it. I told her not to flaunt her background, sweet thing that she is. I can't say she's had an adequate upbringing. Good help is so very hard to find, as are good and loyal friends such as you, dear."

"You were asking about Mr. Teague," Felicia said, coming near. She indicated a broad-shouldered, wavy-haired man watching everyone from the doorway. Then she swept on as if carrying out very important business. She was not about to be brushed aside again, not by anyone.

"If you'll excuse me," Agatha said, leaving Victoria and Gettie open-mouthed. She giggled to herself to think how quickly her fancies would spread about the room. Given enough lies to build upon, Cherry's background would be forever a subject for speculation, and the truth would never surface. Even if it did, she scarcely cared. By then Cherry would be beyond it all. Agatha lumbered toward the wavy-haired man. "Mr. Teague," she said, "we haven't been introduced but..."

He exuded tension, and when he glanced down at her he seemed very preoccupied indeed. Then he said, looking surprised, "You can't be Agatha, Betz's employer?"

"Indeed, conjured up for the occasion by Fate and the gods, such as they are." She gazed steadily into the man's eyes, judging his character. "I have formed quite an attachment for my granddaughter's chaperone, Mr. Teague."

His keen brown eyes swept across the crowd. His brow tightened. Whatever he was looking for, he did not seem to see it.

"Could you excuse me, Lady Ryburn? I want very much to give you my full attention, but just now I can't."

"One question, if you please. Are you a man of principles, Mr. Teague?"

"If you're asking me if I love Betz Witherspoon, the answer is yes. And now, I must go."

He went off at a fast clip toward the stairs.

Agatha smiled to herself, but her eyes were narrow. He was up to something, that one. But she liked him. He reminded her of Cyrus—direct, blunt, and very, very masculine.

• • •

With nearly everyone comfortably situated at the ball, with champagne punch flowing and the orchestra playing, Felicia could safely slip away to fetch Mr. Bonaventure.

Younger men, indeed! That Agatha looked dreadful, and was as overweening as ever. Felicia went upstairs thinking just how delightful it was going to be to appear in the ballroom with Mr. Bonaventure smiling up at her. And soon, soon, they would be in France, away from the gossips and fools…

When she tapped at Charles's door she thought about the packet of money which had been delivered to her that afternoon. Randolph might be divorcing her, but she was going to Europe with a younger man who wanted only love from her. She was luckier than them all.

"Charles?" she called when he failed to acknowledge her knock. "Are you all right?"

Like once before, she heard the sound of movement within his room, and this time she opened the door. He was standing near the dressing table, his wheeled chair across the room. He was in his shirtsleeves, and his nurse was standing behind him with her arms around his chest.

"Felicia!" he said, drooping instantly into Althea Tully's embrace. "I wanted to look so nice for you. Nurse Tully agreed to help me dress—tie my tie—but it's so hard to see if I'm doing it properly when I'm sitting down."

Felicia came into the room, saying coldly, "If you need help, Charles, I am quite ready to give it. Nurse Tully, you may leave." Felicia didn't let herself think. She didn't dare. She felt poised on the precipice of madness once again. Her heart nearly shivered to a stop.

A look passed between Charles and Nurse Tully and the young woman hurried from the room. When the door closed, Felicia approached Charles. He was, amazingly, still standing before the dressing table. She felt as if she would plummet through space.

He bent to reach for something in a case next to the table.

"I don't think you should allow such familiarities with your nurse, Charles—" Felicia began, her voice quavering. Before she could react Charles straightened, with something in his right hand.

He swung. Completely unprepared for any show of strength on his part, she didn't even duck.

Something struck her on the left side of the head and she went down, hitting the other side of her head on the lower comer of the bed's footboard.

Dazed and half-conscious, she was unable to stop Charles from plucking her rings from her fingers and the diamond necklace from her throat.

Vision blurring, she felt him drag her along the floor to the far side of the bed. Then she was forced to watch in terror as he raised the pistol in his hand to strike her again. A thousand images flashed before her bleary eyes…and the butt of his pistol came down on her temple.

With a sense of satisfaction, Charles straightened and wiped the bloody pistol on the bed-linen. Walk in on him, would she? What did she think, that she was buying him body and soul?

Now, because of her, all he must accomplish this night was going to start ahead of schedule. He slipped out into the corridor and locked his door behind him. Seconds later he was picking the lock to Felicia's suite. Letting himself in, he helped himself to everything of value he knew she possessed. What was most satisfying about the entire effort was that she had left her cash in an envelope in plain sight on the desk…and he wasn't going to have to kiss her even once to get his hands on it.

Back in his room moments later, he packed Felicia's valuables in his case and checked on her inert body. Gullible old bitch, he thought, gazing down at her. She had been one of his easiest victims. If only they were all as stupid.

Everyone was occupied in the ballroom, so it was easy for Charles to creep about the halls, picking locks and lifting what valuables he knew to be hidden away. While he took care of the more delicate operations, Althea was doing what she could to get to the others, especially Fitch and Reinhold.

In less than an hour he and his accomplice would be on their way south, to the gaming tables and races that were his passion. By summer next he would assume yet another name and guise, and lay in wait for another victim.

As he tiptoed out of Victoria Whitgift's suite with the contents of her jewel case, he wondered if it would be worth the risk to check Witherspoon's room. Althea had been through it only once, weeks before, and returned with an ugly little paste brooch of no value. But the old Ryburn dowager had arrived unexpectedly. She would have brought jewels and traveling cash.

He decided to risk a look in the room. With his pockets already bulging, he crept along the corridor toward the suite Witherspoon shared with the heiress and her grandmother.

Betz was about to slip out of her room in search of Adam when she heard footsteps outside her door. The music coming up from the ballroom was light and cheerful, and she wondered if Cherry was getting along all right. Surely with Agatha there, she would not encounter any trouble.

Betz had just locked Agatha's jewel case into the trunk with the false bottom when she heard the door to the sitting room open. Thinking it was Adam coming to talk to her, she said nothing. Letting the trunk lid drop and lock, she walked back into the sitting room. But instead of finding Adam there, she came face to face with Mr. Bonaventure. He was looking around, trying to decide where to search for loot.

"Oh," Betz said rather undramatically, trying not to let on that she knew why he was there. "Uh, Mr. Bonaventure, what are you doing in here? Do you need some help?"

His expression dark and somewhat amused, he whispered, "You don't seem surprised to find me standing." Then he made an abrupt move toward her, cautioning, "Don't scream. I'm armed."

She tried to think and found her mind blank.

"I, uh, thought you were going away with Felicia tonight," she said deciding that feigning ignorance was a waste of effort.

"You seem to know a lot about me," he said, advancing.

She retreated into the bedroom, wondering suddenly if she had the courage to scream for help even though he carried a weapon. Did she have the courage to jump from the balcony to avoid being shot?

"Everyone knows Felicia is…taken with you."

"She decided not to go. Come along with me, Miss Witherspoon. I do need your help, for now, it seems. Why aren't you at the ball?" He was looking her up and down as if he had another sort of help in mind.

Moving cautiously around the room toward the door with Mr. Bonaventure's eyes riveted on her, Betz was struck by the absurdity of their casual conversation. She went into the sitting room ahead of him, her back crawling with apprehension. He might do *anything.*

"I, uh…couldn't stomach the pretense any longer." Her voice was shaking.

"Ah, I know what you mean. How glad I am to have this ball early, so that I can get out of here. Felicia was driving me insane."

"Is that what you'll pretend to be next time?"

He didn't answer. She had said too much, she thought, worried suddenly. Her carelessness might provoke him to attack her now.

As Mr. Bonaventure urged Betz none too gently down the hall toward his room, he moved up close behind her, jabbing her in the back with what she was sure was a pistol. His arm circled her neck and he jerked her close.

"Miss Witherspoon. I hope you have a little sense now." He unlocked the door to his room and pushed her inside.

"What are we doing here?"

"I need my chair. You're going to help me downstairs. I have to meet someone outside in a few minutes. Then we'll go back to the ball and make small talk a while." His tone had gone bitterly sarcastic.

Standing awkwardly in the room, Betz watched as Mr.

Bonaventure dragged his chair toward the door and sat down in it. He spread the lap robe across his knees.

"If you please, Miss Witherspoon. Downstairs. We'll see Althea in a moment, but you're going to come along with me, aren't you?"

"Yes," she whispered.

As she approached his chair, trembling at the thought of the pistol hidden beneath the lap robe, she saw something on the far side of the bed—the hem of a woman's elegant skirt, and soles of two rather new dancing slippers.

She needed only an instant to realize that whoever was lying there, was possibly dead. She had a sinking feeling it was Felicia, and she felt ill.

Mr. Bonaventure reached back and seized her wrist. "Does old lady Ryburn have anything worthy of my attention?"

"No, I-I think much of my employer's wealth was talk," Betz said, feeling weak. "She is going to fire me, and I don't think I am going to get paid."

Sniffing in amusement, Mr. Bonaventure settled back.

"Let's go then."

Betz took hold of the handles on the chair-back and started to push Mr. Bonaventure out into the corridor. He rattled his room key at her, and watched closely as she locked the door.

"I was sorry when the Howards cleared out," he said casually as she started pushing him toward the stairs. "There was a man worth robbing." His tone was soft and menacing. "If you're thinking of pushing me down the stairs, Miss Witherspoon, let me advise against it. The chances of me dying in a fall are slim, and I swear to you that if I do fall, I will shoot the first person I see."

As they reached the stairs, Cherry was about to help her grandmother up them. Agatha looked weary, and rather startled to see Betz with Mr. Bonaventure. Cherry's face went ashen.

"Which one should it be?" Mr. Bonaventure whispered as he

got to his feet as if scarcely able to stand. He coughed, holding his cocked pistol within folds of the lap robe clutched in his hands. "Shall I shoot your little temptress or the old lady?"

"I'll do whatever you ask of me," Betz said, her voice amazingly calm.

And then her brother George appeared from the dining room. She had forgotten he was there. For the briefest moment she felt a pang of compassion for him. He was a fool, but he was her brother, and she knew suddenly that she would never be a part of his life again. How would she ever be able to make him understand?

Mr. Bonaventure started painstakingly down the stairs, one step at a time, milking the scene for all it was worth. On his person he had a substantial amount of Summersea's valuables, but those watching from below were not the least bit suspicious.

Betz had seen the nurse wrestle the chair down the stairs before, and turned to drag it down backwards. Looking along the hall, she saw Adam standing in the shadows, his own pistol drawn.

A star-burst of surprise exploded in her chest. Almost stumbling, she had to pause and steady herself. Mr. Bonaventure cast her a warning look.

Adam waved Betz on.

She felt ill with fear. She started down the stairs, the chair bumping down after her. Her heart was pounding and her face red when she reached the bottom and waited while Mr. Bonaventure arranged himself. Heaving a delicate sigh, he said, "Thank you for your kind help, Miss Witherspoon. Might we go outside briefly? I may be able to catch my breath there, and then we'll come back inside." He started one of his coughing fits. Everyone cleared a path.

Looking perplexed, Agatha asked, "What are you doing, Miss Witherspoon?"

Quietly, so that other guests watching would not overhear; Betz said, "I felt that since you fired me this afternoon that I needed to accept new employment as quickly as possible. Mr. Bonaventure is displeased with his nurse, and..."

Annoyed with her lie, Mr. Bonaventure frowned at Betz. She

turned away from Cherry and Agatha, and all the others watching in confused amazement, and started for the doors.

Cherry grasped her grandmother's arm and shushed her. Betz and Mr. Bonaventure went out onto the dark veranda.

Again they went through the charade of getting down the stairs, and then she wheeled him around the hotel in the direction of the road leading away from Summersea. She knew there was someone waiting for him there, another thief, and that her usefulness was quickly coming to an end.

What could Adam do to save her, she wondered.

"Let's go," Mr. Bonaventure hissed, vaulting from the chair and waving the pistol at her. "You're coming with me." He tugged a weighted sack from inside his coat that she was sure was filled with all he had taken from the hotel.

"What about your nurse—"

He jabbed the pistol into her side and shoved her forward. "Move! And not a sound!"

Twenty-Five

Wolves among the Sheep

"What's going on?" Agatha said, frowning down at Cherry. "Do you know something about Miss Witherspoon that I don't?"

"I think she's in trouble," Cherry said, craning her neck to see if Adam was around. When she saw him run down the stairs and bolt out the door onto the veranda, she knew he was following Betz and Mr. Bonaventure.

Drew came up behind Cherry, asking cheerfully, "Does your grandmother have enough strength for one more dance?"

"Yes, do dance with Grandmother," Cherry said, urging the two back toward the ballroom. Cherry heard her grandmother quizzing Drew about what she had just said, and the moment they turned away, Cherry slipped out onto the veranda. Miss Witherspoon, Mr. Bonaventure, Mr. Teague running after them…she was not going to miss this!

As she started down the steps to the lawn, she heard Gettie Hobble calling from the end of the veranda, "Yoo-hoo-o-o, Felicia, are you out here?" After a pause, she muttered, "Where is that woman?"

It was odd, Cherry thought, that the ghastly Mrs. Ellison had not been seen in nearly half an hour.

She darted around to the side of the hotel where she'd seen Mr. Bonaventure the night before. For a few seconds, she saw and heard nothing. Then Nurse Tully emerged from the rear of the hotel. Ducking into a shadow, Cherry saw the woman hike up her skirts and run as fast as she could in the direction of the beach. After a moment, Cherry followed.

Betz picked her way among the rocks at the base of the bluff along the beach. Charles Bonaventure was right behind her, prodding her with his pistol. They had passed the steps leading up to the promontory and were now out of sight of Summersea.

Suddenly he caught her by her hair, hissing, "Stop! Don't make a sound."

He eased her into a pocket of darkness and waited, holding his breath, the pistol stabbing hurtfully into her side. The night was quiet, save for the lapping of waves against the rocks and sand.

Betz couldn't hear anything but her drumming heart. After a moment, Bonaventure stiffened at some muffled sound behind them.

"Stay put," he said in a hushed tone, jerking her tightly against him for a moment. He bruised her temple with the pistol muzzle. "Don't run. I'm warning you. If I don't get you with the first shot, I'll get you with the second. Do what I tell you, maybe I won't kill you!"

"I won't move," she whispered.

He pushed her to a crouching position and then crept back toward Summersea.

As Betz waited, she did think of running, but Adam might be close behind. If he was, he would surely catch up to Bonaventure and get the pistol from him.

With a whimper, she hugged herself, wondering what on earth she was doing there. Everything was so quiet and eerie. She felt so helpless.

Then she saw a small rowboat beached nearby. She was thinking of running to it when a man wearing dark clothes pounded past her from the direction of the hotel, shoved the boat back into the waves and threw himself into it. In seconds he had the oars in place and was half standing as if watching for someone.

"Wait!" someone hissed from the darkness behind her.

Seconds later a woman holding her skirts almost to her hips dashed past, stumbled among the rocks and then broke for the boat, too.

Bonaventure was close behind. He found Betz among the rocks and jerked her to her feet, snarling, "Get going!"

Betz stumbled and fell headlong against a jumble of rocks half buried in the sand. With her wind knocked out she lay stunned, unable to move. "Don't," she grunted, "I can't...breathe!"

"Get up!" he shouted, crouching over her, aiming the pistol at her face.

"I-I can't!" She closed her eyes.

"You can't fool me. Get up!" Clutching a handful of her bodice front, he jerked her upright.

As the pain in her chest eased, she managed to stagger a few feet.

The man in the boat was waving frantically and pointing.

From somewhere behind, a shot was fired. Betz felt the bullet whiz by her head.

Dropping to the sand, Betz covered her head with her arms. There was no time to feel afraid. She was numb, moving by instinct.

She was huddled near the sloping tumble of sand, earth and rock that had collapsed around her during the storm weeks before. Bonaventure yelled something to the man in the boat and then started for it. Betz stood now. She would scramble up the sloping portion of the bluff and escape among the rocks above.

Almost before she could think where to begin climbing, though, another shot was fired. The woman was struggling through the water, trying to reach the boat, but the man in it was rowing as fast as he could to get away from the shore.

"Hey!" Bonaventure shouted. "Wait!"

Standing, he bolted for the water, shoving the woman aside and plunging with all his strength into the deep water.

"Not this time!" Adam shouted, racing down the sloping bluff, bringing off yet another shot.

Bonaventure gave a cry of pain and plunged headfirst into the water. The woman nearby screamed and tried to get to the boat. Without thinking, Betz jumped to her feet and ran after her.

Adam had fished the wounded Bonaventure from the waves and was starting to drag him back to shore. The man in the boat had slowed to the point where Nurse Tully was almost able to reach him.

Betz stripped down to her blouse and drawers and splashed noisily into the bay, determined to stop the woman from escaping.

Behind her, Bonaventure and Adam were struggling frantically on the beach. Another shot fired into the chaotic darkness, but Betz couldn't think about that.

She plowed into the nurse, knocking her under water. When the woman surfaced, sputtering, Betz seized her hair, shouted, "You're not leaving!" and jerked her back toward the beach. "I brought one woman back from the bay. I can bring you back, too."

Nurse Tully didn't struggle until they were safely out of the water. Then she struck at Betz, grazing her chest as she tried to get away on foot. Hampered by her wet skirts, however, she couldn't run. Betz tackled her and wrestled her to the sand.

Adam and Bonaventure were scuffling, throwing and receiving punches. A pistol lay only a few feet from Betz.

She scrambled for it and so did Nurse Tully. Screaming, clawing, biting, the two women fought for a hold on the gun. Dazed when the nurse hit her head with her elbow, Betz was thrown back.

She could see Bonaventure's slim silhouette. He was standing over Adam's body on the sand.

Then she saw Bonaventure take aim.

Desperately afraid for Adam, she slammed her arm across the nurse's face. Hearing the woman's grunt of surprise as she fell back unconscious, Betz seized the pistol.

She fired at Bonaventure. The recoil threw her back onto her haunches. Bonaventure yelped with pain as the shot ripped through his shoulder.

After he fell, there was a long terrifying moment of silence.

Then Adam got to his feet, kicked the pistol from Charles's hand and pounced on him.

"Ah-h-h, don't!" Charles wailed. "My shoulder!"

But Adam was forcing big iron handcuffs around the man's slim white wrists. When he had the man subdued, he grabbed his hair and forced Charles to look at him.

"You're going to jail, Charlie Baskley, alias Bradleigh, Bonaventure and all the rest. Damn your eyes, I'm going to see to it you rot there, and if I can convince them to hang you, I'll do it. If you're wondering who I am, my name is Adam Barrett. I'm with Pinkerton's National Detective Agency, out of Chicago. Does the name Veronice Coe strike a chord in your memory?"

"Get off me! It hurts!"

"She hanged herself over you, you Goddamned worm. Get up before I kill you, just to make myself feel better."

Betz edged back against Nurse Tully's inert body, stunned by Adam's words. A Pinkerton! No wonder Felicia had not been able to find out who he was. Betz almost wanted to laugh, but hot tears were running down her cheeks, and she didn't know why.

Then there was the tearing scream of a young girl.

Adam whirled and ducked as a shot came from the man in the boat. Adam lunged, grabbed up Bonaventure's pistol from where it had fallen in the sand and fired every bullet out into the darkness.

The third shot brought a shout and a splash followed by silence.

"Oh, Mr. Teague!" Cherry wailed as she ran past Betz and the inert nurse.

Sagging, Betz abandoned any thought of restraining the girl. She was limp with the realization that she had shot a man.

"Come on, you son of a bitch," Adam grumbled as he forced Bonaventure to stand. "Cherry, get back. See to Betz. My operatives are waiting for us on the road, friend. I've arranged very pleasant accommodations for you at the jail in Huntington Station." He marched the man back toward Summersea.

"Adam?" Betz called softly. "Adam?"

He paused and turned, rubbing a particularly tender bruise on his jaw. His silence grew long. Then he hissed, "Don't move, Charlie," and moved toward Betz.

He reached down and helped her to her feet, his hand cold and trembling slightly. He circled her with his free arm while keeping his arm on Charles's back, saying softly, "I can't…I have to…"

She knew what he was trying to say. She searched his face, made so dark and obscure by the night, then whispered, "I know, you have to go."

This was the end, she told herself. This was their last moment together. She must make it the kind of moment to always remember with fondness and pride.

She must not weep, she told herself. She must not beg. In a few short weeks she had grown to womanhood and independence. She did not need her brother to protect her. She did not even need Adam, though she wanted him with all her being.

"Go," she said with a tender smile, "I love you."

His grip on her shoulder tightened. He was so close she could feel his breath on her forehead, hear him breathing fast through his nose as if he, too, was in pain.

"Betz, I can't say what you want to hear."

"Sh-h-h," she whispered, putting her fingers to his lips. "I understand."

And then his lips brushed against hers in a fleeting touch of warmth she knew she would never forget. She wanted it to last forever, but it was so damned brief, such a tiny intense touch that she would never feel again. There would never be another man like this one, she thought as Adam released her and moved toward Bonaventure.

"Get going," he said harshly, not looking back.

She stood without moving until the sounds of their footsteps were gone. Her heart was breaking. She wanted to wail but the grief was too fresh for that. The weeping would come later, she knew.

Now, she must go back to the hotel. She must carry on.

"Miss Witherspoon?" Cherry whispered from behind her. She was weeping. "Oh, Miss Witherspoon. What will we do?"

"Are you all right, darling? Why did you follow? You're such a little fool."

"He's going! Can't you stop him?"

"No." Betz's heart felt so tight with pain she wondered if she could take a step. But she did move toward Cherry and finally take the girl into her arms. "You've left your grandmother alone. We must get back to her. She loves you very much. We must try our best to please her."

"But I don't know how!" Cherry cried more loudly, sobbing openly now. "He didn't stay with you. Why didn't he stay with you? Why do they always go away from us? Are we always alone and lost from the ones we love?"

"Sometimes, but think how it would be if we had no one we had ever loved. Think how empty life would be. You're thinking of your father and your mama, aren't you?" Betz felt more tears roll down her cheeks.

Cherry sagged against Betz. Her body shaking with sobs. She moaned, "He should have stayed with you!"

"But he has important work," Betz said, but her own own heart cried out the same words, *he should have stayed.* "Come on. We don't want to worry your grandmother."

They walked slowly back to the hotel, quiet and subdued by their thoughts of lost love. Two of Adam's operatives with lanterns were searching the beach for the man shot from the boat.

When Betz and Cherry returned, a number of gentlemen were standing about on the veranda, attracted by the shots fired on the beach. They showered Betz with questions, but she answered none of them as she helped Cherry into the lobby.

When they walked into the glittering ballroom, nearly every person turned to gawk. Victoria emerged from the crush of people, and the look of disapproval on her face was enough to make Betz's fury bubble full force to the surface. She looked angrily from face to face.

Didn't any of them wonder where Felicia was?

Someone was helping Agatha up from a nearby chair. She moved with effort toward Betz, asking, "What has happened?"

Gettie horned in now. "This baggage was courting mischief again. Just look at her." She shook her head, her lips tight.

Betz turned to look at Cherry. Her pretty curls had come undone and were tumbling about her shoulders. There was sand on her slippers and hem, and some of the lace flounces on her dress were dirtied and torn.

Betz's own appearance was much worse. She had been in the water, and was half-dressed. Suddenly she began to laugh. She drew Cherry close and hugged her.

"Cherry looks beautiful. And you, Gettie Hobble, are a pitiful old woman. Get out of our way. We're going upstairs to rest. We're very tired of all of you."

Agatha took Betz's arm, adding, "I will come along, dear." She was smiling inscrutably.

Heavy with regret, Betz whispered, "I'm very sorry, Agatha. I just can't go on here. I must leave. I don't fit in here, and I don't think Cherry does either. I tried so very hard to make her adapt to all this, but my heart was never in it."

"I think you're all horrible cats!" Cherry shouted, lunging at the ranks of old ladies gawking at her. She growled. "Get back! I hate you all, and I'm *glad* he robbed you. What do you think has been going on here tonight! Mr. Bonaventure robbed all of you! And you thought he was so nice. Mr. Teague is a Pinkerton detective, and *he* knew what to do. You're all very nasty, very rich, boring fools. Get out of our way. We're leaving here!" She squealed and dashed partway up the stairs. "Yea, we're leaving!"

Drew broke from the crowd, calling, "But Cherry!"

Her face folded with doubt and suddenly she was sobbing again. She looked torn by her desire to leave and her love for Drew. Sometimes, Betz thought, it was not always the man who had to go on with important business.

Cherry dashed up the stairs and away.

Betz helped Agatha forward saying, "Don't worry, Drew. There will be time to talk to Cherry later. Find a steward and send for the doctor, if you would. Get someone to Mr. Bonaventure's room immediately. I think you'll find Felicia there. Injured."

As they started up the stairs, Betz heard her brother's voice.

"Betty Carlyle, I insist that you come back down here this instant and explain just what has been going on here!"

She looked down at him, he was just as he always had been—officious, stuffy, completely lacking in human understanding. To go back with him would be to go to her grave. She was going to go on, into the uncertain future, into life as she had never known it before. She turned and continued up the stairs, ignoring him.

"Why," she sighed, "do the ones you *want* to go away cling to your back?"

"I am not up to philosophical questions, dear," Agatha said. "By the way, did this thief get my jewel case?"

"No."

Agatha huffed in disgust, snorting, "There was much there I would gladly part with. Thank the gods that you and Cherry are safe. I must however insist that you leave Cherry behind if you so gallivanting in the night ever again with strange men with pistols. What is this about Mr. Teague being a Pinkerton man? Cyrus met Mr. Pinkerton once. A very correct man. I'm quite impressed. Will I be able to retain you in my employ now that you've had this taste of adventure?"

They paused at the door to the suite. Inside, Cherry was still crying. She sounded as if she was throwing things about and muttering obscenities.

"Agatha, have I not failed miserably to safeguard Cherry and prepare her for finishing school? She was never accepted here, not for a moment." Betz felt exasperated by her confusion.

"Heavens, acceptance was never what I wanted for Cherry!" Agatha cried. "Did I fail to make clear that I wanted my granddaughter merely exposed to this sort of life? I did not want her indoctrinated into it. On the contrary, my dear!"

Confused, irritated, Betz blurted, "I don't understand!"

"Ah, then, I must explain myself."

They went into the suite.

"Come here and sit with me, Cherry dear," Agatha said, sinking to a chair. "The time has come to reveal myself. Quiet now. Wipe your nose and use a hankie, not your hem."

Cherry stood sullenly nearby, watching her grandmother suspiciously.

"I'm sorry I was rude, Grandmother."

"Nonsense! You were marvelous! You said just what I have wanted to say on countless occasions. Now listen, dears. I sent you both here to Summersea for a reason. I do not believe in asking people what they believe their character to be. Character is revealed in how a person lives. What they say is mere lip service, or hypocrisy, or sometimes outright stupidity and lies. You, dear Cherry, are to be my heir, and I had to know just what sort of young lady you are."

Cherry hung her head.

Betz was more confused than ever.

"If you had managed to find your niche here among these very tiresome hypocrites, dear, I would have been terribly disappointed in you. I would still have loved you, though possibly not quite so much." She smiled grandly. "But you have proven yourself to be a true blood Ryburn, with spirit and gumption and character. I could not tell you what I wanted from you both. I had to let you both be free to choose your own way."

Bewildered, Cherry said, "You don't *want* me to be like them?"

"Not in the slightest, child! You are far better. Come hug me. I feel very old tonight. Betz, dear, might you give this old woman a hug, too?"

Betz crouched at the woman's side and embraced her, whispering, "You're remarkable." The tears were hot on her cheeks again. "You set us free to be what we are. But all our efforts to be like the others were wasted!"

"No dear, not wasted. Think of what you both know now that you did not know so short a time ago. Cherry, dear child, I hope you will not become hysterical with excitement, but I've sent for your father, and he will soon be joining us at Cyrus Wood. Can you tear yourself away from your infatuation with young Drew long enough to become reacquainted with him?"

Cherry's face lit with wonder.

"You've found my papa?"

"Indeed, I have. We cannot hope to keep him from his world travels long, but for a time we may enjoy his company. And who knows, he may prove to have a spark of character himself!"

Betz laid her head on Agatha's knee. She was watching a dark scene in her memory—Adam walking away from her. It seemed like a lifetime ago. She did not feel complete regret, she thought. She knew now she was capable of great giving love.

Agatha's hand gentle on her hair made Betz feel she had her mother with her again, and she felt a deep relaxation of the aching in her heart.

"When do we go?" she asked softly.

"Whenever you like. I admit to being very weary. Do you think Felicia is all right?"

"I don't know. Perhaps I'll go check on her. And I should speak to my brother before he leaves."

Wearily, Agatha nodded. Betz motioned that Cherry should help her grandmother prepare for bed. Betz sent for a toddy to warm and relax her.

Then she changed her clothes and brushed back her still damp hair, letting it hang loose down her back. Back in the lobby looking for her brother, she was told by the desk clerk that he had given his notice for the coming morning and was probably packing.

She went up to his room and knocked. George looked rather startled to see her.

"I thought you weren't going to speak to me, Sister," he said, ushering her into the two-room suite. "Cynthia has taken the children for a final look at the ocean—a most special treat—so we shall have privacy while we speak."

"I can't really go without sitting down and talking to you," Betz said, accepting an offered chair. "Can we discuss things like two civilized adults, for once?"

"My dear sister—"

"George, I have just been through a very bad experience," Betz said, wincing as she fingered the bruise on her temple. "I just thought it would be nice."

Speechless to hear her address him in such a forceful way, George stared at her.

"I'm going to go on working for Lady Ryburn for a while. I don't know how long. I'm not perfectly suited to the position of chaperone, but it seems I did well in this case. I've fallen in love with Mr. Adam Teague, but I don't know what I'm going to do about that. I think I will just muddle along as best I can. Is there anything else you'd like to know?"

"You're not coming back with me?"

"No, George. I'm sorry to disappoint you."

"I might agree to asking Cynthia to apologize."

"She's not my reason for not wanting to come back. I admit to being hurt by all she said the day I left, but that's all behind us now. I just don't want to come back. I love the children, and I'll visit from time to time, but I believe now I have much to do with the rest of my life. It won't be a conventional life, either. I hope that doesn't distress you too much. It's what I want. I think it'll make me happy."

Frowning in puzzlement, as if happiness was something he had never taken into consideration, George asked, "There's nothing I can say?"

Betz stood. The battle was won and she was free.

"No, dear brother. Take good care of yourself and your family. I'll be in touch…"

"And what about Mother's house?"

Betz was suddenly laughing. She embraced her brother and kissed his cheek.

"You'll never change, George." She started for the door. "I promised Mother. You know that. Accept it, George. The house is for my old age. If you refuse to live there when it belongs to me, then it'll sit empty a while. And don't fret too much about it. I'll see that someone looks after it."

He was still gaping in disbelief as she went out, the weight of her past finally lifted from her shoulders. Out in the corridor, Betz took a deep breath and ran her fingers through her loose, damp hair. What a glorious feeling to be a free woman, a woman who could take care of herself, and love with complete honesty. Oh, Adam would be so proud if he could see her!

At Felicia's room Betz found several people clustered at the door, whispering. Dismissing their curious looks and ignoring warnings that she couldn't go inside, Betz pushed the door open.

Lying on the bed, Felicia looked pale and bewildered. Blood darkened her hair and stained the bodice of her elaborate gown. She looked around her as if unable to bear the attention of the ladies and stewards.

"Is the doctor coming?" Betz asked.

"Get out, all of you!" Felicia wailed, throwing out her arm and then wincing as the movement brought pain to her head. "Except Betz Witherspoon."

The onlookers were scarcely out of the room before Felicia began her tirade.

"You knew he was a swindler! Why didn't you warn me? Make me a laughingstock, will you? I'll smear your name everywhere you go. You'll never get another position."

"Shut up, Felicia," Betz said with a sigh. "I'm sorry you were hurt, and I'm sorry you feel embarrassed. What would you have said if I had tried to warn you? You would have called me a liar. You didn't want to see the truth."

"You're an impertinent—"

Betz sank to the edge of Felicia's bed and put her hand on the woman's shoulder.

"You may not listen to what I have to say, but I will say it anyway, just to please myself. If you persist in acting this way, Felicia, you will someday find yourself a hated, lonely, miserable old woman."

"How dare you!"

"I dare because I see myself in you. You are what I might have become. I was once hurt, as you were hurt this evening. I'm telling you that I care, but your bitterness is driving me away. How many years do you or I have left to waste in such bitterness? In twenty years you'll be like Gettie Hobble. In thirty, people will fear and hate you as they fear and hate Victoria Whitgift. There's still time to do something about that."

Betz stood, feeling immeasurably better.

Felicia was still frowning.

"Agatha, Cherry and I will probably be leaving in the morning," Betz said. "I hope you find what you're looking for, Felicia."

Departing from Summersea

Sunday, July 14, 1889

Cherry was leaning her cheek unprettily against the windowglass in Agatha's private rail car and braiding the fringes on the maroon drapes just as she had on the trip to Summersea.

Betz made no move to stop her charge from fidgeting. She was thinking that the train was moving away from Summersea, the place where her heart had known its first love.

She sighed gently. She had never loved before, and now she must go on with the love still alive, unfulfilled, in her heart.

Agatha lay in her tiny bedchamber in her specially designed brass bed. Her snores were drifting comfortingly over to Betz, making her glad she had work to keep her mind occupied. What might she be thinking if she was returning to George's house instead?

She yawned, having slept not a wink all night. It hadn't been easy to leave without seeing Adam. She wondered how long she would yearn for him, if the joy and pain of her love would ever ease.

Where was Adam now, she wondered. What was he doing now that he had apprehended Bonaventure? Would he soon begin a new assignment? Was he thinking of her?

She could not imagine a time in the future when she would

forget him. Her love for him would live forever in her heart. Perhaps someday there would be another...

The train was just pulling into Morrsey Junction when Betz spied a top buggy waiting just beyond the deserted platform. A broad-shouldered man with wavy hair stood watching the train pull in.

The conductor bellowed; the junction was little more than a whistle-stop.

Cherry sprang back from the window, crying, "It's Mr. Teague!"

"Barrett," Betz corrected, feeling giddy suddenly. "Do you suppose..." Her heart was dancing. Her thoughts were scattering! He had come after her! He had come after her!

"Go to him!" Cherry cried. "I'll explain to Grandmother when she wakes! She'll understand!"

Betz was on her feet, unable to stop herself. "I'll be back. I'll meet you at Cyrus Wood...tonight."

Cherry gave Betz a look of complete disbelief.

"Tomorrow," Betz amended, blushing.

And then she was on the platform, the sea breeze against her face, her blood rushing in her veins, her heart leaping with delight. He had come back! He had come back!

As Betz stepped down from the rear platform, Adam straightened from his casual pose beside the buggy. Walking toward him, she could not feel her feet touching the ground. Tears of happiness were welling in her eyes, and already her imagination had carried them both well beyond the buggy ride to some secluded place where they would make love.

She wanted to say something witty and light, assure him that his appearance in no way obligated him to her. But her mind was a blank, filled with the white light of hope and love and desire.

Suddenly she was running, her arms outstretched, and she was laughing as her tears spilled. To hell with decorum, she thought, watching his face break into a grin. She was in love!

His arms opened to her, and she fell against him, laughing and weeping with delight. He held her tightly for a moment, pressing her head to his shoulder, his face to her hair.

Finally she pulled back enough to look up at him. She was smiling, almost afraid to hear what he might have to say.

There was pain in his eyes, but as he looked down at her he seemed to gain courage to speak.

"I don't see myself pushing a plow or working in an office, Betz. I've always been footloose. I've forgotten what it's like to have a home. I'm not sure I want one. I like my work, Betz. I like it very much."

She nodded, wanting only to hold him, not to force both of them a future on that neither wanted.

"I'm too old for children," she whispered. "I've already spent too many years in one place, dusting one parlor, cooking on one stove. I think I want to travel like Agatha. I think I want to go on working for her."

Like the sun coming out from behind a cloud, Adam began grinning.

"I could do my work and then come back to you."

"And I could do mine. And we could plan times and places to meet…"

"Like clandestine lovers," he teased, squeezing her, his eyes darkening. He covered her mouth with a hungry kiss.

"Always like lovers," she whispered against his lips. "Always."

"Married?" he asked. "Or not. Perhaps we could work together on one of my assignments."

"There's time enough to decide," she said, thrilled by the idea. "For now…"

"For now we must find some place to be alone. Oh, Betz, how I do love you!" he said, and grinned. "Nothing has been the same since I met you."

"And…" she said, touching his cheek with her trembling hand, "nothing will ever be the same again."

Also by Samantha Harte

CACTUS ROSE

In the heat of the southwest, desire is the kindling for two lost souls—and the flame of passion threatens to consume them both.

Rosie Saladay needs to get married—fast. The young widow needs help to protect her late husband's ranch, but no decent woman can live alone with a hired hand. With the wealthy Wesley Morris making a play for her land, Rosie needs a husband or she risks losing everything. So she hangs a sign at the local saloon: "Husband wanted. Apply inside. No conjugal rights."

Delmar Grant is a sucker for a damsel in distress, and even with Rosie's restrictions on "boots under her bed" stated firmly in black and white, something about the lovely widow's plea leaves him unable to turn away her proposal of marriage.

Though neither planned on falling in love, passion ignites between the unlikely couple. But their buried secrets—and enemies with both greed and a grudge—threaten to tear them apart. They'll discover this marriage of convenience may cost them more than they could have ever bargained for.

ANGEL

When her mother dies, fourteen-year-old Angel has no one to turn to but Dalt, a gruff-spoken mountain man with an unsettling leer and a dark past. Angel follows Dalt to the boomtowns of the Colorado territory, where she is thrust into the hardscrabble world of dancehalls, mining camps, and saloons.

From gold mines to gambling palaces, *Angel* tells the story of a girl navigating her way through life, as an orphan, a pioneer, and ultimately a miner's wife and respected madam…a story bound up with the tale of the one man in all the West who dared to love her.

AUTUMN BLAZE

Firemaker is a wild, golden-haired beauty who was taken from her home as a baby and raised by a Comanche tribe. Carter Machesney is the handsome Texas Ranger charged with finding her, and reacquainting her with the life she never really knew.

Though they speak in different tongues, the instant flare of passion between Firemaker and Carter is a language both can speak, and their love is one that bridges both worlds.

HURRICANE SWEEP

Hurricane Sweep spans three generations of women—three generations of strife, heartbreak, and determination.

Florie is a delicate Southern belle who must flee north to escape her family's cruelty, only to endure the torment of both harsh winters and a sadistic husband. Loraine, Florie's beautiful and impulsive daughter, bares her body to the wrong man, yet hides her heart from the right one. And Jolie, Florie's pampered granddaughter, finds herself in the center of the whirlwind of her family's secrets.

Each woman is caught in a bitter struggle between power and pride, searching for a love great enough to obliterate generations of buried dreams and broken hearts.

KISS OF GOLD

From England to an isolated Colorado mining town, Daisie Browning yearns to find her lost father—the last thing she expects to find is love. Until, stranded, robbed, and beset by swindlers, she reluctantly accepts the help of the handsome and rakish Tyler Reede, all the while resisting his advances.

But soon Daisie finds herself drawn to Tyler, and she'll discover that almost everything she's been looking for can be found in his passionate embrace.

SNOWS OF CRAGGMOOR

When Merri Glenden's aunt died, she took many deep, dark secrets to the grave. But the one thing Aunt Coral couldn't keep hidden was the existence of Merri's living relatives, including a cousin who shares Merri's name. Determined to connect with a family she never knew but has always craved, Merri travels to Colorado to seek out her kin.

Upon her arrival at the foreboding Craggmoor—the mansion built by her mining tycoon great-grandfather—Merri finds herself surrounded by antagonistic strangers rather than the welcoming relations she'd hoped for.

Soon she discovers there is no one in the old house whom she can trust...no one but the handsome Garth Favor, who vows to help her unveil her family's secrets once and for all, no matter the cost.

SWEET WHISPERS

Seeking a new start, Sadie Evans settles in Warren Bluffs with hopes of leaving her past behind. She finds her fresh start in the small town, in her new home and new job, but also in the safe and passionate embrace of handsome deputy sheriff, Jim Warren.

But just when it seems as if Sadie's wish for a new life has been granted, secrets she meant to keep buried forever return to haunt her. Once again, she's scorned by the very town she has come to love—so Sadie must pin her hopes on Jim Warren's heart turning out to be the only home she'll ever need.

TIMBERHILL

When Carolyn Adams Clure returns to her family estate, Timberhill, she's there to face her nightmares, solve the mystery of her parents' dark past, and clear her father's name once and for all. Almost upon arrival, however, she is swept up into a maelstrom of fear, intrigue, and, most alarmingly, love.

In a horrifying but intriguing development for Carolyn, cultlike events begin to unfold in her midst and, before long, she finds both her life and her heart at stake.

VANITY BLADE

Orphan daughter of a saloon singer, vivacious Mary Lousie Mackenzie grows up to be a famous singer herself, the beautiful gambling queen known as Vanity Blade. Leaving her home in Mississippi, Vanity travels a wayward path to Sacramento, where she rules her own gambling boat. Gamblers and con men barter in high stakes around her, but Vanity's heart remains back east, with her once carefree life and former love, Trance Holloway, a preacher's son.

Trying to reclaim a happiness she'd left behind long ago, Vanity returns to Mississippi to discover—and fight for—the love she thought she'd lost forever.